HENNING MANKELL

The Man Who
Smiled

TRANSLATED FROM THE SWEDISH BY
Laurie Thompson

VINTAGE BOOKS
London

Published by Vintage 2012

6 8 10 9 7

First published with the title *Mannen som log* in 1994 by
Ordfronts Förlag, Stockholm

First published in Great Britain in 2005 by
The Harvill Press

Vintage
Random House, 20 Vauxhall Bridge Road,
London SW1V 2SA

www.vintage-books.co.uk

Addresses for companies within The Random House Group Limited
can be found at: www.randomhouse.co.uk/offices.htm

The Random House Group Limited Reg. No. 954009

A CIP catalogue record for this book
is available from the British Library

ISBN 9780099571728

Penguin Random House is committed to a sustainable future for
our business, our readers and our planet. This book is made from
Forest Stewardship Council® certified paper.

Printed and bound in Great Britain by Clays Ltd, St Ives plc

It is not so much the sight of immorality of the great that is to be feared as that of immorality leading to greatness.

Alexis de Tocqueville
Democracy in America

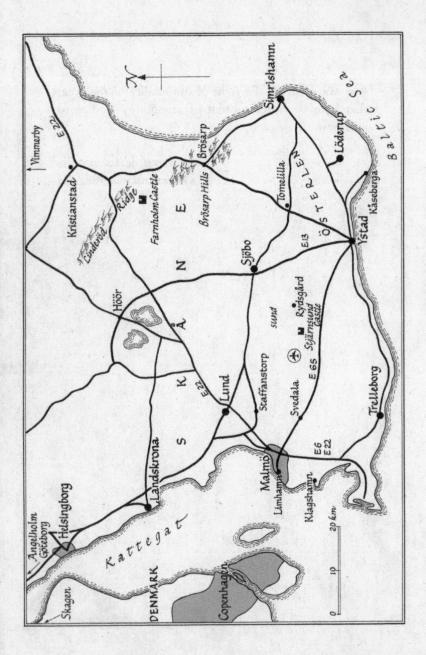

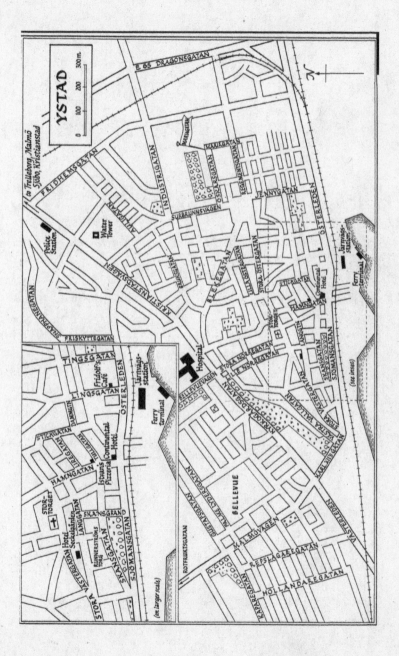

Chapter 1

Fog.

A silent, stealthy beast of prey. Even though I have lived all my life in Skåne, where fog is forever closing in and shutting out the world, I'll never get used to it.

9 p.m., October 11, 1993.

Fog came rolling in from the sea. He was driving home to Ystad and had just passed Brösarp Hills when he found himself in the thick of the white mass.

Fear overcame him straight away.

I'm frightened of fog, he thought. I ought rather to be scared of the man I have just been to see at Farnholm Castle. The friendly man whose menacing staff always lurk in the background, their faces in the shadows. I ought to be thinking about him and what I now know is hidden behind that friendly smile. His impeccable standing in the community, above the very least suspicion. He is the one I ought to be frightened of, not the fog drifting in from Hanö Bay. Not now that I have discovered that he would not hesitate to kill anyone who gets in his way.

He turned on the wipers to try to clear the windscreen. He did not like driving in the dark. He particularly disliked it when rabbits scurried this way and that in the headlights.

Once, more than 30 years ago, he had run over a hare. It was on the Tomelilla road, one evening in early spring. He could still remember stamping his foot down on the brake pedal, but then a dull thud against the bodywork. He had stopped and got out. The hare was lying on the road, its back legs kicking. The upper part of its body was paralysed, but its eyes stared at him. He had had to force himself to find a heavy stone from the verge, and had shut his eyes as he threw it down on to the hare's head. He had hurried back to the car without looking again at the animal.

He had never forgotten those eyes and those wildly kicking legs. The memory kept coming back, again and again, usually at the most unexpected times.

He tried now to put the unpleasantness behind him. A hare that died all of 30 years ago can haunt a man, but it can't harm him, he thought. I have more than enough worries about people still in the land of the living.

He noticed that he was checking his rear-view mirror more often than usual.

I'm frightened, he thought again, and I have only just realised that I am running away. I am running from what I know is hidden behind the walls of Farnholm Castle. And they know that I know. But how much? Enough for them to be afraid that I'll break the oath of silence I once took as a newly qualified solicitor? A long time ago that was, when an oath was just that: a sacred commitment to professional secrecy. Are they nervous about their old lawyer's conscience?

Nothing in the rear-view mirror. He was alone in the

fog, but in under an hour he would be back in Ystad.

The thought cheered him, if only for a moment. So they weren't following him after all. He had made up his mind what he was going to do tomorrow. He would talk to his son, who was also his colleague and a partner in the legal practice. There was always a solution, that was something life had taught him. There had to be one this time too.

He groped on the unlit dashboard for the radio. The car filled with a man's voice talking about the latest research in genetics. Words passed through his brain without his taking them in. He checked his watch: nearly 9.30. Still no-one behind him, but the fog seemed to be getting even thicker. Nevertheless, he squeezed the accelerator a little harder. The further he was from Farnholm Castle, the calmer he felt. Perhaps, after all, he had nothing to fear.

He forced himself to think clearly.

It had begun with a perfectly ordinary telephone call, a message on his desk asking him to contact a man about a contract that urgently needed verifying. He did not recognise the name, but had taken the initiative and made the call: a small solicitors' practice in an insignificant Swedish town could not afford to reject a potential client. He could recall even now the voice on the phone: polite, with a northern accent, but at the same time giving the impression of a man who measured out his life in terms of what each minute cost. He had explained the task, a complicated transaction involving a shipping line registered in Corsica and a number of cement cargoes to Saudi Arabia, where one of his companies was acting as an agent for Skanska. There had been some vague, passing reference to an enormous mosque that was to be built in Khamis Mushayt. Or maybe it was a university building in Jeddah.

They had met a few days later at the Continental Hotel in Ystad. He had got there early, and the restaurant was not yet open for lunch; he had sat at a table in the corner and watched the man arrive. The only other person there was a Yugoslav waiter staring gloomily out of the window. It was the middle of January, a gale was blowing in from the Baltic and it would soon be snowing. But the man approaching him was suntanned. He wore a dark blue suit and was definitely no more than 50. Somehow, he did not belong either in Ystad or in the January weather. He was a stranger, with a smile that did not belong to that suntanned face.

That was the first time he had set eyes on the man from Farnholm Castle. A man without baggage, in a discrete world of his own, in a blue, tailor-made suit, everything centring on a smile, and an alarming pair of shadowy satellites buzzing attentively but in the background.

Oh yes, the shadows had been there even then. He could not recall either of them being introduced. They sat at a table on the other side of the room, and rose without a word when their master's meeting was over.

Golden days, he thought, bitterly, and I was stupid enough to believe in it. A solicitor's vision of the world should not be influenced by the illusion of a paradise to come, not here on earth at least. Within six months the suntanned man had come to be responsible for half of the practice's turnover, and in a year the firm's income

4

had doubled. Bills were paid promptly, it was never necessary to send a reminder. They had been able to afford to redecorate their offices. The man at Farnholm Castle seemed to be managing his business in every corner of the world, and from places that seemed to be chosen more or less at random. Faxes and telephone calls, even the occasional radio transmission, came from the strangest-sounding towns, some he could only with difficulty find on the globe next to the leather sofa in the reception area. But everything had been above board, albeit complex.

The new age has dawned, he remembered thinking. So this is what it's like. As a solicitor, I have to be grateful that the man at Farnholm picked my name from the telephone book.

His train of recollections was cut short. For a moment he thought he was imagining it, but then he clearly made out the headlights in the rear-view mirror.

They had crept up on him.

Fear struck him immediately. They had followed him after all. They were afraid he would betray his oath of silence.

His first reaction was to accelerate away through the fog. Sweat broke out on his forehead. The headlights were on his tail. Shadows that kill, he thought. I'll never get away, just as none of the others did.

The car passed him. He caught a glimpse of the driver's face, an old man. Then the red rear lights vanished into the fog.

He took out a handkerchief and wiped his face and neck.

I'll soon be home, he thought. Nothing is going to happen. Mrs Dunér has recorded in my diary that I was to be at Farnholm today. Nobody, not even he, would send his henchmen to kill off his own elderly lawyer on the way home from a meeting. It would be far too risky.

It was nearly two years before he first realised that something untoward was going on. It was an insignificant assignment, checking contracts that involved the Swedish Trade Council as guarantors for a considerable sum of money. Spare parts for turbines in Poland, combine harvesters for Czechoslovakia. It was a minor detail, some figures that didn't add up. He thought it was probably a misprint, maybe somewhere two digits had been muddled. He had gone through it all again and realised that it was no accident, it was all intentional. Nothing was missing, everything was correct, but the upshot was horrifying. His first instinct had been not to believe it. He had leaned back in his chair – it was late in the evening, he recalled – taking in that there was no doubt that he had uncovered a crime. It was dawn before he had set out to walk the streets of Ystad, and by the time he reached Stortorget he had reluctantly accepted that there was no alternative explanation: the man at Farnholm Castle was guilty of a gross breach of trust regarding the Trade Council, of tax evasion and of a whole string of forgeries.

Thereafter he had been constantly on the lookout for the black holes in every document emanating from Farnholm. And he found them – not every time, but more often than not. The extent of the criminality had slowly dawned on him. He tried not to acknowledge the evidence he could not avoid registering, but in the end he had to face up to the facts. But on the other hand he had done nothing about it. He had not even told his son. Was this because, deep down, he preferred to believe it wasn't true? Nobody else, apparently not even the tax authorities, had noticed anything. Perhaps he had uncovered a secret that was purely hypothetical? Or was it that it was all too late anyway, now that the man from Farnholm Castle was the principal source of income for the firm?

The fog was more or less impenetrable now. He hoped it might lift as he got nearer to Ystad.

He couldn't go on like this, that was certain. Not now that he knew that the man had blood on his hands.

He would talk to his son. The rule of law still applied in Sweden, for heaven's sake, even though it seemed to be undermined and diluted day by day. His own complaisance had been a part of that process. His having for so long turned a blind eye was no reason now for remaining silent.

He would never bring himself to commit suicide.

Suddenly he saw something in the headlights. He slammed on the brakes. At first he thought it was a hare. Then he realised there was something in the road.

He turned his headlights on full beam.

It was a chair, in the middle of the road. A simple kitchen chair. Sitting on it was a human-sized effigy. Its face was white.

Or could it be a real person made up like a tailor's dummy?

He felt his heart starting to pound. Fog swirled in the light of his headlamps. There was no way he could shut out the chair and the effigy. Nor could he ignore his mounting fear. He checked his rear-view mirror. Nothing.

7

He drove slowly forward until the chair and the effigy were no more than ten metres from the car. Then he stopped again.

The dummy looked impressively like a human being. Not just some kind of hastily got-up scarecrow. It's for me, he thought. He switched off the radio, his hand trembling, and pricked up his ears. Fog, and silence. He didn't know what to do next.

What made him hesitate was not the chair out there in the fog, nor the ghostly effigy. There was something else, something in the background, something he couldn't make out. Something that probably existed only inside himself.

I'm very frightened, he said to himself, and fear is undermining my ability to think straight.

Finally, he undid his safety belt and opened the door. He was surprised by how cool it felt outside. He got out, his eyes fixed on the chair and the dummy lit up by the car's headlights. His last thought was that it reminded him of a stage set with an actor about to make his entrance.

He heard a noise behind him, but he didn't turn. The blow caught him on the back of his head.

He was dead before his body hit the damp asphalt. It was 9.53 p.m. The fog was now very dense.

Chapter 2

The wind was gusting from due north.

The man, a long way out on the freezing cold beach, was suffering in the icy blasts. He kept stopping and turning his back to the wind. He would stand there, motionless, staring at the sand, his hands deep in his pockets; then he would go on walking, apparently aimlessly, until he would be lost from sight in the grey twilight.

A woman who every day walked her dog on the sands had grown anxious about the man who seemed to patrol the beach from dawn to dusk. He had turned up out of the blue a few weeks ago, a species of human jetsam washed ashore. People she came across on the beach normally greeted her. It was late autumn, the end of October, so in fact she seldom came across anybody at all. But the man in the black overcoat never acknowledged her. At first she thought he was shy, then rude, or perhaps a foreigner. Gradually she came to feel that he was weighed down by some appalling sorrow, that his beach walks were a pilgrimage taking him away from some unknowable source of pain. His gait was decidedly erratic. He would walk slowly, almost dawdling, then suddenly come to life and break into what was almost a trot. It seemed to her that what dictated his movements was not so much physical as his disturbed spirit. She was convinced that his hands were clenched into fists inside his pockets.

After a week she thought she had worked it out. This stranger had landed on this strand from somewhere or other in order to come to terms with a serious personal crisis, like a vessel with inadequate charts edging its way through a treacherous channel. That must be the cause of his introversion, his restless walking. She had mentioned the solitary wanderer on the beach every night to her husband, whose rheumatism had forced him into early retirement. Once he had even accompanied her and the dog though his condition caused him a great deal of pain and he was much happier staying indoors. He had thought that his wife was right, though he'd found the man's behaviour so strikingly out of the ordinary that he had phoned a friend in the Skagen police and confided in him his own and his wife's observations. Possibly the man was on the run, wanted for some crime, or had absconded from one of the few mental hospitals left in the country? But the police officer had seen so many odd characters over the years, most of them having made the pilgrimage to the furthest tip of Jutland only in search of peace and quiet, that he counselled his friend to be wise: just leave the man alone. The strand between the dunes and the two seas that met there was a constantly changing no man's land for whoever needed it.

The woman with her dog and the man in the black overcoat went on passing each other like ships in the night for another week. Then one day – on October 20, 1993, in point of fact – something happened which she would later connect with the man's disappearance.

It was one of those rare days when there was not a

10

breath of wind, when the fog lay motionless over both land and sea. Foghorns had been sounding in the distance like lost, invisible cattle. The whole of this strange setting was holding its breath. Then she had caught sight of the man in the black overcoat and stopped dead.

He was not alone. He was with a shortish man in a light-coloured windcheater and cap. She noticed that it was the new arrival who was doing the talking, and seemed to be trying to convince the other about something. Occasionally he took his hands from his pockets and gestured to underline what he was saying. She could not hear what they were saying, but there was about the smaller man's manner something that told her he was upset.

After a while they set off along the beach and were swallowed up by the fog.

The following day the man was alone again. Five days later he was gone. She walked the dog on the beach every morning until well into November, expecting to come across the man in black; but he did not reappear. She never saw him again.

For more than a year Kurt Wallander, a detective chief inspector with the Ystad police, had been on sick leave, unable to carry out his duties. During that time a sense of powerlessness had come to dominate his life and affected his actions. Time and time again, when he could not bear to stay in Ystad and had some money to spare, he had gone off on pointless journeys in the vain hope of feeling better, perhaps even of recovering his zest for life, if only he were somewhere other than Skåne. He had taken a package holiday to the Caribbean, but had drunk himself silly on the outward flight and had not

11

been entirely sober for any of the fortnight he spent in Barbados. His general state of mind was one of increasing panic, a sense of being totally alienated. He had skulked in the shade of palm trees, and some days had not even set foot outside his hotel room, unable to overcome a primitive need to avoid the company of others. He had bathed just once, and then only when he'd stumbled on a jetty and fallen into the sea.

Late one evening when he had forced himself to go out and mix with other people, but also in order to replenish his stock of alcohol, he had been solicited by a prostitute. He wanted to wave her away and yet somehow encouraged her at the same time, and was only later overwhelmed by misery and self-disgust. For three days, of which he afterwards had no clear memory, he spent all his time with the girl in a shack stinking of vitriol, in a bed with sheets smelling of mould and cockroaches crawling over his sweaty face. He could not even remember the girl's name or if he had ever discovered what it was. He had taken her in what could only have been a fit of unbridled lust. When she had extracted the last of his money two burly brothers appeared and threw him out. He went back to the hotel and survived by forcing down as much as he could of the breakfast included in the price, eventually arriving back at Sturup airport in a worse state than when he had left.

His doctor, who gave him regular check-ups, forbade him any more such trips as there was a real danger that Wallander would drink himself to death. But two months later, at the beginning of December, he was off again, having borrowed money from his father on the pretext of buying some new furniture in order to raise his spirits. Ever since his troubles started he had avoided his father, who had just married a woman 30 years his junior who used to be his home help. The moment he had the money in his hand, he made a beeline for the Ystad Travel Agency and bought a three-week package holiday in Thailand. The pattern of the Caribbean repeated itself, the difference being that catastrophe was narrowly averted because a retired pharmacist who had sat next to him on the flight and who happened to be at the same hotel took pity on him and stepped in when Wallander began drinking at breakfast and generally acting strangely. The pharmacist's intervention resulted in Wallander's being sent home a week earlier than planned. On this holiday, too, he had surrendered to his self-disgust and thrown himself into the arms of prostitutes, each one younger than the last. There followed a nightmarish winter when he was in constant dread of having contracted the fatal disease.

By the end of April, when he had been off work for ten months, it was confirmed that he was not in fact infected; but he seemed not to react to the good news. That was about the time his doctor began to wonder if Wallander's days as a police officer were over, whether indeed he would ever be fit to work again, or was ready for immediate early retirement on the grounds of ill health.

That was when he went – perhaps "ran away" would be more accurate – to Skagen the first time. By then he had managed to stop drinking, thanks not least to his daughter Linda coming back from Italy and discovering the mess both he and his flat were in. She had reacted in exactly the right way: emptied all the bottles scattered about the flat, and read him the riot act. For the two weeks she stayed with him in Mariagatan, he at last had somebody to talk to. Together they were able to lance most of the abscesses eating into his soul, and by the time she left she felt that she might be able to give a little credence to his promise to stay off the booze. On his own again and unable to face the prospect of sitting around in the empty flat, he had seen an advertisement in the newspaper for an inexpensive guest house in Skagen.

Many years before, soon after Linda was born, he had spent a few weeks in the summer at Skagen with his wife Mona. They had been among the happiest weeks of his life. They were short of money and lived in a tent that leaked, but it seemed to them that the whole universe was theirs. He telephoned that very day and booked himself a room starting in the first week of May.

The landlady was a widow, Polish originally, and she left him to his own devices. She lent him a bicycle. Every morning he went riding along the endless sands. He took a plastic carrier bag with a packed lunch, and did not come back to his room until late in the evening. His fellow guests were elderly, singles and couples, and it was as quiet as a library reading room. For the first time in over a year he was sleeping soundly, and he had the feeling his insides were shedding the effects of his heavy drinking.

During that first stay at the guest house in Skagen he wrote three letters. The first was to his sister Kristina. She had often been in contact during the past year, asking how he was. He had been touched by her concern, but he had scarcely been able to bring himself to write to her, or to telephone. Things were made worse by a vague memory of having sent her a garbled postcard from the Caribbean when he was far from sober. She had never mentioned it, he had never asked; he hoped he had been so drunk that he had got the address wrong, or forgotten to put a stamp on the card. Now he sat in bed one night and wrote to her, resting the paper on his briefcase. He tried to describe the feeling of emptiness, of shame and guilt that had dogged him ever since he had killed a man last year. He had unquestionably acted in self-defence, and not even the most aggressive and police-hating of reporters had taken him to task, but he felt that he would never manage to shake off the burden of guilt. His only hope was that he might one day learn to live with it.

"I feel as if part of my soul has been replaced by an artificial limb," he wrote. "It still doesn't do what I want it to do. Sometimes, in my darkest moments, I'm afraid it might never again obey me, but I haven't given up hope altogether."

The second letter was to his colleagues at the police station in Ystad, and by the time he was about to put it in the red letter box outside the post office in Skagen, he realised that a good part of what he had written was untrue, but that he had to send it even so. He thanked them for the hi-fi system they had clubbed together to give him last summer, and asked them to forgive his not having done so earlier. He meant all that sincerely, of course. But when he ended the letter by saying he was getting better and hoped to be back at work soon, those were just meaningless words: the polar opposite was nearer the truth.

The third letter he wrote during that stay in Skagen was to Baiba Liepa. He had written to her every other month or so over the past year, and she had replied every time. He had begun to think of her as his private patron

15

saint, and his fear of upsetting her so that she might stop replying led him to suppress his feelings for her. Or at least he thought he had. The long, drawn-out process of being undermined by inertia had made him unsure of anything any more. He had brief interludes of absolute clarity, usually when he was on the beach or sitting among the dunes sheltering from the biting cold winds blowing off the sea, and it sometimes seemed to him the whole thing was pointless. He had met Baiba for only a few days in Riga. She had been in love with her murdered husband, Karlis, a captain in the Latvian police force – why in God's name should she suddenly transfer her affections to a Swedish police officer who had done no more than was demanded of him by his profession, even if it had happened in a somewhat unorthodox fashion? But he had no great difficulty dismissing those moments of insight. It was as if he did not dare risk losing what deep down he knew was something he did not even have. Baiba, his dream of Baiba, was his last line of defence. He would defend it to the bitter end, even if it was only an illusion.

He stayed ten days at the guest house, and when he went back to Ystad he had already made up his mind to return as soon as he could. By mid July he was in his old room again. Again the widow lent him a bicycle and he spent his days by the sea. Unlike the first time, the beach was now full of holidaymakers, and he felt as if he was wandering like an invisible shadow among all these people as they laughed, played and paddled. It was as if he had established a territory on the beach where the two seas met, an area under his personal control invisible to everyone else, where he could patrol and keep an eye on himself as he tried to find a way

16

out of his misery. His doctor thought he could detect some improvement in Wallander after his first spell in Skagen, but the indications were still too weak for him to assert that there had been a definite change for the better. Wallander asked if he could stop taking the medication he had been on for more than a year, since it made him feel tired and sluggish, but the doctor urged him to be patient for a little longer.

Every morning he wondered if he would have the strength to get out of bed, but it was easier when he was at the guest house in Skagen. There were moments when he felt he could forget the awful events of the previous year, and there were glimmerings of hope that he might after all have a future.

As he wandered the beach for hour after hour, he began slowly to go through what lay behind it all, searching for a way to overcome and cast off the burden, maybe even to find the strength to become a police officer again, a police officer and a human being.

It was during that visit that he had stopped listening to opera. He would often take his little cassette player on his walks along the beach, but one day it came to him that he had had enough. When he got back to the guest house that evening he packed all his opera cassettes away into his suitcase and put it in the wardrobe. The next day he cycled into Skagen and bought some recordings of pop artists he had barely heard of. What surprised him most was that he did not miss the music that had kept him going for so many years.

I have no space left, he thought. Something inside me has filled up to the brim, and soon the walls will burst.

*

He was back in Skagen in the middle of October. He was firmly resolved this time to work out what he would do with the rest of his life. His doctor had encouraged him to return to the guest house, which obviously did his patient good. There were signs of a gradual return to health, a tentative withdrawal from the depths of depression. Without betraying his oath of confidentiality, he also intimated to Björk, Wallander's boss, that there might just possibly be a chance of the invalid coming back to work at some point.

So Wallander went to Denmark again and set out once more on his walks along the beach. It was late autumn and the sands were deserted. He seldom encountered another human being, and the ones he did see were mostly old, apart from the occasional sweat-stained jogger; and there was a busybody regularly walking her dog. He resumed his patrols, watching over his lonely territory, marching with gathering confidence towards the just visible and constantly shifting line where the beach met the sea.

He was well into middle age now, and the milestone of 50 was not far off. During the last year he had lost so much weight he found himself having to hunt in his wardrobe for clothes he had been unable to get into for the past seven or eight years. He was in better physical shape than he had enjoyed for ages, especially now that he had stopped drinking. That seemed to him a possible starting point for his future plans. Barring accidents, he could have at least 20 more years to live. What exercised him most was whether he would be able to return to police duties, or whether he would have to find something else to do. He refused even to consider early retirement on health grounds. That was a prospect he didn't think he could cope with. He spent his time on the beach, usually enveloped in drifting fog but with occasional days of fresh, clear air, glittering seas and gulls soaring up above. Sometimes he felt like the clockwork man who had lost the key that normally stuck out of his back, and hence lacked the possibility of being wound up, of finding new sources of energy. He pondered his options were he forced to leave the police force. He might become a security guard or the like with some firm or other. He could not see what his service as a police officer actually qualified him for, apart from chasing criminals. His options were limited, unless he decided to make a clean break and put behind him his many years of police work. But who would be willing to employ a former officer approaching 50, whose only expertise was unravelling more or less confused crime scenes?

When he felt hungry he would leave the beach and find a sheltered spot in the dunes. He tucked into his packed lunch and used the plastic carrier bag to sit on, protecting himself from the cold sand. As he ate, he tried hard – without much success – to think of something other than his future. He made every effort to be realistic, but always he had to fend off unrealistic dreams.

Like all other police officers, he was sometimes tempted to go over to the other side. He never ceased to be amazed by the officers who had turned criminals and yet failed to use their knowledge of fundamental police procedures that would have helped them to avoid being caught. He often toyed with schemes which would instantly make him rich and independent, but usually it did not take long to come to his senses and banish any such thoughts with a shudder. What he wanted least of all was to follow in the steps of his colleague Hanson, who seemed to him obsessed, spending so much of his time betting on horses that hardly ever won. Wallander could not imagine himself ever wasting time like that.

He kept coming back to the question of whether he was duty-bound to return to the police force. Start work again, fight off the memories of what happened a year ago, and maybe one day manage to live with them. The only realistic option was for him to go on as before. That was the nearest he came to finding a glimmer of a meaning in life: helping people to lead as secure an existence as possible, removing the worst criminals from the streets. To give up on that would not only mean turning his back on a job he knew he did well – perhaps better than most of his colleagues – it would also mean undermining something deep inside him, the feeling of being a part of something greater than himself, something that made his life worth living.

But eventually, when he had been in Skagen a week, and autumn was showing signs of turning into winter, he was forced to admit that he would not now be up to the job. His career as a police officer was over, the wounds inflicted by what happened the previous year had changed him irrevocably. It was an afternoon when the beach was shrouded in thick fog when he decided that the arguments for and against were exhausted. He would talk to his doctor and to Björk. He would not return to duty.

Deep down he felt a vague sense of relief. Now at least he knew the score. The man he had killed last year in the field with all the sheep hidden in the fog had his revenge.

He cycled in to Skagen that night and got drunk in

a little, smoke-filled bar, where the customers were few and far between and the music too loud. He knew that for once he would not be carrying on his binge the next day. This was merely a way of confirming the fateful conclusion he had reached, that his life as a policeman had come to an end. Riding back to the guest house at the dead of night, he fell off and grazed his cheek. The landlady had noticed his absence and was sitting up, waiting for him. Despite his protests, she insisted on cleaning the blood off his face and on taking his filthy clothes to wash. Then she helped him to unlock the door of his room.

"There was a man here this evening, asking for Mr Wallander," she said, handing him back the key.

He looked blankly at her.

"Nobody asks for me," he said. "Nobody even knows I'm here."

"This man did," she said. "He was anxious to find you."

"Did he give you his name?"

"No, but he was Swedish."

Wallander shook his head and tried to put it out of his mind. He did not want to see anybody, and nobody wanted to see him either, he was sure of that.

The next day he was full of regrets and went back to the beach, never giving a thought to what the landlady had told him. The fog was thick, and he felt very tired. For the first time he asked himself what he thought he was doing on the beach. After only a kilometre or so he wondered if he had the strength to go on, and sat down on the upturned hulk of a large rowing boat half-buried in the sand.

It was then that he noticed a man approaching

21

through the fog. It was as if somebody had intruded on the privacy of his office out there on the boundless sands.

His first impression was of a blurred stranger, wearing a windcheater and a cap that seemed too small for his head. Then he seemed vaguely familiar, but it was not until he had come closer and Wallander had stood up that he realised who it was. They shook hands, and Wallander wondered how on earth his refuge had been discovered. He tried to remember when he had last seen Sten Torstensson, and thought that it must have been in connection with some court proceedings that last fateful spring.

"I came to see you last night at the guest house," Torstensson said. "I don't want to disturb you, of course, but I must talk to you."

Once upon a time I was a police officer and he was a solicitor, Wallander thought, that's all there was to it. We used to sit on either side of criminals, and occasionally but not very often we might argue about whether or not an arrest was justified. We got to know each other a bit better during the difficult period of my divorce from Mona, when he took care of my interests. One day we realised something had clicked, something that might be the beginnings of a friendship. Friendship often develops out of a meeting at which nobody had expected any such miracle to happen. But friendship is a miracle, that's something life has taught me. He invited me out sailing one weekend. It was blowing a gale, and I vowed I would never set foot on a sailing boat again. Then we started meeting, not all that often, not regularly. And now he's tracked me down and wants to talk.

"I heard that somebody had been asking for me,"

22

Wallander said. "How the hell did you find me here?"

He knew he was making it clear he resented being disturbed in his refuge among the dunes.

"You know me," Torstensson said, "I'm not the sort to make a nuisance of myself. My secretary claims I'm sometimes frightened of being a nuisance to myself, whatever she means by that. But I phoned your sister in Stockholm. Or rather, I got in touch with your father and he gave me her number. She knew the name of the guest house, and where it was. And so here I am. I stayed the night at the hotel next to the Art Museum."

They had started walking along the beach, the wind behind them. The woman who was always out with her dog had stopped and was staring at them, and Wallander was sure she would be surprised to see he had a visitor. They walked in silence, and Wallander waited for Torstensson to speak, feeling how odd it was to have someone by his side.

"I need your help," Torstensson said, eventually. "As a friend and as a police officer."

"As a friend," Wallander said. "If I can. Which I doubt. But not as a police officer."

"I know you're still off work," Torstensson said.

"Not only that. You can be the first to know that I'm packing it in altogether."

Torstensson stopped in his tracks.

"That's how it is," Wallander said. "But tell me why you're here."

"My father's dead."

Wallander had known him. He, too, was a solicitor, although he only occasionally appeared in court. As far as Wallander could remember, the older Torstensson spent most of his time advising on financial matters. He tried to work out how old he must have been. Getting on for 70, he supposed, an age by which quite a lot of people are dead already.

"He died in a road accident some weeks ago," Torstensson said. "Just south of Brösarp Hills."

"I'm sorry to hear that," Wallander said. "What happened?"

"That's a good question. That's why I'm here."

Wallander looked at him blankly.

"It's cold," Torstensson said. "They serve coffee at the Art Museum. I have the car with me."

Wallander nodded. His bicycle was sticking out of the boot as they drove through the dunes. There were not many customers in the Art Museum café at that time in the morning. The girl behind the counter was humming a tune Wallander was surprised to recognise from one of his new cassettes.

"It was late in the evening," Torstensson began. "October 11, to be precise. Dad had been to see one of our most important clients. According to the police he'd been driving too fast, lost control, the car had over-turned and he was killed."

"It can happen in a flash," Wallander said. "Lose concentration for just a second, and the result can be catastrophic."

"It was foggy that evening," Torstensson said. "Dad never drove fast. Why would he have done so when it was foggy? He was obsessed by the fear of running over a hare."

Wallander studied him. "What's on your mind?"

"Martinsson was in charge of the case."

"He's good," Wallander said. "If Martinsson says that's what happened, there's no reason to think otherwise."

24

Torstensson looked gravely at him. "I've no doubt Martinsson is a good police officer," he said. "Nor do I doubt they found my father dead in his car, which was upside down and badly knocked about in a field beside the road. But there's too much that doesn't add up. Something more must have happened."

"What?"

"Something else."

"Such as?"

"I don't know."

Wallander went to the counter to refill his cup.

Why don't I tell him the truth? he wondered. That Martinsson is both imaginative and energetic, but can on occasions be careless.

"I've read the police report," Torstensson said, when Wallander had sat down again. "I've taken it with me and read it at the spot where my father died. I've read the post-mortem notes, I've spoken to Martinsson, I've done some thinking and I've asked again. Now I'm here."

"What can I do?" Wallander said. "You're a solicitor, you know that in every case there are a few loose ends that we can never manage to tie up. I take it your father was alone in the car when it happened. If I understand you rightly, there were no witnesses. Which means the only person who could tell us exactly what happened was your father."

"Something happened," Torstensson said. "Something's not right and I want to know what it is."

"I can't help you, although I'd like to."

Torstensson seemed not to hear him. "The keys," he said. "Just to give you one example. They weren't in the ignition. They were on the floor."

"They could have been knocked out," Wallander said. "When a car crashes, anything can happen."

"The ignition was undamaged," Torstensson said. "The ignition key was not even bent."

"There could be an explanation even so."

"I could give you other examples," Torstensson insisted. "I know that something happened. My dad died in a car accident that was really something else."

Wallander thought before replying. "Might he have committed suicide?"

"That possibility did occur to me, but I'm sure it can be discounted. I knew my father well."

"The majority of suicides are unexpected," Wallander said. "But, of course, you know best what you want to believe."

"There's another reason why I cannot accept the accident theory," Torstensson said.

Wallander looked at him sharply.

"My father was a cheerful, outgoing man," Torstensson said. "If I hadn't known him so well, I might not have noticed the change. Little things, barely noticeable, but very definitely a change in his mood during the last six months."

"Can you be more precise?"

Torstensson shook his head. "Not really," he said. "It was just a feeling I had. Something was worrying him. Something he was very keen to make sure I wouldn't notice."

"Did you ever speak to him about it?"

"Never."

Wallander put his empty cup down. "I'd like to help you, but I can't," he said. "As your friend, I can listen to what you have to say. But I no longer exist as a police officer. I don't even feel flattered by the fact that you've come all the way here to talk to me. I just feel numb and tired and depressed."

Torstensson opened his mouth to speak, but thought better of it.

They stood up and left the café.

"I respect what you say, of course," Torstensson said as they stood outside the Art Museum.

Wallander went with him to the car and recovered his bicycle.

"We never know how to handle death," Wallander said in a clumsy attempt to convey his sympathy.

"I'm not asking you to," Torstensson said. "I just want to know what happened. That was no ordinary car accident."

"Have another word with Martinsson," Wallander said. "But it might be best if you don't mention that I suggested that."

They said goodbye, and Wallander watched the car drive off through the dunes.

He was struck by the feeling that matters were getting urgent. He couldn't keep dragging things out any longer. That afternoon he telephoned his doctor and Björk and informed them that he had decided to resign from the police force.

He stayed at Skagen for five more days. The feeling that his soul was a devastated bomb site was as strong as ever. But he felt relieved nevertheless, having had the strength to make up his mind despite everything.

He came back to Ystad on Sunday, October 31, in order to sign the various forms that would draw the line under his police career.

On the Monday morning, November 1, he lay in bed with his eyes wide open after the alarm went off at 6.00. Apart from brief periods of restless dozing, he had been awake all night. Several times he had got out of bed and stood at the window overlooking Mariagatan, thinking that he had made yet another wrong decision. Perhaps there was no obvious path for him to follow for the rest of his life. Without finding any satisfactory answer to that, he had sat on the sofa in the living room listening to the radio. Eventually, just before the alarm rang, he had accepted that he had no choice. He was running away, no doubt about that; but everybody runs away sooner or later, he told himself. Invisible forces get the better of all of us in the end. Nobody escapes.

He got up, dressed, went out for the morning paper, came home, put on the water for coffee and took a shower. It felt odd, going back to the old routine just for a day. As he dried himself down, he tried to recall his last working day almost 18 months ago. It was summer when he cleared his desk and then went to the harbour café to write a gloomy letter to Baiba. He found it hard to decide whether it felt like an age ago, or just yesterday.

He sat at the kitchen table and stirred his coffee.

Then it had been his last day at work for who knew how long. Now it was his last day at work, ever.

He had been in the police force for more than 25 years. No matter what happened in the years to come, those years would be the backbone of his life, nothing could change that. Nobody can ask to have their life declared invalid, and demand that the dice be thrown afresh. There is no going back. The question was whether there was any way forward.

He tried to identify his emotions this cold morning,

28

but all he felt was emptiness. It was as if the autumn mists had penetrated his consciousness.

He gave a sigh, and turned to his newspaper. He leafed through it and had the distinct impression that he had seen all the photographs and read all the articles any number of times before.

He was about to put it down when a death announcement caught his eye. *Sten Torstensson, solicitor, born March 3, 1947, died October 26, 1993.*

He stared hard at the notice. Surely it was the father, Gustaf Torstensson, who was dead? He had talked to Sten just over a week ago, on the sands at Skagen.

He tried to work out what it meant. It must be somebody else. Or the names had got mixed up. He read it again. There was no mistake. Sten Torstensson, the man who'd come to see him in Denmark five days ago, was dead.

He sat there, motionless.

Then he stood up, checked in the phone book and dialled a number. The person he was calling was an early riser.

"Martinsson."

Wallander resisted an urge to put the receiver down. "It's me, Kurt," he said. "I hope I didn't wake you up."

There was a long silence before Martinsson responded. "Is it really you?" he said. "Now there's a surprise!"

"I can imagine," Wallander said. "But there is something I need to ask you."

"It can't be true that you're packing it in."

"That's the way it goes," Wallander said. "But that's not why I'm calling. I want to know what happened to Sten Torstensson, the lawyer."

"Haven't you heard?"

29

"I only got back to Ystad yesterday. I haven't heard anything."

There was a pause. "He was murdered," Martinsson said at last.

Wallander was not surprised. The moment he had seen the notice in the paper, he had known it was not death by natural causes.

"He was shot in his office last Tuesday night," Martinsson said. "It's beyond belief. And tragic. It's only a few weeks since his father was killed in a car accident. But maybe you didn't know that either?"

"No," Wallander lied.

"You've got to come back to work," Martinsson said. "We need you to sort this out. And much more besides."

"No. My mind's made up. I'll explain when we meet. Ystad's a little town. You bump into everybody sooner or later."

Then Wallander said goodbye and hung up.

As he did so, he realised that what he had just said to Martinsson was no longer true. In just a few seconds, everything had changed.

He stood by the phone for more than five minutes. Then he drank his coffee, dressed and went down to his car. At 7.30 he walked through the police-station door for the first time in 18 months. He nodded to the security guard in reception, made a beeline for Björk's office and knocked on the door. Björk stood up as he came in, and Wallander noticed that he was thinner. He could see, too, that Björk was uncertain as to how to deal with the situation.

I'm going to make it easy for him, Wallander thought. He won't understand a thing at first, but then, neither do I.

"Naturally we're pleased to hear you seem to be better," Björk began, hesitantly. "But, of course, we'd prefer you to be coming back to work rather than leaving us. We need you." He gestured towards his desk, piled high with papers. "Today I have to respond to important matters such as a proposed new design for police uniforms, and yet another incomprehensible draft for a change in the system involving relations between the county constabulary and the county police chiefs. Have you kept up with this?"

Wallander shook his head.

"I wonder where we're heading?" said Björk, glumly. "If the new uniform design goes through, it's my belief that in future police officers will look like something between a carpenter and a ticket collector."

He looked at Wallander, inviting a comment, but Wallander said nothing.

"The police were nationalised in the 1960s," Björk said. "Now they're going to do it all over again. Parliament wants to abolish local constabularies and create something entirely new and call it the National Police Force. But the police has always been a national force. What else could it be? The sovereign legal systems of independent provinces were lost in the Middle Ages. How do they think anybody can get on with a day's work when they're buried under an avalanche of woolly memoranda? To cap it all I have to prepare a lecture for a totally unnecessary conference on what they call 'refusal-of-entry techniques'. What they mean is what to do when aliens who can't get a visa have to be loaded on to buses and ferries and deported without too much kerfuffle and protest."

"I realise you're very busy," Wallander said, thinking

31

that Björk hadn't changed an atom. He'd never got his role as Chief of Police under control. The job controlled him.

"I've got all the papers here," Björk went on. "All we need is your signature, and you're an ex-policeman. I have to accept your decision, even if I don't like it. By the way, I hope you don't mind, but I've called a press conference for 9 a.m. You've become a famous police officer in the last few years, Kurt. Even if you've acted a little strangely every now and again, there's no denying you've done a lot for our good name and reputation. They do say that there are police cadets who claim to have been inspired by you."

"I'm sure that's not true," Wallander said. "And you can cancel the press conference."

He could see that this annoyed Björk.

"Out of the question," he said. "It's the least you can do for your colleagues. Besides, *Swedish Police* magazine is going to run a feature on you."

Wallander walked up to Björk's desk.

"I'm not packing it in," he said. "I've come here today to start work again."

Björk stared at him in astonishment.

"There won't be a press conference," Wallander said. "I'm starting work again as of now. I'm going to get the doctor to sign a certificate to say I'm fit. I feel good. I want to work."

"I hope you're not pulling my leg," said Björk, uneasily.

"No," Wallander said. "Something's happened that's changed my mind."

"This is very sudden."

"For me as well. To be precise it's just over an hour

since I changed my mind. But I have one condition. Or rather, a request."

Björk waited.

"I want to be in charge of the Sten Torstensson case," Wallander said. "Who's in charge at the moment?"

"Everybody's involved," Björk said. "Svedberg and Martinsson are in the main team, together with me. Åkeson is the prosecutor in charge."

"Young Torstensson was a friend of mine," Wallander said.

Björk nodded and rose to his feet. "Is this really true?" he said. "Have you really changed your mind?"

"You heard what I said."

Björk walked round his desk and stood face to face with Wallander. "That's the best piece of news I've heard for a very long time," he said. "Let's tear these documents up. Your colleagues are in for a surprise."

"Who's got my old office?" Wallander said.

"Hanson."

"I'd like it back, if possible."

"Of course. Hanson's on a course in Halmstad this week anyway. You can move in straight away."

They walked down the corridor together until they came to Wallander's old office. His nameplate had been removed. That threw him for a moment.

"I need an hour to myself," Wallander said.

"We have a meeting at 8.30 about the Torstensson murder," Björk said. "In the little conference room. You're sure you're serious about this?"

"Why shouldn't I be?"

Björk hesitated before continuing. "You have been known to be a bit whimsical, even injudicious," he said. "There's no getting away from that."

"Don't forget to cancel the press conference," Wallander said.

Björk reached out his hand. "Welcome back," he said.

"Thanks."

Wallander closed the door behind Björk and immediately took the phone off the hook. He looked round the room. The desk was new. Hanson had brought his own. But the chair was Wallander's old one.

He hung up his jacket and sat down.

Same old smell, he thought. Same furniture polish, same dry air, same faint aroma of the endless cups of coffee that get drunk in this station.

He sat for a long time without moving.

He'd agonised for a year and more, searched for the truth about himself and his future. A decision had gradually formed and broken through the indecision. Then he had started reading a newspaper and everything had changed.

For the first time in ages he felt a glow of satisfaction.

He had reached a decision. Whether it was the right one he could not say. But that didn't matter any more.

He reached for a notepad and wrote: *Sten Torstensson*. He was back on duty.

Chapter 3

At 8.30, when Björk closed the door of the conference room, Wallander felt as if he had never been away. The year and a half that had passed since his last investigation meeting had been erased. It was like waking up from a long slumber during which time had ceased to exist.

They were sitting around the oval table, as so often before. As Björk had still not said anything, Wallander assumed his colleagues were expecting a short speech to thank them for their friendship and cooperation over the years. Then he would take his leave and the rest would concentrate on their notes and get on with the search for the killer of Sten Torstensson.

Wallander realised that he had instinctively taken his usual place, on Björk's left. The chair on the other side was empty. It was as if his colleagues did not want to intrude too closely on somebody who did not really belong any more. Martinsson sat opposite him, sniffing loudly. Wallander wondered when he had ever seen Martinsson without a cold. Next to him sat Svedberg, rocking backwards and forwards on his chair and scratching his bald head with a pencil, as usual.

Everything would have been just as before, it seemed

to Wallander, had it not been for the woman in jeans and a blue blouse sitting on her own at the opposite end of the table. He had never met her, but he knew who she was, and even knew her name. It was almost two years since they had started talking about strengthening the Ystad force, and that was when the name Ann-Britt Höglund had cropped up for the first time. She was young, had graduated from Police Training College barely three years before, but had already made a name for herself. She had received one of two prizes awarded on the basis of final examinations and general achievements in the assessment of her fellow cadets. She came from Svarte originally, but had grown up in the Stockholm area. Police forces all over the country had tried to enrol her, but she made it clear she would like to return to Skåne, the province of her birth, and took a job with the Ystad force.

Wallander caught her eye, and she smiled fleetingly at him.

So, it is not the same as it was before, he thought. With a woman among us, nothing can stay as it used to be.

That was as much as he had time to think. Björk had risen to his feet, and Wallander sensed that he was nervous. Perhaps it had been too late. Perhaps his contract had already been terminated without his knowing?

"Monday mornings are normally hard going," Björk said. "Especially when we have to deal with the particularly unpleasant and incomprehensible murder of one of our colleagues, Mr Torstensson. But today I am able to commence our meeting with some good news. Kurt has announced that he is back to good health, and is starting work again as of now. I am the first to welcome him

36

back, of course, but I know all my colleagues feel the same. Including Ann-Britt Höglund, whom you haven't met yet."

There was silence. Martinsson stared at Björk in disbelief, and Svedberg put his head to one side, gaping at Wallander as if he couldn't believe his ears. Ann-Britt Höglund looked as if what Björk had just said hadn't sunk in.

Wallander felt bound to say something. "It's true," he said. "I'm starting work again today."

Svedberg stopped rocking to and fro and slammed the palms of his hands down on the table with a thud. "That's terrific news, Kurt. We couldn't have managed another damned day without you."

Svedberg's spontaneous comment made the whole room burst out laughing. One after another they stood up in a queue to shake Wallander by the hand. Björk tried to organise coffee and pastries, and Wallander had difficulty in hiding the fact that he was moved.

It was all over in a few minutes. There was no more time for emotional outpourings for which Wallander was grateful, at least for now. He opened the notebook he had brought with him from his office, containing nothing but Sten Torstensson's name.

"Kurt has asked me if he can join the murder investigation without more ado," Björk said. "Of course he can. I think the best way to kick off is by making a summary of how things stand. Then we can give Kurt a little time to familiarise himself with the particulars."

He nodded to Martinsson, who had obviously been the one to take on Wallander's role as team leader.

"I'm still a bit confused," Martinsson said, leafing through his papers. "But basically this is how it looks.

On the morning of Wednesday, October 27, in other words five days ago, Mrs Berta Dunér – secretary to the firm of solicitors – arrived for work as usual, a few minutes before 8 a.m. She found Sten Torstensson shot dead in his office. He was on the floor between the desk and the door. He had been hit by three bullets, each one of which would have been enough to kill him. As nobody lives in the building, which is an old stone-built house with thick walls, and located on a main road as well, nobody heard the shots. At least, nobody has come forward as yet. The preliminary post-mortem results indicate he was shot at around 11 p.m. That would fit in with Mrs Dunér's statement to the effect that he often worked late at night, especially after his father died in such tragic circumstances."

Martinsson paused at this point and looked questioningly at Wallander.

"I know his father died in a road accident," Wallander said.

Martinsson nodded and continued: "That's more or less all we know. In other words, we know next to nothing. We don't have a motive, no murder weapon, no witness."

Wallander wondered if he ought to say something about Torstensson's visit to Skagen. All too often he had committed what was a cardinal sin for a police officer and held back information that he should have passed on to his colleagues. On each occasion, it's true, he reckoned that he had good grounds for keeping quiet, but he had to concede that his explanations had almost always been unconvincing.

I'm making a mistake, he thought. I'm starting my second life as a police officer by disowning everything previous experience has taught me. Nevertheless, something told him it was important in this particular case. He treated his instinct with respect. It could be one of his most reliable messengers, as well as his worst enemy. He was certain he was doing the right thing this time.

Something Martinsson had said made him prick up his ears. Or perhaps it was something he had not said.

His train of thought was interrupted by Björk slamming his fist on the table. This normally meant that the Chief of Police was annoyed or impatient.

"I've asked for pastries," he said, "but there's no sign of them. I suggest we break off at this point and that you fill Kurt in on the details. We'll meet again this afternoon. We might even have something to go with our coffee by then."

When Björk had left the room, they all gathered round the end of the table he had vacated. Wallander felt he had to say something. He had no right simply to barge in on the team and pretend nothing had happened.

"I'll try to start at the beginning," he said. "It's been a rough time. I honestly didn't think I'd ever be able to get back to work. Killing a man, even if it was in self-defence, hit me hard. But I'll do my best."

Nobody said a word.

"You mustn't think we don't understand," Martinsson said, at last. "Even if police work trains you to get used to just about everything, making you think there's no end to how awful life can be, it really strikes home when adversity lands on somebody you know well. If it makes you feel any better, I can tell you that we've missed you just as much as we missed Rydberg a few years ago."

Dear old Chief Inspector Rydberg, who died in the spring of 1991, had been their patron saint. Thanks to his enormous abilities as a police officer, and his willingness to treat everybody in a way that was both straightforward and personal, he had always been right at the heart of every investigation.

Wallander knew what Martinsson meant.

Wallander had been the only one who had grown so close to Rydberg that they had been good friends. Behind Rydberg's surly exterior was a person whose knowledge and experience went far beyond the criminal cases they investigated together.

I've inherited his status, Wallander thought. What Martinsson is really saying is that I should take on the mantle that Rydberg had, but never displayed publicly. Even invisible mantles exist.

Svedberg stood up.

"If nobody has any objection I'm going over to Torstensson's offices," he said. "Some people from the Bar Council have turned up and are going through his papers. They want a police officer to be present."

Martinsson slid a pile of case documents over to Wallander.

"This is all we've got so far," he said. "I expect you'd like a bit of peace and quiet to work your way through them."

Wallander nodded. "The road accident. Gustaf Torstensson."

Martinsson looked up at him in surprise. "That's finished and done with," he said. "The old fellow drove into a field."

"If you don't mind, I'd still like to see the reports," Wallander said, tentatively.

Martinsson shrugged. "I'll drop them off in Hanson's office."

"Not any more," Wallander said. "My old room is mine again."

Martinsson got to his feet. "You disappeared one day, and now you're back just as suddenly. Forgive the slip of the tongue."

Martinsson left the room. Only Wallander and Ann-Britt Höglund were left now.

"I've heard a lot about you," she said.

"I'm sure what you've heard is absolutely true, I regret to say."

"I think I could learn a lot from you."

"I very much doubt that."

Wallander got hurriedly to his feet to cut short the conversation, gathering the papers he had been given by Martinsson. Höglund held open the door for him. When he was back in his office and had closed the door behind him, he noticed he was running with sweat. He took off his jacket and shirt, and started drying himself on one of the curtains. Just then Martinsson opened the door without knocking. He hesitated when he caught sight of the half-naked Wallander.

"I was just bringing you the reports on Gustaf Torstensson's car accident," Martinsson said. "I forgot it wasn't Hanson's door any longer."

"I may be old-fashioned," Wallander said, "but please knock in future."

Martinsson put a file on Wallander's desk and beat a hasty retreat. Wallander finished drying himself, put on his shirt, then sat at his desk and started reading.

It was gone 10.30 by the time he finished the reports.

Everything felt unfamiliar. Where should he start? He thought back to Sten Torstensson, emerging out of the fog on the Jutland beach. He asked me for help, Wallander thought. He wanted me to find out what had happened to his father. An accident that was really something else, and not suicide. He talked about how his father's state of mind had seemed to change. A few days later he himself was shot in his office late at night. He had talked about his father being on edge, but he was not on edge himself.

Deep in thought, Wallander pulled towards him the notebook in which he had previously written Torstensson's name. He added another: Gustaf Torstensson. Then he wrote them again in the reverse order.

He picked up the phone and dialled Martinsson's number. No answer. He tried again, still no answer. Then it dawned on him that the numbers must have been changed while he was away. He walked down the corridor to Martinsson's office. The door was open.

"I've been through the investigation reports," he said, sitting down on Martinsson's rickety visitor's chair.

"Nothing much to go on, as you'll have noted," Martinsson said. "One or more intruders break into Torstensson's offices and shoot him. Apparently nothing was stolen. His wallet still in his inside pocket. Mrs Dunér's been working there for more than 30 years and she is sure that nothing is missing."

Wallander nodded. He still hadn't unearthed what it was that Martinsson had said or not said earlier which had made him react.

"You were first on the scene, I suppose?" he said.

"Peters and Norén were there first, in fact," Martinsson said. "They sent for me."

"One usually gets a first impression on occasions like this," Wallander said. "What did you think?"

"Murder with intent to rob," Martinsson said without hesitation.

"How many of them were there?"

"We've found no evidence to suggest whether there was just one, or more than one. But only one weapon was used, we can be pretty sure of that, even if the technical reports are not all in yet."

"So, was it a man who broke in?"

"I think so," Martinsson said. "But that's just a gut feeling with nothing to support or reject it."

"Torstensson was hit by three bullets," Wallander said. "One in the heart, one in the stomach just below the navel, and one in his forehead. Am I right in thinking that that suggests a marksman who knew what he was doing?"

"That struck me too," Martinsson said. "But of course it could have been pure coincidence. They say death is caused just as often by random shots as by shots from a skilled marksman. I read that in some American report."

Wallander got to his feet. "Why should anybody want to break into a solicitor's office?" he asked. "Presumably because lawyers are said to earn huge amounts of money. But would anybody really expect to find the money piled up in their office?"

"There's only one or perhaps two persons who could answer that question," Martinsson said.

"We'll catch them," Wallander said. "I think I'll go there and have a look around."

"Mrs Dunér is pretty shaken, naturally," Martinsson said. "In less than a month the whole fabric of her life has collapsed. First old man Torstensson dies. Hardly has she got over sorting out the funeral arrangements than his son is murdered. She's in shock, but even so it's surprisingly easy to talk to her. Her address is on the transcript of the conversation Svedberg had with her."

"Stickgatan 26," Wallander read. "That's just behind the Continental Hotel. I sometimes park there."

"Isn't that an offence?" Martinsson said.

Wallander collected his jacket and left the station. He had never seen the girl in reception before. He thought that perhaps he ought to have introduced himself. Not least to find out whether Ebba, who had been there for years, had stopped working evenings. But he let it pass. The time he had spent in the station so far today had seemed on the face of it to be nothing dramatic, but that did not reflect the tension inside him. He felt he needed to be on his own. For some considerable time now he had spent most of his days alone. He needed time to make the transformation. He drove down the hill towards the hospital, and just for a moment felt a vague yearning for the solitariness of Skagen, for his isolated sentry duty and his beach patrols that were guaranteed not to be disturbed.

But that was all in the past. He was back at work now.

I'm not used to it, he thought. It'll pass, even if it takes time.

The solicitors' offices were in a yellow-painted stone building in Sjömansgatan, not far from the old theatre that had been getting a facelift. A patrol car was parked outside, and on the opposite pavement a handful of onlookers were discussing what had happened. The wind was gusting in from the sea, and Wallander shuddered as he clambered out of his car. He opened the heavy front door and almost collided with Svedberg on his way out.

"I thought I'd get a bite to eat," he said.

"Go ahead," Wallander said. "I expect to be here for a while."

A young clerk was sitting in the front office with nothing to do. She looked anxious. Wallander remembered from the reports that her name was Sonia Lundin, and that she had been working there only a few months. She had not been able to provide the investigation with any useful information.

Wallander shook hands with her and introduced himself.

"I'm just going to take a look around," he said. "Mrs Dunér's not here, I suppose?"

"She's at home, crying," the girl said.

Wallander had no idea what to say.

"She'll never survive all this," Lundin said. "She'll die too."

"Oh, I don't think so," Wallander said, conscious of how hollow his response sounded.

The Torstensson legal practice had been a workplace for solitary people, he thought. Gustaf Torstensson had been a widower for more than 15 years and so his son Sten had been without a mother all that time and was a bachelor to boot. Mrs Dunér had been divorced since the early '70s. Three solitary people who came into contact with each other day after day. And now two of them were gone, leaving the third more alone than ever.

Wallander had no difficulty in understanding why Mrs Dunér was at home crying.

45

The door to the meeting room was closed. Wallander could hear murmuring from inside. The lawyers' nameplates were on the doors on either side of the meeting room, fancily printed on highly polished brass plates.

On the spur of the moment he opened first the door to Gustaf Torstensson's office. The curtains were drawn and the room was in darkness. There was a faint aroma of cigar smoke. Wallander looked around and had the feeling that he had gone back to an earlier age. Heavy leather sofas, a marble table, paintings on the walls. It occurred to him that he had overlooked one possibility: that whoever murdered Sten Torstensson was there to steal the objets d'art. He walked up to one of the paintings and tried to decipher the signature, trying also to establish whether it was a copy or an original. Without having been successful on either count, he moved on. There was a large globe next to the solid-looking desk, which was empty, apart from some pens, a telephone and a Dictaphone. He sat in the comfortable desk chair and continued to look around the room, thinking again about what Sten Torstensson had said to him in the café at the Art Museum in Skagen.

A car accident that wasn't a car accident. A man who had spent the last months of his life trying to hide something that was worrying him.

Wallander asked himself what would be the characteristics of a solicitor's life. Supplying legal advice. Defending when a prosecutor prosecutes. A solicitor was always receiving confidential information. Lawyers were under a strict oath of confidentiality. It dawned on him that solicitors had a lot of secrets to keep. He hadn't thought of that before.

He got to his feet after a while. It was too soon to draw any conclusions.

Lundin was still sitting motionless on her chair. He opened the door to Sten Torstensson's office. He hesitated for a second, as if half expecting to see the dead man's body lying there on the floor, as it was in the photographs he had seen in the case reports, but all that was left was a plastic sheet. The technical team had taken the dark green carpet away with them.

The room was not unlike the one he had just left. The only obvious difference was a pair of visitors' chairs in front of the desk. This time Wallander refrained from sitting down. There were no papers on the desk.

I'm still only scraping at the surface, he thought. I feel as if I'm listening as much as I am trying to get my bearings by looking.

He went out to the reception area, closing the door behind him. Svedberg was back and was trying to persuade the girl to have one of his sandwiches. Wallander shook his head on being offered one as well. He pointed to the meeting room.

"In there are two worthy gentlemen from the Bar Council," Svedberg said. "They're working their way through all the documents in the place. They record, seal and wonder what to do about them. Clients will be contacted and other solicitors will take over their business. Torstensson Solicitors to all intents and purposes no longer exists."

"We must have access to all the material, of course," Wallander said. "The truth about what happened might well lie somewhere in their relationships with their clients."

Svedberg raised his eyebrows and looked at Wallander. "Their?" he said. "I expect you mean the son's clients."

"You're right. I do mean Sten Torstensson's clients."

"It's a pity really that it's not the other way round."

Wallander almost missed Svedberg's comment. "Why, what do you mean?"

"It would appear that old man Torstensson had very few clients," Svedberg said. "Sten Torstensson, on the other hand, was mixed up in all kinds of things." He nodded in the direction of the meeting room. "They think they'll need a week or more to get through it."

"I'd better not interrupt them, then," Wallander said. "I think I'd rather be having a word with Mrs Dunér."

"Do you want me to come with you?"

"No need, I know where she lives."

Wallander went back to his car and started the engine. He was in two minds. Then he forced himself to come to a decision. He would start with the lead that nobody except him knew about. The lead Sten Torstensson had given him in Skagen.

They have to be connected, Wallander thought as he drove slowly eastwards, passed the courthouse and Sandskogen and soon left the town behind. These two deaths are linked. There is no other rational explanation.

He contemplated the grey landscape he was travelling through. It was drizzling. He turned up the heater.

How can anybody fall in love with all this mud? he wondered. But that's exactly what I have done. I am a police officer whose existence is forever hemmed in by mud. And I wouldn't change this countryside for all the tea in China.

It took him a little more than half an hour to get to the place where Gustaf Torstensson had died on the night of October 11. Wallander had the accident report with him, and stepped out on to the windy road with it in his pocket. He took out his wellingtons and changed into them before he started scouting around. The wind was getting stronger, as was the rain, and he felt cold. A buzzard perched on a crooked fencing pole, watching him.

The scene of the accident was unusually desolate even for Skåne. There was no sign of a farmhouse, nothing but undulating brown fields as far as the eye could see. The road was straight, then started to climb a hundred metres or so ahead before turning sharply left. Wallander unfolded the sketch of the scene of the accident, and compared the map with the ground itself. The wrecked car had been lying upside down to the left of the road, 20 metres into the field. There were no skid marks on the road. It had been thick fog when the accident occurred.

Wallander put the report back into the car before it got soaked. He walked to the crown of the road, and looked around. Not one car had gone past. The buzzard was still on its pole. Wallander jumped over the ditch and squelched his way across muddy clay that immediately clung to the soles of his boots. He paced out 20 metres and looked back towards the road. A butcher's van drove past, and then two cars. The rain was getting heavier all the time. He tried to envisage what had happened. A car with an old man driving is in the midst of a patch of thick fog. The driver loses control, the car leaves the road, spins round once or twice and ends up on its roof. The driver is dead, held into his seat by his safety belt. Apart from some grazing on his face, he has smashed the back of his head against

49

some hard, projecting metallic object. In all probability death was instantaneous. He is not discovered until dawn the next day when a farmer passing on his tractor sees the car.

He need not have been going fast, Wallander thought. He might have lost control and hit the accelerator in panic. The car sped out into the field. What Martinsson wrote up about the scene of the accident was probably comprehensive and correct.

He was about to call it a day when he noticed something half buried in the mud. He bent down and saw that it was the leg of one of those brown wooden kitchen chairs. He threw it away, and the buzzard flew off from its pole, flapping away with its heavy wings.

There's still the wrecked car, Wallander thought, but I don't expect I'll find anything startling there that Martinsson has not noted already.

He went back to his car, scraped as much of the mud off his boots as he could, and changed into his shoes. As he drove back to Ystad he wondered whether he ought to take advantage of the opportunity to call in on his father and his new wife at Löderup, but decided against it. He needed to talk to Mrs Dunér, and if possible also look at the wreck before returning to the police station.

He stopped at the service station just outside Ystad for a cup of coffee and a sandwich, and looked about him. Dour Swedish gloom was nowhere more strikingly in evidence than in cafés attached to petrol stations, he decided. He left his coffee almost untasted, keen to escape the atmosphere. He drove through the rain into town, turned right at the Continental Hotel and then right again into narrow Stickgatan. He parked semi-legally outside the pink house where Berta Dunér lived, both near-side wheels on the pavement. He rang the bell and waited. It was nearly a minute before the door opened. He could just see a pale face through the narrow gap.

"My name's Kurt Wallander and I'm a police officer," he said, searching in vain through his pockets for his identity card. "I'd like to have a chat with you, if I may."

Mrs Dunér opened the door and let him in. She handed him a coat hanger, and he hung up his wet jacket. She invited him into the living room, which had a polished wooden floor and a large picture window looking over a small garden behind the house. He looked around the room and noted that he was in a flat where everything had its place: furniture and ornaments were arranged in orderly fashion, down to the most minuscule detail.

No doubt she ran the solicitors' offices in the same way. Watering the plants and making sure that engagement diaries were impeccably maintained might be two sides of the same coin. A life in which there is no room for chance.

"Please, do sit down," she said in an unexpectedly gruff voice. Wallander had expected this unnaturally thin, grey-haired woman to speak in a soft or feeble voice. He sat on an old-fashioned rattan chair that creaked as he made himself comfortable.

"Can I offer you a cup of coffee?" she said.

Wallander shook his head.

"Tea?"

"No, thank you," Wallander said. "I just want to ask you a few questions. Then I'll be away."

She sat on the edge of a flower-print sofa on the other side of the glass-topped coffee table. Wallander

51

realised he had with him neither pen nor notebook. Nor had he prepared even the opening questions, which had always been his routine. He had learned at an early stage that there is no such thing as an insignificant interview or conversation in the course of a criminal investigation.

"May I first say how much I regret the tragic incidents that have taken place," he began tentatively. "I had only occasionally met Gustaf Torstensson, but I knew Sten Torstensson well."

"He looked after your divorce nine years ago," Berta Dunér said.

As she spoke it came to Wallander that he recognised her. She was the one who had received Mona and himself whenever they had gone to the solicitor's for what usually turned out to be harrowing and annihilating meetings. Her hair had not been so grey then, and perhaps she was not quite so thin. Even so, he was surprised that he had not recognised her straight away.

"You have a good memory," he said.

"I sometimes forget a name," she said, "but never a face."

"I'm the same," Wallander said.

There was an awkward silence. A car passed by. It was clear to Wallander that he ought to have waited before coming to see Mrs Dunér. He did not know what to ask her, did not know where to start. And he had no desire to be reminded of the bitter and long, drawn-out divorce proceedings.

"You have spoken already to my colleague Svedberg," he said after a while. "Unfortunately, it is often necessary to continue asking questions when a serious crime has been committed, and it might not always be the same officer."

He groaned inwardly at the clumsy way he was expressing himself. He very nearly made his excuses and left. Instead, he forced himself to get his act together.

"I don't need to ask about what I already know," he said. "We don't need to go over again how you turned up for work that morning and discovered that Sten Torstensson had been murdered. Unless of course you have since remembered something that you did not mention before."

Her reply was firm and unhesitating. "Nothing. I told Mr Svedberg precisely what happened."

"The previous evening, though?" Wallander said. "When you left the office?"

"It was around 6 p.m. Perhaps five minutes past, but not later. I had been checking some letters that Miss Lundin typed. Then I rang through to Mr Torstensson to check whether there was anything else he wanted me to do. He said there wasn't, and bade me good evening. I put on my coat and went home."

"You locked the door behind you? And Mr Torstensson was all by himself?"

"Yes."

"Do you know what he had in mind to do that evening?"

She looked at him in surprise. "Carry on working, of course. A solicitor with as much work on his hands as Sten Torstensson cannot just go home when it suits him."

"I understand that he was working," Wallander said. "I was just wondering if there had been some special job, something urgent?"

"Everything was urgent," she said. "As his father had been killed only a few weeks before, his workload was immense. That's pretty obvious."

Wallander raised his eyebrows at her choice of words. "You're referring to the car accident, I assume?"

"What else would I be referring to?"

"You said his father had been killed. Not that he'd lost his life in an accident."

"You die or you are killed," she said. "You die in your bed of what is generally called natural causes, but if you die in a car accident, surely you have to accept that you were killed?"

Wallander nodded slowly. He understood what she meant. Nevertheless, he wondered if she had inadvertently said something that might be along the same lines as the suspicions that had led Sten Torstensson to find him at Skagen.

A thought struck him. "Can you remember off the top of your head what Mr Torstensson was doing the previous week?" he said. "Tuesday, October 20, and Wednesday, October 21."

"He was away," she said, without hesitation.

So, Sten Torstensson had made no secret of his visit, he thought.

"He said he needed to get away for a couple of days, to shake off all the sorrow he was feeling after the death of his father," she said. "Accordingly, I cancelled his appointments for those two days."

And then, without warning, she burst into tears. Wallander was at a loss how to react. His chair creaked as he shifted in embarrassment.

She stood up and hurried out to the kitchen. He could hear her blowing her nose. Then she returned.

"It's hard," she said. "It's so very hard."

"I understand."

"He sent me a postcard," she said with a very faint smile. Wallander was sure she would start crying again at any moment, but she was more self-possessed than he had supposed.

"Would you like to see it?"

"Yes, I would," Wallander said.

She went to a bookshelf on one of the long walls, took a postcard from a porcelain dish and handed it to him.

"Finland must be a beautiful country," she said. "I have never been there. Have you?"

Wallander stared at the card in confusion. The picture was of a seascape in evening sunshine.

"Yes," he said slowly. "I've been to Finland. And as you say, it's very beautiful."

"Please forgive me for getting upset," she said. "You see, the postcard arrived the day I found him dead."

Wallander nodded absent-mindedly. It seemed to him there was a lot more he needed to ask Berta Dunér than he had suspected. At the same time, he recognised that this was not the right moment.

So Torstensson had told his secretary that he had gone to Finland. A postcard had arrived from there, apparently as proof. Who could have sent it? Torstensson was in Jutland.

"I need to hang on to this card for a couple of days, in connection with the investigation," he said. "You'll get it back. I give you my word."

"I understand," she said.

"Just one more question before I go," Wallander said. "Did you notice anything unusual those last few days before he died?"

"In what way unusual?"

"Did he behave at all differently from normal?"

"He was very upset and sad about the death of his father."

"Of course, but no other reason for anxiety?"

Wallander could hear how awkward the question sounded, but he waited for her answer.

"No," she said. "He was the same as usual."

Wallander got to his feet. "I'm sure I'll need to talk to you again," he said.

She did not get up from the sofa. "Who could have done such a horrible thing?" she asked. "Walk in through the door, shoot a man and then walk out again, as if nothing had happened?"

"That's what we're going to find out," Wallander said. "I suppose you don't know if he had any enemies?"

"Enemies? How could he have had enemies?"

Wallander paused a moment, then asked one last question. "What do you yourself think happened?"

"There was a time when you could understand things, even things that seemed incomprehensible," she said. "Not now, though. It's just not possible in this country nowadays."

Wallander put on his jacket, which was still wet and heavy. He paused when he went out into the street. He thought about a slogan going the rounds at the time he graduated from Police Training College, sentiments he had adopted as his own. "There's a time for life, and a time for death."

He also thought about what Mrs Dunér had said as he was leaving. He felt that she had said something significant about Sweden, something he ought to come back to. But for now he banished her words to the back of his mind.

I must try to understand the minds of the dead, he thought. A postcard from Finland, postmarked the day when Torstensson was drinking coffee with me in Skagen, makes it clear that he wasn't telling the truth. Not the whole truth, at least. A person can't lie without being aware of it.

He got into his car and tried to make up his mind what to do. For himself, what he wanted most of all was to go back to his flat in Mariagatan, and lie down on the bed with the curtains drawn. As a police officer, however, he must think otherwise.

He checked his watch: 1.45 p.m. He would have to be back at the station by 4.00 at the latest, for the meeting of the investigation team. He thought for a moment before deciding. He started the engine, turned into Hamngatan and bore left to emerge on to the Österleden highway again. He continued along the Malmö road until he came to the turning off to Bjäresjö. The rain had become drizzle, but the wind was gusting. A few kilometres further on he left the main road and stopped outside a fenced-in yard with a rusty sign announcing that this was Niklasson's Scrapyard. The gates were open so he drove in among the skeletons of cars piled on top of each other. He wondered how many times he had been to the scrapyard in his life. Over and over again Niklasson had been suspected of receiving, and been prosecuted for the offence on many occasions. He was legendary in the Ystad police force: he had never once been convicted, in spite of overwhelming evidence of his guilt. But in the last resort there had always been one little spanner that had got stuck in the works, and

Niklasson had invariably been set free to return to the two caravans welded together that constituted both his home and his office.

Wallander switched off the engine and got out of the car. A grubby-looking cat studied him from the bonnet of an ancient, rusty Peugeot. Niklasson emerged from behind a pile of tyres. He was wearing a dark-coloured overcoat and a filthy hat pulled down over his long hair. Wallander had never seen him in any other attire.

"Kurt Wallander!" Niklasson said with a grin. "Long time no see. Here to arrest me?"

"Should I be?" Wallander said.

Niklasson laughed. "Only you can say," he said.

"You have a car I'd like to take a look at," Wallander said. "A dark blue Opel that used to be owned by Gustaf Torstensson, the solicitor."

"Oh, that one. It's over here," he said, starting in the direction he was pointing. "What do you want to see that for?"

"Because a person in it died when the accident took place."

"People drive like idiots," Niklasson said. "The only thing that surprises me is that more of them aren't killed. Here it is. I haven't started cutting it up yet. It's exactly as it was when they brought it here."

Wallander nodded. "I can manage on my own now," he said.

"I've no doubt you can," Niklasson said. "Incidentally, I've always wondered what it feels like, killing somebody."

Wallander was put out. "It feels bloody awful," he said. "What did you think it would feel like?"

Niklasson shrugged. "I just wondered."

When he was on his own, Wallander walked round

the car twice. He was surprised to see that there was hardly any superficial damage. After all, it had gone through a stone wall and then turned over at least twice. He squinted into the driving seat. The car keys were lying on the floor next to the accelerator. With some difficulty he managed to open the door, pick up the keys and fit them into the ignition. Sten had been quite right. Neither the keys nor the ignition were damaged. Thinking hard, he walked once more round the car. Then he climbed inside and tried to work out where Gustaf Torstensson had hit his head. He searched thoroughly, without finding a solution. Although there were stains here and there that he supposed must be dried blood, he could not see anywhere where the dead man could have hit the back of his head.

He crawled out of the car again, the keys still in his hand. Without really knowing why, he opened the boot. There were a few old newspapers and the remains of a broken kitchen chair. He remembered the chair leg he had found in the field. He took out one of the newspapers and checked the date. More than six months old. He shut the boot again.

Then it dawned on him what he had seen without it registering. He remembered clearly what it said in Martinsson's report. It had been quite clear on one matter. All the doors apart from the driver's door had been locked, including the boot.

He stood stock-still.

There's a broken chair locked in the boot. A leg from that chair is lying half buried in the mud. A man is dead in the car.

His first reaction was to get angry about the slipshod examination and the unimaginative conclusions reached. Then he remembered that Sten had not found the chair leg either, and hence had not noticed anything odd about the boot.

He walked slowly back to his car.

So Sten had been right. His father had not lost his life in a car accident. Even though he couldn't envisage what, he was certain that something had happened that night in the fog, on that deserted stretch of road. There must have been at least one other person there. But who?

Niklasson emerged from his caravan.

"Can I get you a coffee?" he said.

Wallander shook his head. "Don't touch that car," he said. "We'll need to take another look at it."

"You'd better be careful," Niklasson said.

Wallander frowned. "Why?"

"What's his name? The son? Sten Torstensson? He was here and had a look at the car. Now he's dead as well. That's all. I'll say no more."

A thought struck Wallander. "Has anybody else been here and examined the car?" he said.

Niklasson shook his head. "Not a soul."

Wallander drove back to Ystad. He felt tired. He could not work out the significance of what he had discovered. But the bottom line was not in doubt: Sten had been right. The accident was a cover for something entirely different.

It was 4.07 p.m. when Björk closed the meeting-room door. Wallander immediately felt that the mood was half-hearted, uninterested. He could sense that none of his colleagues was going to have anything to report which would have a decisive, not to say a dramatic, effect on the investigation. This is one of those moments in the everyday life of a police officer that inevitably ends up on the cutting-room floor. Nevertheless, it's times like this when nothing's happening, when everybody's tired, maybe even hostile towards one another, that are the foundation on which the course of the investigation is built. We have to tell one another that we do not know anything in order to inspire us to move on.

At that point he made up his mind. Whether it was an attempt to find himself an excuse for returning to duty and asking for his job back he could never afterwards be sure. But that half-hearted atmosphere gave him the inspiration to perform again; it was a background against which he could show that he was still a police officer, despite everything, not a burned-out wreck who ought to have had the wit to fade away in silence.

His train of thought was broken by Björk, who was looking at him expectantly. Wallander shook his head, a barely noticeable gesture. He had nothing to say as yet.

"What have we got to report?" Björk said. "Where do we stand?"

"I've been knocking on doors," Svedberg said. "All the surrounding buildings, every single flat. But nobody heard anything unusual, nobody saw anything. Oddly enough we haven't had one single tip-off from the general public. The whole investigation seems to be in limbo."

Björk turned to Martinsson.

"I've been through his flat in Regementsgatan," he said. "I don't think I've ever been so unsure of what I was looking for. What I can say for sure is that Sten Torstensson had a liking for fine cognac, and that he

61

owned a collection of antiquarian books which I suspect must be very valuable. I've also been putting pressure on the technical boys in Linköping about the bullets, but they say they'll be in touch tomorrow."

Björk sighed and turned to Höglund.

"I've been trying to piece together his private life," she said. "His family, friends. But I haven't turned anything up that you could say takes us any further. He didn't exactly put himself about, and you could say he lived almost exclusively for his work as a solicitor. He used to do a fair bit of sailing in the summer, but he had given that up, for reasons I'm unsure about. He doesn't have many relatives. One or two aunts, a couple of cousins. He seems to have been a bit of a hermit, so far as I can understand."

Wallander kept his eye on her while she was talking, without making it obvious. There was something thoughtful and straightforward about her, almost a lack of imagination. But he decided he would reserve judgment. He didn't know her as a person, he was just aware of her reputation as an unusually promising police officer.

The new age, he thought. Perhaps she is the new type of police officer, the type I have often wondered about, what would they look like?

"In other words, we're marking time," Björk said, in a clumsy attempt to sum up. "We know young Torstensson has been shot, we know where and we know when. But not why, nor by whom. Unfortunately, we have to accept that this is going to be a difficult case. Time-consuming and demanding."

Nobody had any quarrel with that assessment. Wallander could see through the window that it was raining again.

He recognised that his moment had come. "As far as Sten Torstensson is concerned, I have nothing to add," he said. "There is not a lot we know. We have to approach it from another angle. We have to look at what happened to his father."

Everyone round the table sat up and took notice.

"Gustaf Torstensson did not die in a road accident," he said. "He was murdered, just as his son was. We can assume that the two cases are linked. There is no other satisfactory explanation."

He looked at his colleagues, who were all staring fixedly at him. The Caribbean island and the endless sands at Skagen were now far, far away. He was aware that he had sloughed off that skin, and returned to the life he thought he had abandoned for good.

"In short, I have only one more thing to say," he said, thoughtfully. "I can prove he was murdered."

Nobody spoke. Martinsson eventually broke the silence.

"By whom?"

"By somebody who made a bad mistake." Wallander rose to his feet.

Soon afterwards they were in three cars in a convoy on their way to that fateful stretch of road near Brösarp Hills.

When they got there dusk was settling in.

Chapter 4

In the late afternoon of November 1, Olof Jönsson, a Scanian farmer, had a strange experience. He was walking his fields, planning ahead for the spring sowing, when he caught sight of a group of people standing in a semicircle up to their ankles in mud, as if looking down at a grave. He always carried binoculars with him when he was inspecting his land – he sometimes saw deer along the edge of one of the copses that here and there separated the fields – so he was able to get a good view of them. One of them he thought he recognised – something familiar about the face – but he could not place him. Then he realised that the four men and one woman were in the place where the old man had died in his car the previous week. He did not want to intrude, so he lowered his binoculars. Presumably they were relatives who had come to pay their respects by visiting the scene of his death. He turned and walked away.

When they came to the scene of the accident Wallander started to wonder, just for a moment, if he had imagined it all. Perhaps it wasn't a chair leg he had found in the mud and thrown away. As he strode into the field the others stayed on the road, waiting. He could hear their voices, but not what they said.

They think I've lost my grasp, he thought, as he searched for the leg. They wonder if I am fit to be back in my old job after all.

But there was the chair leg, at his feet. He examined it quickly, and now he was certain. He turned and beckoned to his colleagues. Moments later they were grouped round the chair leg lying in the mud.

"You could be right," Martinsson said, hesitantly. "I remember there was a broken chair in the boot. This could be a piece of it."

"I think it's very odd, even so," Björk said. "Can you repeat your line of reasoning, Kurt?"

"It's simple," Wallander said. "I read Martinsson's report. It said that the boot had been locked. There's no way that the boot could have sprung open and then reclosed and locked itself. In that case the back of the car would have been scored or dented when it hit the ground, but it isn't."

"Have you been to look at the car?" Martinsson said, surprised.

"I'm simply trying to catch up with the rest of you," Wallander said, and felt as if he were making excuses, as if his visit to Niklasson's had implied that he didn't trust Martinsson to conduct a simple accident investigation. Which was true, in fact, but irrelevant. "It just seems to me that a man alone in a car that rolls over and over and lands up in a field doesn't then get out, open the boot, take out a leg of a broken chair, shut the boot again, get back into the car, fasten his safety belt and then die as a result of a blow to the back of the head."

Nobody spoke. Wallander had seen this before, many times. A veil is peeled away to reveal something nobody expected to see.

Svedberg took a plastic bag from his overcoat pocket and carefully slotted the chair leg into it.

"I found it about five metres from here," Wallander said, pointing. "I picked it up, and then tossed it away."

"A bizarre way to treat a piece of evidence," Björk said.

"I didn't know at the time that it had anything to do with the death of Gustaf Torstensson," Wallander said. "And I still don't know what the chair leg is telling us exactly."

"If I understand you rightly," Björk said, ignoring Wallander's comment, "this must mean that somebody else was there when Torstensson's accident took place. But that doesn't necessarily mean he was murdered. Somebody might have stumbled upon the crashed car and looked to see if there was anything in the boot worth stealing. In that case it wouldn't be so odd if the person concerned didn't get in touch with the police, or if he threw away a leg from the broken chair. People who rob dead bodies very rarely publicise their activities."

"That's true," Wallander said.

"But you said you could prove he was murdered," Björk said.

"I was overstating the case," Wallander said. "All I meant was that this goes some way towards changing the situation."

They made their way back to the road.

"We'd better have another look at the car," Martinsson said. "The forensic boys will be a bit surprised when we send them a broken kitchen chair, but that can't be helped."

Björk made it plain that he would like to put an end to this roadside discussion. It was raining again, and the wind was getting stronger.

"Let's decide tomorrow where we go from here," he said. "We'll investigate the various leads we've got, and unfortunately we don't have very many. I don't think we're going to get any further at the moment."

As they returned to their cars, Höglund hung back. "Do you mind if I go in your car?" she said. "I live in Ystad itself, Martinsson has child seats everywhere and Björk's car is littered with fishing rods."

Wallander nodded. They were the last to leave. They drove in silence for several kilometres. It felt odd to Wallander to have somebody sitting beside him. He realised he had not spoken properly to anybody apart from his daughter since the day 18 months ago when he had lapsed into his long silence.

She was the one who finally started talking. "I think you're right," she said. "There must be a connection between the two deaths."

"It's a possibility we'll have to look into in any case," Wallander said.

They could see a patch of sea to the left. There were white horses riding on the waves.

"Why does anybody become a police officer?" Wallander wondered aloud.

"I can't answer for others," she said, "but I know why I became one. I remember from Police Training College that hardly anybody had the same dreams as the other students."

"Do police officers have dreams?" Wallander said, in surprise.

She turned to him. "Everybody has dreams," she said. "Even police officers. Don't you?"

Wallander didn't know what to say, but her question was a good one, of course. Where have my dreams gone to? he thought. When you're young, you have dreams that either fade away or develop into a driving force that spurs you on. What have I got left of all my ambitions?

"I became a police officer because I decided not to become a vicar," she said. "I believed in God for a long time. My parents are Pentecostalists. But one day I woke up and found it had all gone. I agonised for ages over what to do, but then something happened that made my mind up for me, and I resolved to become a police officer."

"Tell me," he said. "I need to know why people still want to become police officers."

"Some other time," she said. "Not now."

They were approaching Ystad. She told him how to get to where she lived, to the west of the town, in one of the newly built brick houses with a view over the sea.

"I don't even know if you have a family," Wallander said, as they turned into a road that was still only half finished.

"I have two children," she said. "My husband's a service mechanic. He installs and repairs pumps all over the world, and is hardly ever at home. But he's earned enough for us to buy the house."

"Sounds like an exciting job."

"I'll invite you round one evening when he's at home. He can tell you himself what it's like."

He drew up outside her house.

"I think everybody's pleased you've come back," she said as a parting shot.

Wallander felt immediately that it wasn't true, that it was more of an attempt to cheer him up, but he muttered his appreciation.

Then he drove straight home to Mariagatan, flung his wet jacket over the back of a chair, and lay on the bed, still in his dirty shoes. He dozed off and dreamed that he was asleep among the sand dunes at Skagen.

When he woke up an hour later, he did not know where he was at first. Then he took his shoes off and went to the kitchen to make coffee. He could see through the window how the street light beyond was swaying in the gusting wind.

Winter is almost upon us, he thought. Snow and storms and chaos. And I am a police officer again. Life tosses us all hither and thither. Is there anything we can truly decide for ourselves?

He sat for a long time staring into his coffee cup. It was cold by the time he got up to fetch a notepad and pencil from a kitchen drawer.

Now I really must become a police officer again, he told himself. I get paid for thinking constructive thoughts, investigating and sorting out cases, not for worrying about my own petty problems.

It was gone midnight by the time he put down his pen and stretched his back. Then he pored over the summary he had written in his notepad. All about his feet the floor was littered with crumpled-up sheets of paper.

I can't see any pattern, he admitted. There are no obvious connections between the accident that wasn't an accident and the fact that a few weeks later Sten Torstensson was shot dead in his office. It doesn't even necessarily follow that Sten's death was a direct result of what happened to his father. It could be the other way round.

He remembered something Rydberg had said in the last year of his life, when he was stuck in the middle of an apparently insoluble investigation into a string of arson cases. "Sometimes the effect can come before the cause," he had said. "As a police officer you have always to be prepared to think back to front."

He lay on the living-room sofa.

An old man is found dead in his car in a field on a morning in October, he thought. He was on his way home from a meeting with a client. After a routine investigation, the case is written off as a car accident. But the dead man's son starts to question the accident theory. For two crucial reasons: first, that his father would never have been driving fast in the fog; second, that for some time he had been worried or upset, but had kept whatever it was to himself.

Wallander sat bolt upright. His instinct told him he had hit upon a pattern, or rather, a non-pattern, a pattern falsified so that the true facts would not come to light.

He continued his train of thought. Sten had not been able to prove that his father's death had not been a straightforward accident. He had not seen the chair leg in the field, nor had he thought about the broken chair itself in the boot of his father's car. Precisely because he had not been able to find any proof, he had turned to Wallander. He had gone to the trouble of tracking him down, of coming to see him.

At the same time he had laid a false trail. A postcard from Finland. Five days later he was shot. No-one could doubt that it was murder.

Wallander had lost the thread. What he thought he had sensed – a pattern created to cover up another one – had drifted off into no man's land.

He was tired. He wasn't going to get any further tonight. He knew, too, from experience that if his suspicions had any basis they would come back.

He went to the kitchen, washed the dishes and cleared up the crumpled papers lying all over the floor. I have to start all over again, he told himself. But where is the start? Sten or Gustaf Torstensson?

He went to bed, but could not sleep despite being so tired. He wondered vaguely about what had happened to make Ann-Britt Höglund decide to become a police officer.

The last time he looked at the clock it was 2.30 a.m.

He woke up shortly after 6.00, still feeling tired; but he got up, with a sense that he had slept in. It was almost 7.30 by the time he walked through the police-station door and was pleased to see that Ebba was in her usual chair in reception. When she saw him she came to greet him. He could see that she was moved, and a lump came into his throat.

"I couldn't believe it!" she said. "Are you really back?"

"Afraid so," Wallander said.

"I think I'm going to cry," she said.

"Don't do that," Wallander said. "We can have a chat later."

He got away as quickly as he could and hurried down the corridor. When he got to his office he noticed that it had been thoroughly cleaned. There was also a note on his desk asking him to phone his father. Judging by the obscure handwriting, it was Svedberg who had taken the message the previous evening. He reached for the telephone, then changed his mind. He took out the summary he had prepared and read through it. The feeling he had had of being able to detect an obscure but nevertheless definite pattern linking the various incidents would not resurrect itself. He pushed the papers to one side. It's too soon, he decided. I come back after 18 months in the cold, and I've got less patience than ever. Annoyed, he reached for his notepad and found an empty page.

It was clear that he would have to start again from the beginning. Apparently nobody could say with any certainty where the beginning was, so they would have to approach the investigation with no preconceived ideas. He spent half an hour sketching out what needed to be done, but all the time he was nagged by the idea that it was really Martinsson who ought to be leading the investigation. He himself had returned to duty, but he did not want to take on the whole responsibility right away.

The telephone rang. He hesitated before answering.

"I hear we've had some great news." It was Per Åkeson. "I have to say I'm delighted." Åkeson was the public prosecutor with whom Wallander had, over the years, established the best working relationship. They had often had heated discussions about the best way of interpreting case data, and Wallander had many times been angry because Åkeson had refused to accept one of his submissions as sufficient grounds for an arrest. But they had more or less always seen eye to eye. And they shared a particular impatience at cases being carelessly handled.

"I have to admit it all seems a bit strange," Wallander said.

"Rumour had it that you were about to retire on health grounds," Åkeson said. "Somebody ought to tell Björk to put a stop to all these rumours that keep flying around."

"It wasn't just a rumour," Wallander said. "I had made my mind up to chuck it in."

"Might one ask why you changed your mind?"

"Something happened," Wallander said evasively. He could tell that Åkeson was waiting for him to continue, but he did not oblige.

"Anyway, I'm pleased you've come back," Åkeson said, after an appropriately long silence. "I'm also certain that I'm expressing the sentiments of my colleagues in saying that."

Wallander began to feel uncomfortable about all the goodwill that was flowing in his direction, but which he found hard to believe. We go through life with one foot in a rose garden and the other in quicksand, he thought.

"I assume you'll be taking over the Torstensson case," Åkeson said. "Maybe we ought to get together later today and work out where we stand."

"I don't know about 'taking over'," Wallander said. "I'll be involved, I asked to be. But I suppose that one of the others will be leading the investigation."

"Hmm, none of my business," Åkeson said. "I'm just pleased you're back. Have you had time to get into the details of the case?"

"Not really."

"Judging by what I've heard so far, there doesn't seem to have been any significant development."

"Björk thinks it's going to be a long haul."

"What do you think?"

Wallander hesitated before replying. "Nothing at all as yet."

"Insecurity seems to be on the increase," Åkeson said. "Threats, often in the form of anonymous letters, are more common. Public buildings which used to keep open house are now barricading themselves like fortresses. No question, you'll have to go through his clients with a fine-tooth comb. You might find a clue there. Someone among them might have a grudge."

"We've already started on that," Wallander said.

They agreed to meet in Åkeson's office that afternoon.

Wallander forced himself to return to the investigation plan he had started to sketch out, but his concentration wandered. He put his pen down in irritation and went to fetch a cup of coffee. He hurried back to his office, not wanting to meet anybody. It was 8.15 by now. He drank his coffee and wondered how long it would be before he lost his fear of being with people. At 8.30 he gathered his papers together and went to the conference room. On the way there it struck him that unusually little had been achieved during the five or six days that had passed since Sten Torstensson had been found murdered. All murder investigations are different, but there always used to be a mood of intense urgency among the officers involved. Something had changed while he had been away. What?

They were all present by 8.40, and Björk tapped the table as a sign that work was about to commence. He turned at once to Wallander.

"Kurt," he said, "you've just come into this case and can view it with fresh eyes. What do you think we should do now?"

"I hardly think I'm the one to decide that," Wallander said. "I haven't had time to get into it properly."

"On the other hand, you're the only one who's so far come up with anything useful," Martinsson said. "If I know you, you'll have sat up last night and sketched out an investigation plan. Am I right?"

Wallander nodded. He realised that in fact he had no objection to taking over the case.

"I have tried to write a summary," he began. "But first let me tell you about something that happened just over a week ago, when I was in Denmark. I ought to have mentioned it yesterday, but it was all a bit hectic for me, to say the least."

Wallander told his astonished colleagues about Sten Torstensson's trip to Skagen. He tried hard to leave out no detail. When he finished, there was silence. Björk eventually spoke, making no attempt to conceal the fact that he was cross.

"Very odd," he said. "I don't know why it is that you always seem to find yourself in situations that are out of normal procedures."

"I did refer him to you," Wallander objected, and could feel his anger rising.

"It's nothing for us to get excited about now," Björk said impassively. "But it is a bit strange, you must agree. What is of course clear is that we have to reopen the investigation into Gustaf Torstensson's accident."

"It seems to me both natural and necessary that we advance on two fronts," Wallander said. "The assumption being that two people have been murdered, not one. It's a father and a son, moreover. We have to think two thoughts at the same time. There may be a solution to be found in their private lives, but it might also be something to do with their work, two lawyers working for the same firm of solicitors. The fact that Sten came to see me to talk about his father being on edge might suggest that the key concerns Gustaf Torstensson. But that is not a foregone conclusion – for one thing, there's the postcard Sten sent to Mrs Dunér from Finland when at the time he was in Denmark."

"That tells us something else as well," Höglund said.

Wallander nodded. "That Sten also thought that he was under threat. Is that what you mean?"

"Yes," Höglund said. "Why else would he have laid a false trail?"

Martinsson put his hand up, indicating he wanted to say something. "It would be simplest if we split into two groups," he said. "One to concentrate on the father, and the other on the son. Then let's see if we come up with anything that points in the same direction."

"I agree with that," Wallander said. "At the same time I can't help thinking there's something odd about all this. Something we ought to have discovered already."

"All murder cases are odd, surely," Svedberg said.

"Yes, but there's something more," Wallander said. "And I can't put my finger on it."

Björk indicated it was time to conclude the meeting.

"As I've already started delving into what happened to Gustaf Torstensson, I might as well go on," Wallander said. "If nobody has any objections."

"The rest of us can devote ourselves to Sten Torstensson, then," Martinsson said. "Can I assume that you'll want to work on your own to start with, as usual?"

"Not necessarily. But if I understand it rightly, the Sten case is much more complicated. His father didn't have so many clients. His life seems to be more transparent."

"Let's do that then," Björk said, shutting his diary with a thud. "We'll meet every day at 4.00, as usual, to see how far we've got. Oh, and I need help with a press conference later today."

"Not me," Wallander said. "I haven't got the strength."

"I thought Ann-Britt might do it," Björk said. "It won't do any harm for people to know she's here with us now."

"That's fine by me," she said, to the others' surprise. "I need to learn about such things."

After the meeting Wallander asked Martinsson to stay behind. When the others had left, he closed the door.

"We need to have a few words," Wallander said. "I feel as though I'm barging in and taking over, when what I was really supposed to be doing was confirming my resignation."

"We're all a bit surprised, certainly," Martinsson said. "You must accept that. You're not the only one who's a bit unsure of what's going on."

"I don't want to stand on anybody's toes."

Martinsson burst out laughing. Then blew his nose. "The Swedish police force is full of officers suffering from sore toes and heels," he said. "The more bureaucratic the force becomes, the more people get obsessed about their careers. All the regulations and the paperwork – it gets worse every day – result in misunderstandings and a lack of clarity, so it's no wonder people stand on each other's toes and kick their heels. Sometimes I think I understand why Björk is worried about the way things are going. What's happening to ordinary straightforward police work?"

"The police force has always reflected society at large," Wallander said. "But I know what you mean. Rydberg used to say the same thing. What's Höglund going to say?"

"She's good," Martinsson said. "Hanson and Svedberg are both frightened of her precisely because she's so good. Hanson especially is worried that he might get left behind. That's why he spends most of his time on courses nowadays, picking up extra qualifications."

"The new-age police officer," Wallander said, getting to his feet. "That's what she is." He paused in the doorway. "You said something yesterday that rang a bell. Something about Sten Torstensson. I'm not sure what, but I have the feeling it was more important than it sounded."

"I was reading aloud from my notes," Martinsson said. "You can have a copy."

"I dare say I'm imagining things," Wallander said.

When he got back to his office and had closed the door, he knew that he had experienced something he had almost forgotten existed. It was as if he had rediscovered his drive. Not everything, it seemed, had been lost during the time he had been away.

He sat at his desk, feeling that he could now examine himself at arm's length: the man staggering around in the West Indies, the miserable trip to Thailand, all those days and nights when everything seemed to have ground to a halt apart from his automatic bodily functions. He was looking at himself, but he realised that that person was somebody he no longer knew. He had been somebody else.

He shuddered to contemplate the catastrophic consequences that some of his actions could have had. He thought hard about his daughter Linda. It was only when

Martinsson knocked on the door and delivered a photo-copy of his notes from the previous day that Wallander succeeded in banishing all the memories. Everybody had within himself a secret room, it seemed to him, where memories and recollections were all jumbled up together. Now he had bolted the door, and attached a strong pad-lock. Then he went to the toilet and flushed away the antidepressants he had been carrying around in a tube in his pocket.

He returned to his office and started work. It was 10 a.m. He read carefully through Martinsson's notes without identifying what it was that had caught his atten-tion. It's too soon, he thought. Rydberg would have advised patience. Now I have to remember to advise myself.

He wondered briefly where to begin. Then he looked up Gustaf Torstensson's home address in the file for the car accident. Timmermansgatan 12. That was in one of Ystad's oldest and most affluent residential districts, beyond the army barracks, near Sandskogen. He tele-phoned the solicitors' and spoke to Sonia Lundin, who told him that the house keys were in the office. He left the station and noted that the rain clouds had dispersed, the sky was clear. He had the feeling he was breathing in the first of the cold winter air that was slowly advancing. As he drew up outside the solicitors' offices, Lundin came out and handed him the keys.

He took two wrong turnings before he reached the correct address. The big, brown-painted wooden house was a long way back in a large garden. He swung open the creaking gate and started along the gravel drive. It was quiet, and the town seemed a long way away. A world inside a world, he thought. The Torstensson firm of solicitors must have been a very profitable business. He doubted if there were many more expensive houses in Ystad than this one. The garden was well tended but strangely lifeless. A few deciduous trees, some neatly clipped bushes, some dull flower beds. Perhaps an elderly lawyer needed to surround himself with straight lines, a traditional garden with no surprises or improvisations. Someone had told him that as a solicitor Torstensson had the reputation of dragging out court proceedings to an unprecedented level of boredom. One spiteful opponent claimed that Torstensson could get a client off by driving the prosecutor to distraction with his plodding, colourless presentation of the case for the defence. He should ask Per Åkeson what he thought of Gustaf Torstensson. They must have dealt with each other many times over the years.

He went up the steps to the front door and found the right key. It was an advanced Chubb lock of a type he had not come across before. He let himself into a large hall with a broad staircase at the back leading to the upper floor. Heavy curtains were drawn across the windows. He opened one set and saw that the window was barred. An elderly man living alone, experiencing the fear that inevitably goes with age. Was there something here he needed to protect, apart from himself? Or was his fear something that originated beyond these walls? He made his way round the house, starting on the ground floor with its library lined with sombre portraits of family ancestors, and the large open-plan living room and dining room. Everything, from furniture to wallpaper, was dark, giving him a feeling of melancholy and silence. Nowhere even a small patch of light colour, no trace of a light touch that could raise a smile.

He went upstairs. Guest rooms with neatly made beds, deserted like a hotel closed for the winter. The door to Torstensson's own bedroom had a barred inner door. He went back downstairs, oppressed by the gloom. He sat at the kitchen table and rested his chin on his hands. All he could hear was a clock ticking.

Torstensson was 69 when he died. He had been living alone for the last 15 years, since his wife died. Sten was their only child. Judging by one of the portraits in the library, the family was descended from Field Marshal Lennart Torstensson. Wallander's vague memory from his schooldays was that during the Thirty Years' War the man had a reputation for exceptional brutality towards the peasants wherever his army had set foot.

Wallander stood up and went down the stairs to the basement. Here, too, everything was pedantically neat. Right at the back, behind the boiler room, Wallander discovered a steel door that was locked. He tried the various keys until he found the right one. Wallander had to feel his way until he located the light switch.

The room was surprisingly big. The walls were lined with shelves laden with icons from Eastern Europe. Without touching them, Wallander scrutinised them from close up. He was no expert, nor had he ever been particularly interested in antiques, but he reckoned that this collection was extremely valuable. That would explain the barred windows and the lock, if not the wrought-iron safety door to the bedroom. Wallander's uneasiness grew. He felt he was intruding on the privacy of a rich old man whom happiness had abandoned, who had barricaded his house, and who was watched over by greed in the shape of all these Madonna figures.

He pricked up his ears. There were footsteps upstairs, then a dog barking. He hurried out of the room, up the steps and into the kitchen.

He was astonished to be confronted by Peters, his colleague, who had drawn his pistol and was pointing it at him. Behind him was a security guard with a growling dog tugging at a lead. Peters lowered his gun. Wallander could feel his heart racing. The sight of the gun had momentarily revived the memories he had spent so long trying to banish.

Then he was furious. "What the hell's going on here?" he snarled.

"The alarm went off at the security company, and they called the police," Peters said, clearly worried. "So we came rushing here in a hurry. I had no idea it was you."

Peters' partner Norén entered on cue, also wielding a pistol.

"There's a police investigation going on here," Wallander said, noting that his anger had subsided as quickly as it had broken out. "Torstensson, the solicitor who died in the car accident, lived here."

"If the alarm goes off, we turn out," the man from the security company said, bluntly.

"Turn it off," Wallander said. "You can turn it on again in a few hours' time. But let's all work our way through the house first."

"This is Chief Inspector Wallander," Peters explained. "I expect you recognise him."

The security man was very young. He nodded, but Wallander could tell that he had not recognised him.

"We don't need you any more. And get that dog out of here," Wallander said.

The guard withdrew, taking the reluctant Alsatian with him. Wallander shook Peters and Norén by the hand.

"I'd heard you were back," Norén said. "It's good to see you again."

"Thank you."

"Things haven't been the same since you were on sick leave," Peters said.

"Well, I'm in harness again now," Wallander said, hoping to steer the conversation back to the investigation.

"The information we get isn't exactly reliable," Norén said. "We'd been told you were going to retire. After that we didn't expect to find you in a house when the alarm went off."

"Life is full of surprises," Wallander said.

"Anyway, welcome back," Peters said.

Wallander had the feeling for the first time that the friendliness was genuine. There was nothing artificial about Peters: his words were straightforward and clear.

"It's been a difficult time," Wallander said. "But it's over now. I think so, at least."

He walked down to the car with them and waved as they drove off. He wandered around the garden, trying to sort out his thoughts. His personal feelings were intertwined with thoughts about what had happened to the two lawyers. In the end he decided to go and talk again to Mrs Dunér. Now he had a few questions to put to her which needed answering.

It was almost noon when he rang her doorbell and was let in. This time he accepted her offer of a cup of tea.

"I'm sorry to disturb you again so soon," he began, "but I do need help in building up a picture of both of them, father and son. Who were they? You worked with the older man for 30 years."

"And 19 years with Sten Torstensson," she said.

"That's a long time," Wallander said. "You get to know people as time goes by. Let's start with the father. Tell me what he was like."

"I can't," she said.

"And why not?"

"I didn't know him."

Her reply astonished him, but it sounded genuine. Wallander decided to feel his way forward, to take all the time his impatience told him he did not have.

"You will not mind my saying that your response is a bit odd," Wallander said. "I mean, you worked with him for a very long time."

"Not *with* him," she said. "*For* him. There's a big difference."

Wallander nodded. "Even if you didn't know the man, you must know a lot about him. Please, tell me what you can. If you don't I'm afraid we may never be able to solve the murder of his son."

"You're not being honest with me, Inspector Wallander," she said. "You haven't told me what really happened when he died in that car crash."

She was evidently going to go on surprising him. He made his mind up on the spot to be straight with her.

"We don't know yet," he said. "But we suspect it was more than just an accident. Something might have caused it, or happened afterwards."

"He'd driven along that road lots of times," she said. "He knew it inside out. And he never drove fast."

"If I understand it rightly, he'd been to see one of his clients," Wallander said.

84

"The man at Farnholm," was all she said.

"The man at Farnholm?"

"Alfred Harderberg. The man at Farnholm Castle."

Wallander knew that Farnholm Castle was in a remote area to the south of the Linderöd Ridge. He had often driven past the turning, but had never been there.

"He was our biggest client," Mrs Dunér went on. "For the last few years he'd been in effect Gustaf Torstensson's only client."

Wallander wrote the name on a scrap of paper he found in his pocket.

"I've never heard of him," he said. "Is he a farmer?"

"He's the man who owns the castle," Mrs Dunér said. "But he's a businessman. Big business, international."

"I'll be in touch with him, obviously," Wallander said. "He must be one of the last people to see Mr Torstensson alive."

A packet of mail suddenly dropped through the letter box. Wallander noticed that Mrs Dunér gave a start.

Three scared people, he thought. Scared of what?

"Gustaf Torstensson," he started again. "Let's try again. Tell me what he was like."

"He was the most private person I have ever met," she said, and Wallander detected a hint of aggression. "He never allowed anybody to get close to him. He was a pedant, never varied his routine. He was one of those people folk say you could set your watch by. That was absolutely true in Gustaf Torstensson's case. He was a sort of bloodless, cut-out silhouette, neither nice nor nasty. Just boring."

"According to Sten Torstensson, he was also cheerful," Wallander said.

"You could have fooled me," Mrs Dunér said.

"How did the two of them get on?"

She did not hesitate, she answered directly to the point. "Gustaf Torstensson was annoyed that his son was trying to modernise the business," she said. "And naturally enough, Sten Torstensson thought his father was a millstone round his neck. But neither of them revealed their true feelings to the other. They were both afraid of fighting."

"Before Sten Torstensson died he said something had been upsetting and worrying his father for several months," Wallander said. "Can you comment on that?"

This time she paused before answering.

"Maybe," she said. "Now that you mention it, there was something distant about him in the last months of his life."

"Have you any explanation for that?"

"No."

"Nothing unusual that happened?"

"No, nothing."

"Please think carefully. This could be very important."

She poured another cup of tea while she was thinking. Wallander waited. Then she looked up at him.

"I can't say," she said. "I can't explain it."

Wallander knew she was not telling the truth, but he decided not to press her. Everything was still too vague and uncertain. The time wasn't ripe.

He pushed his cup to one side and rose to his feet. "I won't disturb you any longer," he said. "But I'll be back, I'm afraid."

"Of course," Mrs Dunér said.

"If you think of anything you'd like to say, just give me a ring," Wallander said as he left. "Don't hesitate. The slightest detail could be significant."

"I'll bear that in mind," she said as she closed the door behind him.

Wallander sat in his car without starting the engine. He felt very uneasy. Without being able to say exactly why, he had the feeling there was something very serious and disturbing behind the deaths of the two lawyers. They were still only scratching the surface.

Something is pointing us in the wrong direction, he thought. The postcard from Finland might not be a red herring, might be the thing we really ought to be looking into. But why?

He was about to start the engine and drive off when he noticed that somebody was standing on the opposite pavement, watching him.

It was a young woman, hardly more than 20, of some Asiatic origin. When she saw that Wallander had noticed her, she hurried away. Wallander could see in his rear-view mirror that she had turned right into Hamngatan without looking back.

He was certain he had never seen her before.

That didn't mean she had not recognised him. Over the years as a police officer he had often come up against refugees and asylum seekers in various contexts.

He drove back to the police station. The wind was still squally, and clouds were building up from the east. He had just turned into Kristianstadsvägen when he slammed his foot on the brake. A lorry behind him sounded its horn.

I'm reacting far too slowly, he thought. I'm not seeing the wood for the trees.

He made an illegal U-turn, parked outside the post office in Hamngatan and made his way swiftly into the side street that led into Stickgatan from the north. He positioned himself so that he could see the pink building where Mrs Dunér lived.

It was getting chilly, and he started walking up and down while keeping an eye on the building. After an hour he wondered whether he ought to give up. But he was sure he was right. He kept on watching the building. By now Åkeson was waiting for him, but he would wait in vain.

At 3.43 p.m. the door to the pink building suddenly opened. Wallander hid behind a wall. He *was* right. He watched that woman with the vaguely Asiatic appearance leave Berta Dunér's house. Then she turned the corner and was gone.

It had started raining.

Chapter 5

The meeting of the investigation team started at 4 p.m. and finished exactly seven minutes later. Wallander was the last to arrive and flopped down on his chair. He was out of breath, and sweating. His colleagues around the table observed him in surprise, but no-one made any comment.

It took Björk a few minutes to establish that no-one had any significant progress to report or matters to discuss. They had reached a point in the investigation where they had become "tunnel diggers", as they used to say. They were all trying to break through the surface layer to find what might be concealed underneath. It was a familiar phase in criminal investigations, and no discussion was needed. The only one who came up with a question at the end of the meeting was Wallander.

"Who is Alfred Harderberg?" he asked, after consulting a scrap of paper on which he'd written down the name.

"I thought everybody knew that," Björk said. "He's one of Sweden's most successful businessmen just now. Lives here in Skåne. When he's not flying all over the world in his private jet, that is."

"He owns Farnholm Castle," Svedberg said. "It's said that he has an aquarium with genuine gold dust at the bottom instead of sand."

"He was a client of Gustaf Torstensson's," Wallander said. "His principal client, in fact. And his last. Torstensson had been to see him the night he met his death in the field."

"He organises collections for the needy in parts of the Balkans ravaged by war," Martinsson said. "But maybe that's not so extraordinary when you have the limitless amounts of money he does."

"Alfred Harderberg is a man worthy of our respect," Björk said.

Wallander could see he was getting annoyed. "Who isn't?" he wondered aloud. "I intend to pay him a visit even so."

"Phone first," Björk said, getting to his feet.

The meeting was at an end. Wallander fetched a cup of coffee and repaired to his office. He needed time on his own to think over the significance of Mrs Dunér being visited by a young Asian woman. Maybe there was nothing to it at all, but Wallander's instinct told him otherwise. He put his feet on his desk and leaned back in his chair, balancing his coffee cup between his knees.

The telephone rang. Wallander stretched to answer it, lost his grip on the cup, and coffee spilled all over his trouser leg as the cup fell to the floor.

"Shit!" he shouted, the receiver halfway to his ear.

"No need to be rude," said his father. "I only wanted to ask why you never get in touch."

Wallander was instantly assailed by his bad conscience, and that in turn made him angry. He wondered

90

if there would ever be a time when dealings with his father could be conducted on a less tense footing.

"I spilled a cup of coffee," he said, "and scalded my leg."

His father seemed not to have heard what he said. "Why are you in your office?" he asked. "You're supposed to be on sick leave."

"Not any more. I've started work again."

"When?"

"Yesterday."

"Yesterday?"

Wallander could tell that this conversation was going to be a very long one if he did not manage to cut it short. "I owe you an explanation, I know," he said, "but I just haven't time at the moment. I'll come and see you tomorrow evening, and tell you what's happened."

"I haven't seen you for ages," his father said, and hung up.

Wallander sat for a moment with the receiver in his hand. His father would be 75 next year, and invariably managed to arouse in him contradictory emotions. Their relationship had been complicated for as long as he could remember. Not least on the day he told his father he intended to join the police. More than 25 years had passed since then and the old man never missed an opportunity of criticising that decision. Nevertheless, Wallander had a guilty conscience about the time he devoted to him. The previous year, when he had heard the astonishing news that his father was going to marry a woman 30 years younger than himself, a home help who came to his house three times a week, he had reckoned his father would not lack for company any more.

Now, sitting there with the receiver in his hand, he realised that nothing had really changed.

He replaced the receiver, picked up the cup and wiped his trouser leg with a sheet torn from his notepad. Then he remembered he was supposed to get in touch with Åkeson, the prosecutor. Åkeson's secretary put him straight through. Wallander explained that he had been held up and Åkeson suggested a time for the next morning instead.

Wallander went to fetch another cup of coffee. In the corridor he bumped into Höglund carrying a pile of files.

"How's it going?" Wallander said.

"Slowly," she said. "And I can't shake off the feeling that there's something fishy about those two dead lawyers."

"That's exactly how I feel," Wallander said. "What makes you think so?"

"I don't know."

"Let's talk about it tomorrow," Wallander said. "Experience tells me you should never underestimate the significance of what you can't put into words, can't put your finger on."

He went back to his office, unhooked the phone and pulled over his notepad. He went back in his mind to the freezing cold beach at Skagen, Sten Torstensson walking towards him out of the fog. That's where this case started for me, he thought. It started while Sten was still alive.

He went over everything he knew about the two solicitors. He was like a soldier cautiously retreating, keeping a close watch to his left and his right. It took him an hour to work his way through every one of the facts he and his colleagues had so far assembled.

What is it I can see and yet do not see? He asked himself this over and over as he sifted through the case notes. But when he tossed aside his pen all he had managed to achieve was a highly decorative and embellished question mark.

Two lawyers dead, he thought. One killed in a strange accident that was in all probability not an accident. Whoever killed Gustaf Torstensson was a cold, calculating murderer. That lone chair leg left in the mud was an uncharacteristic mistake. There's a *why* and a *who*, but there may well be something else.

It came to him that there was something he could and should do. He found Mrs Dunér's telephone number in his notes.

"I'm sorry to trouble you," he said. "Inspector Wallander here. I have a question I'd be grateful for an answer to right away."

"I'd be pleased to help if I can," she said.

Two questions in fact, Wallander thought, but I'll save the one about the Asian woman for another time.

"The night Gustaf Torstensson died he had been to Farnholm Castle," he said. "How many people knew he was going to visit his client that evening?"

There was a pause before she replied. Wallander wondered whether that was in order to remember, or to give herself time to think of a suitable answer.

"I knew, of course," she said. "It's possible I might have mentioned it to Miss Lundin, but nobody else knew."

"Sten Torstensson didn't know, then?"

"I don't think so. They kept separate engagement diaries."

"So most probably you were the only one who knew," Wallander said.

"Yes."

"Thank you. I apologise for disturbing you," Wallander said, and hung up.

He returned to his notes. Gustaf Torstensson drives out to see a client, and is attacked on the way home, murder disguised as a road accident.

He thought about Mrs Dunér's reply. I'm sure she was telling the truth, he thought, but what interests me is what lies behind that truth. What she said means that apart from herself the only other person who knew what Gustaf Torstensson was going to do that evening was the man at Farnholm Castle.

He continued his walk through the case. The landscape of the investigation constantly shifted. The cheerless house with its sophisticated security systems. The collection of icons hidden in the basement. When he thought he'd walked as far as he could go he switched to Sten Torstensson. The landscape shifted yet again and became almost impenetrable. Sten's unexpected appearance in Wallander's windswept haven, against a background of melancholy foghorns, and then the deserted café at the Art Museum – they seemed to Wallander like the ingredients of an unconvincing operetta. But there were moments in the plot when life was taken seriously. Sten had found his father restless and depressed. And the postcard from Finland, sent by an unknown hand but arranged by Sten: clearly there was a threat and a false trail was required. Always assuming that the false trail wasn't in fact the right trail.

Nothing takes us on to a next stage, Wallander thought, but these are facts that one can categorise. It's harder to know what to do with the mystery ingredients, the Asian woman, for example, who doesn't want anybody to see her visiting Berta Dunér's pink house. And Mrs Dunér herself, who's a good liar, but not good enough to deceive a detective inspector from the Ystad police – or, at least, for him not to notice that something isn't quite right.

Wallander stood up, stretched his back and stood at the window. It was 6 p.m., and it had grown dark. Noises could be heard from the corridor, footsteps approaching and then fading away. He remembered something Rydberg had said during the last year of his life: "A police station is essentially like a prison. Police officers and criminals live their lives as mirror images of each other. It's not really possible to decide who's incarcerated and who isn't."

Wallander suddenly felt listless and lonely. He resorted to his only consolation: an imagined conversation with Baiba Liepa in Riga, as though she were standing there in front of him, and as if his office were a room in a grey building with dilapidated façades in Riga, in that flat with the dimmed lighting and the thick curtains permanently drawn. But the image became blurred, faded like the weaker of two wrestlers. Instead, Wallander pictured himself crawling on his muddy hands and knees through the Scanian fog with a shotgun in one hand and a pistol in the other, like a pathetic copy of some unlikely film idol, and then suddenly the illusion was ripped to shreds and reality imposed itself through the slits, and death and killing were not rabbits plucked out of a conjuror's hat. He watches himself witnessing a man being shot by a bullet through the head, and then he also shoots and the only thing he can be sure of is that his only hope is for the man he's aiming at to die.

I'm a man who doesn't laugh enough, he thought. Without my noticing, middle age has marooned me on a coast with too many dangerous submerged rocks.

He left all his papers on his desk. In reception, Ebba was busy on the telephone. When she signalled to him to wait, he shook his head and waved to indicate he was in a hurry.

He drove home and cooked a meal he would have been incapable of describing afterwards. He watered the five plants he had on his window ledges, filled the washing machine with clothes that had been strewn around the flat, discovered he had no washing powder, then sat on the sofa and cut his toenails. Occasionally he looked around the room, as if he expected to find that he wasn't alone after all. Shortly after 10.00 he went to bed and fell asleep almost immediately.

Outside the rain had eased off and become light drizzle.

When Wallander woke up the next morning it was still dark. The alarm clock with the luminous hands indicated that it was barely 5.00. He turned over and tried to go back to sleep, but found it impossible. His long stay out in the cold was still making itself felt. Whatever has changed, whatever is still the same, I will spend the rest of my life in two timescales, "before" and "after". Kurt Wallander exists and doesn't exist.

He got up at 5.30, made coffee, waited for the newspaper to arrive and saw from the outside thermometer that it was 4°C outside. Driven by a feeling of unrest he did not have the strength to analyse or fight, he left the flat at 6 a.m. He got into his car and started the engine, thinking he might just as well pay a visit to

Farnholm Castle. He could stop somewhere on the way, have a coffee and telephone to warn them he was coming. He drove east out of Ystad, averting his gaze as he passed the military training ground on his right where 18 months earlier he had fought the old Wallander's last battle. Out there in the fog he had discovered that there are people who would not shrink from any form of violence, who would not hesitate to commit murders in cold blood. Out there, on his knees in the mud, he had fought desperately for his own life and somehow, thanks to an incredibly accurate shot, he had killed a man. It was a point of no return, a birth and a burial at the same time.

He drove along the road to Kristianstad and slowed down as he passed the place where Gustaf Torstensson had died. When he came to Skåne-Tranås he stopped at the café and went in. It was getting windy: he ought to have put on a thicker jacket. In fact, he ought to have given more thought to his clothes in general: the worn Terylene trousers and dirty windcheater he had on were perhaps not ideal for visiting a lord of the manor. As he entered the café he wondered what Björk would have worn for a visit to a castle, supposing it had been on business.

He was the only customer. He ordered coffee and a sandwich. It was 6.45, and he leafed through a well-thumbed magazine on a shelf. He soon tired of that, and tried to think instead about what he was going to say to Alfred Harderberg, or whoever might be able to tell him about Gustaf Torstensson's last visit to his client. He waited until 7.30, then asked to use the telephone on the counter next to the old-fashioned cash register, and first called the police station in Ystad. The only one of his colleagues there that early was Martinsson. He explained where he was, and said that he expected the visit to take an hour or two.

"Do you know the first thing that entered my head when I woke up this morning?" Martinsson said.

"No."

"That it was Sten Torstensson who killed his father."

"How do you explain what then happened to the son?" Wallander said.

"I don't," Martinsson said. "But what seems to me to be clearer and clearer is that the explanation has to do with their professional rather than their private lives."

"Or a combination of the two."

"What do you mean?"

"Just something I dreamed last night," Wallander said, ducking the question. "Anyway, I'll be back at the station in due course."

He hung up, lifted the receiver again and dialled the number of Farnholm Castle. It was answered on the very first ring. "Farnholm Castle," said a woman's voice. She had a slight foreign accent.

"This is Detective Chief Inspector Wallander of the Ystad police. I'd like to speak to Mr Harderberg."

"He's in Geneva," the voice said.

Wallander ought to have foreseen the possibility that an international businessman might be abroad.

"When will he be back?"

"He hasn't said."

"Do you expect him tomorrow or next week?"

"I can't give you that information over the telephone. His schedule is strictly confidential."

"Maybe so, but I am a police officer," Wallander said, his anger rising.

"How am I to know that?" the woman said. "You could be anybody."

"I'll be at Farnholm Castle in half an hour," Wallander said. "Who shall I ask for?"

"That's for the guards at the main gate to decide," the woman said. "I hope you have some acceptable form of identification with you."

"What do you mean by 'acceptable'?" Wallander shouted, but she had hung up.

Wallander slammed down the receiver. The powerfully built waitress was putting buns out on a plate, and looked up at him with displeasure. He put some coins on the counter, and left without a word.

Fifteen kilometres further north he turned to the west and was soon swallowed up by the dense forest to the south of Linderöd Ridge. He braked when he came to the turning for Farnholm Castle and a granite plaque with gold lettering told him he was on course. Wallander thought the plaque looked like an expensive gravestone.

The castle road was asphalted and in good condition. Tucked discreetly into the trees was a high fence. He stopped and wound down his window to get a better view. It was a double fence with about a metre gap. He drove on. Another kilometre or so and the road swung sharply to the right. Just beyond the turn were the gates. Next to them was a grey building with a flat roof looking more like a pillbox than anything else. He drove forward and waited. Nothing happened. He sounded his horn. Still no reaction. He got out of the car, he was getting annoyed. He had a vague feeling of being humiliated by all these fences and closed gates. Just then a man emerged through one of the steel doors in the pillbox. He was wearing a dark red uniform Wallander had never seen before. He still had not familiarised himself with these new security companies that were popping up all over the country.

The man in the uniform came up to him. He was about the same age as Wallander.

Then he recognised him.

"Kurt Wallander," said the guard. "Long time no see."

"Indeed," Wallander said. "How long ago was it we last met? Fifteen years?"

"Twenty," the guard said. "Maybe more."

Wallander had dug out the man's name from his memory. Kurt Ström. They had been colleagues on the Malmö police force. Wallander was young then and inexperienced, and Ström was a year or so older. They had never had more than professional contact with each other, but Wallander had moved to Ystad and many years later he had heard that Ström had left the force. He had a vague memory that Ström had been sacked, something had been hushed up, possibly excessive force on a prisoner, or stolen goods vanishing from a police storeroom. He didn't know for sure.

"I was warned you were on your way," Ström said.

"Lucky for me," Wallander said. "I was told I'd have to produce an 'acceptable form of identification'. What do you find acceptable?"

"We have a high level of security at Farnholm Castle," Ström said. "We're pretty careful about who we let in."

"What kind of treasure do you have hidden away here?"

"No treasure, but there's a man with very big business interests."

"Harderberg?"

"That's the one. He has something a lot of people would like to get their hands on."

"What's that?"

"Knowledge, know-how. Worth more than owning your own mint."

Wallander had no patience with the servile manner Ström was displaying as he spoke of the great man.

"Once upon a time you were a police officer," Wallander said. "I still am. Perhaps you understand why I'm here?"

"I read the papers," Ström said. "I suppose it's got something to do with that lawyer."

"Two lawyers have died, not just one," Wallander said. "But if I understand it right, only the elder one worked with Harderberg."

"He came here a lot," Ström said. "A nice man. Very discreet."

"He was last here on October 11, in the evening," Wallander said. "Were you on duty then?"

Ström nodded.

"I take it you make notes on all the cars and people that come in and out?"

Ström laughed out loud. "We stopped that a long time ago," he said. "It's all done by computer nowadays."

"I'd like to see a printout for the evening of October 11," Wallander said.

"You'll have to ask them up at the castle," Ström said. "I'm not allowed to do things like that."

"But I dare say you're allowed to remember," Wallander said.

"I know he was here that evening," Ström said. "But I can't remember when he arrived and when he left."

"Was he on his own in the car?"

"I can't say."

"Because you're not allowed to say?"

Ström nodded again.

"I've sometimes thought about applying for a job with a security company," Wallander said, "but I think I'd find it hard to get used to not being allowed to answer questions."

"Everything has its price," Ström said.

Wallander thought he could say "hear, hear" to that. He watched Ström for a few moments. "Harderberg," he said eventually. "What's he like as a person?"

The reply surprised him.

"I don't know," Ström said.

"You must have some sort of an opinion, surely? Or aren't you allowed to comment on that either?"

"I've never met him," Ström said.

"And you have been working for him how long?"

"Nearly five years."

"You've never once seen him?"

"Never."

"He's never passed through these gates?"

"His car has one-way glass in the windows."

"I take it that's part of the security system?" Wallander thought for a moment. "In other words, you are never completely sure whether he's here or not. You don't know if he's in the car when it passes in or out through the gates?"

"No. It's all to do with security," Ström said.

Wallander went back to his car. Ström disappeared through the steel door, and shortly afterwards the gates opened without a sound. It's like entering a different world, Wallander thought.

After about a kilometre the forest opened up. The castle stood on a hill, surrounded by extensive and well-tended grounds. The large main building, like the free-standing outbuildings surrounding it, was in dark red brick. The castle had towers and steeples, balustrades and balconies. The only thing to break the mood of another world, another age, was a helicopter on a concrete pad. Wallander had the impression of a large insect with its wings half folded, a wild beast at rest but liable to come back to life with a jerk.

He drove slowly up to the main entrance. Peacocks strolled leisurely around on the road, in front of the car. He parked behind a black BMW and got out. It was very quiet all around. The tranquillity reminded him of the previous day when he'd walked up the gravel drive to Gustaf Torstensson's house. Perhaps tranquillity is what distinguishes the environment in which wealthy people live, he thought. It's not the orchestral fanfares, but the tranquillity.

Just then one of the double doors at the main entrance to the castle opened. A woman in her thirties, dressed in well-fitting and, Wallander guessed, expensive clothes emerged on to the steps.

"Please come in," she said with a ready smile, a smile that seemed to Wallander just as cold and unwelcoming as it was correct.

"I don't know if I have any identification papers you would regard as acceptable," he said, "but the guard who goes by the name of Ström recognised me."

"I know," said the woman.

It was not the woman who'd answered the phone when he rang from the café. He went up the steps, held out his hand and introduced himself. She ignored his hand but simply reproduced the same distant smile. He followed her in through the doors. They walked across a large entrance hall. Modernistic sculptures on stone pedestals were dotted around, illuminated by invisible spotlights. In the background, by the wide staircase leading to the upper floor, he detected two men lurking in the shadows. Wallander could sense their presence, but could not make out their faces. Tranquillity and shadows, he thought. The world of Harderberg, as I know it so far. He followed her through a door on the left, leading into a large oval room that was also decorated with sculptures. But as a reminder of the fact that they were in a castle with a history going back deep into the Middle Ages, there were also some suits of armour keeping watch over him. In the centre of the highly polished oak parquet floor was a desk and a single visitor's chair. There was no paper on the desk, only a computer and an advanced telephone exchange that was hardly any bigger than an ordinary telephone. The woman invited him to sit down, then keyed a command into the computer. She handed him a sheet from a printer invisible somewhere under the desk.

"I gather you wanted a printout of the gate-control data for the evening of October 11," the woman said. "You can see from this when Mr Torstensson arrived, and when he left Farnholm."

Wallander took the printout and put it on the floor beside him.

"That's not the only reason why I've come," he said. "I have several other questions."

"Fire away."

The woman had sat down behind the desk. She pressed various buttons on the telephone exchange. Wallander assumed she was switching all incoming calls to another exchange somewhere in the huge building.

"The information I've received informs me that Gustaf Torstensson had Alfred Harderberg as a client," Wallander said. "If I understand it rightly, he's out of the country at present."

"He's in Dubai," the woman said.

Wallander frowned. "An hour ago he was in Geneva," he said.

"That's right," the woman said without batting an eyelid. "But he's now left for Dubai."

Wallander took a notebook and pencil from his jacket pocket.

"May I ask your name and what you do here?"

"I'm one of Alfred Harderberg's secretaries," she said. "My name's Anita Karlén."

"Does Mr Harderberg have many secretaries?" Wallander wondered.

"That depends on how you look at it," Anita Karlén replied. "Is that really relevant?"

Once again Wallander started to get annoyed at the way in which he was being treated. He decided he would have to change his approach if the whole visit to Farnholm were not to be a waste of time.

"I shall decide if the question is relevant or not," he said. "Farnholm Castle is a private property and you have a legal right to surround it with as many fences as you like, as high as you like. Provided you have planning permission and are not contravening any laws or regulations. You also have the right to deny entry to whoever you like. With one exception: the police. Is that understood?"

"We haven't denied you entry, Mr Wallander," she said, still without batting an eyelid.

"Let me express myself more clearly," Wallander said, noting that the woman's indifference was making him feel insecure. Perhaps he was also distracted by the fact that she was strikingly beautiful.

Just as he opened his mouth to continue, a door opened and a woman came in with a tray. To his surprise Wallander saw that she was black. Without saying a word she put the tray down on the desk, then disappeared again just as noiselessly as she'd appeared.

"Would you like a cup of coffee, Mr Wallander?"

He said he would. She poured and then handed him the cup and saucer. He examined the china.

"Let me ask you a question that's relevant," he said. "What will happen if I drop this cup on the floor? How much will I owe you?"

For the first time her smile seemed genuine.

"Everything's insured, of course," she said. "But that's a classic Rörstrand special edition."

Wallander put the cup and saucer gingerly down by the side of the printout on the oak parquet floor, and started again.

"I'll express myself very precisely," he said. "That same evening, October 11, barely an hour after Mr Torstensson had been here, he died in a car accident."

"We sent flowers to the funeral," she said. "One of my colleagues attended the service."

"But not Alfred Harderberg, of course?"

"My employer avoids appearing in public whenever possible."

"I've gathered that," Wallander said. "But the fact is that we've reason to believe this wasn't in fact a car accident. Many things suggest Mr Torstensson was murdered. And to make matters worse, his son was shot dead in his office a few weeks later. Perhaps you sent flowers to his funeral as well?"

She stared at him uncomprehendingly.

"We only dealt with Gustaf Torstensson," she said.

Wallander nodded, and went on: "Now you know why I've come. And you still haven't told me how many secretaries there are working here."

"And you haven't understood that it depends on how you look at it, Inspector Wallander," she said.

"I'm all ears."

"Here at Farnholm Castle there are three secretaries," she said. "Then there are two more who accompany him on his travels. In addition Dr Harderberg has secretaries stationed in various places around the world. The number can vary, but it's rarely fewer than six."

"I make it eleven," Wallander said.

She agreed.

"You referred to your employer as Dr Harderberg," Wallander said.

"He has several honorary doctorates," she said. "You can have a list if you'd like one."

"Yes, I would," Wallander said. "I also want an overview of Dr Harderberg's business empire. But you can let me have that later. What I want now is to know what happened that evening when Gustaf Torstensson was here for the last time. Which one of all those secretaries can tell me that?"

"I was on duty that evening."

Wallander thought for a moment. "That's why you're here," he said. "That's why you are receiving me. But what would have happened if this had been your day off? You couldn't know the police were going to come this day of all days."

"Of course not."

Even as he spoke Wallander realised he was wrong. And he also realised how it would be possible for people at Farnholm Castle to know. The thought worried him. He had to force himself to concentrate before continuing.

"What happened that evening?" he asked.

"Mr Torstensson arrived shortly after 7 p.m. He had a private conversation with Dr Harderberg and some of his closest colleagues, lasting an hour. Then he had a cup of tea. He left Farnholm at exactly 8.14."

"What did they talk about that evening?"

"I can't answer that."

"But you said a moment ago that you were on duty."

"It was a conversation with no secretary present. No notes were taken."

"Who were the colleagues?"

"I beg your pardon?"

"You said Mr Torstensson had a private conversation with Dr Harderberg and some of his closest colleagues."

"I can't answer that."

"Because you're not allowed to?"

"Because I don't know."

"Don't know what?"

"Who those colleagues were. I'd never seen them before. They had arrived that day and they left the following day."

Wallander didn't know what to ask next. It seemed as if all the answers he was getting were peripheral. He decided to approach matters from a different angle.

"You said a moment ago that Dr Harderberg has eleven secretaries. Might I ask how many solicitors he has?"

"Presumably at least as many."

"But you're not allowed to say exactly how many?"

"I don't know."

Wallander nodded. He could see he was entering another cul-de-sac.

"How long had Mr Torstensson been working for Dr Harderberg?"

"Ever since he bought Farnholm Castle and made it his headquarters. About five years ago."

"Mr Torstensson worked as a solicitor in Ystad all his life," said Wallander. "All of a sudden he's considered to be qualified to advise on international business matters. Doesn't that seem a little remarkable?"

"That's something you'll have to ask Dr Harderberg."

Wallander closed his notebook. "Absolutely right," he said. "I'd like you to send him a message, whether he's in Geneva or Dubai or wherever, and inform him that Inspector Wallander wants to talk to him as soon as possible. The day he gets back here, in other words."

He stood up and gingerly placed the cup and saucer on the desk.

"The Ystad police don't have eleven secretaries," he said, "but our receptionists are pretty efficient. You can leave a message with them saying when he can see me."

He followed her out into the hall. Next to the front door, lying on a marble table, was a thick leather-bound file.

"Here's the overview of Dr Harderberg's business affairs you asked for," Anita Karlén said.

Somebody's been listening in, Wallander thought. Somebody's overheard the whole of our conversation. Presumably a transcript is already on its way to

Harderberg, wherever he is. In case he's interested. Which I doubt.

"Don't forget to stress that it's urgent," Wallander said. This time Anita Karlén did shake hands with him.

Wallander glanced at the big unlit staircase, but the shadows had gone.

The sky had cleared. He got into his car. Anita Karlén was standing on the steps, her hair fluttering in the wind. As he drove off he could see her in his rear-view mirror, still on the steps, watching him. This time he didn't need to stop at the gates, which started opening as he approached. There was no sign of Kurt Ström. The gates closed automatically behind him, and he drove slowly back to Ystad. It was only three days since he'd suddenly made up his mind to return to work, but even so, it seemed like a long time. As if he were on his way somewhere while his memories went dashing off at an enormous pace in an entirely different direction.

Just after the turning into the main highway there was a dead hare lying on the road. He drove round it, and thought how he was still no nearer to finding out what had happened to Gustaf Torstensson or his son. It seemed to him highly unlikely that he would find any connection between the dead solicitors and the people in the castle behind that double fence. Nevertheless, he would go through that leather file before the day was out, and try to get some idea of Alfred Harderberg's business empire.

His car phone started ringing. He picked it up and heard Svedberg's voice.

"Svedberg here," he shouted. "Where are you?"

"Forty minutes from Ystad."

"Martinsson said you were going to Farnholm Castle."

"I've been there. Drew a blank."

The conversation was cut off by interference for a few seconds. Then Svedberg's voice returned.

"Berta Dunér phoned and asked for you," he said. "She was keen for you to get in touch with her right away."

"Why?"

"She didn't say."

"If you give me her number I'll give her a call."

"It would be better if you drove round there. She seemed very insistent."

Wallander glanced at the clock. It was 8.45 already.

"What happened at the meeting this morning?"

"Nothing special."

"I'll drive straight to her place when I get back to Ystad," Wallander said.

"Do that," Svedberg said.

Wallander wondered what Mrs Dunér wanted that was so urgent. He could feel himself growing tense, and increased his speed.

At 9.25 he parked any old how opposite the pink house. He hurried across the street and rang her bell. The moment she opened the door he could see something was amiss. She looked to be in shock.

"You've been asking for me," he said.

She nodded and ushered him in. He was about to take off his shoes when she grasped his arm and dragged him into the living room that overlooked her little garden. She pointed.

"Somebody's been there during the night," she said.

She looked really frightened. Something of her anxiety rubbed off on Wallander. He stood at the French windows and examined the lawn: the flower beds, dug over ready for winter, the climbers on the whitewashed wall between Mrs Dunér's garden and her neighbour's.

"I can't see anything," he said.

She had been hovering in the background, as if she did not dare go up to the window. Wallander began to wonder if she was suffering from some temporary mental aberration as a result of the violent events that had shaken her life to its foundations.

She came to his side, and pointed. "There," she said. "There. Somebody's been there during the night, digging."

"Did you see anybody?"

"No."

"Did you hear anything?"

"No. But I know somebody's been there during the night."

Wallander tried to follow where she was pointing. He had the vague impression he could see that a tiny piece of lawn had been trodden down.

"It could be a cat," he said. "Or a mole. Even a mouse."

She shook her head. "No, somebody's been there during the night," she said.

Wallander opened the French windows and stepped out into the garden. He walked on to the lawn. From close up it looked as if a square of turf had been lifted and then put back. He squatted down and ran his hand over the grass. His fingers touched something hard, something plastic or iron, a little spike sticking up out of the turf. Very carefully, he bent back the blades of grass. A greyish-brown object was buried just under the surface.

Wallander stiffened. He pulled his hand back and rose gingerly to his feet. For a moment he thought he had gone mad – it could not possibly be what he thought it was. That was too unlikely, too far-fetched even to be considered.

He walked backwards to the French windows, placing his feet exactly where they had been before. When he got to the house he turned round. He still could not believe it was true.

"What is it?" she said.

"Please go and fetch the telephone directory," Wallander said, and he could hear his voice was tense.

"What do you want the directory for?"

"Do as I say," he said.

She went out into the hall and returned with the directory for Ystad and District. Wallander took it and weighed it in his hand.

"Please go into the kitchen and stay there," he said.

She did as she was told.

Wallander tried to tell himself that this was all in his imagination. If there'd been the slightest possibility that the improbability was in fact true, he ought to have reacted quite differently. He went in through the French windows and positioned himself as far back in the room as he could. Then he aimed the phone book and threw it at the spike sticking up out of the grass.

The explosion deafened him.

Afterwards, he was amazed to find the windows hadn't shattered.

He eyed the crater that had formed in the lawn. Then he hurried into the kitchen where he'd heard Mrs Dunér scream. She was standing as if petrified in the middle of the floor, her hands over her ears. He took hold of her and sat her down on one of the kitchen chairs.

"There's no danger," he said. "I'll be back in a second. I must just make a phone call."

113

He dialled the number to the police station. To his relief it was Ebba who answered.

"Kurt here," he said. "I have to speak to Martinsson or Svedberg. Failing that, anybody will do."

Ebba recognised his voice, he could tell. That's why she asked no questions, just did as he had asked. She had grasped how serious he was.

Martinsson answered.

"It's Kurt," Wallander said. "Any minute now the police are going to get an emergency call about a violent explosion behind the Continental Hotel. Make sure there's no emergency call-out. I don't want fire engines and ambulances rushing here. Get here quick and bring somebody with you. I'm with Mrs Dunér, Torstensson's secretary. The address is Stickgatan 26. A pink house."

"What's happened?" Martinsson said.

"You'll see when you get here," Wallander said. "You wouldn't believe me if I tried to explain."

"Try me," Martinsson said.

"If I told you that somebody had planted a landmine in Mrs Dunér's back garden, would you believe me?"

"No," Martinsson said.

"I thought not."

Wallander hung up and went back to the French windows.

The crater was still there.

Chapter 6

Kurt Wallander would remember Wednesday, November 3 as a day that he was never entirely convinced had existed. How could he ever have dreamed that he would one day come across a landmine buried in a garden in the middle of Ystad?

When Martinsson arrived at Mrs Dunér's house with Höglund, Wallander still had difficulty in believing it was a mine that had exploded. Martinsson, however, had greater faith in what Wallander had said on the telephone, and on the way out from the police station he had already sent a message to Nyberg, their technical expert. He arrived at the pink house only a few minutes after Martinsson and Höglund had stood transfixed before the crater in the lawn. As they couldn't be sure there weren't any more mines hidden in the grass, they all stayed close to the house wall. Off her own bat Höglund then went to the kitchen with Mrs Dunér, who was a little calmer by now, to question her.

"What's going on?" Martinsson said, indignantly.

"Are you asking me?" Wallander replied. "I have no idea."

No more was said. They continued contemplating the hole in the ground. Shortly afterwards the forensic team arrived, led by the skilful but irritable Sven Nyberg. He stopped in his tracks when he caught sight of Wallander.

"What are *you* doing here?" he said, making Wallander feel that he had committed an indecent act by returning to duty.

"Working," he said, going on the defensive.

"I thought you were packing it in?"

"So did I. But then I realised you couldn't manage without me."

Nyberg was about to say something, but Wallander raised a hand to stop him.

"More important is this hole in the lawn," he said, remembering that Nyberg had served several times with Swedish troops for the UN. "From your years of duty in Cyprus and the Middle East you can verify if this was in fact a mine. But first can you tell us if there are any more of them?"

"I'm not a dog," Nyberg said, squatting by the house wall. Wallander told him about the spike he had found with his fingers, and then the telephone book that had triggered the explosion.

Nyberg nodded. "There are very few explosive substances or compounds that are detonated on impact – apart from mines. That's the whole point of them. People or vehicles are supposed to be blown up if they put a foot or a wheel on a landmine. For an anti-personnel mine a pressure of just a few kilos can be enough – a kiddie's foot or a telephone directory will do. If the target's a vehicle, 200 kilos would be the pressure required." He stood up and looked questioningly at Wallander and Martinsson. "But what the hell kind of person lays a mine in somebody's garden? They had better be caught in very short order."

"You're quite certain it was a mine?" Wallander said.

"I'm never certain of anything," Nyberg said, "but I'll send for a mine detector from the regiment. Until it gets here nobody should set foot in this garden."

While they were waiting for the mine detector Martinsson made a few calls. Wallander sat on the sofa, trying to come to terms with what had happened. From the kitchen he could hear Höglund patiently asking Mrs Dunér questions that Mrs Dunér answered even more slowly.

Two dead lawyers, Wallander thought. Then somebody lays a mine in their secretary's garden. Even if everything else is still obscure, we can be sure of one thing: the solution must lie somewhere in the activities of the firm of solicitors. It's hardly credible any more that the private or social lives of these three individuals is relevant.

Wallander was interrupted in his train of thought by Martinsson finishing his calls.

"Björk asked me if I'd taken leave of my senses," he said, pulling a face. "I must admit that I wasn't quite sure at first how I should answer that. He says it's inconceivable that it could be a landmine. Even so, he wants one of us to update him as soon as possible."

"When we've got something to say," Wallander said. "Where's Nyberg disappeared to?"

"He's gone to the barracks himself to fetch a mine detector," Martinsson said.

Wallander looked at the time. 10.15. He thought about his visit to Farnholm Castle, but didn't really know what conclusion to draw.

Martinsson was standing in the doorway, studying the hole in the lawn. "There was an incident about 20

117

years ago in Söderhamn," he said. "In the municipal law courts. Do you remember?"

"Vaguely," Wallander said.

"There was an old farmer who'd spent countless years bringing just as countless a series of lawsuits against his neighbours, his relatives, anybody and everybody. It ended up by becoming a clinical obsession that nobody diagnosed as such soon enough. He thought he was being persecuted by all his imagined opponents, not least by the judge and his own solicitor. In the end he snapped. He drew a revolver in the middle of a case and shot both the judge and his solicitor. When the police tried to get into his house afterwards, it turned out he'd booby-trapped all the doors and windows. It was sheer luck that nobody was injured once the fireworks started."

Wallander remembered the incident.

"A prosecutor in Stockholm has his house blown up," Martinsson went on. "Lawyers are threatened and attacked. Not to mention police officers."

Wallander nodded without replying. Höglund emerged from the kitchen, notebook in hand. Somewhat to his surprise, Wallander noticed that she was an attractive woman. It had not occurred to him before. She sat on a chair opposite him.

"Nothing," she said. "She hadn't heard a thing during the night, but she is certain the lawn hadn't been messed with by nightfall. She's an early riser and as soon as it got light she saw that somebody had been in her garden. She says she has no idea why anybody would want to kill her. Or at the very least blow her legs off."

"Is she telling the truth?" Martinsson said.

"It's not easy to tell if a person in shock is telling the truth," Höglund said, "but I am positive she thinks

118

the mine was put in her lawn during last night. And that she doesn't have a clue why."

"Something about it worries me," Wallander said. "I'm not sure if I can get a handle on it."

"Try," Martinsson said.

"She looks out of the window this morning and sees that somebody has been digging up her lawn. So what does she do?"

"What *doesn't* she do?" Höglund said.

"Precisely," Wallander said. "The natural thing for her to do would have been to open the French windows and go out and investigate. But what does she do instead?"

"She phones the police," Martinsson said.

"As if she'd suspected there was something dangerous out there," said Höglund.

"Or known," Wallander said.

"An anti-personnel mine, for instance," Martinsson said. "She was in quite a state when she phoned the police station."

"She was in a state when I got here," Wallander said. "In fact, I've had the impression that she was nervous every time I've spoken to her. Which could be explained by all that's happened over the last week or two, of course, but I'm not convinced."

The front doorbell rang and in marched Nyberg ahead of two men in uniform carrying an implement that reminded Wallander of a vacuum cleaner. It took the soldiers a quarter of an hour to go over the little garden with the mine detector. The police officers stood at the window watching intently as the men worked. Then they announced that it was all clear, and prepared to leave. Wallander accompanied them out into the street where their car was waiting for them.

"What can you say about the mine?" he asked them. "Size, explosive power? Can you guess where it might have been made? Anything at all could be of use to us."

LUNDQVIST, CAPTAIN, it said on the identity disc attached to the tunic of the older of the two soldiers. He was also the one who replied to Wallander's question.

"Not a particularly powerful mine," he said. "A few hundred grams of explosive at most. Enough to kill a man, though. We usually call this kind of mine a Four."

"Meaning what?" Wallander said.

"Somebody treads on a mine," Captain Lundqvist said. "You need three men to carry him out of battle. Four people removed from active duty."

"And the origin?"

"Mines aren't made the same way as other weapons," Lundqvist said. "Bofors makes them, as do all the other major arms manufacturers. But nearly every industrialised country has a factory making mines. Either they're manufactured openly under licence, or they're pirated. Terrorist groups have their own models. Before you can say anything about where the mine comes from, you have to have a fragment of the explosive and preferably also a bit of the material the casing was made from. It could be iron or plastic. Even wood."

"We'll see what we can find," Wallander said. "Then we'll get back to you."

"Not a nice weapon," Captain Lundqvist said. "They say it's the world's cheapest and most reliable soldier. You put him somewhere and he never moves from the spot, not for a hundred years if that's how you want it. He doesn't require food or drink or wages. He just exists, and waits. Until somebody comes and treads on him. Then he strikes."

120

"How long can a mine remain active?" Wallander asked.

"Nobody knows. Landmines that were laid in the First World War are still going off now and then."

Wallander went back into the house. Nyberg was in the garden and had already started his meticulous investigation of the crater.

"The explosive and if possible also a piece of the casing," Wallander said.

"What else do you suppose we're looking for?" Nyberg snarled. "Bits of bone?"

Wallander wondered whether he should let Mrs Dunér calm down for a few more hours before talking to her, but he was getting impatient again. Impatient at never seeming to be able to see any sign of a breakthrough, or finding any clear starting point for this investigation.

"You two had better go and put Björk in the picture," he said to Martinsson and Höglund. "This afternoon we'll go through the whole case in detail, to see where we've got to."

"Have we got anywhere at all?" Martinsson said.

"We've always got somewhere," Wallander said, "but we don't always know exactly where. Has Svedberg been talking to the lawyers going through the Torstensson archives?"

"He's been there all morning," Martinsson said. "But I reckon he'd rather be doing something else. He's not much of a one for reading papers."

"Go and help him," Wallander said. "I have an idea that it's urgent."

He went back into the house, hung up his jacket and went to the toilet in the hall. He gave a start when he saw his face in the mirror. He was unshaven and red-eyed, and his hair was on end. He wondered at the impression he must have made at Farnholm Castle. He rinsed his face in cold water, asking himself where he was going to start in order to get Mrs Dunér to understand that he knew she was holding back information – and he did not know why. I must be friendly, he decided. Otherwise she'll put up the shutters.

He went to the kitchen where she was still slumped on a chair. The forensic team were busy in the garden. Occasionally Wallander heard Nyberg's agitated voice. He had the sense of having experienced exactly what he was now seeing, feeling, a moment before, the bewildering sensation of having gone round in a circle and returned to a point way in the distant past. He closed his eyes and took a deep breath. Then he sat at the kitchen table and looked at the woman facing him. Just for a moment he thought she reminded him of his long-dead mother. The grey hair, the thin body that seemed to have been compressed inside a tiny frame. He could not conjure up a picture of his mother's face, though: it had faded from his memory.

"You're very upset, I know," he began, "but we have to have a talk."

She nodded without replying.

"Let's see, this morning you discovered that somebody had been in your garden during the night," Wallander said.

"I could see it straight away," she said.

"What did you do then?"

She looked at him in surprise. "I've already told you," she said. "Do I have to go through everything again?"

"Not everything," Wallander said, patiently. "You only need to answer the questions I ask you."

"It was getting light," she said. "I'm an early riser. I looked out at the garden. Somebody had been there. I called the police."

"Why did you call the police?" Wallander said, watching her carefully.

"What else should I have done?"

"You might have gone out to see what damage had been done, for instance."

"I didn't dare."

"Why not? Because you knew there was something out there that could be dangerous?"

She didn't answer. Wallander waited. Nyberg shouted angrily in the garden.

"I don't think you've been completely honest with me," Wallander said. "I think there is something that you ought to be telling me."

She put a hand over her eyes, as if the light in the kitchen was affecting her. Wallander waited. The clock on the kitchen wall showed 11 a.m.

"I've been frightened for so long," she said suddenly, peering up at Wallander as if it were his fault. He waited for more, but in vain.

"People aren't usually frightened unless there is a cause," Wallander said. "If the police are going to be able to find out what happened to Gustaf and Sten Torstensson, you have got to help us."

"I can't help you," she said.

Wallander could see that she was liable to break down at any moment. But he pressed on nevertheless.

"You can answer my questions," he said. "Start by telling me why you're frightened."

"Do you know what's the most scary thing there is?" she said. "It's other people's fear. I'd worked 30 years for Gustaf Torstensson. I wasn't close to him, but I couldn't avoid noticing the change. There came to be a strange smell about him. His fear."

"When did you first notice it?"

"Three years ago."

"Had anything specific happened?"

"Everything was exactly as usual."

"It's very important that you try to remember."

"What do you think I've been trying to do all this time?"

Wallander tried to think how best to keep Mrs Dunér going – despite everything she seemed willing to answer his questions now.

"You never spoke to Mr Torstensson about it?"

"Never."

"Not to his son either?"

"I don't think he'd noticed anything."

She could be right, Wallander thought. She was Gustaf Torstensson's secretary, after all.

"Have you really no explanation for what happened today? You realise that you could have been killed if you had gone into the garden. I think you suspected as much and that's why you phoned the police. You've been expecting something to happen. But you have no explanation?"

"People started coming to the office during the night," she said. "Both Gustaf and I noticed. A pen lying differently on a desk, a chair somebody had been sitting on and put back nearly in its proper place but not quite."

"You must have asked him about it," Wallander said.

"I wasn't allowed to. He forbade me."

"So he did speak about these nocturnal visits, then?"

124

"You can see by looking at a person what you're not allowed to mention."

The conversation was interrupted by Nyberg tapping on the window.

"I'll be back in a moment," Wallander said. Nyberg was standing outside the kitchen door, holding out his hand. Wallander could see something badly burned, hardly half a centimetre across.

"A plastic landmine," Nyberg said. "I can confirm that even at this stage. We might possibly be able to find out what type it is, even where it was made. But it'll take time."

"Can you say anything about whoever it was who laid the mine?"

"I might have been able to if you hadn't thrown a directory at it," Nyberg said.

"It was easy to see," Wallander said.

"A person who knows what he's doing can plant a mine so that it's invisible," Nyberg said. "Both you and that woman in the kitchen could see that somebody had been digging up the lawn. We're dealing with amateurs."

Or somebody who wants us to think that, Wallander thought. But he didn't say so and went back to the kitchen. He only had one more question.

"Yesterday afternoon you had a visit from an Asian woman," he said. "Who was she?"

She looked at him in astonishment. "How do you know that?"

"Never mind how," Wallander said. "Just answer the question."

"She's a cleaner, she works at the Torstensson offices," Mrs Dunér said.

So that was it! Wallander was disappointed.

125

"What's her name?"

"Kim Sung-Lee."

"Where does she live?"

"I have her address at the office."

"What did she want?"

"She was wondering if she'd keep her job."

"I'd be grateful if you could let me have her address," Wallander said, standing up.

"What will happen now?"

"You don't need to be afraid any more," Wallander said. "I'll make sure there's a police officer at hand. For as long as it's necessary."

He told Nyberg he was leaving and went back to the police station. On the way there he stopped at Fridolf's Café and bought some sandwiches. He shut himself in his office and prepared for his meeting with Björk. But when he went to his office, Björk was not there. The conversation would have to wait.

It was 1 p.m. by the time Wallander knocked on the door of Åkeson's office at the other end of the long, narrow police station. Every time he was there he was surprised by the chaos that seemed to prevail. The desk was piled high with paper, files were strewn around the floor and on the visitors' chairs. Along one wall was a barbell and a hastily rolled-up mattress.

"Have you started working out?"

"Not only that," Åkeson replied with a self-satisfied grin, "I've also acquired the good habit of taking a nap after lunch. I've just woken up."

"You mean you sleep here on the floor?"

"A 30-minute nap," Åkeson confirmed. "Then I get back to work full of energy."

"Maybe I should try that," Wallander said doubtfully.

Åkeson made room for him on one of the chairs by tipping a heap of files on to the floor. Then he sat down and put his feet on the desk.

"I'd almost given you up for lost," he said with a smile, "but deep down I always knew you'd be back."

"It's been a hell of a time," Wallander said.

Åkeson became serious. "I really can't imagine what it must be like killing a man. Never mind if it was self-defence. It must be the only human act from which there's no going back. I haven't enough imagination to conjure up anything except a vague image of the abyss."

"You can never get away from it," Wallander said. "But maybe you can learn to live with it."

They sat without speaking. Somebody in the corridor was complaining that the coffee machine had broken down.

"We're the same age, you and me," Åkeson said. "Six months ago I woke up one morning and thought: Good God! Was that all it was, life? Was there no more to it than that? I felt panic-stricken. But now, looking back, I have to acknowledge that it was useful. It made me do something I ought to have done ages ago."

He fished a sheet of paper out of one of the piles on his desk and handed it to Wallander. It was an advertisement from various UN organisations for legally qualified people to fill a variety of posts abroad, including refugee camps in Africa and Asia.

"I sent in an application," Åkeson said, "Then I forgot all about it. But a month ago I was called for an interview in Copenhagen. There's a chance I might be offered a two-year contract in a big camp for Ugandan refugees who are going to be repatriated."

"Jump at it if the offer comes," Wallander said. "What does your wife say?"

"She doesn't know about it," Åkeson said. "I don't honestly know what will happen."

"I need you to give me some information," Wallander said.

Åkeson took his feet off the desk and cleared aside some of the papers from in front of him. Wallander told him about the explosion in Mrs Dunér's back garden. Åkeson shook his head incredulously.

"That's not possible."

"Nyberg was positive," Wallander said. "And he's usually right, as you know."

"What do you think about the whole business?" Åkeson said. "I've spoken to Björk, and of course I go along with your tearing up the previous investigation into Gustaf Torstensson's accident. Do we really have nothing to go on?"

Wallander thought before replying. "The one thing we can be completely sure about is that it's no strange co-incidence that two solicitors are dead and a mine is planted in Mrs Dunér's garden. It's all planned. We don't know how it started, and we don't know how it will end."

"You don't think what happened to Mrs Dunér was just meant to frighten her?"

"Whoever put that mine in her garden intended to kill her," Wallander said. "I want her protected. Perhaps she ought to move out of the house."

"I'll arrange for that," Åkeson said. "I'll have a word with Björk."

"She's scared," Wallander said. "But I can see now, after talking to her again, that she doesn't know what she's scared of. I thought she was holding something back, but I now realise she knows as little as the rest of us. Anyway, I thought you might be able to help by telling me about Gustaf and Sten Torstensson. You must have had quite a bit to do with them over the years."

"Gustaf was an odd bird," Åkeson said. "And his son was well on the way to becoming one."

"Gustaf Torstensson," Wallander said. "I think that's the starting point. But don't ask me why."

"I didn't have that much to do with him," Åkeson said. "It was before my time when he used to appear in court as a defence lawyer. These last few years he seems to have been busy exclusively with financial consultancy."

"For Alfred Harderberg," Wallander said. "Of Farnholm Castle. Which also strikes me as odd. A run-of-the-mill lawyer from Ystad. And a businessman with a global business empire."

"As I understand it, that's one of Harderberg's chief attributes," Åkeson said. "His knack of finding and surrounding himself with just the right associates. Perhaps he noticed something about Gustaf that nobody else had suspected."

"Are there any skeletons in Harderberg's cupboard?"

"Not as far as I know," Åkeson said. "Which in itself might seem odd. They say there's a crime behind every fortune. But Harderberg appears to be a model citizen. And he does his bit for Sweden as well."

"Meaning what?"

"He doesn't channel all his investments abroad. He's even set up businesses in other countries and moved the actual manufacturing to Sweden. That's pretty unusual nowadays."

"No skeletons roaming the corridors at Farnholm Castle, then," Wallander said. "Were there any blots in Torstensson's copybook?"

"None at all," Åkeson said. "Honest, pedantic, boring. Old-fashioned sense of honour. Not a genius, not an idiot. Discreet. Not the type ever to wake up one morning and ask himself where his life had disappeared to."

"Yet he was murdered," Wallander said. "There must have been *one* blot somewhere. Maybe not in his copybook, but in somebody else's."

"I'm not sure I follow you."

"A solicitor must be a bit like a doctor," Wallander said. "He knows a lot of people's secrets."

"You're no doubt right," Åkeson agreed. "The solution must be somewhere in his relations with his clients. Something that involves everybody working for the firm. Including the secretary, Mrs Dunér."

"We're searching."

"I haven't much more to say about Sten Torstensson," Åkeson said. "A bachelor, a bit old-fashioned as well. I've heard the odd rumour to the effect that he was interested in persons of the same sex, but that's a rumour that circulates about all bachelors who are getting on in years. Thirty years ago, we could have guessed it might be blackmail."

"That might be worth bearing in mind," Wallander said. "Anything else?"

"Not really. Very occasionally he would come out with a joke, but he wasn't exactly the type you wanted to invite for dinner. He was said to be a good sailor, though."

The phone rang. Åkeson answered, then handed the receiver to Wallander.

Wallander recognised Martinsson's voice, and could hear straight away that it was important. Martinsson's voice was loud and shrill.

"I'm at the solicitors' offices," he said. "We've found something that might be what we've been looking for."

"What?"

"Threatening letters."

"Who to?"

"To all three."

"Mrs Dunér as well?"

"Her as well."

"I'm on my way."

Wallander handed the receiver back to Åkeson and rose to his feet.

"Martinsson's found some threatening letters," he said. "It looks as if you might have been right."

"Phone me here or at home the moment you've got anything to tell me," Åkeson said.

Wallander went out to his car without going back to his office for his jacket. He exceeded the speed limit all the way to the solicitors' offices. Lundin was in reception as he hurried through the door.

"Where are they?" he said.

She pointed at the conference room. Wallander went straight in before he remembered that there were people from the Bar Council there as well. Three solemn men, each one in his sixties, who clearly resented his barging in. He thought of the unshaven face he had seen in the mirror earlier – he did not look exactly presentable.

Martinsson and Svedberg were at the table, waiting for him.

"This is Inspector Wallander," Svedberg said.

"A police officer with a national reputation," said one of the men, stiffly, shaking hands. Wallander shook hands with the other two as well, and sat down.

"Fill me in," Wallander said, looking at Martinsson. But the reply came from one of the lawyers from Stockholm.

"Perhaps I should start by informing Inspector Wallander of the procedure undertaken when a firm of solicitors is liquidated," said the man whose name Wallander had gathered was Wrede.

"We can do that later," Wallander intervened. "Let's get straight down to business. You've found some threatening letters, I understand?"

Wrede looked at him disapprovingly, but said no more. Martinsson pushed a brown envelope across the table to Wallander, and Svedberg handed him a pair of plastic gloves.

"They were at the back of a drawer in a filing cabinet," Martinsson said. "They weren't listed in any diary or ledger. They were hidden away."

Wallander put on the gloves and opened the large brown envelope. Inside were two smaller envelopes. He tried without success to decipher the postmark. On one of the envelopes was a patch of ink, suggesting that some of the text had been crossed out. He took out the two letters, written on white paper, and put them on the desk in front of him. They were handwritten, and the text was short: *The injustice is not forgotten, none of you shall be allowed to live unpunished, you shall die, Gustaf Torstensson, your son and also Dunér.*

The second letter was even shorter, the handwriting the same: *The injustice will soon be punished.*

The first letter was dated June 19, 1992, and the second August 26 of the same year. Both letters were signed *Lars Borman*.

Wallander slid the letters carefully to one side and took off the gloves.

"We've searched the ledgers," Martinsson said, "but neither Gustaf nor Sten Torstensson had a client by the name of Lars Borman."

"That's correct," Wrede confirmed.

"The man writes about an injustice," Martinsson said. "It must have been something major, or he wouldn't have had cause to threaten the lives of all three."

"I'm sure you're right," Wallander said, his thoughts miles away.

Once again he had the feeling there was something he ought to understand, but he couldn't put his finger on it.

"Show me where you found the envelope," he said, standing up.

Svedberg led him to a big filing cabinet in the office where Mrs Dunér had her desk. Svedberg pointed to one of the lower drawers. Wallander opened it. It was filled with suspension files.

"Fetch Miss Lundin," he said.

When Svedberg came back with her, Wallander could see she was very nervous. Even so, without being able to say why, he was convinced that she had nothing to do with the mysterious events at the solicitors' offices.

"Who had a key to this filing cabinet?" he said.

"Mrs Dunér," Lundin replied, almost inaudibly.

"Please speak a bit louder," Wallander said.

"Mrs Dunér," she repeated.

"Only her?"

"The solicitors had their own keys."

133

"Was it kept locked?"

"Mrs Dunér used to open it in the morning and lock it again when she went home."

Wrede interrupted the conversation. "We have signed for a key from Mrs Dunér," he said. "Sten Torstensson's key. We opened the cabinet today."

Wallander nodded. There was something else he ought to ask Lundin, he was sure, but he couldn't think what it was. Instead he turned to Wrede.

"What do you think about these threatening letters?" he said.

"The man must obviously be arrested at once," Wrede said.

"That's not what I asked," Wallander said. "I asked for your opinion."

"Solicitors are often placed in an exposed situation."

"I take it all solicitors receive this kind of letter sooner or later?"

"The Bar Council might be able to supply the statistics."

Wallander looked at him for some time before asking his final question.

"Have you ever received a threatening letter?"

"It has happened."

"Why?"

"I'm afraid I'm not at liberty to reveal that. It would break my oath of confidentiality as a lawyer."

Wallander could see his point. He replaced the letters in the brown envelope.

"We'll take these with us," he said to the men from the Bar Council.

"It's not quite so straightforward as that," Wrede said. He seemed always to be the one speaking on behalf of the others. Wallander felt like he was in a court facing a judge.

"It's possible that just at this moment our interests are not identical," Wallander interrupted him, irritated by his way of speaking. "You're here to work out what to do with the firm's property, if that's what you can call it. We are here to identify one or more murderers. The brown envelope is going with me."

"We cannot allow any documents to be removed from these premises until we have discussed the matter with the prosecutor in charge of the investigation," Wrede said.

"Phone Per Åkeson," Wallander said, "and send him my regards."

Then he picked up the envelope and marched out of the room. Martinsson and Svedberg hastened after him.

"Now there'll be trouble," Martinsson said as they left the building. Wallander could tell that Martinsson was not altogether displeased at the prospect.

Wallander felt cold. The wind was gusting and seemed to be getting stronger.

"What now?" he said. "What's Höglund up to?"

"Looking after her sick child," Svedberg said. "Hanson would be pleased to know that. He has always said women police officers are no good when it comes to investigations."

"Hanson has always said all kinds of things," Martinsson said. "Police officers who are forever absent on further-education courses are not much good at investigations either."

"The letters are a year old," Wallander said. "We have a name, Lars Borman. He threatens the lives of Gustaf and Sten Torstensson. And Mrs Dunér. He writes a letter, and then another one two months later. One was posted in some form of company envelope. Nyberg is good. I think he'll be able to tell us what it says under the ink on that envelope. And where they were postmarked, of course. In fact, I don't know what we're waiting for."

They returned to the police station. While Martinsson phoned Nyberg, who was still at Mrs Dunér's house, Wallander sat down and tried to puzzle out the postmarks.

Svedberg had gone to look for the name Lars Borman in various police registers. When Nyberg came to Wallander's office a quarter of an hour later he was blue with cold and had dark grass stains on the knees of his overalls.

"How's it going?" Wallander said.

"Slowly," Nyberg said. "What did you expect? A mine exploded into millions of tiny particles."

Wallander pointed to the two letters and the brown envelope on the desk in front of him.

"These have to be thoroughly examined," he said. "First of all I'd like to know where the letters were post-marked. And what it says under the ink stain on one of the envelopes. Everything else can wait."

Nyberg put on his glasses, switched on Wallander's desk lamp, found a clean pair of plastic gloves and examined the letters.

"We'll be able to decipher the postmarks using a microscope," he said. "Whatever is written on the envelope has been painted over with Indian ink. I can try a bit of scraping. I think I should be able to sort that out without having to send it to Linköping."

"It's urgent."

Nyberg took off his glasses in irritation. "It's always urgent," he said. "I need an hour. Is that too much?"

"Take as long as you need," Wallander said. "I know you work as fast as you can."

Nyberg picked up the letters and left. Martinsson and Svedberg appeared almost immediately.

"There is no Borman in any of the registers," Svedberg said. "I've found four Bromans and one Borrman. I thought maybe it could have been misspelled. Evert Borrman wandered around the Östersund area at the end of the 1960s cashing false cheques. If he's still alive he must be about 85 by now."

Wallander shook his head. "We'd better wait for Nyberg," he said. "At the same time, I think we'd be wise not to expect too much of this. The threat is brutal alright. But vague. I'll give you a shout when Nyberg reports back."

When Wallander was on his own he took out the leather file he had been given at Farnholm Castle. He spent almost an hour acquainting himself with the extent of Harderberg's business empire. He had still not finished when there was a knock on the door and Nyberg came in. Wallander noticed to his surprise that he was still in his dirty overalls.

"Here are the answers to your questions," he said, flopping down on Wallander's visitor's chair. "The letters are postmarked in Helsingborg, and on one of the envelopes it says 'The Linden Hotel'."

Wallander pulled over a pad and made a note.

"Linden Hotel," Nyberg said. "Gjutargatan 12. It even gave the phone number."

"Where?"

"I thought you'd grasped that," Nyberg said. "The letters were postmarked in Helsingborg. That's where the Linden Hotel is as well."

"Well done," Wallander said.

"I just do as I'm told," Nyberg said. "But as this went so quickly, I did something else as well. I think you're going to have problems."

Wallander looked questioningly at him.

"I rang that number in Helsingborg," Nyberg said. "I got the 'number unobtainable' tone. It no longer exists. I asked Ebba to look into it. It took her ten minutes to establish that the Linden Hotel went out of business a year ago."

Nyberg stood up and brushed down the seat of the chair. "Now I'm off for lunch," he said.

"Do that," Wallander said. "And thanks for your help."

When Nyberg had left, Wallander thought over what he had heard. Then he summoned Svedberg and Martinsson. A few minutes later they had collected a cup of coffee and were in Wallander's office.

"There must be some kind of hotel register," Wallander said. "I mean, a hotel is a business enterprise. It has an owner. It can't go out of business without it being recorded somewhere."

"What happens to old hotel ledgers?" Svedberg said. "Are they discarded? Or are they kept?"

"That's something we'll have to find out," Wallander said. "Now, right away. Most important is to get hold of the Linden Hotel's owner. If we divide the task up between us, it shouldn't take us more than an hour or so. We'll meet again when we're ready."

Wallander called Ebba and asked her to look for the name Borman in the directories for Skåne and Halland first. He had only just put down the receiver when the phone rang. It was his father.

"Don't forget you're coming to see me this evening," his father said.

"I'll be there," Wallander said, thinking that in fact he was too tired to drive out to Löderup. But he knew he could not say no, he could not change the arrangement.

"I'll be there at about 7.00," he said.

"We'll see," his father said.

"What do you mean by that?" Wallander asked, and could hear the anger in his voice.

"I just mean we'll see if that is in fact when you come," his father said.

Wallander forced himself not to start arguing.

"I'll be there," he said, and put down the phone.

His office suddenly seemed stifling. He went out into the corridor, and kept going as far as reception.

"There is nobody called Borman in the directories," Ebba said. "Do you want me to keep looking?"

"Not yet," Wallander said.

"I'd like to ask you round for dinner," Ebba said. "You must tell me how you are."

Wallander nodded, but he said nothing.

He went back to his office and opened the window. The wind was getting stronger still, and he felt very cold. He closed the window and sat at his desk. The file from Farnholm Castle was lying open, but he pushed it aside. He thought about Baiba Liepa in Riga.

Twenty minutes later he was still there, thinking, when Svedberg knocked on the door and came in.

"Now I know all there is to know about Swedish hotels," he said. "Martinsson will be here in a minute."

When Martinsson had closed the door behind him, Svedberg sat at one corner of the desk and started reading from a pad in which he had made his notes.

"The Linden Hotel was owned and run by a man called Bertil Forsdahl," he began. "I got that information from the County Offices. It was a little family hotel that was no longer viable. And Forsdahl is getting on a bit, he's 70. I've got his number here. He lives in Helsingborg."

Wallander dialled the number as Svedberg read out the digits. The telephone rang for a considerable time before it was answered. It was a woman.

"I'm trying to reach Bertil Forsdahl," Wallander said.

"He's gone out," the woman said. "He'll be back late this evening. Who shall I tell him called?"

Wallander thought for a moment before replying.

"My name's Kurt Wallander," he said. "I'm calling from the police station in Ystad. I have some questions to ask your husband about the hotel he used to run a year or so ago. No cause for concern, it's just some routine questions."

"My husband's an honest man," the woman said.

"I've no doubt about that," Wallander said. "This is just a routine inquiry. When exactly do you expect him back?"

"He's on a senior citizens' excursion to Ven," the woman said. "They're due to have dinner in Landskrona, but he's bound to be home by ten. He never goes to bed before midnight. That's a habit he got into when he ran the hotel."

"Tell him I'll get back to him," Wallander said. "And there's absolutely nothing to be worried about."

"I'm not worried," the woman said. "My husband's an honest man."

Wallander hung up. "I'll drive out and visit him tonight," Wallander said.

"Can't it wait until tomorrow?" Martinsson asked.

"I'm sure it can," Wallander said. "But I've nothing else on tonight."

An hour later they met to assess the situation. Björk had left a message to say he could not be there as he had been summoned to an urgent meeting with the District Police Chief. Höglund suddenly put in an appearance. Her husband had come home and was looking after the sick child.

Everybody agreed they should concentrate on the threatening letters. Wallander could not escape the nagging thought that there was something odd about the dead solicitors, something he ought to have cottoned on to. He remembered that Höglund had had the same feeling the previous day.

After the meeting they bumped into each other in the corridor.

"If you're going to Helsingborg tonight, I'll go with you," she said. "If I may."

"It's not necessary," he said.

"But I'd like to, even so."

He nodded. They agreed to meet at the police station at 9.00.

Wallander drove to his father's house at Löderup shortly before 7 p.m. He stopped on the way to buy some buns to eat with the coffee. When he got there his father was in his studio, painting the same old picture: an autumn landscape, with or without a grouse in the foreground.

My father's what people call a "kitsch" artist, Wallander thought. I sometimes feel like a kitschy police officer.

141

His father's wife, who used to be his home help, was visiting her parents. Wallander expected his father to be cross when he heard that his son could only stay an hour, but to his surprise, he simply nodded. They played cards for a short while and Wallander told him in detail why he returned to work. His father did not seem interested in his reasons. It was an evening when, just for once, they did not quarrel. As Wallander drove back to Ystad, he racked his brains to remember when that had last happened.

At 8.55 they were in Wallander's car, heading for the Malmö road. It was still windy, and Wallander could feel a draught from the ill-fitting rubber strip round the windscreen. He could smell the faint aroma of Höglund's discreet perfume. When they emerged on to the E65 he speeded up.

"Do you know your way around Helsingborg?" she said.

"No."

"We could call our colleagues in Helsingborg and ask."

"Best to keep them out of it for the time being," Wallander said.

"Why?"

"When police officers intrude into others' territory there are always problems," Wallander said. "No point in making things difficult for ourselves unnecessarily."

They drove on in silence. Wallander thought reluctantly about the conversation he would have to have with Björk. When they came to the road for Sturup airport, Wallander turned off. A few kilometres further on he turned off again, towards Lund.

"Tell me why you became a police officer," Wallander said.

"Not yet," she said. "Another time."

There was not much traffic. The wind seemed to be getting worse all the time. They passed the roundabout outside Staffanstorp and saw the lights from Lund. It was 9.25.

"That's odd," she said suddenly.

Wallander noticed straight away there was something different about her voice. He glanced at her face, which was lit up by the glow from the dashboard. He could see she was staring intently into the mirror on her side. He looked in his rear-view mirror. There were headlights some way behind.

"What's odd?" he asked.

"I've never experienced this before," she said.

"What?"

"Being chased," she said. "Or, at least, being followed."

Wallander could see that she was serious. He looked again at the lights in his mirror.

"How can you be so sure the car is following us?" he said.

"That's easy. It's been behind us ever since we set off."

Wallander looked at her doubtfully.

"I'm positive," she said. "That car has been following us ever since we left Ystad."

Chapter 7

Fear was like a beast of prey.

Afterwards, Wallander remembered it as being like a claw clamped round his neck – an image that seemed even to him childish and inadequate, but it was the comparison he eventually used even so. Who would he describe the fear to? His daughter Linda, and perhaps also Baiba, in one of the letters he sent regularly to Riga. But hardly to anyone else. He never discussed with Höglund what he had felt in that car; she never asked, and he was never sure whether she had noticed he was frightened. Nevertheless, he had been so terrified that he was shaking, and was convinced he would lose control of the car and plunge into the ditch at high speed, perhaps even hurtle to his death. He remembered with crystal clarity that he wished he had been alone in the car. That would have made everything much simpler for him. A large part of his fear, the weight of the giant beast, was the worry that something might happen to her, the woman in the passenger seat. Superficially, he had played the role of the experienced police officer who was unmoved by a minor matter like discovering that he was being followed from Staffanstorp to Lund, but he had been scared out of his wits until they reached the outskirts of the city. Shortly after crossing the boundary, when she had announced that the car was still following them, he had pulled in to one of the big petrol stations that had 24-hour service. They had seen the car drive past, a dark blue Mercedes, but had been unable to catch the registration number or make out how many people were inside. Wallander had stopped by one of the pumps.

"I think you're wrong," he said.

She shook her head. "The car was following us," she said. "I can't swear that it was waiting for us outside the police station, but I noticed it early on. It was there when we passed the roundabout on the E65. It was just a car then, any old car. But when we'd turned off a couple of times and it still hadn't overtaken us, it started to be something else."

Wallander got out and unscrewed the petrol cap. She stood by his side, watching him. He was thinking as hard as he could.

"Who would want to follow us?" he asked as he replaced the pipe.

She remained standing by the car while he went to pay. She couldn't possibly be right, he thought. His fear had started to wear off.

They continued through the town. The streets were deserted, and the traffic lights seemed very reluctant to change. Once they had left Lund behind them and Wallander increased speed along the motorway heading north, they started to check the traffic behind them once again. But the Mercedes had gone, and it didn't reappear. When they took the exit for Helsingborg south, Wallander slowed down. A dirty lorry overtook them, then a dark red Volvo. Wallander pulled up at the side of the road, released his safety belt and got out. He walked round to the back of the car and crouched down, as if he were inspecting one of the back wheels. He knew she would keep an eye on every car that passed. He counted four cars overtaking them, and a bus which had a fault in one of its cylinders, to judge by the sound of its engine. He got back into the car and turned to her.

"No Mercedes?"

"A white Audi," she said. "Two men in front, maybe another in the back."

"Why pick on that one?"

"They were the only ones who didn't look at us. They also picked up speed."

Wallander pointed to the car phone. "Phone Martinsson," he said. "I take it you made a note of the registration number. Not just the Audi, the others as well. Give them to him. Tell him it's urgent."

He gave her Martinsson's home number and drove on, keeping his eye open for a telephone box where he hoped he might find a phone book with a map of the area. He heard her speaking to one of Martinsson's children, probably his little daughter. After a short pause Martinsson came on the line and she gave him the registration numbers. Then she handed the phone to Wallander.

"He wants to speak to you," she said.

Wallander braked and pulled in to the side before taking the phone.

"What's going on?" Martinsson asked. "Can't these cars wait until tomorrow?"

"If Ann-Britt calls you and says it's urgent, then it's urgent," he said.

"What have they done, these cars?"

146

"It would take too long now. I'll tell you tomorrow. When you've got the information you can phone us here in the car."

He brought the call to an end, so as to give Martinsson no chance to ask any more questions. He saw that Höglund had been offended.

"Why can't he trust me? Why does he have to check with you?"

Her voice had become shrill. Wallander wondered if she could not control her disappointment, or did not want to.

"It's nothing to worry about," he said. "It takes time to get used to changes. You are the most shattering thing that's happened to the police station in Ystad for years. You're surrounded by a pack of old dogs who haven't the slightest desire to learn new tricks."

"Does that include you?"

"Of course it does," Wallander said.

Wallander failed to find a phone box before they had reached the ferry terminal. There was no sign of the white Audi. Wallander parked outside the railway station, and found a dirty map on the wall inside showing Gjutargatan on the eastern edge of the town. He memorised the route, and returned to the car.

"Who could it be that's following us?" she said as they turned left and passed the white theatre building.

"I don't know," Wallander said. "There's too much about Gustaf and Sten Torstensson that's odd. I get the feeling we're always shooting off in the wrong direction."

"I have the feeling we're standing still," she said.

"Or that we're going round in circles," Wallander said. "And we don't see that we're treading in our own footsteps."

Still no sign of the Audi. They drove into a housing estate. There was no-one about. Wallander parked at number 12, and they got out of the car. The wind threatened to blow the doors off their hinges. The house was a red-brick bungalow with garage incorporated, and a modest garden. Wallander thought he could see the outline of a boat under a tarpaulin.

The door opened before he had chance to ring the bell. An elderly, white-haired man in a tracksuit eyed them up and down with an inquisitive smile.

Wallander produced his ID.

"My name's Wallander," he said. "I'm a detective inspector, and this is Ann-Britt Höglund, a colleague. We're from the Ystad police."

The man took Wallander's ID and scrutinised it – he was obviously short-sighted. His wife appeared in the hall, and bade them welcome. Wallander had the impression he was standing on the threshold of a contented couple's home. They invited them into their living room, where coffee and cakes were prepared. Wallander was about to sit down when he noticed a picture on one of the walls. He could not believe his eyes at first – it was one of his father's paintings, one without a grouse. He saw that Höglund had noticed what he was looking at, and she gave him a questioning look. He shook his head, and sat down. This was the second time in his life he had gone into a strange house and discovered one of his father's paintings. Four years ago he had found one in a flat in Kristianstad, but there had been a grouse in the foreground of that one.

"I apologise for calling on you so late," Wallander said, "but I'm afraid we have some questions that simply can't wait."

"I hope you've time for a cup of coffee," said the lady of the house.

They said that of course they had. It occurred to Wallander that Höglund had been keen to accompany him so that she could find out how he conducted an interview of this nature, and he felt insecure. There's been a lot of water under this bridge, he thought. It's not a case of me teaching her, but of me relearning how to do it, trying to remember all that I had written off as the end of an era in my life, until a couple of days ago.

His mind went back to those limitless beaches at Skagen. His private territory. Just for a moment, he wished he were back there. But that was history. More water under the bridge.

"Until a year ago you ran a hotel, the Linden Hotel," he began.

"For 40 years," Bertil Forsdahl said, and Wallander could hear he was proud of what he had achieved.

"That's a long time," he said.

"I bought it in 1952," Forsdahl said. "It was called the Pelican Hotel in those days, a bit on the scruffy side and with not a good reputation. I bought it off a man called Markusson. He was an alcoholic, and just wasn't bothered. The last year of his tenancy the rooms were used mainly by his drunken cronies. I have to admit I got the hotel cheaply. Markusson died the following year. His wake was a drunken orgy in Elsinore. We renamed the hotel. In those days there was a linden tree outside. It was next to the old theatre – that's been demolished now, of course, like everything else. The actors used to stay with us sometimes. Inga Tidblad was our overnight guest on one occasion. She wanted an early-morning cup of tea."

"I expect you've kept the ledger with her name in it," Wallander said.

"I've kept all of them," Forsdahl said. "I've got 40 years of history tucked away downstairs."

"We sometimes sit down after dinner," Forsdahl's wife said, "and we leaf through them all, remembering the good old days. You see the names and you remember the people."

Wallander exchanged glances with Höglund. They already had the answer to one of their key questions.

A dog started barking in the street outside.

"Next door's guard dog," Forsdahl explained apologetically. "He keeps an eye on the whole street."

Wallander took a sip of the coffee, and noticed that it said Linden Hotel on the cup.

"I'll explain why we're here," he said. "You have the name of your hotel on the coffee cups, and you had printed letterheads and envelopes. In July and August last year, two letters were posted from here in Helsingborg. One was in one of your printed envelopes. That must have been during the last few weeks you were open."

"We closed on September 15," Forsdahl said. "We made no charge for the final night."

"Might I ask why you closed down?" Höglund said.

Wallander was irritated by her intervention, but he hoped she would not notice his reaction. As if it were natural for a woman to be answered by another woman, it was Forsdahl's wife who responded.

"What else could we do?" she said. "The building was condemned, and the hotel wasn't making any money. No doubt we could have kept going for another year or two if we'd wanted, and if we'd been allowed. But that wasn't how it turned out."

"We tried to maintain the highest standards for as long as we could," Forsdahl said. "But in the end it was just too expensive for us. Colour TV in every room and such like. It was just too much outlay."

"It was a very sad day, September 15," his wife said. "We still have all the room keys. We had number 17. The site's a car park now. And they've cut the linden tree down. They said it was rotten. I wonder if a tree can die of a broken heart."

The dog was still barking. Wallander thought about the tree that no longer existed.

"Lars Borman," he said eventually. "Does that name mean anything to you?"

The response was a complete surprise. "Poor man," Forsdahl said.

"A very sad story," his wife said. "Why are the police interested in him now?"

"So you know who he is?" Wallander said. He saw that Höglund had produced a notebook from her handbag.

"Such a nice man," Forsdahl said. "Calm, quiet. Always friendly, always polite. They don't make them like him any more."

"We'd very much like to get in touch with him," Wallander said.

Forsdahl exchanged looks with his wife. Wallander had the impression they were ill at ease.

"Lars Borman's dead," Forsdahl said. "I thought the police knew that."

Wallander thought for a while before answering. "We know next to nothing about Borman," he said. "All we do know is that last year he wrote two letters, and one of them was in one of your hotel's envelopes. We wanted to get in touch with him. Obviously that isn't possible now. But we'd like to know what happened. And who he was."

"A regular customer," Forsdahl said. "He stayed with us about every four months for many years. Usually two or three nights."

"What was his line of work? Where was he from?"

"He worked at the County Offices," Mrs Forsdahl said. "Something to do with finance."

"An accountant," Forsdahl said. "A very conscientious and honest civil servant at the Malmöhus County Offices."

"He lived in Klagshamn," his wife added. "He had a wife and children. It was a terrible tragedy."

"What happened?" Wallander said.

"He committed suicide," Forsdahl said. Wallander could see it pained him to revive the memory. "If there was one person we'd never have expected to take his own life it was Lars Borman. Evidently he had some kind of secret we never imagined."

"What happened?" Wallander asked again.

"He'd been in Helsingborg," Forsdahl said. "It was a few days before we closed down. He did whatever he had to do during the day and spent the evenings in his room. He would read a lot. That last morning he paid his bill and checked out. He promised to keep in touch even though the hotel was closing. Then he drove away. A few weeks later we heard that he'd hanged himself in a clearing outside Klagshamn, a few kilometres from his house. There was no explanation, no letter to his wife and children. It came as a shock to us all."

Wallander nodded slowly. He had grown up in Klagshamn, and wondered which clearing it was

Borman had hanged himself in. Perhaps it was somewhere he had played as a child?

"How old was he?"

"He'd passed 50, but he can't have been much more," Mrs Forsdahl said.

"So he lived in Klagshamn," Wallander said, "and worked as an accountant at the County Offices. It strikes me as being a bit odd, staying in a hotel. It's not that far between Malmö and Helsingborg."

"He didn't like driving," Forsdahl said. "Besides, I think he enjoyed it here. He could shut himself away in his room in the evening and read his books. We used to leave him in peace, and he appreciated that."

"You have his address in your ledgers, of course," Wallander said.

"We heard his wife had sold the house and moved," Mrs Forsdahl said. "She couldn't cope with staying there after what had happened. And his children are grown up."

"Do you know where she moved to?"

"To Spain. Marbella, I think it's called."

Wallander looked at Höglund, who was making copious notes.

"Do you mind if I ask *you* a question now?" Forsdahl said. "Why are the police interested in Borman so long after his death?"

"It's pure routine," Wallander said. "I'm afraid I can't tell you more than that. Except that there's no question of his being suspected of any crime."

"He was an honest man," Forsdahl insisted. "He thought people ought to lead a simple life and always do the right thing. We talked quite a lot over the years. He would always get angry when we touched on the

153

dishonesty that seems to be common nowadays in society."

"Was there really no explanation as to why he had committed suicide?" Wallander asked.

Both Forsdahl and his wife shook their heads.

"OK," Wallander said. "Just one more thing. We'd like to take a look at the record books for the final year, if you don't mind."

"They're in the basement," Forsdahl said, getting to his feet.

"Martinsson might ring," Höglund said. "I'd better fetch the car phone."

Wallander gave her the keys and Mrs Forsdahl went with her. He heard her slamming the car door without the neighbour's dog starting to bark. When she returned they all went down into the basement. In a room that was surprisingly big for a basement was a long row of ledgers on a shelf running the whole length of one wall. There was also the old hotel sign, and a board with 17 room keys hanging on it. A museum, Wallander thought, how touching. This is where they hide their memories of a long working life. Memories of a little hotel that got to the point where it was viable no more.

Forsdahl took down the last of their ledgers and put it on a table. He looked up August, then the 26th, and pointed to one of the columns. Wallander and Höglund leaned forward to examine it. Wallander recognised the handwriting. He also thought the letter had been written by the same pen as Borman used when he signed the register. He was born on October 12, 1939, and described himself as a County Offices accountant. Höglund noted his address in Klagshamn: Mejramsvägen 23. Wallander

154

did not recognise the street name. It was probably one of the housing estates that had sprung up after he had left. He turned back to the records for June, and found Borman's name there again, on the day that the first of the letters had been posted.

"Do you understand any of this?" Höglund said, quietly.

"Not a lot," Wallander said.

The mobile phone rang, and Wallander nodded to indicate she should answer it. She sat down on a stool and started writing down what Martinsson had to say. Wallander closed the ledger and watched Forsdahl return it to its place. When the call was finished they went back upstairs, and on the way Wallander asked what Martinsson had said.

"It was the Audi," she said. "We can talk about it later."

Wallander and Höglund prepared to leave.

"I am sorry for it being so late," Wallander said. "Sometimes the police can't wait."

"I hope we've been of some help," Forsdahl said. "Even though it's painful to be reminded of poor old Lars Borman."

"I understand how you feel," Wallander said. "If you should remember anything else, please phone the Ystad police."

"What else is there to remember?" asked Forsdahl, in surprise.

"I don't know what it might be," Wallander said, shaking hands.

They left the house and got into the car. Wallander switched on the inside light. Höglund had taken out her notebook.

"I was right," she said, looking at Wallander. "It was the white Audi. The number didn't fit the car. The registration plate had been stolen. It should have been on a Nissan that hasn't even been sold yet. It's registered with a showroom in Malmö."

"And the other cars?"

"All in order."

Wallander started the engine. It was 11.30, and there was no sign of the wind dropping. They drove out of town. There was not much traffic on the motorway. And there were no cars behind them.

"Are you tired?" Wallander said.

"No," she replied.

"In that case let's stop for a while," he said. He drove into a 24-hour petrol station with a café attached just south of Helsingborg. "We can have a little late-night conference, just you and me, and see if we can work out how far we got this evening. We can also see what other cars stop. The only one we don't need to bother about is a white Audi."

"Why so?"

"If they do come back they'll be using a different car," Wallander said. "Whoever they are, they know what they're doing. They won't appear twice in the same car."

They went into the café. Wallander ordered a hamburger, but Höglund didn't want anything. They found a seat with a view of the parking area. A couple of Danish lorry drivers were drinking coffee, but the other tables were empty.

"So, what do you think?" Wallander said. "About an accountant with the County Offices writing threatening letters to a couple of lawyers, then going out to the forest to hang himself."

"It's hard to know what to say," she said.

"Try," Wallander said.

They sat in silence, lost in thought. A lorry from a rental firm pulled up outside. Wallander's burger was called; he fetched it and returned to the table.

"The accusation in Borman's letter is injustice," she said. "But it doesn't say what the injustice was. Borman wasn't a client. We don't know what their relationship was. In fact, we don't know anything at all."

Wallander put down his fork and wiped his mouth with a paper napkin. "I'm sure you've heard about Rydberg," he said. "An old detective inspector who died a couple of years ago. He was a wise bird. He once said that police officers always tend to say they know nothing, whereas in fact we always know a lot more than we think."

"That sounds like one of those pearls of wisdom they were forever feeding us at college," she said. "The kind we used to write down and then forget as quickly as possible."

Wallander was annoyed. He did not like anybody questioning Rydberg's competence. "I couldn't care less what you wrote down or didn't write down at Police Training College," he said. "But at least take notice of what I say. Or what Rydberg said."

"Have I made you angry?" she said, surprised.

"I never get angry," Wallander said, "but I think your summary of what we know about Lars Borman was poor."

"Can you do any better, then?" she said, her voice shrill again.

She's thin-skinned, he thought. No doubt it's a lot harder than I think to be a lone woman among the Ystad detectives.

"I don't really mean your summary was poor," he said. "But I do think you're overlooking a few things."

"I'm listening," she said. "I know I'm good at that."

Wallander slid his plate to one side and went to fetch a cup of coffee. The Danish lorry drivers had left, leaving the two police officers as the only customers. A radio could be heard faintly from the kitchen.

"It's obviously impossible to draw any reliable conclusions," Wallander said, "but we can make a few assumptions. We can try fitting a few pieces of the puzzle together and see what they look like, see if we can work out a motive perhaps."

"I'm with you so far," she said.

"Borman was an accountant," Wallander said. "We also know that he seemed to be an honest, upright man. That was the most characteristic thing about him, according to the Forsdahls. Apart from the fact that he was quiet and liked reading. In my experience it's quite rare for anybody to start by categorising a man like that. Which suggests he really was a passionately honest man."

"An honest accountant," she said.

"This honest man suddenly writes two threatening letters to the Torstenssons' firm of solicitors in Ystad. He signs them with his own name, but he crosses out the name of the hotel on one of the envelopes. This provides us with several assumptions we can deduce."

"He didn't want to be anonymous," Höglund said. "But he didn't want to involve the hotel in the business. An honest man upset about injustice. The question is, what injustice?"

"Here we can make my last assumption but one," Wallander said. "There's a missing link. Borman wasn't a client of the Torstenssons', but there might have been somebody else, somebody who was in contact both with Borman and with the firm of solicitors."

"What does an accountant actually do?" Höglund said. "He checks that money is being used properly. He goes through receipts, he certifies that the proper practices have been adhered to. Is that what you mean?"

"Gustaf Torstensson gave financial advice," Wallander said. "An accountant makes sure the rules and regulations are obeyed. The emphasis is a bit different, but an accountant and a solicitor in fact do very similar things. Or should do."

"And your last assumption?" she said.

"Borman writes two threatening letters. He may have written more, but we don't know that. What we do know is that the letters were simply put away in an envelope."

"But now both the solicitors are dead," Höglund said, "and someone tried to kill Mrs Dunér."

"And Borman committed suicide," Wallander said. "I think that's where we should begin. With his suicide. We have to get in touch with our colleagues in Malmö. There must be a document somewhere that rules out the possibility that the death was murder. There has to have been a doctor's certificate."

"There's a widow living in Spain," she said.

"The children are presumably still in Sweden. We must talk to them as well."

They stood up and left the café.

"We should do this more often," Wallander said. "It's fun talking to you."

"Even though I don't understand anything," she said, "and make poor summaries?"

Wallander shrugged. "I talk too much," he said.

They got back into the car. It was almost 1.00. Wallander shuddered at the thought of the empty flat that awaited him in Ystad. It felt as if something in his life had come to an end a long time ago, long before he knelt in the fog in the military training ground near Ystad. But he hadn't worked out what it was. He thought about his father's painting that he had seen in the house in Gjutargatan. In the old days, his father's paintings had always seemed to him something to be ashamed of, to be taking advantage of people's bad taste. It now seemed to him there might be another way of looking at it. Perhaps his father painted pictures that gave people a feeling of balance and normality they were looking everywhere for, but only found in those unchanging landscapes.

"A penny for your thoughts," she said.

"Not sure," he said vaguely. "I think I'm just tired."

Wallander drove on towards Malmö. Even though it was a longer way round, he wanted to stick to the main roads back to Ystad. There was not much traffic, and there was no sign of anybody following them. The gusting wind was buffeting the car.

"I didn't think that kind of thing happened around here," she said suddenly. "Being followed by some stranger in a car, I mean."

"I didn't think so either until a few years ago," Wallander said. "Then things changed. They say Sweden changed slowly and imperceptibly, but I think it was rather open and obvious. If you only knew where to look."

"Tell me," she said, "what it used to be like. And what happened."

"I don't know if I can," he said. "I just see things from the point of view of the man in the street. But in our everyday work, even in an insignificant little town like Ystad, we could see a change. Crime became more frequent and more serious: different, nastier, more complicated. And we started finding criminals among people who'd previously been irreproachable citizens. But what set it all off I have no idea."

"That doesn't explain why we have a record for solving crimes worse than practically everywhere else in the world, either," she said.

"Speak to Björk about that," Wallander said. "It keeps him awake at night. I sometimes think that his ambition is for the Ystad force to make up for the rest of the country put together."

"But there must be an explanation," she insisted. "It can't just be that the Swedish force is undermanned, and that we don't have the resources which everybody talks about without anybody being able to say what they actually should be."

"It's like two different worlds meeting head on," Wallander said. "Many police officers think as I do, that we got our training and experience at a time when everything was different, when crime was more transparent, morals were clearer and the authority of the police unchallenged. Nowadays, we need a different kind of training and different experiences in order to be as efficient. But we don't have that. And the ones who come after us, such as you, don't as yet have much chance to influence what we do, to decide where our priorities should lie. It often feels as if there's nothing to stop criminals getting even further ahead of us than they are already. And all society does in response is to manipulate the statistics. Instead of giving the police rein to solve every crime committed, a lot of them are just written off. What used to be considered a crime ten years ago is now judged a non-crime. Things change by the day. What people were punished for yesterday can be something nobody thinks twice about today. At best it might spark off a report that then disappears in some invisible shredder. All that's left is something that never happened."

"That can't be good," she said hesitantly.

Wallander glanced at her. "Who said that it was?"

They had passed Landskrona and were approaching Malmö. An ambulance overtook them at high speed, blue light flashing. Wallander was tired. Without really knowing why, just for a moment he felt sorry for the woman sitting beside him. Over the coming years she would constantly have to reassess her work as a police officer. Unless she was an exceptional person, she would experience an unbroken sequence of disappointments, and very little joy.

He had no doubt about that. But he also thought that the reputation that had preceded her seemed to be true. He could remember Martinsson's first year when he'd just left Police Training College to join the Ystad force. He had not been a lot of use then, but now he was one of their best detectives.

"Tomorrow we'll make a thorough assessment of all the material we have," he said in an attempt to cheer her up. "There must be a chance of breaking through somewhere along the line."

"I hope you're right," she said. "But one of these days things could get so bad here that we start to regard certain types of *murder* as incidents that are best left alone."

"If that happens, the police force will have to mutiny," Wallander said.

"The Police Commissioner would never go along with that."

"We'll rise up when he's out of the country eating posh dinners in the name of PR," Wallander said.

"We'll have plenty of opportunities, then," she said.

The conversation died out. Wallander stayed on the motorway to the east of Malmö, concentrating on the road with only the occasional vague thought about what had happened during the day.

It was when they had left Malmö behind and were heading for Ystad on the E65 that Wallander suddenly had the feeling that something was wrong. Höglund had closed her eyes and her head had sunk down on one shoulder. There was no sign of headlights in the rear-view mirror.

He was suddenly wide awake. I've been on the wrong track, he thought. Instead of establishing that we weren't being followed, I ought to have been wondering why. If Ann-Britt Höglund was right, and I've no reason to doubt that somebody has been following us from the moment we left the police station, then the absence of a car behind us could indicate that they no longer considered it necessary.

He thought about the mine in Mrs Dunér's garden.

Without a second thought he braked and pulled up on the hard shoulder with his warning lights blinking. Höglund woke up. She stared at him drowsily.

"Get out of the car," Wallander said.

"Why?"

"Do as I say," he shouted.

She flung aside her safety belt and was out of the car before he was.

"Take cover," he said.

"What's wrong?" she said, as they stood staring at the warning lights. It was cold, and the wind was gusty.

"I don't know," Wallander said. "Maybe nothing. I got worried because nobody was following us."

He did not need to explain further. She understood right away. That convinced Wallander on the spot that she was already a good police officer. She was intelligent, she knew how to react to the unexpected. But he also felt for the first time in ages that he now had somebody with whom he could share his fear. On that stretch of hard shoulder, just before the Svedala exit, he had the feeling that all that endless walking up and down the beach at Skagen had come to an end.

Wallander had been sufficiently alert to take the car phone with him. He started to dial Martinsson's number. "He'll think I've gone out of my mind," he said as he waited for a reply.

"What do you think's going to happen?"

"I don't know. But people who can bury a mine in a garden in Sweden would have no problem doing something to a car."

"If it's the same people," she said.

"Yes," Wallander said. "If it's the same people."

Martinsson answered. Wallander could tell that he was half asleep.

"It's Kurt," he said. "I'm on the E65 just outside Svedala. Ann-Britt's here with me. I'd like you to phone Nyberg and ask him to come out here."

"What's happened?"

"I want him to have a look at my car."

"If your engine's packed up you could phone a breakdown firm," Martinsson said, puzzled.

164

"I haven't got time to explain," Wallander said, and could feel his irritation coming on. "Do as I say. Tell Nyberg he should bring with him equipment to test whether I've been driving round with a bomb under my feet."

"A car bomb?"

"You heard."

Wallander switched off and shook his head. "He's right, of course," he said. "It sounds ridiculous – we're on the E65 in the middle of the night and think there might be a bomb in the car."

"Is there?"

"I don't know," Wallander said. "I'm not sure."

It took Nyberg an hour to reach them. By then Wallander and Höglund were frozen to the bone. Wallander expected Nyberg to be annoyed, being woken up by Martinsson for reasons that must have seemed dodgy, to say the least, but to his surprise Nyberg was friendly and prepared to believe that something serious had happened. Despite her protests, Wallander insisted that Höglund should get into Nyberg's car and warm up.

"There's a thermos in the passenger seat," Nyberg said. "I think the coffee's still hot."

Then he turned to Wallander, who could see that he was still in his pyjamas under his overcoat. "What's wrong with the car?" he asked.

"I was hoping you could tell me that," Wallander said. "There's a real possibility that there's nothing wrong at all."

"What am I supposed to be looking for?"

"I don't know. All I can tell you is an assumption. The car was left unwatched for about half an hour. It was locked."

"Do you have an alarm?" Nyberg said.

"I've got nothing," Wallander said. "It's an old car. Rubbish. I've always assumed nobody would want to steal it."

"Go on," Nyberg said.

"Half an hour," Wallander repeated. "When I started the engine, nothing happened. Everything was normal. From Helsingborg to here is about 100 kilometres. We stopped on the way and had a cup of coffee. I'd filled the tank in Helsingborg. It must be about three hours since the car was left unattended."

"I shouldn't touch it," Nyberg said. "Not if you suspect it might blow up."

"I thought that happened when you started the engine," Wallander said.

"Nowadays you can set explosions to go off whenever you like," Nyberg said. "They could be anything from inbuilt, self-triggering delay mechanisms to radio-controlled ignition devices that can be set off from miles away."

"Maybe it's best just to leave it," Wallander said.

"Could be," Nyberg said. "But I'd like to take a look at it even so. Let's say I'm doing it of my own free will. You're not ordering me to do it."

Nyberg went back to his car and came back with a powerful torch. Wallander accepted a mug of coffee from Höglund, who had now got out of the car again. They watched Nyberg as he lay down beside the car and shone his torch underneath. Then he started to walk round it, slowly.

"I think I'm dreaming," Höglund murmured.

Nyberg had stopped by the open door on the driver's side. He peered inside and shone his torch in. An overloaded Volkswagen van with Polish number plates drove past on its way to the ferry in Ystad. Nyberg switched off his torch and came back towards them.

"Did I hear wrongly?" he asked. "Didn't you say you'd filled up with petrol on the way to Helsingborg?"

"I filled up in Lund," Wallander said. "Right to the top."

"Then you drove to Helsingborg? And to here?"

Wallander thought a moment. "It can't have been more than about 150 kilometres," he said.

Nyberg frowned.

"What's the matter?" Wallander asked.

"Have you ever had reason to think there was something wrong with your petrol gauge?"

"Never. It's always been spot on."

"How many litres does the tank hold?"

"Sixty."

"Then explain to me why the indicator suggests you've only got a quarter of a tank left," he said.

It didn't sink in at first. Then Wallander realised the significance of what Nyberg had said. "Somebody must have drained the tank," he said. "The car uses less than one litre per ten kilometres."

"Let's move further back," Nyberg said. "I'm going to move my own car further back as well."

They watched him drive further away. The warning lights were still flashing on Wallander's car. The wind was still gusty. Another overfull car with Polish number plates passed them going east. Nyberg came to join them. They all looked at Wallander's car.

167

"If somebody drains petrol from a tank, they do it to make room for something else," Nyberg said. "Somebody might have planted explosives with some kind of delayed ignition that is gradually eaten away by the petrol. Eventually it blows up. Does your petrol indicator usually go down when the engine's ticking over?"

"No."

"Then I reckon we should leave the car here till tomorrow," Nyberg said. "In fact, we ought to close off the E65 altogether."

"Björk would never agree to that," Wallander said. "Besides, we don't know for sure that anybody's put anything in the petrol tank."

"I think we should call people out to cordon the area off, no matter what," Nyberg said. "This is the Malmö police district, isn't it?"

"I'm afraid it is," Wallander said. "But I'll phone them even so."

"My handbag's still in the car," Höglund said. "Can I fetch it?"

"No," Nyberg said. "It'll have to stay there. And the engine can keep running."

Höglund got back into Nyberg's car. Wallander called the police in Malmö. Nyberg had wandered off to the side of the road for a pee. Wallander looked up and contemplated the stars while he waited to be connected.

It was 3.04 in the morning.

Malmö answered. Wallander saw Nyberg zipping up his flies.

Then the night exploded in a flash of white. The telephone was ripped from Wallander's hand.

Chapter 8

The painful silence.

Afterwards, Wallander recalled the explosion as a large space with all the oxygen squeezed out, the sudden arrival of a strange vacuum on the E65 in the middle of a November night, a black hole in which even the blustery wind had been silenced. It happened very quickly, but memory has the ability to stretch things out and in the end he remembered the explosion as a series of events, each one rapidly replacing the other but nevertheless distinct.

What surprised him most was that his telephone was lying on the wet asphalt just a few metres away. That was the most incomprehensible bit, not the fact that his car was enveloped by intense flames and seemed to be melting away.

Nyberg had reacted quickest. He grabbed hold of Wallander and dragged him away, possibly afraid there would be another explosion from the blazing car. Höglund had flung herself out of Nyberg's car and sprinted to the other side of the road. Perhaps she had screamed, but it seemed to Wallander he might have been the one to scream, or Nyberg, or none of them; perhaps he had imagined it.

169

On the other hand, he thought he ought to have screamed. He ought to have screamed and yelled and cursed the fact that he had gone back to duty, that Sten Torstensson had been to see him in Skagen and dragged him into a murder investigation he should never have been involved in. He should never have gone back, he should have signed the documents Björk had prepared for him, attended the press conference and allowed himself to be interviewed for a feature in *Swedish Police* magazine, on the back page no doubt, and been out of it all.

In the confusion following the explosion there had been a moment of painful silence when Wallander had been able to think perfectly clearly as he looked at the telephone lying in the road and his old Peugeot going up in flames on the hard shoulder. His thoughts had been lucid and he had been able to reach a conclusion: the first indication that the double murder of the solicitors, the mine in Mrs Dunér's garden and now the attempted murder of himself had a pattern, not itself clear as yet and with many locked doors still to open.

But a conclusion had been possible and unavoidable, amid the chaos, and it had been a terrifying one: somebody thought Wallander knew something they did not want him to know. He was convinced that whoever had put the explosives in the petrol tank had not planned to kill Ann-Britt Höglund. That merely revealed another aspect of the people who lurked in the shadows: they didn't care about human life.

Wallander recognised, with a mixture of fear and despair, that these people who hid in cars with stolen number plates were wrong. He could have made an honest public statement that it was all based on a mistake and that he knew nothing of what lay behind the murders, or the mine, or even the suicide of the accountant Lars Borman, if indeed it was suicide.

The truth was that he knew nothing. But while his car was still ablaze and Nyberg and Höglund were directing inquisitive late-night drivers away from the scene and calling the police and fire brigade, he had gone on standing in the middle of the road, thinking things through to their conclusion. There was only one starting point for the awful mistake of thinking he knew something, and that was Sten's visit to Skagen. The postcard from Finland had not been sufficient. They had followed Sten to Jutland, they had been there among the dunes, hidden in the fog. They had been watching the Art Museum where Wallander had drunk coffee with Sten, but they had not been close enough to hear what was said, for if they had been, they would have known that Wallander knew nothing, since Sten knew nothing either; the whole business was no more than suspicions. But they had not been able to take the risk. That's why his old Peugeot was burning away by the side of the road; and that's why the neighbour's dog had been barking while they had been talking to the Forsdahls.

The painful silence, he thought. That's what's enveloping me, and there is one more conclusion to draw, perhaps the most vital one of all. For it means we have made a breakthrough in this awful case, we have found a point around which we can all gather and say: this is our starting point. It might not take us to the Holy Grail, but it might lead to something else that we need to find.

The chronology was right, he thought. It started with that muddy field where Gustaf Torstensson met his end

171

almost a month ago. Everything else, including the execution of his son, must derive from what happened that night, when he was on his way home from Farnholm Castle. We know that now, which means we now know what we should be doing.

He bent to retrieve his telephone. The emergency number for the Malmö police was staring him in the face. He switched the phone off and established that it had not been damaged by the blast or by being dropped on the road.

The fire engine had arrived. He watched as they put out the flames, covering the car with white foam. Nyberg appeared at his side. Wallander could see that he was sweating and afraid.

"That was a close call," he said.

"Yes," Wallander said. "But not close enough."

Nyberg looked at him in surprise.

At that moment a senior officer from the Malmö police came up to Wallander. They had met before but Wallander could not remember the man's name.

"I gather it was your car that got torched," he said. "Rumour had it you'd left the force. But you come back, and your car gets burned out."

Wallander was not sure if the man was being ironic, but he decided he wasn't, that it was a natural reaction. At the same time he wanted to ensure that there were no misunderstandings.

"I was on my way home with a colleague," he said.

"Ann-Britt Höglund," said the man from Malmö. "I've just spoken to her. She passed me on to you."

Well done, Wallander thought. The fewer people who comment, the easier it is to keep the thing under control. She's learning fast.

"I had the feeling something wasn't as it should be," Wallander said. "We stopped and got out. I phoned my colleague Nyberg here. The car blew up almost as soon as he got here."

The high-up from Malmö eyed him sceptically. "This is the official version, I assume," he said.

"Well, the car will have to be examined," Wallander said. "But nobody's been hurt. For the moment you can report just what I said. I'll ask Björk to get in touch with you – he's the Chief of Police in Ystad. Forgive me, but I'm afraid I can't remember your name."

"Roslund."

Wallander remembered.

"We'll cordon the scene off," Roslund said. "I'll leave a car here."

Wallander checked his watch. It was 4.15.

"I think it's time for us to go home to bed."

They all got into Nyberg's car. Nobody had anything to say. They dropped Höglund outside her house, then Nyberg drove Wallander home to Mariagatan.

"We'll have to get to grips with this a few hours from now," Wallander said before getting out. "We can't put it off."

"I'll be at the station by 7.00," Nyberg said.

"Eight will be soon enough. Thanks for your help."

Wallander had a quick shower then stretched himself out between the sheets. He was still awake at 6.00. He got up again shortly before 7.00. He knew it was going to be a long day. He wondered how he would cope.

Thursday, November 4, began with a sensation.

Björk came to work unshaven. This had never happened before. But when the door of the conference

173

room was closed at 8.05, everybody could see that Björk had more bristle than anybody could have imagined. Wallander knew that he was still not going to have the opportunity to talk to Björk about what had happened before his visit to Farnholm Castle. But it could wait: they had more important things to sort out first.

Björk slapped his hands down on the table and looked round the room.

"What's going on?" he demanded to know. "I get a phone call at 5.30 in the morning from a senior officer in Malmö who wants to know if they should send their own forensic people to examine Inspector Wallander's burned-out car that's standing near Svedala on the E65, or were we going to send Nyberg and his team? There I am in my kitchen, it's 5.30 in the morning, wondering what on earth I should say because I haven't the slightest idea what's going on. What's happened? Has Kurt been injured or even killed in a crash that ended with his car going up in flames? I know nothing at all. But Roslund from Malmö is a sensible man who is able to fill me in. I am grateful to be told roughly what's being going on. But the fact is that I'm a good deal in the dark."

"We have a double murder to solve," Wallander said. "We have an attempted murder on Mrs Dunér to keep us occupied. Until yesterday we had next to nothing to go on. The investigation was up against a brick wall, we all agree on that, I think. Then we hear about these threatening letters. We discover a name and a link with a hotel in Helsingborg. Ann-Britt and I go there to investigate. That could have waited until today, I admit. We pay a visit to some people who knew Borman. They are able to supply us with useful information. On the way to Helsingborg, Ann-Britt notices that we're being followed. When we get to Helsingborg we stop, and manage to get one or two relevant registration numbers. Martinsson gets on the trail of those numbers. While Ann-Britt and I are talking to Mr and Mrs Forsdahl, who used to run the Linden Hotel that's closed down now, somebody plants explosives in our petrol tank. Purely by chance, on the way home I get suspicious. I get Martinsson to phone Nyberg. Shortly after he gets there the car blows up. Nobody is hurt. This happens outside Svedala, in the Malmö police district. That's what happened."

Nobody spoke when Wallander finished. It seemed to him he might just as well continue. He could give them the whole picture, everything he had thought about as he stood there in the road while his car was burning before his very eyes.

The moment of painful silence.

Also the moment of clarity.

He reported scrupulously on his thoughts, and noticed straight away that his deductions won the meeting's approval. His colleagues were experienced police officers. They could distinguish between sensible theories, and a fantastic but nevertheless plausible series of events.

"I can see three lines of attack," Wallander said in conclusion. "We can concentrate on Gustaf Torstensson and his clients. We must delve deeply but rapidly into just what he was up to those last five years while he devoted himself more or less exclusively to financial advice and similar matters. But to save time we should start off with the last three years during which time, according to Mrs Dunér, he started to change. I would also like somebody to have a word with the Asian woman who cleans the offices. Mrs Dunér has her address. She might have seen or heard something."

"Does she speak Swedish?" Svedberg said.

"If not we'll have to arrange for an interpreter," Wallander said.

"I'll talk to her," Höglund said.

Wallander took a sip of his cold coffee before going on. "The second line of attack is Lars Borman. I have a suspicion that he can still be of help to us, even though he's dead."

"We'll need the support of our colleagues in Malmö," Björk said. "Klagshamn is in their territory."

"I would rather not," Wallander said. "It would be quicker to deal with it ourselves. As you keep pointing out, there are all kinds of administrative problems when police officers from different districts try to help each other."

While Björk pondered his response, Wallander took the opportunity to finish what he had to say. "The third line is to find out who's following us. Perhaps I should ask whether anybody else has had a car trailing them?"

Martinsson and Svedberg shook their heads.

"There's every reason for you to keep your eyes peeled," Wallander said. "I could be wrong, it might not just be me they're after."

"Mrs Dunér is being guarded," Martinsson said. "And in my view you ought to be as well."

"No," Wallander said. "That's not necessary."

"I can't go along with that," Björk said firmly. "In the first place you must never go out on duty alone. And furthermore you must be armed."

"Never," Wallander said.

"You'll do as I say," Björk said.

Wallander didn't bother to argue. He knew what he was going to do anyway.

They divided the work between them. Martinsson and Höglund would go to the solicitors' offices and begin sifting through the Gustaf Torstensson files. Svedberg would do a thorough search into the cars that had been following them to Helsingborg. Wallander would concentrate on Borman.

"For some days now I have had the feeling that it's all very urgent," he said. "I don't know why. But let's get a move on."

The meeting broke up and they went their different ways. Wallander could sense the resolve in everybody's attitude, and he noted that Höglund was coping well with her exhaustion.

He fetched another cup of coffee and went back to his office to work out what to do next. Nyberg stuck his head round the door and announced that he was about to set off for the burned-out car at Svedala.

"I take it you want me to see if there's any similarity to the explosion in Mrs Dunér's garden," he said.

"Yes," Wallander said.

"I don't expect to be able to establish that," Nyberg said, "but I'll have a go."

Nyberg went on his way and Wallander called reception.

"It's awful, these terrible things happening," Ebba said.

"Nobody was hurt," Wallander said. "That's the main thing." He came straight to the point.

"Can you get hold of a car for me, please? I have to go to Malmö in a few minutes. Then I'd like you to phone Farnholm Castle and get them to send me a copy

177

of their overview of Alfred Harderberg's business empire. I did have a file but it got burned up in the car."

"I'd better not tell them that," Ebba said.

"Maybe not. But I need that file as quickly as they can manage it."

He hung up. Then a thought struck him. He went down the corridor to Svedberg's office, and found him just starting to go through Martinsson's notes about the cars from the previous night.

"Kurt Ström," he said. "Does that name mean anything to you?"

Svedberg thought for a moment. "A police officer in Malmö? Or am I wrong?"

"That's right," Wallander said. "I'd like you to do something for me when you've finished with the cars. Ström left the force many years ago. There was a rumour that he resigned before he was sacked. Try and find out what happened. Be discreet."

Svedberg made a note of the name. "Might I ask why? Has it anything to do with the solicitors? The car that got blown up? The mine in the garden?"

"Everything has to do with that," Wallander said. "Ström is working now as top security guard at Farnholm Castle. Gustaf Torstensson had been there the night he died."

"I'll look into it," Svedberg said.

Wallander went back to his office and sat down at his desk. He was very tired. He didn't even have the strength to think about how close he and Höglund had been to getting killed. Later, he thought. Not now. Borman dead is more important just now than Wallander alive.

He looked up the Malmöhus County Offices in the phone book. He knew from past experience that it was located in Lund. He dialled the number and got a reply immediately. He asked the operator to put him through to one of the bosses in the finance department.

"They're not available today," the operator said.

"There must be somebody available, surely?"

"They're in a budget meeting all day," the girl explained patiently.

"Where?"

"At the conference centre in Höör," the girl said. "But there's no point in phoning there."

"What's the name of the man in charge of auditing? Is he there as well?"

"His name's Thomas Rundstedt," the girl said. "Yes, he's in Höör too. Perhaps you could try again tomorrow?"

"Many thanks for your help," Wallander said, and hung up.

He had no intention of waiting until the next day. He fetched yet another cup of coffee and thought through all he knew about Lars Borman. He was interrupted by Ebba who called to say there was a car waiting for him outside the police station.

It was 9.15. A clear autumn day, blue skies, and Wallander noted that the wind had died down. He found himself looking forward to his drive.

It was just turning 10.00 when he drove up to the conference centre near Höör. He parked the car and went to reception. A notice on a blackboard and easel informed him that the big conference hall was occupied by the County Offices Budget Conference. A red-haired man behind the desk gave Wallander a friendly smile.

"I'm trying to get hold of some people taking part in the budget conference," he said.

"They've just had their coffee break," the receptionist replied. "They'll be in session now right through until lunch at 12.30. I'm afraid it's not possible to disturb them before then."

Wallander produced his police ID. "I'm afraid it's sometimes necessary to disturb people," he said. "I'll write a note for you to take in."

He pulled over a notepad and started writing.

"Has something happened?" the receptionist said, sounding worried.

"Nothing too serious. But it can't wait, I'm afraid." He tore off the page. "It's for a man called Thomas Rundstedt, the chief auditor," he said. "I'll wait here."

The receptionist went out. Wallander yawned. He felt hungry. He could see a dining room through a half-open door. He went to investigate. There was a plate of cheese sandwiches standing on a table. He took one and ate it. Then another. Then he went back to the sofa in reception.

It was another five minutes before the receptionist reappeared. He was accompanied by a man Wallander assumed was the person he was looking for, Mr Rundstedt.

The man was tall and broad-shouldered. It occurred to Wallander that he had always thought accountants were short and thin. The man facing him could have been a boxer. He was also bald, and eyed Wallander up and down suspiciously.

"My name's Kurt Wallander and I'm a detective inspector with the Ystad police," he said, reaching out his hand. "I take it you're Thomas Rundstedt and Auditor-in-Chief at the Malmöhus County Offices."

The man nodded abruptly. "What's this all about?" he said. "We specifically asked not to be disturbed. The financial affairs of the County Offices are not to be trifled with. Especially just now."

"I'm sure they're not," Wallander said. "I won't keep you long. Does the name Lars Borman mean anything to you?"

Rundstedt raised his eyebrows in surprise. "That was before my time," he said. "Borman was an accountant at the County Offices, but he's dead. I've only been working there for six months."

Shit, Wallander thought. I've come here for nothing.

"Was there anything else?" Rundstedt said.

"Who did you replace?" Wallander asked.

"Martin Oscarsson," Rundstedt said. "He retired."

"And he was Lars Borman's boss?"

"Yes."

"Where can I get hold of him?"

"He lives in Limhamn. On the Sound. In Möllevägen. I can't remember the number. I assume he'll be in the phone book."

"That's all, thank you very much," Wallander said. "I apologise for disturbing you. Do you know how Borman died, by the way?"

"They say it was suicide," Rundstedt said.

"Good luck with the budget," Wallander said. "Will you be putting the council tax up?"

"Who knows?" Rundstedt said, and went back to his meeting.

Wallander waved a salute to the receptionist and went back to his car. He phoned Directory Enquiries and wrote down Martin Oscarsson's address, Möllevägen 32.

He was there before noon.

The house was stone-built, around the turn of the century – it said 1912 over the big entrance. He went through the gate and rang the bell. The door was opened by an old man in a tracksuit. Wallander explained who he was, showed his ID and was invited in. In contrast to the dreary façade, the house inside was filled with light-coloured furniture, had pretty curtains in pastel shades, and large, uncluttered spaces. Music could be heard from another room. Wallander thought he recognised the voice of Ernst Rolf, the popular variety artist. Oscarsson showed him into the living room and asked if Wallander might like a cup of coffee. He declined.

"I've come to talk to you about Lars Borman," he said. "I was given your name by Thomas Rundstedt. About a year ago, shortly before you retired, Borman died. The official explanation was suicide."

"Why do you want to talk about Lars Borman?" Oscarsson said, and Wallander noted the unfriendly tone in his voice.

"His name has cropped up in a criminal investigation we're dealing with," Wallander said.

"What sort of criminal investigation?"

Wallander decided that he might as well not beat about the bush. "You'll have seen in the newspapers that a solicitor in Ystad was murdered a few days ago," he said. "The questions I need to ask are about Borman's connection with that investigation."

Oscarsson stared at him for some time before replying. "Although I'm an old man, tired but perhaps not yet quite finished, I admit to being curious. I'll answer your questions, if I can."

"Borman was an accountant at the County Offices,"

Wallander said. "What exactly did he do? And how long had he been working there?"

"An accountant is an accountant," Oscarsson said. "The job title tells you what he did. He kept the books, in this case the County Council books. He checked that all the regulations were being observed, that budgets laid down by the appropriate authority were not exceeded. He also checked to make sure people were paid what they should be paid. You have to remember that a county office is like a large business, or rather an industrial empire associated with a small duchy. Its main responsibility is health spending, but it oversees a lot of other things as well. Education, culture, and so on. Borman wasn't our only accountant, of course. He came to the County Offices from the municipal corporation at the beginning of the '80s."

"Was he a good accountant?"

"He was the best accountant I ever came across."

"Why so?"

"He worked quickly but with no loss of accuracy. He was very involved in his work and was always coming up with suggestions as to how we could save money for the council."

"I've heard it said that he was a particularly honest man," Wallander said.

"Of course he was," Oscarsson said. "But that's not exactly earth-shattering – accountants are mostly honest. There are exceptions, of course, but they could never survive in an environment such as you get at county offices."

Wallander thought for a moment before continuing.

"And out of the blue he committed suicide," he said. "Was that unexpected?"

"It certainly was unexpected," Oscarsson said.

Looking back, Wallander was never quite sure what had happened when those words were spoken. There was a slight change of tone in Oscarsson's voice, a faint trace of doubt, perhaps reluctance, that made itself felt in the way he replied. As far as Wallander was concerned, the conversation changed character at that moment, and straightforward question and answer was replaced by alertness.

"You worked closely with Borman," Wallander said. "You must have known him well. What was he like as a man?"

"We were never friends. He lived for his work and for his family. He had an integrity that nobody ever questioned. And if anybody came too close, he would withdraw into his shell."

"Could he have been seriously ill?"

"That I don't know."

"You must have thought a good deal about his death."

"It was a very unpleasant time. It cast a shadow over my final months at work before I retired."

"Can you tell me about his last day at work?"

"He died on a Sunday, so the last time I saw him was on the Friday afternoon. There was a meeting of the financial heads of the County Council. It was quite a lively meeting, unfortunately."

"In what way?"

"There were arguments about how a particular problem ought to be resolved."

"Which problem was that?"

Oscarsson looked hard at Wallander. "I'm not sure I ought to answer that question," he said.

"Why not?"

"In the first place I'm retired now. And also there are laws regarding those aspects of public administration that are confidential."

"We have a right-of-access principle in Sweden," Wallander said.

"But that doesn't apply to specific cases which for various reasons are deemed unsuitable to be made public."

"On the last day Borman was at work, he was at a meeting with the finance heads of the County Council," he said. "Is that right?"

Oscarsson nodded.

"And at that meeting a problem was discussed, sometimes heatedly, which was later designated unsuitable, et cetera. In other words, the minutes of that meeting are locked away somewhere. Correct?"

"No, not correct," Oscarsson said. "There were no minutes."

"In which case it can't have been an official meeting," Wallander said. "If it had been, minutes would have to have been taken and kept, and in due course submitted for approval and signed."

"It was a confidential discussion," Oscarsson said. "But it's all water under the bridge now, and I don't think I'm going to answer any more questions. My memory isn't what it was. I've forgotten what happened."

Wallander thought, Oscarsson has forgotten nothing. What was it they were discussing that Friday?

"I can't oblige you to answer my questions, of course," Wallander said. "But I can resort to a public prosecutor who can. Or I can go to the Executive Committee of the County Council. I can do all sorts of things to find out what the problem was, it's just that it would take time and I don't have that luxury."

"I'm not going to answer any more questions," Oscarsson said, getting to his feet.

Wallander remained seated. "Sit down," he said firmly. "I have a suggestion."

Oscarsson hesitated, but then sat down again.

"Let's do what you did that Friday afternoon," Wallander said. "I'm not going to make any notes. Let's call this a confidential conversation. There are no witnesses to say that it ever took place. I can give you my word that I shall never refer to you, irrespective of what you're going to say."

Oscarsson thought over the proposal. "Rundstedt knows you've come to see me."

"He doesn't know what about," Wallander said.

He waited while Oscarsson struggled with his conscience. But he knew what would happen. Oscarsson was a wise old bird.

"I'll go along with your suggestion," he said eventually, "but I don't guarantee to be able to answer all your questions."

"Be able to or be willing to?"

"That's a matter for me and me alone," Oscarsson said.

Wallander nodded. They had a deal.

"The problem," Wallander said. "What was it?"

"Malmöhus County Council had been swindled," Oscarsson said. "We didn't know at the time how much money was involved, but we do now."

"How much?"

"Four million kronor. Of taxpayers' money."

"What had happened?"

"So that it makes sense, I'll start by sketching in how a county council works," Oscarsson said. "Our annual turnover runs to several million, handled by a variety of departments and activities. Financial supervision is centralised and computerised. Safety devices are built in at various levels to protect against embezzlement and other illegal practices. There are even precautions checking what the top executives do, but I don't need to go into detail about them in this case. What it's important to understand, though, is that there is a constant, continuous audit of all payments. Anyone who wants to defraud a county council is going to have to be very familiar with methods of juggling sums of money between accounts. Anyway, that's the background in brief."

"I think I understand," Wallander said.

"What happened made it clear that our precautions were inadequate," Oscarsson said. "They've been radically altered since then. A similar fraud wouldn't be possible now."

"Take your time," Wallander said. "I'd like to have as much detail as possible about what happened."

"There are things we still don't know," Oscarsson said. "But what we do know is this: as you may be aware, the whole of the administration of public services in Sweden has undergone far-reaching change in recent years. In many ways you could say it's undergone an operation without quite enough anaesthetic. Those of us civil servants from the older generation especially have found it hard to cope with the enormous changes. The reforms are still not finished, and it will be some time before we can make a judgment on

187

all the consequences. The bottom line is that public authorities should be managed in the same way as business enterprises, taking market forces and competition into account. Some public authorities have been turned into limited companies, and others have been sent out to tender from the private sector. All of them have had to satisfy increased demands for efficiency. One of the outcomes, as far as we were concerned, was that a company had to be formed in order to handle all the purchases made by the council. Having the County Council as a customer is one of the best things that can happen to a private enterprise, whether it's lawnmowers or washing powder they're manufacturing or selling. In connection with the formation of that company we hired a firm of consultants with a wide-ranging mandate, one item being to evaluate the applications for the newly established top executive posts that had been advertised. And that is where the fraud took place."

"What is the name of the firm of consultants?"

"They're called STRUFAB. I can't remember what the acronym stands for."

"Who was behind the firm?"

"It belonged to a division of the investment company Smeden, which is a listed company."

"Is there one principal owner?"

"As far as I know, both Volvo and Skanska had large shareholdings in Smeden at that time. It might be different now, though."

"We can come back to that," Wallander said. "Let's get back to the fraud. What happened?"

"We had a series of meetings in late summer and early autumn to put the finishing touches to the formation of the company. The consultants were very efficient and our lawyers gave them full marks, as did the financial supremos at the County Council. We even went so far as to propose that STRUFAB should be given a long-term contract by the council."

"Who were the individual consultants?"

"Egil Holmberg and Stefan Fjällsjö. On a few occasions a third one was there as well, but I'm afraid I've forgotten his name."

"And all of these people turned out to be swindlers?" Oscarsson's reply surprised him.

"I don't know," he said. "The fraud was carried out in such a way that, in the end, it wasn't possible to put a finger on any one individual. Nobody was guilty. But the money had disappeared."

"That sounds pretty odd," Wallander said. "What actually happened?"

"We have to go back to the afternoon of Friday, August 14, 1992," Oscarsson said. "That's when the scam was set up, and carried out in a very short space of time. As far as we could determine with hindsight, it was all very carefully planned. We met the consultants in a conference room at the Finance Unit. We started at 1 p.m. and thought we'd be finished by 5.00. When the meeting started, Holmberg announced that he had to leave at 4.00, but that need have no effect on the meeting. At 1.55 the Finance Director's secretary came in to announce that there was an important phone call for Fjällsjö. I think it was said to be from the Ministry of Technology. Fjällsjö apologised and went out with the secretary in order to take the call in her office. She explained later that she intended to leave the room so that Fjällsjö could take the call in private and he told her that the call would last for at least ten minutes. What happened next we can't be absolutely sure, but we are clear on the outline. Fjällsjö laid the receiver on his desk – we don't know where the call came from, except that it wasn't from the Ministry of Technology. He then went from the secretary's office through the connecting door to the Finance Director's office, and authorised the transfer of four million kronor to a business account at Handelsbanken in Stockholm. It was described specifically as a consultancy fee. No counter-signature was required, so there was no problem. The authorisation referred to a contract number with the non-existent consultancy firm, which I seem to remember was called Sisyphus. Fjällsjö confirmed the transfer in writing, forging the signature of the Finance Director and using the appropriate form. Then he keyed his authorisation into the computer. He put the hard copy in the internal mail, then went back to the secretary's office, went on talking to whoever it was at the other end of the line, and hung up when the secretary returned. That was the end of the first stage of the fraud. Fjällsjö returned to the conference room. Less than a quarter of an hour had passed."

Wallander was listening intently. Because he was not making notes, he was fearful of forgetting details.

Oscarsson continued: "Just before 4.00 Holmberg made his apologies and left. We realised afterwards that he didn't leave the building, but went down to the next floor where the Chief Clerk had his office. I should perhaps mention that it was empty, because the Chief Clerk was attending our meeting. He didn't usually do so, but on this occasion the consultants had specifically asked for him to be present. In other words, the whole thing was meticulously prepared. Holmberg hacked into his computer, entered the invented contract number, and inserted an authorisation for a payment of four million kronor backdated a week. He phoned the Handelsbanken head office in Stockholm and requested payment. And then he sat back and waited calmly for the response. Ten minutes later Handelsbanken rang back to check. He took the call and confirmed the transaction. There was only one thing left to do: he called the County Council's own bank and authorised the payment, and then left the premises. Early the following Monday morning, somebody collected the money from Handelsbanken in Stockholm. The person was authorised by Sisyphus to sign on behalf of the company, and claimed to be called Rickard Edén. We have reason to believe that it was Fjällsjö who collected the money, using this alias. It was about a week before the fraud was discovered. The police were called in, and it did not take long to work out what must have happened. But there was no proof, naturally. Needless to say, Fjällsjö and Holmberg were vociferous in denying all knowledge. We severed all links with the consultancy firm, but we were unable to get any further. In the end, the Public Prosecutor wrote the whole thing off and we managed to hush it up. Everybody agreed that was what we had to do – apart from one person."

"Borman?"

Oscarsson nodded slowly. "He was most upset. We all were, of course, but Borman took it hardest. He seemed to take it personally because we weren't prepared to force the Public Prosecutor and the police to follow the case up. I suppose he took it so badly because he thought we'd failed in our duty."

"Did he take it badly enough to commit suicide?"

"I believe so."

Some progress, Wallander thought. But where does the firm of solicitors in Ystad fit in? They must be involved, in view of Borman's letters.

"Do you know what Holmberg and Fjällsjö are doing now?"

"Their consultancy firm changed its name. That's all I know. We warned county councils the length and breadth of the country about them, discreetly to be sure."

"You said that the consultancy firm was part of a bigger concern, an investment company. But you didn't know who owned it. Who was chairman of the board of Smeden?"

"From what I've read in the newspapers, Smeden has been transformed during the last year or so. It's been split up, several sectors have been sold off, and new elements have been acquired. It might not be going too far to say that Smeden has quite a poor reputation. Volvo have sold their shares. I forget who bought them. But somebody at the Stock Exchange could tell you."

"You've been a great help," Wallander said.

"You won't forget our agreement?"

"I never forget anything," Wallander said. "But tell me, did it ever occur to you that Borman might have been murdered?"

Oscarsson stared at him in evident unease.

"No," he said. "Never. Why on earth should I have thought that?"

"I was only asking," Wallander said. "Many thanks for your help. I might need to be in touch again."

Oscarsson stood on the steps, watching him leave. Wallander was now so exhausted he wanted nothing more than to lie down in the car and go to sleep, but he forced himself to think ahead. The natural thing would have been to return to Höör, call Thomas Rundstedt out from his budget conference and ask him some quite different questions.

He set off for Malmö while allowing a decision to mature in his mind, then he stopped on the hard shoulder and called the Malmö police. He asked for Roslund, gave his name, and said he had an urgent matter to discuss. It took the operator less than a minute to find Roslund.

"It's Wallander here, from Ystad," he said. "We met last night."

"I haven't forgotten," Roslund said. "They told me you had something urgent to discuss."

"I'm in Malmö," Wallander said. "I'd like to ask you a favour."

"I'm listening."

"About a year ago, at the beginning of September, the first or second Sunday in the month, a man called Lars Borman hanged himself in a clearing in the woods at Klagshamn. There must be a call-out report, and some notes about death by unnatural causes, and a post-mortem report. I'd be very grateful if you could dig them out for me. If at all possible I'd like to get in touch with one of the officers who answered the call and took the body down. Do you think this might be possible?"

"What was the name again?"

Wallander spelled it out.

"I don't know how many suicides we get per year," Roslund said. "I don't recall this one. But I'll look for the documents and see if one of the officers called out is in today."

Wallander gave him his mobile number.

193

"I'll drive to Klagshamn in the meantime," he said.

It was 2.00. He tried in vain to shake off his exhaustion, but was forced to give in and turned off on to a road that he knew led to an old quarry. He switched off the engine and pulled his jacket tightly around him. A minute later he was asleep.

He woke up with a start. He was freezing cold and didn't know where he was at first. Something had strayed into his consciousness, something he had dreamed, but he couldn't remember what it was. A feeling of depression gripped him when he looked around at the grey landscape on every side. It was 2.35, so he had been asleep for half an hour. He felt as if he had been roused from a long period of unconsciousness.

That is about as close as one can get to the greatest loneliness of all, he thought. Being all alone in the world. The final human being, forgotten about.

He was roused from his thoughts by the phone ringing. It was Roslund.

"You sound half asleep," he said. "Have you been having a snooze in the car?"

"Not at all," Wallander said. "I have a bit of a cold."

"I've found the stuff you asked for," Roslund said. "I have the papers here on my desk. I also have the name of the police officer: Magnus Staffansson. He was in the car that was called out when a jogger found a body hanging from a birch tree. No doubt he can explain how a man can hang himself in a birch, of all trees. Where would you like to meet him?"

Wallander could feel his exhaustion slipping away. "At the slip road for Klagshamn," he said.

"He'll be there in a quarter of an hour," Roslund said. "By the way, I spoke to Sven Nyberg a few minutes ago. He hasn't found anything in your car."

"I'm not surprised," Wallander said.

"You won't have to see the wreck when you drive back home," Roslund said. "We've just arranged for it to be taken away."

"Thanks for your help."

He drove straight to Klagshamn and parked at the meeting place. After a few minutes a police car drove up. Wallander had got out of his car and was walking up and down; Magnus Staffansson was in uniform, and saluted. Wallander responded with an awkward wave. They sat in Wallander's car. Staffansson handed over a plastic file containing photocopies.

"I'll have a glance through this," Wallander said. "Meanwhile, you can try to remember what happened."

"Suicide is something you'd prefer to forget," Staffansson said, in a thick Malmö accent. Wallander smiled to hear how he too used to speak, before his move to Ystad had changed his dialect.

He read swiftly through the terse reports, the post-mortem document and the record of the decision to abandon the investigation. There were no suspicious circumstances.

I wonder, Wallander thought. Then he put the file on the shelf on the dashboard and turned to Staffansson.

"I think it would be a good idea to take a look at the place where it happened. Can you remember how to get there?"

"Yes," he said. "It's a few kilometres outside the village. I'll go ahead."

They left Klagshamn and drove south along the coast.

A container ship was on its way through the Sound. A bank of cloud hovered over Copenhagen. The housing estates petered out and soon they were surrounded by fields. A tractor made its way slowly over one of them.

They were there almost before he knew it. There was a stretch of deciduous woods to the left of the road. Wallander pulled up behind Staffansson's police car and got out. The path was wet and he thought he ought to put on his wellingtons, but on his way to the boot to collect them he realised they had been in his car.

Staffansson pointed to a birch tree, bigger than the rest. "That's where he was hanging," he said.

"Tell me about it," Wallander said.

"Most of it's in the report," Staffansson said.

"It's always better from the horse's mouth."

"It was a Sunday morning," Staffansson began. "About 8.00. We'd been called out to calm down an angry passenger on the morning ferry from Dragør who claimed he had got food poisoning from the breakfast during the crossing. That was when we got the emergency call: a man hanging from a tree. We got a location and headed there. A couple of joggers had come across him. They were in shock, of course, but one of them had run to the house on the hill over there and phoned the police. We did what we're trained to do and took him down, as it sometimes happens that they're still alive. Then the ambulance arrived, the CID took over, and eventually it was put down as a suicide. That's all I can remember. Oh, I forgot to say he had got there on a bike. It was lying here among the bushes."

Wallander examined the tree while listening to what Staffansson had to say. "What kind of a rope was it?" he said.

"It looked like a hawser from a boat, about as thick as my thumb."

"Do you remember the knot?"

"It was an ordinary running noose."

"How did he do it?"

Staffansson stared at him, bewildered.

"It's not all that easy to hang yourself," Wallander said. "Did he stand on something? Had he climbed up the tree?"

Staffansson pointed at the trunk. "He probably pushed off from that bulge in the trunk," he said. "That's what we supposed. There was nothing he could have stood on."

Wallander nodded. The post-mortem made it clear Borman had choked to death. His neck was not broken. He had been dead for an hour at most when the police arrived.

"Can you remember anything else?" he asked.

"Such as what?"

"Only you can answer that."

"You do what you have to do," Staffansson said. "You write your report and then you try to forget it as soon as you can."

Wallander knew how it was. There's an atmosphere of depression about a suicide unlike anything else. He thought of all the occasions when he himself had been forced to deal with suicides.

He went over what Staffansson had said. It lay like a sort of filter over what he had already read in the report. But he knew that there was something that did not add up.

He thought of all he had heard about Borman: even if the descriptions were incomplete, even if there had been some murky areas, it seemed clear that Borman had been in every way a well-organised sort of person. And yet when he had decided to take his own life he had cycled out to some woods and chosen a tree that was highly unsuitable for what he planned to do. That already told Wallander there was something fishy about Borman's death. But there was something else. He could not put his finger on it at first, but then he stared down at the ground a few metres from the tree.

The bicycle, he thought. That's telling quite a different story.

Staffansson had lit a cigarette and was pacing up and down to keep warm.

"The bicycle," Wallander said. "There are no details about it in your reports."

"It was a very good one," Staffansson said. "Ten gears, good condition. Dark blue, as I remember."

"Show me exactly where it was."

Staffansson pointed straight at the spot.

"How was it lying?" Wallander asked.

"Well, what can one say? It was just lying on the ground."

"It hadn't fallen over?"

"There was a stand, but it hadn't been opened."

"Are you sure?"

He thought for a moment. "Yes," he said, "I'm certain."

"So he had just let the bike fall down any old how? More or less like a kid does when he's in a hurry?"

"Exactly," Staffansson said. "It had been flung down. As if he was in a hurry to get it all over with."

Wallander nodded thoughtfully. "Just one more thing," he said. "Ask your colleague if he can confirm that the stand hadn't been opened up."

"Is that so important?"

"Yes," Wallander said. "It's much more important than you think. Phone me if your colleague disagrees."

"The stand wasn't opened," Staffansson said. "I'm absolutely certain."

"Call me anyway," Wallander said. "Now let's get out of here. Many thanks for your help."

Wallander started the drive back to Ystad, thinking about Borman. An accountant at the County Council. A man who would never have just tossed his bicycle to the ground, not even *in extremis*.

One more step forward, Wallander thought. I am on to something without knowing quite what it is. Somewhere between Borman and the solicitors' offices in Ystad there is a link. I need to find it.

He had passed the spot where his car had blown up before he noticed. He turned off at Rydsgård and had a late lunch at the local inn. He was the only person in the dining room. He really must ring Linda that night, no matter how tired he was. Then he would write to Baiba.

He was back at the station in Ystad by 5.00. Ebba informed him that there was not going to be a meeting – everybody was busy and didn't have time to advise their colleagues that they had nothing of significance to advise them about. They would meet the following morning instead, at 8.00.

"You look dreadful," she said.

"Thank you," he said. "I'll get some sleep tonight."

He went to his office and shut the door behind him. There were several notes on his desk, but nothing so important that it could not wait until morning.

He hung up his jacket and spent half an hour writing a summary of what he had done during the day. Then he dropped his pen and leaned back in his chair.

We really must break through now, he thought. We just have to find the missing link.

He had just put on his jacket when there was a knock on the door and Svedberg came in. Wallander could see right away that something had happened. Svedberg seemed worried.

"Have you got a moment?" he said.

"What's happened?"

Svedberg looked uneasy, and Wallander could feel the last of his patience dwindling away.

"I assume there's something you want to say seeing as you've come here," he said. "I was just going home."

"I'm afraid you'll have to go to Simrishamn," Svedberg said.

"Why must I?"

"They phoned."

"Who did?"

"Our colleagues."

"The police in Simrishamn? What did they want?"

Svedberg seemed to make sure both feet were planted firmly on the ground before replying.

"They've had to arrest your father," he said.

"The Simrishamn police have arrested my father? What for?"

"Apparently he's been involved in a violent fight," Svedberg said.

Wallander stared at him for quite a while without speaking. Then he sat down at his desk.

"Tell me again," he said. "Slowly."

"They rang about an hour ago," Svedberg said. "As you were out they spoke to me. A few hours ago they arrested your father. He had started fighting in the off-licence in Simrishamn. It was evidently pretty violent. Then they discovered he was your father. So they phoned here."

Wallander sighed, but said nothing. He got slowly to his feet.

"I'll drive over then," he said.

"Would you like me to come with you?"

"No thanks."

Wallander left the station. He didn't know whether he was coming or going.

An hour later he walked into the police station in Simrishamn.

Chapter 9

On the way to Simrishamn Wallander had thought about the Silk Knights. It was many years since he had needed to remind himself that they had once been real.

The last time his father had been arrested by the police was when Wallander was eleven. He could remember it very clearly. They were still living in Malmö, and his reaction to his father's arrest had been a strange mixture of shame and pride.

That time, however, his father had not been arrested in an off-licence, but in a public park in the centre of town. It was a Saturday in the early summer of 1956, and Wallander had been allowed to accompany his father and some of his friends on a night out.

His father's friends, who came to their house at irregular intervals and always unexpectedly, were great adventurers in his young eyes. They rolled up in shiny American cars, always wore silk suits, and they often had broad-brimmed hats and heavy gold rings on their fingers. They came to call at the little studio that smelled of turps and oil paint, to view and perhaps to buy some of the pictures his father had painted. Sometimes he ventured into the studio himself and hid behind the pile of junk in the darkest corner, old canvases that mice had been nibbling at, and he would shudder as he listened to the bargaining that always ended with a couple of swigs from a bottle of brandy. He had realised that it was thanks to these great adventurers – the Silk Knights, as he used to call them in his secret diaries – that the Wallanders had food on the table. It was one of those supreme moments in life when he witnessed a bargain being struck, and the unknown men peeling banknotes from enormous bundles with their ring-adorned fingers and handing over rather smaller bundles which his father would stuff into his pocket before giving a little bow.

He could still recall the conversations, the terse, almost stuttering repartee, often followed by lame protests from his father and chuckling noises from the visitors.

"Seven landscapes without grouse and two with," one of them would say. His father rummaged among the piles of finished paintings, had them approved, and then the money would land on the table with a gentle thud. Wallander was eleven years old, standing in his dark corner, almost overcome by the turpentine fumes, and thinking that what he was observing was the grown-up life that also lay in store for him, once he had crossed the river formed by Class Seven – or was it Class Nine in those days? He was surprised to find that he could not remember. Then he would emerge from the shadows when it was time to carry the canvases out to the shiny cars, where they were to be loaded into the boot or on to the back seat. This was a moment of great significance, because now and then one of the Knights would notice the boy helping with the carrying and covertly slip him a five-kronor note. Then he and his father would stand at the gate and watch the car roll away, and once it was gone his father would go through a metamorphosis: the obsequious manner would be gone in a flash, and he would spit after the man who had just driven off and say with contempt in his voice that yet again he had been swindled.

This was one of the great childhood mysteries. How could his father think he had been swindled when every time he had collected a wad of banknotes in exchange for those boring paintings, all identical, with a landscape illuminated by a sun that was never allowed to set?

Just once he had been present at a visit of these unknown men when the ending turned out otherwise. There were two of them, and he had never seen them before – as he skulked in the shadows behind the remains of an old mangle, he gathered from the conversation that they were new business contacts. It was an important moment, for it was not a foregone conclusion that they would approve of the paintings. He had helped to carry the canvases to the car, a Dodge on this occasion (he had learned how to open the boot of all the different makes of car). Then the two men had suggested they should all go out for something to eat. He remembered that one of them was called Anton and the other something foreign, possibly Polish. He and his father had squeezed in among the canvases on the back seat; the fantastic men even had a gramophone in the car, and they had listened to Johnny Bohde as they drove to the park. His father had gone to one of the restaurants with the two men, and Wallander had been given a handful of one-krona pieces and sent to play on the roundabouts. It was a warm day in early summer, a gentle breeze was blowing in from the Sound, and he worked out in great detail what he would be able to buy for his money. It would have been unfair to save the money, it had been given to him for spending, to help him enjoy that afternoon and evening in the park. He had been on the roundabouts and taken two rides on the big wheel which took you so high you could see as far as Copenhagen. Occasionally he checked to make sure that his father, Anton and the Pole were still there. He could see even from a distance that lots of glasses and bottles were being carried to their table, and plates of food and white napkins that the men tucked into their shirt collars. He remembered thinking how, when he had crossed that river after Class Seven or Nine or whatever, he would be like one of those men who drove in a shiny car and rewarded artists by peeling off banknotes and dropping them on a table in a dirty studio.

The afternoon had turned into evening, and rain threatened. He decided to have one more ride on the big wheel, but he never did. Something had happened. The big wheel and the roundabouts and the rifle range suddenly lost all their attraction, and people started hurrying towards the restaurant. He had gone along with the tide, elbowed his way to the front and seen something he could never forget. It had been a rite of passage, something he had not realised existed, but it taught him that life is made up of a series of rites of passage of whose existence we are unaware until we find ourselves in the midst of them.

When he pushed and shoved his way to the front he found his own father in a violent fight with one of the Silk Knights and several security guards, waiters and other complete strangers. The dining table had been overturned, glasses and bottles were broken, a beefsteak dripping with gravy and dark brown onion rings was dangling from his father's arm, his nose was bleeding and he was throwing punches left, right and centre. It had all happened so quickly. Wallander shouted his father's name, in a mixture of fear and panic – but then it was all over. Burly, red-faced bouncers intervened; police officers appeared from nowhere, and his father was dragged away along with Anton and the Pole. All that was left was a battered broad-brimmed hat. He tried to run after them and grab hold of his father, but he was pulled back. He stumbled to the gate, and burst into tears as he watched his father driven away in a police car.

He walked all the way home, and it started raining before he got there. Everything was in turmoil, his universe had crumbled away and he only wished he could have erased everything that had happened. But you cannot erase reality. He hurried on through the downpour and wondered whether he would ever see his father again. He sat all night in the studio, waiting for him. The smell of turps almost choked him, and every time he heard a car he would run out to the gate. He fell asleep in the end, curled up on the floor.

He woke up to find his father bending over him. He had a piece of cotton wool in one of his nostrils, and his left eye was swollen and discoloured. He stank of drink, a sort of stale oil smell, but the boy sat up and flung his arms round his father.

"They wouldn't listen to me," his father said. "They wouldn't listen. I told them my boy was with us, but they wouldn't listen. How did you get home?"

Wallander told him that he had walked all the way home through the rain.

"I'm sorry it turned out like that," his father said. "But I got so angry. They were saying something that just wasn't true."

His father picked up one of the paintings and studied it with his good eye. It was one with a grouse in the foreground.

"I got so angry," he said again. "Those bastards maintained it was a partridge. They said I had painted the bird so badly, you couldn't tell if it was a grouse or a partridge. What else can you do but get angry? I'm not having them put my honour and competence in doubt."

"Of course it's a grouse," Wallander had said. "Anybody can see it isn't a partridge."

His father regarded him with a smile. Two of his front teeth were missing. His smile's broken, Wallander thought. My father's smile's broken.

Then they had a cup of coffee. It was still raining, and his father had slowly cooled down.

"Fancy not being able to tell the difference between a grouse and a partridge," he kept protesting, half incantation, half prayer. "Claiming I can't paint a bird the way it looks."

All this went through Wallander's mind as he drove to Simrishamn. He also recalled that the two men, the one called Anton and the Pole, had kept coming back every year to buy paintings. The fight, the sudden anger, the excessive tipples of brandy, everything had turned into a hilarious episode they could now remember and laugh about. Anton had even paid the dentist's bills. That's friendship, he thought. Behind the fight there was something more important, friendship between the art dealers and the man who kept on at his never-changing pictures so that they had something to sell.

He thought about the painting in the flat in Helsingborg, and about all the other flats he had not seen but where nevertheless the grouse was portrayed against a landscape over which the sun never set.

For the first time he thought he had gained an insight. Throughout his life his father had prevented the sun from setting. That had been his livelihood, his message. He had painted pictures so that people who bought them to hang on their walls could see it was possible to hold the sun captive.

He came to Simrishamn, parked outside the police station and went in. Torsten Lundström was at his desk. He was due to retire and Wallander knew him for a kind man, a police officer of the old school who wanted nothing but good for his fellow men. He nodded at Wallander and put down the newspaper he was reading. Wallander sat on a chair in front of his desk and looked at him.

"Can you tell me what happened?" he said. "I know my father got mixed up in a fight at the off-licence, but that's about all I know."

"Well, it was like this," Lundström said with a friendly smile. "Your father drove up to the off-licence in a taxi at about 4.00 in the afternoon, went inside, took the ticket with his queue number from the machine and sat down to wait. It seems he didn't notice when his number came up. After a while he went up to the counter and demanded to be served even though he had missed his turn. The shop assistant handled the whole thing really badly, apparently insisting that your father get a new number and start at the back of the queue.

Your father refused, another customer whose number had come up pushed his way past and told your father to get lost. To everybody's surprise your father was so angry he turned and thumped this man. The assistant intervened, so your father started fighting with him as well. You can imagine what happened next. But at least nobody got hurt. Your father might have some pain in his right hand, though. He seems to be pretty strong, despite his age."

"Where is he?"

Lundström pointed to a door in the background.

"What'll happen now?" Wallander asked.

"You can take him home. I'm afraid he'll be charged with causing an affray. Unless you can sort it out with the man he punched and the shop assistant. I'll have a word with the prosecutor and do what I can."

He handed Wallander a piece of paper with two names and addresses on it.

"I don't think the fellow in the shop will give you any difficulty," he said. "I know him. The other man, Sten Wickberg, could be a bit of a problem. He owns a firm of haulage contractors. Lives in Kivik. He seems to have made up his mind to come down on your poor father from a great height. You could try calling him. The number's there. And Simrishamn Taxis are owed 230 kronor. In all the confusion, he never got round to paying. The driver's name is Waldemar Kåge. I've had a word with him. He knows he'll get his money."

Wallander took the sheet of paper and put it in his pocket. Then he motioned towards the door behind him.

"How is he?"

"I think he's simmered down. But he still insists he had every right to defend himself."

"Defend himself?" Wallander said. "But he was the one who started it all."

"Well, he feels he had a right to defend his place in the queue," Lundström said.

"For Christ's sake!"

Lundström stood up. "You can take him home now," he said. "By the way, what's this I hear about your car going up in flames?"

"There could have been something wrong with the electrics," Wallander said. "Anyway, it was an old banger."

"I'll disappear for a few minutes," Lundström said. "The door locks itself when you close it."

"Thanks for your help," Wallander said.

"What help?" Lundström said, putting on his cap and going out.

Wallander knocked and opened the door. His father was sitting on a bench in the bare room, cleaning his fingernails with a nail. When he saw who it was, he rose to his feet and was clearly annoyed.

"You took your time," he said. "How long did you intend making me wait here?"

"I came as quickly as I could," Wallander said. "Let's go home now."

"Not until I've paid for the taxi," his father said. "I want to do the right thing."

"We'll sort that out later."

They left the police station and drove home in silence. Wallander could see that his father had already forgotten what had happened. It wasn't until they reached the turning to Glimmingehus that Wallander turned to him.

"What happened to Anton and the Pole?" he asked.

"Do you remember them?" his father asked in surprise.

"There was a fight on that occasion as well," Wallander said with a sigh.

"I thought you would have forgotten about that," his father said. "I don't know what became of the Pole. It's getting on for 20 years since I last heard of him. He had gone over to something he thought would be more profitable. Pornographic magazines. I don't know how he got on. But Anton's dead. Drank himself to death. That must be nearly 25 years ago."

"What were you doing at the off-licence?" Wallander asked.

"What you normally do there," his father said. "I wanted to buy some brandy."

"I thought you didn't like brandy."

"My wife enjoys a glass in the evening."

"Gertrud drinks brandy?"

"Why shouldn't she? Don't start thinking you can tell her what to do and what not to do, like you've been trying to do to me."

Wallander could not believe his ears. "I've never tried to tell you what to do," he said angrily. "If anybody's been trying to tell somebody else what to do, it's been you telling me."

"If you'd listened to me you'd never have joined the police force," his father said. "And in view of what's happened these last few years, that would have been to your advantage, of course."

Wallander realised the best he could do was to change the subject. "It was a good job you weren't injured," he said.

"You have to preserve your dignity," his father said. "And your place in the queue. Otherwise they walk all over you."

"I am afraid you might be charged."

"I shall deny it."

"Deny what? Everybody knows it was you who started the fight. There's no way you can deny it."

"All I did was preserve my dignity," his father said. "Do they put you in prison for that nowadays?"

"You won't go to prison," Wallander said. "You might have to pay damages, though."

"I shall refuse," his father said.

"I'll pay them," Wallander said. "You punched another customer on the nose. That sort of thing gets punished."

"You have to preserve your dignity."

Wallander gave up. Shortly afterwards they turned into his father's drive.

"Don't mention this to Gertrud," his father said as he got out of the car. Wallander was surprised by his insistent tone.

"I won't say a word."

Gertrud and his father had married the year before. She had started to work for him when he had begun to show signs of senility. She introduced a new dimension into his solitary life – she had visited him three days a week – and there had been a big change in his father, who no longer seemed to be senile. She was 30 years his junior, but that apparently did not matter to either of them. Wallander was aghast at the thought of their marrying, but he had discovered that she was good-hearted and determined to go through with it. He did not know much about her, beyond the fact that she was local, had two grown-up children and had been divorced for years. They seemed to have found happiness together, and Wallander had often felt a degree of jealousy. His own life seemed

212

to be so miserable and was getting worse all the time so that what he needed was a home help for himself.

Gertrud was preparing the evening meal when they went in. As always, she was delighted to welcome him. He apologised for not being able to join them for supper, blaming pressure of work. Instead, he went with his father to the studio, where they drank a cup of coffee which they made on the filthy hotplate.

"I saw one of your pictures on a wall in Helsingborg the other night," Wallander said.

"There've been quite a few over the years," his father said.

"How many have you made?"

"I could work it out if I wanted to," his father said. "But I don't."

"It must be thousands."

"I'd rather not think about it. It would be inviting the Reaper into the parlour."

The comment surprised Wallander. He had never heard him refer to his age, never mind his death. It struck him that he had no idea how frightened his father might be of dying. After all these years, I know nothing at all about my father, he thought. And he probably knows equally little about me.

His father was peering at him short-sightedly.

"So, you're fit again, are you?" he said. "You've started work again. The last time you were here, before you went to that guest house at Skagen, you said you were going to pack it in as a police officer. You've changed your mind, have you?"

"Something happened," Wallander said. He would rather not get involved in a discussion about his job. They always ended up quarrelling.

213

"I gather you're a pretty good police officer," his father said suddenly.

"Who told you that?" Wallander said.

"Gertrud. They've been writing about you in the newspapers. I don't read them, but she claims they say you're a good police officer."

"Newspapers say all kinds of things."

"I'm only repeating what she says."

"What do *you* say?"

"That I tried to put you off joining, and I still think you should be doing something else."

"I don't suppose I'll ever stop," Wallander said. "I'm coming up to 50. I'll be a police officer as long as I work."

They heard Gertrud shouting that the food was on the table.

"I'd never have thought you'd have remembered Anton and the Pole," said his father as they walked over to the house.

"It's one of the most vivid memories I have of my childhood," Wallander said. "Do you know what I used to call all those strange people who came to buy your paintings?"

"They were art dealers," his father said.

"I know," Wallander said. "But to me they were the Silk Knights."

His father stopped in his tracks and stared at him. He burst out laughing.

"That's an excellent name," he said. "That's exactly what they were. Knights in silk suits."

They said goodbye at the bottom of the steps.

"Are you sure you wouldn't like to stay?" Gertrud asked. "There's plenty of food."

"I've got work to do," Wallander said.

He drove back to Ystad through the dark autumn countryside. He tried to think what it was about his father that reminded him of himself.

But he could not find the answer.

On Friday, November 5, Wallander arrived at the station shortly after 7.00, feeling that he had caught up on his sleep and was raring to go. He made himself coffee, then spent the next hour preparing for the meeting of the investigation team that was due to start at 8.00. He drew up a schematic and chronological presentation of all the facts and tried to work out where they should go from there. He was bearing in mind that one or more of his colleagues might have come up with something the previous day that would throw new light on existing facts.

He had the feeling still that there was no time to spare, that the shadows behind the two dead solicitors were growing and becoming more frightening.

He put down his pen, leaned back in his chair and closed his eyes. He was at once back at Skagen, the beach stretching away in front of him, shrouded in fog. Sten Torstensson was there somewhere. Wallander tried to see past him to catch a glimpse of the people who must have followed him and were watching his meeting with the police officer on sick leave. They must have been close, for all that they were invisible, hidden among the dunes.

He thought of the woman walking her dog. Could it have been her? Or the girl working in the Art Museum café? That seemed impossible. There must have been somebody else there in the fog, somebody neither Sten nor he had seen.

He glanced at the clock. Time for the meeting. He gathered up his papers.

The meeting went on for more than four hours, but by the end of it Wallander felt that they had made a breakthrough, that a pattern was now beginning to appear, although there was much that was still obscure and the evidence of the involvement of any particular individuals was as yet inconclusive. Nevertheless, they had agreed that there could hardly be any doubt that what they were dealing with was not a string of unassociated events, but a deliberate chain of acts, even if at this stage they could not be clear about the links. By the time Wallander was able to summarise their conclusions, the atmosphere was stuffy and Svedberg had started to complain of a headache, and they were all exhausted.

"It's possible, even probable, that this investigation will take a long time, but we'll get all the bits of the jigsaw sooner or later. And that will lead to the solution. We must exercise the greatest care: we've already met with one booby trap, a mine. There may be more, metaphorically speaking. But now is the time to start ferreting away."

They had spent the morning going over their material – point by point – discussing it, evaluating it. They had scrutinised every detail from all possible points of view, tested various interpretations, and then agreed on how to proceed. They had reached a crucial moment in the investigation, one of the most critical stages at which it could so easily go wrong if any one of them had a lapse of concentration. All contradictory evidence had to be taken as the starting point of a positive and constructive re-examination, not as grounds for automatic oversimplification or too-swift judgments. It's like being at the exploratory stage of designing a house, Wallander thought. We're constructing many of different models, and we must not dismantle any one of them too hastily. All the models are built on the same foundation.

It was almost a month since Gustaf Torstensson had died in the muddy field near Brösarp Hills. It was ten days since his son had been in Skagen and then murdered in his office. They kept coming back to those starting points.

The first to give their report that morning was Martinsson, supported by Nyberg.

"We've received the forensic analysis on the weapon and ammunition used to kill Sten Torstensson," Martinsson said, holding up the documents. "There's at least one point which we need to pay attention to."

Nyberg took over. "Sten Torstensson was hit by three 9 mm rounds. Standard ammunition. But the most interesting thing is that the experts believe the weapon used was an Italian pistol known as a Bernadelli Practical. I won't go into technical details as to why they think so. It could have been a Smith & Wesson 3914 or 5904, but it's more likely to have been a Bernadelli. That is a rather rare pistol in Sweden. There are no more than 50 or so registered. Of course, nobody knows how many illegal ones there might be floating about, but an informed guess would be about 30."

"Who would want to use that Italian pistol?" Wallander said.

"Somebody who knows a lot about guns," Nyberg said. "Somebody who chose it for specific reasons."

"Are you saying it could be a foreign professional hit man?"

"We shouldn't disregard that possibility," Nyberg said.

"We're going to go through the list of Bernadelli owners," Martinsson said. "From first checks, no registered owner of a Bernadelli pistol has reported it missing."

They moved to the next point.

"The number plate on one of the cars that followed you was stolen," Svedberg said. "From a Nissan in Malmö. Malmö are looking into it. They've found lots of fingerprints, but we shouldn't set our hopes very high."

Wallander agreed. "Anything else?" he said.

"You asked me to dig out some facts about Kurt Ström," Svedberg said.

Wallander gave a brief account of his visit to Farnholm Castle and his meeting with the former policeman at the castle gates.

"Kurt Ström was not a good advertisement for the police force," Svedberg said. "He had dealings with several fences. What they never managed to prove but was almost certainly the case was that he tipped them off about police raids. He was kicked out, but there was no publicity."

Björk spoke for the first time. "This sort of thing is deplorable. We can't afford to have people like Ström in the force. What's worrying is that they then turn up in one of these security firms, no problem. The checks made on them are obviously nowhere near thorough enough."

Wallander refrained from commenting on Björk's outburst. He knew from experience the risk of being side-tracked into a discussion that had no direct bearing on the case.

"As to the explosion in your car," Nyberg said, "we can be sure that the device was planted in your petrol tank. I gather that this method of using the petrol to eat its way through a fuse and delay the explosion is common in Asia."

"An Italian pistol," Wallander said, "and an Asian car bomb. Where does that leave us?"

"With a false conclusion, if we're not careful," Björk said firmly. "It needn't be people from the other end of the world behind all this. Nowadays Sweden is a crossroads and a meeting place for everything you can think of."

"What did you find at the solicitors' offices, Ann-Britt?"

"Nothing as yet that could be considered significant," Höglund said. "It will take us ages to take stock of all the material. The only thing that's already definite is that Gustaf Torstensson's clients diminished in number drastically over the last years. And that he seemed to spend all his time setting up companies, on financial advice, and drawing up contracts. I wonder whether we might need some help from the national CID, a specialist on financial crime. Even if no crime has been committed it's probably beyond us to make out what may be behind all the various transactions."

"Make use of Åkeson," Björk said. "He knows a lot about financial matters and crime. Then he can decide if he's sufficiently well up, or whether we need to send for reinforcements."

Wallander agreed and returned to his checklist.

"What about the cleaner?" he said.

"I'm going to meet her," Höglund said. "I've spoken to her on the phone. She speaks Swedish well enough for an interpreter to be unnecessary."

Then it was Wallander's turn. He told the meeting of his visit to Martin Oscarsson and the drive to Klagshamn and the birch woods where Borman was supposed to have hanged himself. As so often before, Wallander felt he had discovered new details when he reported to his colleagues on what had happened. Retelling the story sharpened his concentration.

When he had finished, the atmosphere in the conference room was tense. We're close to making significant progress, Wallander thought. "We have to find the link between Borman and the Torstensson firm of solicitors. What upset Borman so much that he sent threatening letters to the Torstenssons and even involved Mrs Dunér? He accused them of what he called a serious injustice. We can't be certain that it had anything to do with the scam inflicted on the County Council, but I think we would do well to assume that, for the time being, this is what it was. In any case, this is the black hole in our investigation, and we must dredge our way into it with as much energy as we can muster."

The discussion was tentative at first. Everybody needed time for what Wallander had described to sink in.

"I'm thinking about those threatening letters," Martinsson said hesitantly. "I can't get away from the feeling that they are so naive. So childish, almost innocent. I can't get a clear sense of Borman's nature."

"We'll have to find out more," Wallander said. "Let's start by tracing his children. We should also telephone his widow in Marbella."

"I'd be happy to do that," Martinsson said. "Borman interests me."

"The whole business of that investment firm Smeden will have to be thoroughly looked into," Björk said. "I suggest we contact the fraud squad in Stockholm. Or maybe it would be better for Åkeson to do that. There are people there who know as much about the business world as the most skilful investment analysts."

"I'll speak to Per," Wallander said.

They went backwards and forwards through the case all morning. Eventually they reached a point where everybody was losing their sharpness, and nobody seemed to have anything else to say. Björk had already left for one of his countless meetings with the District Chief of Police. Wallander decided it was time to bring the meeting to an end.

"Two solicitors murdered," he said. "Plus Lars Borman's suicide, if that is what it was. We have the mine in Mrs Dunér's garden, and we have my car. Let no-one forget that we're dealing with extremely dangerous people, people who are keeping a close watch on everything we do. That means we all have to be tirelessly watchful ourselves."

They gathered their papers and left.

Wallander drove to a restaurant nearby for lunch. He needed to be on his own. He was back at the police station just after 1.00, and spent the rest of the afternoon talking to the national CID and their fraud specialists. At 4.00 he went over to the prosecutor's offices and spoke at length to Åkeson. Then he returned to his own office, and did not leave until nearly 10.00.

He felt the need for fresh air. He was missing his long walks at Skagen, so he left his car at the station and walked home to Mariagatan. It was a mild evening,

221

and he occasionally paused to look in shop windows. He was home by 11.00.

Half an hour later he was surprised by the phone ringing. He had just poured himself a glass of whisky and settled to watch a film on the television. He went out to the hall and answered. It was Höglund.

"Am I disturbing you?" she said.

"Not in the least."

"I'm at the station," she said. "I think I'm on to something."

Wallander did not hesitate. She would not have rung if it hadn't been very important. "I'll be there in ten minutes," he said.

She was in the corridor, waiting for him.

"I need a cup of coffee," she said. "There's nobody in the canteen just now. Peters and Norén left a few minutes ago. There's been an accident at the Bjäresjö crossroads."

They sat down at a table with their mugs of coffee.

"There was a fellow student at college who paid his way through his studies by dealing on the Stock Exchange," she said.

Wallander looked at her in surprise.

"I phoned him," she said, almost apologetically. "It can be quicker to do things through personal contacts, if you've got any. Anyway, I told him about STRUFAB, Sisyphus and Smeden. I gave him the names Fjällsjö and Holmberg. He phoned me at home an hour ago. I came straight here."

Wallander could hardly wait to hear what was coming next.

"I made notes of everything he said. The investment company Smeden has undergone a lot of changes in recent years. Boards of directors have come and gone, and on several occasions their shares have been suspended because of suspicions of insider trading and other infringements of Stock Exchange regulations. Substantial shareholdings have been changing hands with bewildering frequency, and it's difficult to keep track of them. Smeden seems to have been a prime example of the irresponsible goings-on in the financial world. Until a few years ago. Then a number of foreign brokers, including firms in Britain, Belgium and Spain, started buying shares, very discreetly. At first there was nothing to suggest that the same purchaser was acting through these various brokerage firms. It was all done stealthily, and the brokers did nothing to attract attention to themselves. By this time everybody was so fed up with Smeden that nobody was taking the company seriously any more, least of all the mass media. Every time the Secretary-General of the Stockholm Stock Exchange met reporters, he would begin by asking them not to put questions about Smeden because he was so irritated by everything to do with the company. Then one day such substantial holdings were acquired by the same group of brokers that it was no longer possible to avoid wondering who was so interested in this dodgy company with such a bad reputation. It transpired that Smeden had fallen into the hands of a not exactly unknown Englishman called Robert Maxwell."

"The name means nothing to me," Wallander said. "Who is he?"

"Was. He's dead. He fell overboard from his luxury yacht off the Spanish coast a couple of years ago. There were rumours that he had been murdered. Something to do with Mossad, the Israeli secret service, and shadowy but large-scale arms deals. He owned newspapers and publishing houses, all registered in Liechtenstein, but when he died his empire collapsed like a house of cards. It was all built on borrowings, borrowings and embezzled pension funds. The bankruptcy was instantaneous and set off a tremendous crash."

"An Englishman?" Wallander said in astonishment. "What does that tell us?"

"That it didn't end there. The shares were passed on to somebody else."

"Who?"

"There was something going on behind the scenes," Höglund said. "Maxwell had been acting on behalf of somebody else who preferred to remain invisible. And that person was a Swede. A mysterious circle was finally closed." She stared intently at him. "Can you guess who that person is?"

"No."

"Have a guess."

The penny dropped. "Alfred Harderberg."

She nodded.

"The man at Farnholm Castle," Wallander said slowly. They sat in silence for a while.

"In other words, he also controlled STRUFAB, via Smeden," she said eventually.

Wallander looked hard at her. "Well done," he said. "Very well done."

"Thank my fellow student," she said. "He's a police officer in Eskilstuna. But there's something else as well. I don't know if it's important, but while I was waiting for you I came to think about something. Torstensson

Senior died on the way home from Farnholm Castle. Borman hanged himself. But it might be that both of them, in different ways, had discovered the same thing. What can that have been?"

"You could be right," Wallander said. "But I think we can draw one other conclusion. We might regard it as unproven but definite even so. Borman did not commit suicide. Just as Torstensson was not killed in a car accident."

They sat in silence again for a while.

"Alfred Harderberg," she said at last. "Can he really be the man behind everything that's happened?"

Wallander stared into his coffee mug. He had never asked himself that question, but he had suspected something of the kind. Yes, he could see that now.

He looked at her. "Of course it could be Harderberg," he said.

Chapter 10

Wallander would always think of the following week as a time in which the police surrounded the difficult murder investigation with invisible barricades. It was like making preparation for a complicated military campaign – in a very short time and under great pressure. It was not so outrageous a comparison, since they had designated Harderberg their enemy – a man who was not only a living legend but also a man whose power was not unlike that of a medieval prince, and this before he had even reached the age of 50.

It had all started on the Friday night, when Höglund had revealed the link with the English contact man, Robert Maxwell, and his crooked share dealings; and also the fact that the owner of the investment company Smeden was the man at Farnholm Castle, who thus took an enormous step out of the shadows of anonymity and into centre stage of the murder investigation. Wallander would afterwards agonise about not having suspected Harderberg much earlier. He would never find a satisfactory answer as to why. Whatever explanation he found, it was no more than an excuse for carelessly and negligently granting Harderberg exemption from suspicion in the early stages of the inquiry, as if Farnholm

Castle had been a sovereign territory with some kind of diplomatic immunity.

The next week changed all that. But they had been forced to proceed cautiously, not just because Björk insisted on it, with some support from Åkeson, but mainly because the facts they had to go on were very few. They knew that Gustaf Torstensson had acted as financial adviser to Harderberg, but they could not know exactly what he had done, what precisely his remit had been. And in any case, there was no evidence to suggest that Harderberg's business empire was involved in illegal activities. But now they had discovered another link: Borman and the fraud to which Malmöhus County Council had been subjected and which had been hushed up and quietly buried. On the night of Friday, November 5, Wallander and Höglund had discussed the situation until the small hours, but it had been mostly speculation. Even so, they had begun to evolve a plan for how the investigation should proceed, and it was clear to Wallander from the start that they would have to move discreetly and circumspectly. If Harderberg really was involved, and Wallander kept repeating that *if* during the next week, it was clear that he was a man with eyes and ears wherever they turned, all round the clock, no matter what they did or where they were. They had to bear in mind that the existence of links between Borman, Harderberg and one of the murdered solicitors did not necessarily amount to a beginning of a solution to the case.

Wallander was also doubtful for quite different reasons. He had spent his life in the loyal and unhesitating belief that Swedish business practices were as above reproach as the emperor's wife. The men and women at the top of the big Swedish concerns were the bedrock of the welfare state. The Swedish export industry was at the heart of the country's prosperity, and as such was simply above suspicion. Especially now, now that the whole edifice of the welfare state was showing signs of crumbling, its floorboards teeming with termites. The bedrock on which it all rested must be protected from irresponsible interference, irrespective of where it came from. But even if he had his doubts, he was still aware that they might be on the track to the solution, no matter how unlikely it might seem at first glance.

"We don't have anything substantial," he said to Höglund that Friday night at the police station. "What we do have is a link, a connection. We shall investigate it. And we'll do that with all the stops out. But we can't take it for granted that doing so will lead us to the person responsible for our murders."

They were ensconced in Wallander's office. He was surprised she had not wanted to go home as soon as possible: it was late, and unlike him she had a family to get back to. They were not going to solve anything then, it would have been better to get a good night's rest and start fresh the next morning. But she had insisted on continuing their discussions, and he was reminded of what he had been like at her age. So much police work is dull routine, but there could occasionally be moments of inspiration and excitement, an almost childish delight in playing around with feasible alternatives.

"I know it doesn't necessarily mean anything," she said. "But remember that a master criminal like Al Capone was caught out by an accountant."

"That's hardly a fair comparison," Wallander said. "You're talking about a gangster known by one and all to have built his fortune on theft, smuggling, blackmail, bribery and murder. In this case all we know is that a successful Swedish businessman has a majority shareholding in an apparently fraudulent investment company which has many activities, just one of which is that it controls a consultancy employing certain individuals who have swindled a county council. We *know* no more than that."

"They used to say that concealed behind every fortune was a major crime," she said. "Why just 'used to'? Whenever you open your newspaper nowadays it looks more like the rule than the exception."

"You can find a quotation for every situation," Wallander said. "The Japanese say that business is a form of warfare. But that doesn't justify somebody in Sweden killing people to put a few accounts into the clear. If that's what they were trying to do."

"This country is also awash with sacred cows," Höglund said. "Such as the idea that we don't need to chase up criminals with names that tell us they come from noble families, and who belong to some ancient line in Skåne with a family castle to maintain. We would rather not haul them into the courts when they've been caught with their fingers in the till."

"I've never thought like that," Wallander said, realising at once that he was not telling the truth. And what was it he was trying to defend? Or was it just that he could not allow Höglund to be right, not when she was so much younger than he was and a woman?

"I think that's how everybody thinks," she insisted. "Police officers are no different. Or prosecutors. Sacred cows must graze in peace."

They had been sailing around hidden rocks without finding a clear channel. It seemed to Wallander that their differing views indicated something he had been thinking for a long time, that the police force was being split by a generation gap. It wasn't so much that Höglund was a woman, but rather that she brought with her quite different experiences. We are both police officers, but we do not have the same view of the world, Wallander thought. We may live in the same world, but we see it differently.

Another thought occurred to him, and he did not like it one bit. What he had been saying to Höglund could just as easily have been said by Martinsson. Or Svedberg. Even Hanson, for all his non-stop further-education courses. He sat there on the Friday night talking not just with his own voice, but with that of the others. He was speaking for a whole generation. The thought annoyed him, and he blamed Höglund, who was all too self-confident, all too definite in her views. He did not enjoy being reminded of his own laziness, his own very vague views about the world and the age he was living in.

It was as if she were describing an unknown land to him. A Sweden that she was not making up, unfortunately, but one which really existed just outside the confines of the police station, filled with real people.

But the discussion petered out in the end, when Wallander had poured enough water on the fire. They went out to fetch more coffee, and were offered a sandwich by a patrolman who seemed to be worn out, or just bored stiff, and was sitting in the canteen staring into space. They went back to Wallander's office, and to avoid further discussion about sacred cows, Wallander asserted himself and proposed a session of constructive thinking.

"I had an elegant leather folder in my car when it

went up in flames," he said. "An overview I was given when I went to Farnholm Castle. I had begun reading it. It was a summary of Harderberg's empire and of the man himself, his various honorary doctorates, all his good deeds: Harderberg the patron of the arts, Harderberg the humanist, Harderberg the young people's friend, Harderberg the sports fan, Harderberg the sponsor of our cultural heritage, the enthusiastic restorer of old Öland fishing boats, Harderberg the honorary doctor of archaeology who provides generous funding for digs at what might be Iron Age dwellings in Medelpad, Harderberg the patron of music who sponsors two violinists and a bassoonist in the Gothenburg Symphony Orchestra. Founder of the Harderberg Prize for the most gifted young opera singer in the country. Generous donor to peace research in Scandinavia. And all the other things I can't remember. It was as if he were being portrayed as a one-man Swedish Academy. Without a drop of blood on his hands.

"I've asked Ebba to get hold of another copy of the file. It must be studied and investigated. As discreetly as possible we must obtain access to reports and balance sheets for all his companies. We have to find out how many companies he in fact owns. Where they are located. What they do. What they sell. What they buy. We have to examine his tax returns and his tax status. In that respect I accept what you say about Al Capone. We have to find out where Gustaf Torstensson was allowed to poke his nose in. We have to ask ourselves: why him of all people? We have to take a look into every secret room we can find. We have to wriggle our way into Harderberg's mind, not just his bank accounts. We have to talk to eleven secretaries without his noticing. Because if he does notice, a tremor will run through the whole enterprise. A tremor that will result in every door closing simultaneously. We must never forget that no matter how many resources we put into this, he will be able to send yet more troops into battle. It's always easier to close a door than it is to open it again. It's always easier to maintain a cleverly constructed lie than it is to find an unclear truth."

She listened to what he had to say with what looked to him to be genuine interest. He had set it all out for her as much to clarify things in his own mind, but he could not deny having made some small effort to squash her. He was still the senior officer around here, and she could consider herself just a snotty-nosed kid, albeit a talented one.

"We have to do all that," he said. "It could be that we end up once more with the magnificent reward of having discovered absolutely nothing. But the most important thing for the moment, and the most difficult thing, is how we are going to do all this without attracting attention. If what we suspect is true, and it's on Harderberg's orders that we're being watched, that efforts are being made to blow us up, and that it was an extension of his hand that planted the mine in Mrs Dunér's garden, then we must keep reminding ourselves all the time that he sees things and hears things. He must not notice that we are repositioning our troops. We must camouflage everything we do in thick fog. And in that fog we have to make sure that we follow the right road and that he goes astray. Where's the investigation going? That is the question we have to keep asking ourselves, and then we have to provide a very good answer."

"We have to do the opposite of what we seem to be doing, then," she said.

"Exactly," Wallander said. "We have to send out signals that say: we're not remotely interested in Alfred Harderberg."

"What happens if it's too obvious?" she said.

"It mustn't be," Wallander said. "We have to send out another signal. We have to tell the world that yes, naturally, Dr Harderberg is involved in our routine inquiries. He even attracts our special interest in certain respects."

"How can we be sure that he swallows our bait?"

"We can't. But we can send a third signal. We can say that we have a lead that we believe in. That it points in a certain direction. And that it seems to be reliable. So reliable that Harderberg can be convinced that we really are following a false trail."

"He's bound to take out a few insurance policies even so."

"Yes. We shall have to make sure we find out what they are," he said. "And we mustn't show him that we know. We must not give the impression we are stupid, a bunch of blind and deaf police officers who are leading one another in the wrong direction. We must identify his insurance tactics, but appear to misinterpret them. We must hold up a mirror to our own strategy, and then interpret the mirror image."

She eyed him thoughtfully. "Are we really going to be able to manage this? Will Björk go along with it? What will Mr Åkeson have to say?"

"That will be our first big problem," Wallander said. "Convincing ourselves that we've got the right strategy. Our Chief of Police has an attribute which makes up for a lot of his weaker points: he sees through us if we don't believe in what we say or suggest as the starting point for our investigation. In such circumstances he puts his foot down, and rightly so."

"And when we've convinced ourselves? Where do we start?"

"We have to make sure we do not fail in too much of what we set ourselves to do. We have to lose our way so cleverly in the fog that Harderberg believes it. We have to lose our way and be following the right road at the same time."

She went back to her office to fetch a notepad. Meanwhile, Wallander sat listening to a dog barking somewhere inside the station. When she came back, it struck him again that she was an attractive woman, despite the fact that she was very pale, and had blotchy skin and dark rings under her eyes.

They went through Wallander's pronouncements once again. All the time Höglund kept coming up with relevant comments, finding flaws in Wallander's reasoning, homing in on contradictions. He noticed, however reluctantly, that he was inspired by her, and that she was very clear-headed. It struck him – at 2 a.m. – that he had not had a conversation like this since Rydberg died. He imagined Rydberg coming back to life and putting his vast experience at the disposal of this pale young woman.

They left the station together. It was cold, the sky was full of stars, the ground was covered in frost.

"We'll have a long meeting tomorrow," Wallander said. "There'll be any number of objections, but I'll talk to Björk and Åkeson ahead of time. I'll ask Per to sit in on the meeting. If we don't get them on our side, we'll lose too much time trying to dig up new facts just in order to convince them."

She seemed surprised. "Surely they must see we're right?"

"We can't be sure of that."

"It sometimes seems to me that the Swedish police force is very slow to catch on to things."

"You don't need to be a recent graduate of Police Training College to reach that conclusion," Wallander said. "Björk has calculated that given the current increase in administrators and others who don't actually do work in the field, as investigators or on traffic duties, that kind of thing, all normal police work will grind to a halt around 2010. By which time every police officer will just sit around all day passing bits of paper to other police officers."

She laughed. "Maybe we're in the wrong job," she said.

"Not the wrong job," Wallander said, "but maybe we're living at the wrong time."

They said goodnight and drove home in their own cars. Wallander kept an eye on the rear-view mirror, but could not see anybody following him. He was very tired, but at the same time inspired by the fact that a door had opened up into the current investigation. The coming days were going to be very strenuous.

On the morning of Saturday, November 6, Wallander phoned Björk at 7.00. His wife answered, and asked Wallander to try again a few minutes later as her husband was in the bath. Wallander used the time to phone Åkeson, who he knew was an early riser and generally up and about by 5.00. Åkeson picked up the phone immediately. Wallander summarised briefly what had happened, and why Harderberg had become relevant to the investigation in quite a new light. Åkeson listened without interruption. When Wallander had finished, he made just one comment.

"Are you convinced you can make this stick?"

Wallander replied without a moment's hesitation: "Yes," he said. "I think this can solve the problem for us."

"In that case, of course, I've no objection to our concentrating on digging deeper. But make sure it's all discreet. Say nothing to the media without consulting me first. What we need least of all is a Palme situation here in Ystad."

Wallander could quite see what Åkeson meant. The unsolved assassination of the Swedish prime minister, a mystery now getting on for ten years old, had not only stunned the police but had also shocked nearly everyone in Sweden. Too many people, both inside and outside the police force, were aware that in all probability the murder had not been solved because at an early stage the investigation had been dominated and mishandled in scandalous fashion by a district police chief who had put himself in charge in spite of being incompetent to run a criminal investigation. Every local force discussed over and over, sometimes angrily and sometimes contemptuously, how it had been possible for the murder, the murderer and the motive to be brushed under the carpet with such nonchalance. One of the most catastrophic errors in that disastrous investigation had been the insistence of the officers in charge on pursuing certain leads without first establishing priorities. Wallander agreed with Åkeson: an investigation had to be more or less concluded before the police had the green light to put all their eggs into one basket.

"I'd like you to be there when we discuss the case this morning," Wallander said. "We have to be absolutely clear about what we're doing. I don't want the investigation team to be split. That would prevent us from being able to react rapidly to any new development."

"I'll be there," Åkeson said. "I was supposed to be playing golf today. Mind you, given the weather, I'd rather not."

"It's probably pretty hot in Uganda," Wallander said. "Or was it the Sudan?"

"I haven't even raised the subject with my wife yet," Åkeson said in a low voice.

After that call, Wallander drank another cup of coffee and then called Björk again. This time it was the man himself who answered. Wallander had decided not to say anything about what had happened the first time he visited Farnholm Castle. He would rather not do that on the phone, he needed to be face to face with Björk. He was brief and to the point.

"We need to meet and discuss what's happened," Wallander said. "Something, that is, which is going to change the whole direction of the case."

"What's happened?" Björk said.

"I'd sooner not discuss it over the phone," Wallander said.

"You're not suggesting our phones are being tapped, I hope?" Björk said. "We need to keep things in perspective after all."

"It's not that," Wallander said, although it struck him that he had never considered that possibility. It was too late to do anything about it now – he had already told Åkeson how things were going to develop from now on.

"I need to see you briefly before the investigation meeting starts," he said.

"OK, half an hour from now," Björk said. "But I don't understand why you're being so secretive."

"I'm not being secretive," Wallander said. "But it's sometimes better to discuss crucial things face to face."

"That sounds pretty dramatic to me," Björk said. "I wonder if we shouldn't contact Per."

"I've done that already," Wallander said. "I'll be in your office in half an hour."

Before meeting Björk, Wallander sat in his car outside the police station for a few minutes, gathering his thoughts. He considered cancelling the whole thing, perhaps there were more important things to do; but then he acknowledged that he had to make it clear to Björk that Harderberg must be treated like any other Swedish citizen. Failure to reach that understanding would lead inevitably to a crisis of confidence that would end up with Wallander's resignation. He thought how quickly things had moved. It was only just over a week since he had been pacing up and down the beach at Skagen, preparing to say goodbye for ever to his life as a police officer. Now he was feeling that he had to defend his position and his integrity as a police officer. He must write about all this to Baiba as soon as he could.

Would she be able to understand why everything had changed? Did he really understand it himself?

He went to Björk's office and sat on his visitors' sofa.

"What on earth's happened?" Björk said.

"There's something I must say before we go into the

meeting," Wallander said, and realised his voice sounded hesitant.

"Don't tell me you've decided to resign again," Björk said, looking worried.

"No," Wallander said. "I have to know why you phoned Farnholm Castle and warned them that the Ystad police were going to contact them in connection with the murder investigation. I have to know why you didn't tell me or the others that you had phoned."

Wallander could see Björk was put out and annoyed.

"Alfred Harderberg is an important man in our society," Björk said. "He's not suspected of any criminal activity. It was purely politeness on my part. Might I ask how you know about the phone call?"

"They were too well prepared when I got there."

"I don't see that as being negative," Björk said. "Given the circumstances."

"But it was inappropriate even so," Wallander said. "Inappropriate in more ways than one. And besides, such goings-on can create unrest in the investigation team. We have to be absolutely frank with one another."

"I have to say that I find it difficult being lectured by you – of all people – on frankness," Björk said, no longer hiding the fact that he was furious.

"My shortcomings are no excuse for others acting in that way," Wallander said. "Not my superior in any case."

Björk rose to his feet. "I will not allow myself to be addressed in that manner," he said, going red in the face. "It was pure politeness, nothing more. In the circumstances, a routine conversation. It couldn't have had any adverse effect."

"Those circumstances no longer apply," Wallander

said, realising he was not going to get any further. The important thing now was to apprise Björk as quickly as possible as to how the whole situation had changed.

Björk was staring at him, still on his feet. "Express yourself more clearly," he said. "I don't understand what you mean."

"Information has come to light which suggests that Alfred Harderberg could be behind everything that's happened," Wallander said. "That would surely imply that the circumstances have changed quite dramatically."

Björk sat down again, incredulous. "What do you mean?"

"I mean that we have reason to believe that Harderberg is directly or indirectly mixed up in the murder of the two solicitors. And the attempted murder of Mrs Dunér. And the blowing up of my car."

Björk stared at him in disbelief. "Am I really expected to take that seriously?"

"Yes, you are," Wallander said. "Åkeson does."

Wallander gave Björk a brisk summary of what had happened. When he had finished, Björk sat looking at his hands before responding.

"It would be very unpleasant, of course, if this were to turn out to be true," he said in the end.

"Murder and explosions are certainly unpleasant things," Wallander said.

"We must be very, very careful," Björk said, apparently ignoring Wallander's comment. "We can't accept anything short of conclusive proof before we consider making a move."

"We don't normally do that," Wallander said. "Why should this case be any different?"

"I have no doubt at all that this will turn out to be

a dead end," Björk said, getting to his feet to indicate that the conversation was over.

"That is a possibility," Wallander said. "So is the opposite."

It was 8.10 when he left Björk's office. He fetched a cup of coffee and called in at Höglund's office, but she had not yet arrived. He went to his office to telephone Waldemar Kåge, the taxi driver in Simrishamn. He got through to him on his mobile and explained what it was about. He made a note that he should send Kåge a cheque for 230 kronor. He wondered if he should phone the haulage contractor his father had punched and try to persuade him not to take the case to court, but decided against it. The meeting was due to start at 8.30. He needed to concentrate until then.

He stood at the window. It was a grey day, very cold and damp. Late autumn already, winter just round the corner. I'm here, he thought: I wonder where Harderberg is right now. At Farnholm Castle? Or 30,000 feet up, in his Gulfstream, on the way to and from some intricate negotiation? What had Gustaf Torstensson and Borman discovered? What had really happened? What if Höglund and I are right, if two police officers of different generations, each with their own view of what the world is like, have come to the same conclusion? A conclusion that might even lead us to the truth?

Wallander came into the conference room at 8.30. Björk was already at the short end of the table, Åkeson was standing by the window, looking out, and Martinsson and Svedberg were deep in conversation about what sounded to Wallander like salaries. Höglund was in her usual place opposite Björk at the other short end of the table. Neither Martinsson nor Svedberg seemed to be worried by Åkeson being there.

Wallander said good morning to Höglund. "How do you think this is going to go?" he asked softly.

"When I woke up I thought I must have dreamed it all," she said. "Have you spoken yet to Björk and Åkeson?"

"Åkeson knows most of what happened," he said. "I only had time to give Björk the short version."

"What did Åkeson say?"

"He'll go along with us."

Björk tapped on the table with a pencil and those who were still standing sat down.

"All I have to say is that Kurt is going to do the talking," Björk said. "Unless I am much mistaken, it looks as though there might have been a dramatic development."

Wallander wondered what to say, his mind a sudden blank. Then he found the thread and began. He went through in detail what Höglund's colleague in Eskilstuna had been able to enlighten them about, and he set out the ideas that had developed in the early hours of the morning, about how they should proceed without waking the sleeping bear. When he had finished – and his account lasted 25 minutes – he asked Höglund if she had anything to add, but she shook her head: Wallander had said all there was to say.

"So, that's where we've got to," Wallander said. "Because this means that we have no choice but to reassess our priorities for the investigation, we have got Per with us. Another consideration is whether we need to call in outside help at this stage. It's going to be a very tricky and in many ways a laborious process, penetrating

Harderberg's world, especially since we can't afford to let him notice how interested in him we are."

Wallander was not sure whether he had succeeded in putting across all the things he had wanted to. Höglund smiled and nodded at him, but when he studied the other faces around the table he still could not tell.

"This really is something for us to get our teeth into," Åkeson said when the silence had lasted long enough. "We must be clear about the fact that Alfred Harderberg has an impeccable reputation in the Swedish business community. We can expect nothing but hostility if we start questioning that reputation. On the other hand, I have to say there are sufficient grounds for us to start taking a special interest in him. Naturally, I find it difficult to believe that Harderberg was personally involved in the murders or the other events, and of course it might be that things happen in his set-up over which he has no control."

"I've always dreamed of putting one of those gentlemen away," Svedberg suddenly said.

"A most regrettable attitude in a police officer," Björk said, unable to control his displeasure. "It shouldn't be necessary for me to remind you all of our status as neutral civil servants – "

"Let's stick to the point," Åkeson interrupted. "And perhaps we should also remind ourselves that in our role as servants of the law we are paid to be suspicious in circumstances in which normally we would not need to be."

"So we have the go-ahead to concentrate on Harderberg, is that right?" Wallander asked.

"On certain conditions," Björk said. "I agree with Per that we have to be very careful and prudent, but I also want to stress that I shall regard it as dereliction of duty if anything we do is leaked outside these four walls. No statements are to be made to the press without their first having been authorised by me."

"We gathered that," said Martinsson, speaking for the first time. "I'm more concerned to find out how we're going to manage to run a vacuum cleaner over the whole of Harderberg's empire when there are so few of us. How are we going to coordinate our investigation with the fraud squads in Stockholm and Malmö? How are we going to cooperate with the tax authorities? I wonder if we shouldn't approach it quite differently."

"How would we do that?" Wallander said.

"Hand the whole thing over to the national CID," Martinsson said. "Then they can arrange cooperation with whichever squads and authorities they like. I think we have to concede that we're too small to handle this."

"That thought had occurred to me too," Åkeson said. "But at this stage, before we've even made an initial investigation, the fraud squads in Stockholm and Malmö would probably turn us down. I don't know if you realise this, but they're probably even more overworked than we are. There are not many of us, but they are so understaffed they're verging on collapse. We'll have to take charge of this ourselves for the time being at least. Do the best we can. Nevertheless, I'll see if I can interest the fraud squads in helping us. You never know."

Looking back, Wallander had no doubt that it was what Åkeson had to say about the hopeless situation the national CID were in that established once and for all the basis of the investigation. The murder investigation would be centred on Harderberg and the links between him and Lars Borman and him and the dead solicitors.

Wallander and his team would also be on their own. It was true that the Ystad police were always having to deal with fraud cases of various kinds, but this was so much bigger than anything they had come across before, and they did not know of any financial impropriety associated with the deaths of the two solicitors.

In short, they had to start looking for an answer to the question: what were they really looking for?

When Wallander wrote to Baiba in Riga a few nights later and told her about "the secret hunt", as he had started to call the investigation, he realised that as he wrote to her in English, he would have to explain that hunting in Sweden was different from an English fox hunt. "There's a hunter in every police officer," he had written. "There is rarely, if ever, a fanfare of horns when a Swedish police officer is after his prey. But we find the foxes we are after even so. Without us, the Swedish hen house would long since have been empty: all that remained would have been a scattering of bloodstained feathers blowing around in the autumn breeze."

The whole team approached their task with enthusiasm. Björk removed the lid of the box where generally he kept overtime locked away. He urged everybody on, reminding them again that not a word of their activities must leak out. Åkeson had removed his jacket, loosened his tie which was usually so neatly knotted, and become one of the workers, even if he never let slip his authority as ultimate leader of the operation that was now getting under way.

But it was Wallander who called the shots; he could feel that, and it gave him frequent moments of deep satisfaction. Thanks to unexpected circumstances and the goodwill of his colleagues, which he scarcely deserved, he had been given an opportunity to atone for some of the guilt he felt after rejecting the confidence Sten Torstensson had shown in him by coming to Skagen and asking for his help. Leading the search for Sten's murderer and the murderer of his father was enabling Wallander to redeem himself. He had been so preoccupied with his own private woes that he had failed to hear Sten's cry for help, had not allowed it to penetrate the barricades he had built around his all-consuming depression.

He wrote another letter to Baiba that he never posted. In it he tried to explain to her, and hence also to himself, just what it meant, killing a man last year and now, adding to his guilt, rejecting Sten Torstensson's plea for help. The conclusion he seemed to reach, even though he doubted it deep down, was that Sten's death had started to trouble him more than the events of the previous year on the fog-bound training area, surrounded by invisible sheep.

But nothing of this was discernible to those around him. In the canteen his colleagues would comment in confidence that Wallander's return to duty and to health was as much a surprise as it would have been if he had taken up his bed and walked when he had been at his lowest. Martinsson, who was sometimes unable to hold his cynicism in check, said: "What Kurt needed was a challenging murder. Not some nervous, carelessly executed manslaughter committed on the spur of the moment. The dead solicitors, a mine in a garden and some Far Eastern explosive mixture in his petrol tank – that was just what he needed to bring him back to the fold."

The others agreed that there was more than a grain of truth in what Martinsson said.

It took them a week to complete the exhaustive survey of Harderberg's empire that would be the platform for the rest of the investigation. During that week neither Wallander nor any of his colleagues slept for more than five hours at a time. They would later look back at that period and conclude that a mouse really could roar if it had to. Even Åkeson, who was rarely impressed by anything, had to doff his non-existent hat to what the team had achieved.

"Not a word of this must get out," he said to Wallander one evening when they had gone outside for a breath of fresh autumn air, trying to drive away their tiredness. Wallander did not at first understand what he meant.

"If this gets out, the Central Police Bureau and the Ministry of Justice will set up an inquiry that will eventually lead to something called the 'Ystad Model' being presented to the Swedish public: how to achieve outstanding results with minimal resources. We'll be used as proof that the Swedish police force is not undermanned at all. We'll be used as evidence to show that in fact there are too many police officers. So many that they keep getting in each other's way and that gives rise to a great waste of money and deteriorating clear-up rates."

"But we haven't achieved any results at all yet," Wallander said.

"I'm talking about the Central Police Bureau," Åkeson said. "I'm talking about the mysterious world of politics. A world where masses of words are used to camouflage the fact that they're doing nothing but straining at a gnat and swallowing a camel. Where they go to bed every night and pray that the next day they'll be able to turn water into wine. I'm not talking about the fact that we haven't yet discovered who killed the two solicitors. I'm talking about the fact that we now know that Alfred Harderberg is not the model citizen, superior to all others, that we thought he was."

That was absolutely true. During that hectic week they had managed to build a bird's-eye view of Harderberg's empire that naturally was by no means comprehensive, but they could see that the gaps – indeed, the black holes – indicated quite clearly that the man who lived in Farnholm Castle should not be allowed out of their sight for one minute.

When Åkeson and Wallander stood outside the police station that night, on November 14 to be exact, they had got far enough to be able to draw certain conclusions. The first phase was over, the beaters had done their work and the hunters could prepare to move in. Nothing had leaked out, and they had begun to discern the shape and nature of the leviathan in which Lars Borman and more especially Gustaf Torstensson must have discovered something it would have been safer for them not to have seen.

The question was: what?

It had been a hectic time, but Wallander had organised his troops well and had not hesitated to take on the most boring work himself – which often proved to produce the most interesting information. They had gone through the story of Harderberg's life, from the day he was born, the son of an alcoholic timber merchant in Vimmerby, when he was known as Hansson, to the present day when he was the driving force of an enterprise with

248

a turnover of billions in Sweden and abroad. At one point during the laborious exercise, wading through company reports and accounts, tax returns and share brochures, Svedberg said: "It's simply not possible for a man who owns as much as this to be honest." In the end it was Sven Nyberg, the surly and irritable forensic specialist, who gave them the information they needed. As so often happens, it was pure coincidence that he stumbled upon the tiny crack in Harderberg's immaculately rendered wall, the barely visible fault they had craved. And if Wallander, despite his exhaustion, had not picked up on a remark Nyberg made as he was on his way out of Wallander's office late one night, the opportunity might have slipped away.

It was nearly midnight on Wednesday and Wallander was poring over a résumé Höglund had drawn up on Harderberg's worldly possessions when Nyberg belted on the door. Nyberg was not a discreet person; he stamped down corridors and he belted on doors, as if he were about to make an arrest, when he visited his fellow officers. That night he had just completed the forensic lab's preliminary report on the mine in Mrs Dunér's garden and the blowing up of Wallander's car.

"I thought you would want the results right away," he said after flopping down on one of Wallander's visitors' chairs.

"What have you got?" Wallander said, peering at Nyberg with red-rimmed eyes.

"Nothing," Nyberg said.

"Nothing?"

"You heard." Nyberg was irritated. "That's also a result. It's not possible to say for certain where the mine was manufactured. We think it might be from a factory

249

in Belgium, a company called Poudreris Réunie de Belgique or however you pronounce it. The explosive used suggests that. And we didn't find any splinters, which means that the force of the mine was upwards. That also suggests Belgian in origin. But it could also have been from somewhere else entirely. As for your car, we can't say definitely that there was explosive material in your petrol tank. In other words we can't say anything at all for sure. So the result is nothing."

"I believe you," Wallander said, searching through his pile of papers for a note he had made about what he wanted to ask Nyberg.

"And that Italian pistol, the Bernadelli, we don't know any more about that either," Nyberg said while Wallander made notes. "There's no report of one having been stolen. All the people registered in Sweden as owning one have been able to produce it. Now it's up to you and Per Åkeson to decide whether we should call them all in and give them a test firing."

"Do you think that would be worth it?"

"Yes and no," Nyberg said. "Personally, I think we ought to run a check on stolen Smith & Wessons first. That'll take a few more days."

"We'll do as you suggest, then," Wallander said, making a note. Then they went on going through Nyberg's points.

"We didn't find any fingerprints in the solicitors' offices," Nyberg said. "Whoever shot Sten Torstensson didn't press his thumb helpfully on the window pane. An inspection of the threatening letters from Lars Borman produced negative results as well. But we did establish that it was his handwriting. Svedberg has samples from both of his children."

"What did they say about the language?" Wallander asked. "I forgot to ask Svedberg."

"What do you mean, the language?"

"The letters were very oddly phrased."

"I have a vague memory from one of our meetings that Svedberg said that Borman was word blind."

"Word blind?" Wallander frowned. "I don't remember hearing that."

"Maybe you'd left the room to fetch more coffee?"

"Could be. I'll have a word with Svedberg. Have you got anything else?"

"I went to give Gustaf Torstensson's car the once-over," Nyberg said. "No fingerprints there either. I examined the ignition and the boot, and I've spoken to the pathologist in Malmö. We're almost certain that he didn't get the fatal blow to the back of his head by hitting it against the car roof. There's nothing anywhere in the bodywork that matches the wound. So it's more probable that somebody hit him. He must have been outside the car when it happened. Unless there was somebody in the back seat."

"I thought about that," Wallander said. "The likelihood is that he stopped on the road and got out of the car. Somebody came up behind him and hit him. Then the accident was faked. But why did he stop in the fog? Why did he get out?"

"I couldn't say," Nyberg said.

Wallander put down his pen and leaned back in his chair. His back ached, and he needed to go home and get some sleep.

"The only thing of note we found in the car was a plastic container made in France," Nyberg said.

"What was in it?"

"Nothing."

"Why is it interesting, then?"

Nyberg shrugged and got up to leave. "I've seen a similar one before. Four years ago. When I was on a study visit at the hospital in Lund."

"The hospital?"

"I have a good memory. It was identical."

"What was it used for?"

Nyberg was already at the door. "How should I know?" he said. "But the container we found in Torstensson's car was chemically clean. Only a container that's never contained *anything* could be as clean as that one."

Nyberg left. Wallander could hear him stamping down the corridor.

Then he pushed the heap of paper to one side and stood up to go home. He put on his jacket, then paused. There was something Nyberg had said. Just before he left the room. Something about the plastic container.

Then it came to him, and he sat down again.

There's something funny there, he thought. Why would there be a plastic container that has never been used in Torstensson's car? An empty container, but evidently a very special one? There was only one possible answer.

When Torstensson left Farnholm Castle, the container had not been empty. There had been something in it. Which meant that this was not the same container. It had been exchanged for the other one. On the road in the fog. When Torstensson stopped and got out of his car. And was killed.

Wallander checked his watch. After midnight. He waited for a quarter of an hour, then he phoned Nyberg at home.

"What the hell do you want now?" Nyberg said as soon as he recognised Wallander's voice.

"Get yourself over here," Wallander said. "Now, right away."

He expected Nyberg to explode in fury, but he said nothing, just put down the receiver.

At 12.40 a.m., Nyberg was back in Wallander's office once more.

Chapter 11

That conversation with Nyberg in the middle of the night was crucial. It seemed to Wallander that yet again he had confirmation of the fact that criminal investigations achieve a breakthrough when it is least expected. Many of Wallander's colleagues thought this proved that even police officers needed a bit of luck now and again to find their way out of a cul-de-sac. Wallander said nothing, but he thought that what it really proved was that Rydberg was right to maintain that a good police officer must always listen to what his intuition tells him – without discarding his critical faculties, of course. He had known – without knowing why he knew – that the plastic container in Torstensson's wrecked car was important. And although he was exhausted, he also knew that he could not wait until the next day to have his suspicions confirmed. That's why he had phoned Nyberg, who had just walked into his office. He had anticipated an angry outburst from his temperamental colleague, but none had been forthcoming. Nyberg had simply sat down in the visitor's chair, and Wallander noted to his surprise that he was wearing pyjamas under his overcoat. He had wellingtons on as well.

"You must have gone straight to bed," Wallander said. "If I'd known that I wouldn't have phoned."

"Are you telling me you've called me out for nothing?"

Wallander shook his head. "It's the plastic container," he said. "Tell me more about it."

"I've no more to say than I have already," Nyberg said.

Wallander sat down at his desk and looked hard at Nyberg. He knew that Nyberg was not only a good forensic officer, but that he had imagination too, and was blessed with an exceptional memory.

"You said you'd seen a similar container before," he said.

"Not a similar one," Nyberg said. "An identical one."

"That means it must be special," Wallander said. "Can you describe it for me?"

"Wouldn't it be better if I fetched it?"

"Let's go and look at it together," Wallander said, getting up.

The police station was deserted as they walked down the corridor. A radio could be heard in the distance. Nyberg unlocked the room where the police kept objects material to ongoing investigations. The container was on a shelf. Nyberg took it down and handed it to Wallander. It was rectangular, and reminded Wallander of a cool box. He put it on a table and tried to open the lid.

"It's screwed down," Nyberg said. "Notice also that it's perfectly airtight. There's a window on this side. I don't know what it's for, but I suspect there ought to be a thermometer mounted on the inside."

"You saw a similar one at the hospital in Lund," Wallander said, scrutinising the container. "Can you remember where? Which ward?"

255

"It was moving around," Nyberg said. "It was in a corridor outside the operating theatres. A nurse came with it. I seem to remember she was in a hurry."

"Anything else?"

"No, nothing."

"It reminds me of a cool box," Wallander said.

"I think that's what it is," Nyberg said. "For blood, possibly."

"I need you to find out," Wallander said. "I also want to know what that container was doing in Torstensson's car the night he died."

When they were back in Wallander's office, he remembered something Nyberg had said earlier in the evening.

"You said you thought it was made in France."

"It said 'Made in France' on the handle."

"I didn't notice that."

"The text on the one I saw in Lund was more obvious," Nyberg said. "I think we can excuse you."

"I may be wrong," Wallander said, "but I reckon the fact that this container was in Torstensson's car *is* remarkable. What was it doing there? Are you sure it was unused?"

"When I unscrewed the lid I could see that it was the first time it had been opened since it left the factory. Do you want me to explain how I knew?"

"It's enough to know that you're sure," Wallander said. "I wouldn't understand anyway."

"I can see you believe this container is important," Nyberg said, "but it's not unusual to find unexpected items in crashed cars."

"In this case we can't overlook a single detail," Wallander said.

"But we've never done that."

Wallander stood up. "Thank you for coming back," he said. "I'd like to know what the plastic container was used for sometime tomorrow."

They said goodnight outside the station. Wallander drove home and had a couple of sandwiches before going to bed. He couldn't sleep, and after tossing and turning for some time he got up again and went into the kitchen. He sat at the table without switching on the light. He felt uneasy and impatient. This investigation had too many loose ends. Even though they had decided on a way forward, he was still not convinced it was the right way. Had they overlooked something vital? He thought back to the day when Sten Torstensson came to see him on the Jutland coast. He could recall their conversation word for word. Even so, he wondered if he had missed the real message, whether there had been some other significance behind Sten's words.

It was gone 4.00 by the time he went back to bed. A wind had got up outside, and the temperature had plummeted. He shivered when he slid between the sheets. He did not think he had got anywhere. Nor had he succeeded in convincing himself that he would have to be patient. What he demanded of his colleagues was something he could not manage himself on this occasion.

When Wallander arrived at the station just before 8 a.m. there was a gale blowing. They told him in reception there were forecasts of hurricane-strength gusts before lunch. As he walked to his office he wondered if his father's house in Löderup would survive the winds. His conscience had been nagging him for some time over his failure to have the roof repaired, and there was a real risk that one violent storm would blow it right off. He sat at his desk thinking that he had better phone his father – he hadn't spoken to him since the fight at the off-licence. He was about to pick up the receiver when the phone rang.

"There's a call for you," Ebba said. "And have you noticed how strong the wind is?"

"I can console you with the news that it's going to get worse," Wallander said. "Who is it?"

"Farnholm Castle."

Wallander stretched out in his chair.

"Put them on," he said.

"It's a lady with a remarkable name," Ebba said. "She introduced herself as Jenny Lind."

"It sounds normal enough to me."

"I didn't say it was abnormal, I said it was remarkable. You must have heard of the Swedish Nightingale, the great singer Jenny Lind?"

"Put her through," Wallander said.

The voice he heard was that of a young woman. One more of all those secretaries, Wallander thought.

"Inspector Wallander?"

"Speaking."

"You were here the other day and expressed a wish to have an audience with Dr Harderberg."

"I don't do audiences," Wallander said in irritation. "I need to speak to him in connection with a murder investigation."

"I do realise that. We have received a telex this morning informing us that Dr Harderberg will be back home this afternoon and will be able to receive you tomorrow."

"Where did the telex come from?"

"Does that matter?"

"I wouldn't have asked otherwise," Wallander lied.

"Dr Harderberg is at the moment in Barcelona."

"I don't want to wait until tomorrow," Wallander said. "I need to talk to him as soon as possible. If he gets back to Sweden this afternoon he should be able to see me this evening."

"He has nothing in his diary for this evening," Lind said. "But I shall need to contact him in Barcelona before I can give you an answer."

"Do that if you wish," Wallander said. "Tell him he'll be receiving a visit from the Ystad police at 7 p.m."

"I'm afraid I can't agree to that. Dr Harderberg always decides on the time of visits himself."

"Not in this case," Wallander said. "We'll be there at 7.00."

"There will be someone else with you?"

"Yes."

"Could I ask for that person's name?"

"You may ask, but you won't get it. There will be another police officer from Ystad."

"I'll contact Dr Harderberg," Lind said. "You should be aware that he sometimes changes his plans at very short notice. He could be forced to go somewhere else before coming home."

"I can't allow that," Wallander said, fearing that he was far exceeding his authority in saying so.

"I must say you surprise me," Lind said. "Can a police officer really decide what Dr Harderberg does or doesn't do?"

Wallander continued to exceed his authority. "I have only to speak to a prosecutor – he can issue demands," Wallander said.

He realised his mistake even as he spoke. They had decided to tread carefully. Harderberg would be asked some questions, but as important as his answers was convincing him that their interest in him was purely routine. He tried to tone down what he had said.

"Dr Harderberg is suspected of nothing illegal, let me make that clear," he said. "It's just that we need to speak to him at the earliest possible moment, for reasons to do with our investigation. No doubt a prominent citizen like Dr Harderberg will be anxious to help the police solve a serious crime."

"I'll contact him," Lind repeated.

"Thank you for ringing," Wallander said and replaced the receiver.

A thought had struck him. With Ebba's help he tracked down Martinsson and asked him to come to his office.

"Harderberg has been in touch," he said. "He's in Barcelona, but on his way home. I thought of taking Ann-Britt with me and going to see him this evening."

"She's at home. Her kid's not well," Martinsson said. "She's just phoned."

"You can come instead, in that case," Wallander said.

"That's fine by me," Martinsson said. "I want to see that aquarium with gold dust for sand."

"There's another matter," Wallander said. "What do you know about aeroplanes?"

"Not a lot."

"I had a thought," Wallander said. "Harderberg has a private jet. A Gulfstream, whatever that is. It must be registered somewhere. There must be flight logs showing when he's out on his travels, and where he goes to."

"If nothing else he must have a few pilots," Martinsson said. "I'll look into it."

"Give that job to somebody else," Wallander said. "You've got more important things to do."

"Ann-Britt can do it from her phone at home," Martinsson said. "I think she'll be pleased to be doing something useful."

"She could develop into a good police officer."

"Let's hope so," Martinsson said. "But to tell you the truth, we have no way of knowing. All we know is that she did well at college."

"You're right," Wallander said. "It's awfully hard to imitate reality at a college."

After Martinsson had left, Wallander sat down to prepare for the meeting at 9.00. When he had woken that morning, all the thoughts he had had during the night about the loose ends of the investigation were still in the forefront of his mind. He had decided they would have to write off anything they judged to be of no immediate relevance to the investigation. If eventually they concluded that the route they had decided on was a cul-de-sac, they could always go back to the loose ends. But only then could the loose ends be allowed to occupy their attention.

Wallander pushed aside all the papers piled up on his desk and put an empty sheet in front of him. Many years ago Rydberg had taught him a way of approaching an investigation in a new light. We have to keep moving from one lookout tower to another, Rydberg had said. If we don't, our overviews become meaningless. No matter how complicated an investigation is, it has to be possible to describe it to a child. We have to see things simply, but without simplifying.

Wallander wrote: "Once upon a time there was an old solicitor who paid a visit to a rich man in his castle. On the way back home somebody killed him and tried to make us believe it had been a car accident. Soon afterwards his son was shot dead in his office. He had begun to suspect there hadn't been a car accident after all, and so he had been to see me to ask for help. He had made a secret trip to Denmark although his secretary was told he had gone to Finland. She had also had a postcard from there. A few days later somebody planted a mine in the garden of the secretary. A wide-awake officer from Ystad noticed that I was being followed by a car as we drove to Helsingborg. The solicitors had received threatening letters from an accountant working for a county council. The accountant later committed suicide by hanging himself in a tree near Malmö, although the probability is that he, too, was murdered. Just as with the car accident, the suicide was contrived. All these incidents are linked, but there is no obvious thread. Nothing has been stolen and there is no sign of passions such as hatred or jealousy running high. All that was left behind was a strange plastic container. And now we start all over again. Once upon a time there was an old solicitor who paid a visit to a rich man in his castle."

Wallander put down his pen.

Alfred Harderberg, he thought. A modern-day Silk Knight. Lurking in the background, everybody's background. Flying all over the world and doing his business deals that are so difficult to penetrate, as if it were all a kind of ritual for which only the initiated know the rules.

He read through what he had written. The words were transparent, but there was nothing in them to put the investigation in a new light. Least of all was there anything to suggest that Harderberg might be involved.

This must be something very big, Wallander thought. If my suspicions are right and he really is behind all this, then Gustaf Torstensson – and Borman too – must have discovered something that threatened his whole empire. Presumably Sten did not know what it was or he would have told me. But he came to visit me and he suspected he was being watched, and that turned out to be true. They could not take the risk of him passing on what he knew. Nor could they risk Mrs Dunér knowing anything.

This must be something very big, he thought again. Something so big that might nevertheless fit into a plastic container that reminds you of a cool box.

Wallander went to fetch another cup of coffee. Then he phoned his father.

"It's blowing a gale," Wallander said. "There's a risk your roof might get blown off."

"I'm looking forward to that," his father said.

"Looking forward to what?"

"Seeing my roof flying off over the fields like a bird. I've never seen anything like that before."

"I ought to have had it repaired ages ago," Wallander said, "but I'll make sure it's done before winter sets in."

"I'll believe that when I see it," his father said. "It would mean you'd have to come here."

"I'll make time. Have you thought over what happened in Simrishamn?"

"What is there to think over?" his father said. "I just did what was right."

"You can't just attack people at the drop of a hat," Wallander said.

"I'm not going to pay any fines," his father said. "I'm not going to prison either."

"There's no question of that," Wallander said. "I'll phone you tonight to find out what's happened to the roof. There might be hurricane-strength gusts."

"Maybe I ought to climb up on the chimney."

"What on earth for?"

"So that I can go flying myself."

"You'll kill yourself. Isn't Gertrud there?"

"I'll take her with me," said his father, and put the receiver down.

Wallander was left sitting there with the telephone in his hand. Björk came in at that very moment.

"I can wait if you're going to make a call," Björk said.

Wallander put the receiver down.

"I heard from Martinsson that Dr Harderberg has shown signs of life," Björk said.

"Was that a question?" he said. "If so, I can confirm that what Martinsson says is correct. Except that it wasn't Harderberg who phoned. He's in Barcelona and is expected back later today. I asked for a meeting this evening."

Wallander could see Björk was put out.

"Martinsson said that he would be going with you," Björk said. "I wonder if that's appropriate."

"Why shouldn't it be?" Wallander said, surprised.

"I don't mean that Martinsson isn't suitable," Björk said. "I just thought perhaps I ought to go."

"Why?"

"Well, after all, Harderberg isn't just anybody."

"You're not as familiar with the case as Martinsson is. We're not going on a social call."

"If I went with you it might have a calming effect on the whole thing. We agreed we should be careful – Dr Harderberg mustn't be upset."

Although Wallander was annoyed that Björk wanted to go with him to make sure he did not behave in a way that Björk considered inappropriate, anything that might damage the force's reputation, nevertheless Björk had a point: they did not want Harderberg worrying about the interest the police were showing in him.

"I take your point," Wallander said, "but it could also have the opposite effect. It could raise eyebrows if the Chief of Police is there for what's supposed to be a routine inquiry."

"I merely wanted to put the idea to you," Björk said.

"It'll be best if Martinsson goes," Wallander said, getting to his feet. "I think our meeting is due to start."

On the way to the conference room Wallander told himself that one of these days he really would have to learn to be honest. He should have told Björk the truth, that he did not want him to come because he could not abide his subservient attitude towards Harderberg. There was something in Björk's behaviour that was typical of the peasant's awe of those in power. He had barely thought about it before, even though he knew it to be true of society at large. There was always somebody at the top who dictated the terms, specifically or by implication, that those below had to accept. As a child he remembered seeing workers doffing their caps whenever one of those who decided their fate went by. He thought about how his father used to bow to the Silk Knights. Caps were still being doffed even today, albeit invisible ones.

I, too, have a cap in my hand, Wallander thought. Sometimes I don't notice it's there.

They gathered around the conference-room table. Svedberg glumly produced a proposal for a new police uniform that had been sent out to all police stations.

"Do you want to see what we'll look like in future?" he said.

"We never wear uniform," Wallander said as he sat down.

"Ann-Britt's not as negative as the rest of us," Svedberg said. "She thinks it could look rather smart."

Björk had sat down and dropped his hands on the table as a signal for the meeting to start.

"Per isn't here this morning," he said. "He has to try to make sure those twins who robbed the bank last year are convicted."

"What twins?" Wallander said.

"Can anybody have failed to be aware that Handelsbanken was robbed by two men who turned out to be twins?"

"I was away last year," Wallander said. "I haven't heard a thing about it."

"We got them in the end," Martinsson said. "They'd got themselves a basic university qualification in economics and then needed some capital so that they could put their ideas into practice. They had visions of a floating pleasure palace called Summerland that would travel back and forth along the south coast."

"Not such a bad idea in fact," Svedberg said, scratching his head ruminatively.

Wallander looked round the room.

"Alfred Harderberg has phoned," he said. "I'm going to Farnholm Castle this evening and taking Martinsson

266

with me. There's a slight possibility that his travel plans may change, but I've made it clear that he cannot count on our unlimited patience."

"Mightn't that make him suspicious?" Svedberg said.

"I've stressed that it's a routine inquiry," Wallander said. "He was the one Gustaf Torstensson had been to see the night he died."

"It's about time," Martinsson said. "But we'd better think pretty carefully about what we're going to say to him."

"We've got all day to do that," Wallander said.

"Where has he been this time?" Svedberg wanted to know.

"Barcelona."

"He owns a lot of property in Barcelona," Svedberg said. "He also has an interest in a holiday village under construction near Marbella. All through a company called Casaco. I've seen the share brochures somewhere. I rather think the whole thing's run by a bank in Macao. Wherever that is."

"I don't know," Wallander said, "but it's not important just now."

"It's south of Hong Kong," Martinsson said. "Didn't anybody do geography at school?"

Wallander poured himself a glass of water and the meeting proceeded on its usual course. They took it in turns to report on what they had been doing since the last time they had met, each one concentrating on their allocated field. Martinsson passed on some messages he had received from Höglund. The most important of which was that she was going the following day to meet Borman's children, and also his widow who was over from Spain on a visit. Wallander started by reporting on the plastic container. He soon saw that his colleagues could not make out why that particular detail should be so significant. Perhaps that's no bad thing, he thought. It might help me scale down my own expectations.

After half an hour or so the discussion became more general. Everybody agreed with Wallander that loose ends not directly linked with Farnholm Castle should be left dangling for the time being.

"We're still waiting to hear what the fraud squads in Stockholm and Malmö have to say," Wallander said as he drew the meeting to a close. "What we can say for now is that Gustaf and Sten Torstensson were killed for reasons which we have not yet identified. I incline towards robbery rather than revenge. Obviously we have to be prepared to continue investigating all their clients if the Farnholm lead goes cold, but for the moment we have to concentrate on Harderberg and Borman. Let's hope Ann-Britt can squeeze something important out of the widow and the children."

"Do you think she can handle it?" Svedberg said.

"Why ever not?"

"Let's face it, she's not very experienced," Svedberg said. "I was only asking."

"I have no doubt she will cope in exemplary fashion," Wallander said. "If there's nothing else, the meeting is closed."

Wallander went back to his office. He stood for a while looking out of the window, his mind a blank. Then he sat at his desk yet again and went through the material he had on Harderberg and his business empire. He had read most of it before, but he went through it one more time with a fine-tooth comb. There was a lot he did not understand. The most complicated commercial transactions – the way in which a company melted away and became something different, and the complex business of shares and bonds – made him feel that he was entering a world he could not begin to comprehend. Occasionally he broke off to try to get hold of Nyberg, but he had no luck. He gave lunch a miss, and did not leave the station until 3.30. There had been no word from Nyberg, and that was strange. Wallander began to accept that he would not know what that plastic container had been used for until after he had been to Farnholm Castle. He struggled through the gale as far as Stortorget and ordered a kebab. He was thinking all the time about Harderberg.

When he got back to the police station there was a note on his desk saying that someone in the office at Farnholm Castle had phoned and Dr Harderberg would expect him at 7.30 p.m. He went to look for Martinsson. They needed to prepare themselves, go through the questions they were going to ask, and which ones they would save for the time being. In the corridor he bumped into Svedberg, who was on his way out.

"Martinsson wants you to phone him at home," Svedberg said. "He left some time ago. I don't know why."

Wallander went back to his room and dialled Martinsson's number.

"I have to cry off, I'm afraid," Martinsson said. "My wife's ill. I haven't been able to find a babysitter. Can you take Svedberg instead?"

"He's just left," Wallander said. "I've no idea where he's going."

"I'm sorry about this," Martinsson said.

"Don't worry, of course you have to stay at home," Wallander said. "I'll find a solution somehow."

"You could take Björk," Martinsson said ironically.

"You're right, I could," Wallander said in all seriousness. "I'll think about it."

The moment he put down the phone he decided to go to Farnholm Castle on his own. He realised that was what he had really wanted to do all along. My biggest weakness as a police officer, he thought. I always prefer to go alone. Over the years he had begun to question whether it really was a weakness.

In order to concentrate in peace and quiet, he left the police station without further ado, got into his car and drove out of Ystad. The gale really was gusting up to hurricane strength. The car swayed and rattled. Ragged clouds raced across the sky. He wondered how his father's roof was faring at Löderup. He felt a sudden need to listen to some opera, drove on to the hard shoulder and switched on the inside light. But he couldn't find any of his cassettes – and then it dawned on him that this wasn't his own car. He carried on towards Kristianstad. He tried to think through what he was going to say to Harderberg, but discovered that what he was most looking forward to was the meeting itself. There had not been a single photograph of the man at Farnholm, or in any of the press reports he had read, and Höglund had said that he actively disliked being photographed. On the few occasions he appeared in public his staff ensured that there were no photographers around. An enquiry to Swedish Television revealed that they did not have a single clip of him in their archives.

Wallander thought back to his first visit to the castle. What had struck him then was that very rich people are characterised by silence and remoteness. Now he could add another characteristic: they were invisible. Faceless people in beautiful surroundings.

Just before he got to Tomelilla he ran over a hare that seemed hypnotised by his headlights. He stopped and got out into a wind that almost blew him over. The hare was lying on the verge, its hind legs kicking. Wallander searched for a big enough stone, but by the time he found one the hare was dead. He toed it into the ditch, and returned to his car with an ugly taste in his mouth. The gusts were so strong that they almost ripped the car door out of his grasp.

He drove on to Tomelilla where he stopped at a café and ordered a sandwich and a cup of coffee. It was 5.45. He took out his notebook and wrote down questions that he could use as a framework for his interview. He felt tense. What concerned him was that this must mean he hoped he was going to come face to face with the murderer.

He stayed in the café for nearly an hour, refilling his cup and allowing his thoughts to wander. He found himself thinking about Rydberg. For a moment he had trouble conjuring up his face, and that worried him. If I lose Rydberg, he thought, I lose the only real friend I've got. Dead or alive.

He paid and left. A sign outside the café had been toppled by the wind. Cars flashed past but he couldn't see any people. A real November storm, he thought, as he drove off. Winter is blowing open its portals.

He arrived at the castle gates at 7.25. He expected Ström to come out and greet him, but nobody did. The bunker appeared to be deserted. Then the gates glided open without a sound. He drove towards the castle. Powerful spotlights lit up the façade and the grounds. It was like a stage set – an image of reality, not reality itself.

He stopped by the steps and switched off his engine. The castle door opened as he climbed out of the car. When he was halfway up the steps a powerful gust made him stumble and he dropped his notebook. It was carried away by the wind. He shook his head and continued up the steps. A young woman with close-cropped hair was waiting to receive him.

"Was that something important?" she asked.

Wallander recognised her voice. "It was only a notebook," he said.

"We'll send somebody out for it," Jenny Lind said.

Wallander contemplated her heavy earrings and the blue ribbons in her black hair.

"There was nothing in it," he said.

She let him in and the door closed behind them.

"You said you would have somebody with you," she said.

"They couldn't make it."

Wallander noticed two men hovering in the shadows by the great staircase. He recalled the shadows he had seen on his first visit. He could not make out their faces, and wondered fleetingly if they really were alive, or just two suits of armour.

"Dr Harderberg will be here in a moment," the girl said. "You can wait in the library."

She led him through a door to the left of the hall. Wallander could hear his footsteps echoing on the stone floor. He wondered how the woman in front of him could move so quietly, then he saw to his surprise that she was barefoot.

"Isn't it cold?" he said, indicating her feet.

"There's under-floor heating," she said impassively, and showed him into the library.

"We'll look for your notes," she said, then left him and closed the door behind her.

Wallander found himself in a large, oval-shaped room lined with bookshelves. In the middle was a group of leather chairs and a serving table. The lights were dim and, unlike the entrance hall, the library had oriental carpets on the floor. Wallander stood quite still and listened. He was surprised to hear no sound from the storm raging outside. Then he realised that the room was soundproof. This was where Gustaf Torstensson had spent the last evening of his life, where he had met his employer and several other, unknown, men.

Wallander looked about him. Behind a column he discovered a large aquarium with strangely shaped fish slowly swimming around. He went closer to see if there was gold dust on the bottom: the sand certainly glittered. He continued his tour of the room. I am no doubt being observed, he thought. I can't see any cameras, but they'll be there, hidden among the books, and they'll be sensitive enough to beam adequate pictures despite the dim lighting. There'll be hidden tape recorders as well, of course. They expected me to have somebody with me. They would have left us alone together for a while in order to listen in on our conversation.

Wallander did not hear Harderberg come into the room, but at a certain moment he knew he was no longer alone. He turned and saw a man standing beside one of the sumptuous leather chairs.

"Inspector Wallander," the man said, and smiled. What Wallander would remember afterwards was that the smile never seemed to leave the man's tanned face. He could never forget it.

"Alfred Harderberg," Wallander said. "I'm very grateful you were able to receive me."

"We all need to do our bit when the police call in," Harderberg said.

The voice was unusually pleasant. They shook hands. Harderberg was wearing an immaculate and no doubt very expensive pinstriped suit. Wallander's first impression was that everything about him was perfect – his clothes, his way of moving, his way of speaking. And that smile never left his face.

They sat down.

"I've arranged for tea," Harderberg said in a friendly tone. "I hope you take tea, Inspector?"

"Yes, please," Wallander said. "Especially in weather like this. The walls here at Farnholm must be very thick."

"You're referring to the fact that we can't hear the wind, I suppose," Harderberg said. "You're right. The walls are indeed very thick. They were built to offer resistance, both to enemy soldiers and to raging gales."

"It must have been rather difficult to land today," Wallander said. "Did you come to Everöd or Sturup?"

"I use Sturup," Harderberg said. "You can get straight out into the international routes from there. But the landing was excellent. I have only the best pilots."

The African woman Wallander had met on his first visit emerged from the shadows. They sat in silence while she poured tea.

"This is a very special tea," Harderberg said.

Wallander thought of something he had read that afternoon.

"I expect it's from one of your own plantations," he said.

The constant smile made it impossible to tell whether Harderberg was surprised that Wallander knew that he owned tea plantations.

"I see you are well informed, Inspector Wallander," he said. "It is true that we have a share in Lonrho's tea plantations in Mozambique."

"It's very good," Wallander said. "It's hard for me to imagine what is involved in doing business in all four corners of the world. A policeman's existence is rather different. But then, I suppose you must have found it pretty hard yourself in the early days: from Vimmerby to tea plantations in Africa."

"They were indeed very long strides," Harderberg said.

Wallander noted that Harderberg ended the opening exchanges with an invisible full stop. He put down his teacup, feeling rather insecure. The man opposite radiated controlled but apparently unlimited authority.

"I think we can keep this very brief," Wallander said after a moment's pause, during which he could not hear the slightest whisper from the storm outside. "The solicitor Gustaf Torstensson, who died in a car accident after visiting your castle, was in fact murdered. The accident was contrived in order to conceal the crime. Apart from whoever it was who killed him, you were the last person to see him alive."

"I must admit I find the whole business inconceivable," Harderberg said. "Who on earth would want to kill poor old Gustaf Torstensson?"

"That's precisely the question we are asking ourselves," Wallander said. "And who could be sufficiently cold-blooded to disguise it as a car accident?"

"You must have some idea?"

"Yes, we do, but I'm afraid I can say no more."

"I understand," Harderberg said. "You will realise how disturbed we were by what happened. Old Torstensson was a trusted colleague."

"Things didn't get any easier when his son, too, was murdered," Wallander said. "Did you know him?"

"I never met him. But I am aware of what happened, of course."

Wallander was feeling increasingly insecure. Harderberg seemed unmoved. Normally, Wallander could very quickly surmise whether or not a person was telling the truth, but this man, the man sitting opposite him, was different.

"You have business interests all over the world," Wallander said. "You preside over an empire with a turnover of billions. If I understand it rightly, yours is close to being listed among the world's biggest enterprises."

"We shall overtake Kankaku Securities and Pechiney International next year," Harderberg said. "And when we do, yes, we'll be one of the top one thousand companies in the world."

"I've never heard of the companies you referred to."

"Kankaku is Japanese, and Pechiney is French," Harderberg said.

"It's not a world I am at all familiar with," Wallander said. "It must have been quite unfamiliar to Gustaf Torstensson too. For most of his life he was a simple provincial solicitor. But nevertheless you found a place for him in your organisation."

"I freely admit that I was surprised myself. But when we decided to move our Swedish base to Farnholm Castle, I needed a lawyer with some local know-how. Torstensson was recommended to me."

"By whom?"

"I'm afraid I can no longer remember that."

That's it, Wallander thought. He knows very well who it was, but he prefers not to say. A barely perceptible shift in his impassive features had not escaped Wallander's notice.

"I gather he dealt exclusively with financial advice," Wallander said.

"He made sure the transactions we had with the rest of the world were in accordance with Swedish law," Harderberg said. "He was most meticulous. I had great faith in him."

"That last evening," Wallander said. "I suppose you were sitting in this very room. What was the meeting about?"

"We had made an offer for some properties in Germany that were owned by Horsham Holdings in Canada. I was due to meet Peter Munk a few days later to try to clinch the deal. We discussed if there were any formal obstacles in the way. Our proposal was that we should pay partly in cash and partly in shares."

"Peter Munk? Who is he?"

"The principal shareholder in Horsham Holdings," Harderberg said. "He's the one who runs the business."

"The discussions you had that night were routine?"

"As I remember, yes."

"I understand that other persons were present," Wallander said.

"There were two directors from Banca Commerciale Italiana," Harderberg said. "We'd intended paying for the German properties with some of our holdings in Montedison. The transaction was to be handled by the Italian bank."

"I'd be grateful for the names of those persons," Wallander said. "In case it arises that we need to speak to them as well."

"Of course."

"Gustaf Torstensson left Farnholm Castle immediately after the meeting, I take it," Wallander said. "Did you notice anything out of the ordinary about him that night?"

"Nothing at all."

"And you have no idea why he was murdered?"

"I find it totally incomprehensible. An old man who led a solitary life. Who would want to kill him?"

"That's just it," Wallander said. "Who would want to kill him? And who would want to shoot his son as well, a couple of weeks later?"

"I thought you indicated that the police had a lead?"

"We do have a lead," Wallander said, "but we don't have a motive."

"I wish I could help you," Harderberg said. "If nothing else I'd like the police to keep me informed about developments in the case."

"It's very possible that I may need to come back to you with some more questions," Wallander said, getting to his feet.

"I'll answer them as best I can," Harderberg said.

They shook hands again. Wallander tried to look beyond the smile, beyond those ice-blue eyes. But somewhere along the line he came up against an invisible wall.

"Did you buy those buildings?" Wallander asked.

"Which buildings?"

"In Germany."

The smile became even broader.

"Of course. It was a very good deal. For us."

They took leave of each other at the door. Miss Lind was standing there in her bare feet, waiting to escort him out.

"We've found your notebook," she said as they walked through the big entrance hall, and she handed him an envelope.

Wallander noticed that the shadows were no longer there. "This has the names of the two Italian bank directors," Wallander said.

She smiled.

Everybody smiles, Wallander thought. Does that include the men in the shadows?

Jenny Lind closed the door behind him. The gates opened silently, and Wallander felt relieved once he had passed through them. The gale hit him the moment he emerged from the castle grounds.

This is where Gustaf Torstensson drove that night, he thought. At more or less the same time. He felt scared. He looked over his shoulder to make sure there was nobody in the back seat. But he was alone. A cold draught was forcing its way through the windows.

He thought about Dr Harderberg, the man who smiled. He's the one, Wallander thought, the one who knows exactly what happened.

Chapter 12

The hurricane-force gusts that had hit Skåne slowly moved away.

Kurt Wallander had spent another sleepless night in his flat. By dawn the storm seemed to be over. During the night he had several times stood at his kitchen window, watching the light hanging over the street writhing about in the wind like a snake.

Wallander had returned from the strange stage-set world of Farnholm Castle with the sense of having been put down. The smiling Dr Harderberg had made him play the same obsequious role his father had performed before the Silk Knights when he was a child. As he watched the storm raging outside, he thought how Farnholm Castle was but a variation of the sleek American cars that had swayed to a halt outside the house in Malmö where he had grown up. The loud-voiced Pole in his silk suit was a distant relation of the man in the castle with the soundproof library. Wallander had sat in Harderberg's leather armchair, invisible cap in hand, and afterwards he had the feeling of having been vanquished.

OK, that was an exaggeration. He had done what he set out to do, asked his questions, met the man with so much power whom so few people had ever seen, and he had put Harderberg's fears at rest, he was sure of that. Harderberg had no reason to think that he was thought anything but a prominent citizen beyond suspicion.

At the same time Wallander was convinced now that they were on the right track, that they had turned the stone which hid the secret of why the two solicitors had been murdered, and under that stone he had seen Alfred Harderberg's image. What he would have to do now was not merely wipe that smile off the man's face, he had also to slay a giant.

Over and over through that sleepless night he had replayed his conversation with Harderberg. He had pictured his face and tried to interpret the slight shifts in that silent smile, the way one tries to crack a secret code. Once he had hovered on the brink of an abyss, he was certain of that. This was when he had asked Harderberg who had recommended Gustaf Torstensson to him. The smile had shown signs of cracking, if only for a second, no doubt about it. So there were moments when Harderberg could not avoid being human, vulnerable, exposed. But there again, it did not necessarily mean much. It might just have been the momentary and irresistible weariness of the ever-busy world traveller, the barely discernible weakness of a man who no longer had the strength to put on a polite front while allowing himself to be questioned by this insignificant police officer from Ystad.

Wallander believed that this was where he should make the first move if he was going to slay the giant, wipe that smile off his face and discover the truth behind the death of the two solicitors. He had no doubt that the skilful and persistent officers in the fraud squad would uncover information that would be of use to them in the investigation. But as the night wore on Wallander had become increasingly convinced that it was Harderberg himself who would put them on the right track. Somewhere, sometime, the man with the smile would leave a trail which would enable them to hunt him down and use what they found to finish him off.

Wallander knew that it had not been Harderberg himself who had committed the murders. Nor had he planted the mine in Mrs Dunér's garden. Or been in the car that had followed Wallander and Höglund to Helsingborg. Nor put the explosives in the petrol tank. Wallander had noticed that Harderberg had repeatedly said *we* and *us*. Like a king, or a Crown prince. But also like a man who knew the importance of surrounding himself with loyal colleagues who never questioned the instructions they were given.

It seemed to Wallander that this trait also applied to Gustaf Torstensson, and he could understand why Harderberg had chosen to include him among his staff. He could expect total loyalty from Torstensson. Torstensson would always understand that his place at table was below the salt. Harderberg had presented him with an opportunity he could never have imagined in his wildest dreams.

Maybe it's as simple as that, Wallander thought as he watched the swaying street light. Maybe Gustaf Torstensson had discovered something he would not or could not accept? Had he also discovered a crack in that smile? A crack which gave him occasion to confront himself with the unpleasant role he had in fact been playing?

From time to time Wallander had left the window

and sat at his kitchen table. Written his thoughts on a notepad and tried to make sense of them.

At 5 a.m. he had made himself a cup of coffee. Then he had gone to bed and dozed until 6.30. Got up again, showered and had another cup of coffee. Then he had made his way to the police station at 7.30. The storm had given way to a clear blue sky, and it felt distinctly colder. Although he had hardly slept, he felt full of energy as he stepped into his office. Second wind, he had thought on his way to the station. We're no longer feeling our way into an investigation, we're in the thick of it. He flung his jacket over the back of the visitor's chair, fetched a coffee, phoned Ebba in reception and asked her to get hold of Nyberg for him. While he was waiting he read through his summary of the conversation with Harderberg. Svedberg stuck his head round the door and asked how it had gone.

"You'll hear all about it shortly," Wallander said. "But I do reckon the murders and all the rest of it originate from Farnholm Castle."

"Ann-Britt phoned to say she would be going straight to Ängelholm," Svedberg said. "To meet Lars Borman's widow and children."

"How's she getting on with Harderberg's jet?"

"She didn't mention that," Svedberg said. "I suppose it will take a while."

"I feel so impatient," Wallander said. "I wonder why?"

"You always have been. And you're the only one who doesn't seem to be aware of it," Svedberg said, as he left.

As soon as Nyberg came in, Wallander could see that something was up. He asked him to close the door behind him.

"You were right," Nyberg said. "The plastic container we were examining the other night is hardly the sort of thing that belongs in a solicitor's car."

Wallander waited expectantly.

"You were also right in thinking it was a sort of cool box. But it's not for medicine or blood. It's for body organs intended for transplants. A kidney, for instance."

Wallander looked at him thoughtfully. "Are you sure?"

"If I'm not sure, I'll tell you," Nyberg said.

"I know," Wallander said, brushing Nyberg's annoyance aside.

"This is a very advanced kind of plastic container. There aren't a lot of them around, so it should be possible to track it down. If what I've managed to find out so far is correct, the sole importers into Sweden are a company based in Södertälje called Avanca. I'm about to investigate further."

"Good," Wallander said. "One other thing – don't forget to find out who owns the company."

"I take it you want to know whether Avanca is a part of Harderberg's empire?"

"That would be a start," Wallander said.

Nyberg paused in the doorway. "What do you know about organ transplants?"

"Not a lot," Wallander said. "I know they happen, that they're getting more common, and that more organs are being transplanted. For myself, I hope I never have to have one. It must be very strange to have somebody else's heart in your body."

"I spoke to a Dr Strömberg in Lund," Nyberg said. "He gave me quite a bit of insight. He says there's a side to transplants that's murky, to say the least. It's not just that poor people in the Third World sell their own organs in desperation to survive – obviously that's a business with lots of grey areas, from a moral point of view anyway. He also hinted at something much worse."

Wallander looked questioningly at Nyberg.

"Go on," he said, "I've got time."

"It was beyond me," Nyberg said, "but Strömberg persuaded me that there's no limit to what some people are prepared to do to earn money."

"Surely you know that already?" Wallander said.

Nyberg sat down on Wallander's visitor's chair.

"Like so much else, there's no proof," he said, "but Strömberg maintains that there are gangs in South America and Asia who take orders for particular organs, then go out and commit murder to get them."

Wallander said nothing.

"He said this practice is more widespread than anybody suspects. There are even rumours that it goes on in Eastern Europe and in the US. A kidney doesn't have a face, it doesn't have an individual identity. Somebody kills a child in South America and extends the life of someone in the West whose parents can afford to pay and don't want to wait in the queue. The murderers earn serious money."

"It can't be easy to extract an organ," Wallander said. "That means there must be doctors involved."

"Who's to say that doctors are any different from the rest of us when it comes to morals?"

"I find it difficult to believe," Wallander said.

"I expect everybody does," Nyberg said. "That's why the gangs can continue to operate in peace and quiet."

He took a notebook out of his pocket and thumbed through the pages.

"The doctor gave me the name of a journalist who's

digging into this," he said. "A woman. Her name's Lisbeth Norin. She lives in Gothenburg and writes for several popular-science magazines."

Wallander made a note. "Let's think an outrageous thought," he said, looking Nyberg in the eye. "Let's suppose that Alfred Harderberg goes round killing people and selling their kidneys or whatever on the black market that apparently exists. And let's suppose that Gustaf Torstensson somehow or other discovered that. And took the cool box with him as proof. Let's think that outrageous thought."

Nyberg stared at Wallander, eyebrows raised. "Are you serious?"

"Of course not," Wallander said. "I'm just posing an outrageous thought."

Nyberg stood up to leave. "I'll see if I can trace that container," he said. "I'll make that the number-one priority."

When he had gone Wallander went to the window and thought over what Nyberg had said. He told himself that it really was an outrageous thought. Harderberg was a man who donated money for research. Especially for illnesses affecting children. Wallander also recalled that he had given money to support health care in several African and South American countries.

The cool box in Torstensson's car must have some other significance, he concluded. Or no significance at all.

Even so, he could not resist calling Directory Enquiries and getting Lisbeth Norin's number. When he called her, he found himself talking to an answering machine. He left his name and number.

*

286

Wallander spent the rest of the day waiting for things to happen. No matter what he did, what he was waiting for – reports from Höglund and Nyberg – was more important. He phoned his father and discovered that the studio had somehow survived the gales. Then he turned his wavering attention to everything he could find about Harderberg. He could not help but be fascinated by the brilliant career that had started inauspiciously in Vimmerby. Wallander appreciated that Harderberg's commercial genius had made itself felt very early on. At nine he had sold Christmas cards. He had also used his savings to buy previous years' leftovers. These he had snapped up for next to nothing. The boy had sold cards for a number of years, adjusting his prices to whatever the market would stand. Clearly, Harderberg had always been a *trader*. He bought and sold what other people made. He created nothing himself, but he bought cheap and sold less cheap. He discovered value where nobody else had found it. At 14 he had recognised that there was a demand for veteran cars. He had got on his bike, cycled round the Vimmerby area, poked his nose into sheds and backyards, and bought up any clapped-out vehicle he thought he might be able to sell on. Very often he got them for nothing, as people were too high-minded to think that they should exploit an inexperienced young chap who cycled round the country districts and seemed to be interested in old wrecks. All the while he had saved the money he did not need to plough back into the business. To celebrate his seventeenth birthday, he had travelled to Stockholm. He had been accompanied by an older friend from a village near Vimmerby, an amazing ventriloquist. Harderberg paid all their expenses, and appointed himself the ventriloquist's manager. It seemed that Harderberg had established himself early on as an efficient and unfailingly smiling aide who could further the careers of the up-and-coming. Wallander read several reports about Harderberg and the ventriloquist. They had often featured in *Picture Parade*, a magazine Wallander thought he could remember; and the articles kept referring to how well bred, well dressed and how capable of a friendly smile the young manager was. There were photographs of the ventriloquist, but not – even then – of his manager. It seemed he had shed his Småland dialect and adopted the way Stockholmers spoke. He paid for lessons from a speech therapist. After a while the ventriloquist was sent back to Vimmerby and anonymity, and Harderberg turned to new commercial projects. By the end of the 1960s his tax returns showed him to be a millionaire, but his big breakthrough came in the mid '70s. He had spent time in Zimbabwe, or Southern Rhodesia as it was then, and made some profitable investments in copper and gold mines together with a businessman called Tiny Rowland. Wallander assumed that this was when he had acquired the tea plantation.

At the beginning of the 1980s Harderberg had been married to a Brazilian woman, Carmen Dulce da Silva, but they divorced without having had any children. All the time Harderberg had remained as invisible as possible. He had never put in an appearance when hospitals he had helped to finance were opened, nor did he ever send anybody to represent him. But he did write letters and telex messages in which he was modesty itself, expressing his thanks for all the kindness that had been extended to him. He was never present at the ceremony when he was awarded an honorary doctorate.

His life is one long absence, Wallander thought. Until out of the blue he turned up in Skåne and installed himself behind the walls of Farnholm Castle, nobody had any idea where he was. He was constantly moving from one house to another, being driven in curtained cars, and from the early '80s he had owned a jet.

But there were a few exceptions. One of them seemed to be more surprising and even stranger than the rest. According to something Mrs Dunér had said in a conversation with Höglund, Harderberg and Gustaf Torstensson had met for the first time over lunch at the Continental Hotel in Ystad. Torstensson had described Harderberg afterwards as likeable, suntanned and strikingly well dressed.

Why had he chosen to meet Torstensson at a restaurant so openly? Wallander wondered. Well-known journalists specialising in international commerce have to wait for years before getting a glimpse of the man. Could that be significant? Does he sometimes change tack to create even more confusion? Uncertainty can be a hiding place, Wallander thought. The world is allowed to know he exists, but never where he is.

Around midday Wallander went home for lunch. He was back by 1.30. He had just settled down to his files when Höglund knocked and came in.

"Back so soon?" Wallander said in surprise. "I thought you were supposed to be in Ängelholm?"

"It didn't take long to talk to Borman's family," she said. "Unfortunately."

Wallander could hear she was unhappy with the trip, and her mood immediately rubbed off on him. It's no good, then, he thought gloomily. Nothing here to help us break down the walls of Farnholm Castle.

She had sat down on his visitor's chair and was leafing through her notebook.

"How's the sick child?" Wallander said.

"Children don't stay ill for long nowadays," she said. "I've found out quite a bit about Harderberg's jet, by the way. I'm glad Svedberg phoned and gave me that to keep me occupied. Women always have a guilty conscience when they can't work."

"The Bormans first," Wallander said. "Let's start with them."

"There really isn't much to say," she said. "There's no doubt they think he committed suicide. I don't think the widow's got over it, nor the son or daughter. I think it's the first time I've realised what it must mean to a family when somebody takes his own life, and for no reason."

"He really hadn't left anything? No letter?"

"Not a thing."

"That doesn't fit with the picture we have of Borman. He wouldn't just drop his bike on the ground, and he wouldn't have taken his life without leaving some kind of explanation, or an apology."

"I went over everything I thought was important. He wasn't in debt, he didn't gamble, and he hadn't been involved in any kind of swindle."

"You mean you asked about that?" Wallander said, astonished.

"Indirect questions can produce direct answers," she said.

Wallander thought he understood what she meant. "People who know the police are coming make preparations," he said. "Is that it?"

"All three of them had decided to defend his reputation," she said. "They listed all his good qualities without my needing to ask if he had any weaknesses."

"The only question is whether what they said is true."

"They weren't lying. I don't know what he might have got up to in private, but he does not seem to have been the kind of man who leads a double life."

"Go on," Wallander said.

"It came as a total shock to them," she said. "And they haven't come to terms with it yet. I think they spend night and day worrying about why he would have taken his own life. Without being able to find an answer."

"Did you give any indication that it might not have been suicide?"

"No."

"Good. Go on."

"The only thing of any interest to us is that Borman was in touch with Gustaf Torstensson. They were able to confirm that. They could also tell me why. Torstensson and Borman were members of a society for the study of icons. Gustaf Torstensson occasionally used to visit the Bormans. And Borman visited Torstensson in Ystad now and then."

"You mean they were friends?"

"I wouldn't say that. I don't think they were that close. And that's what's interesting, it seems to me."

"I don't follow you," Wallander said.

"What I mean is this," she said. "Torstensson and Borman were both loners. One was married, the other a widower, but they were loners even so. They didn't meet very often, and when they did, it was to talk about icons. But don't you think that these two solitary men, caught up in a difficult situation, might confide in each other? They didn't have any real friends, but they did have each other."

"It's conceivable," Wallander said. "But it doesn't explain Borman's threatening letters to the whole firm of solicitors."

"The filing clerk, Lundin, wasn't threatened," she objected. "That might be more significant than we think."

Wallander leaned back in his chair and looked intently at her. "You think you're on to something."

"It's only speculation," she said. "Probably far-fetched."

"We have nothing to lose by thinking," Wallander said. "I'm all ears."

"Let's suppose that Borman told Torstensson what had happened at the County Council. Fraud. I mean, they can't have talked about nothing but icons all the time. We know that Borman was disappointed and offended because there was no proper police investigation into what happened. Let's suppose, too, that Torstensson knew there was a link between Harderberg and that swindling company STRUFAB. He might have mentioned that he worked for Harderberg. Let's go a step further and suppose that Borman saw in Torstensson a solicitor with the same feelings about justice as he had himself, a sort of guardian angel. He asked for help. But Torstensson did nothing. You can interpret threatening letters in different ways."

"Can you?" Wallander said. "Threatening letters are threatening letters."

"Some more serious than others," she said. "Perhaps we should not have overlooked that Torstensson did not in fact take them seriously. He did not record them, he did not turn to the police or to the Bar Council. He just hid them away. The most dramatic discovery can sometimes be finding that an incident wasn't really very dramatic. The fact that Lundin wasn't mentioned might be because he did not know she existed."

"Good thinking," Wallander said. "Your speculations are no worse than any others. On the contrary. But there's just one thing you don't explain. The most important detail of all. Borman's murder. A carbon copy of Gustaf Torstensson's death. Executions disguised as something else."

"I think you might have given the answer yourself," she said. "Their deaths were similar."

Wallander thought for a moment. "You could be right," he said. "If we suppose that Gustaf Torstensson was already suspect in Alfred Harderberg's eyes. If he was being watched. Then what happened to Lars Borman could be a copy of what nearly happened to Mrs Dunér."

"That's exactly what I was thinking," she said.

Wallander stood up. "We can't prove any of this," he said.

"Not yet," she said.

"We don't have much time," Wallander said. "I suspect Per Åkeson will switch on the red light and demand that we broaden the investigation if nothing happens. Let's say we have a month in which to concentrate on our so-called prime suspect, Alfred Harderberg."

"That might be long enough," she said.

"I'm having a bad day today," Wallander said. "I think the whole investigation's going off the rails. That's why it's good to hear what you have to say. Detectives whose resolve starts to falter have no business to be in the force."

They went to fetch some coffee, but paused in the corridor.

"The private jet," Wallander said. "What do we know about that?"

"Not a great deal," she said. "It's a Grumman Gulfstream dating from 1974. Its Swedish base is at Sturup. It gets serviced in Germany, in Bremen. Harderberg employs two pilots. One's from Austria and is called Karl Heider. He's been with Harderberg for many years and lives in Svedala. The other pilot has only been in the post a couple of years. His name is Luiz Manshino, originally from Mauritius. He has a flat in Malmö."

"Where did you get all that information from?"

"I pretended to be from a newspaper running a feature on the private jets of Swedish business executives. I spoke to somebody in charge of PR at the airport. I don't think Harderberg will be suspicious, even if he gets to hear about it. Obviously, though, I couldn't start asking if there were logbooks that recorded his travels."

"The pilots interest me," Wallander said. "People who travel that often with each other and spend so much time together must have a special relationship. They know a lot about each other. Don't they have to have some kind of stewardess with them? For safety reasons?"

"Evidently not," she said.

"We'll have to try to make contact with the pilots," Wallander said. "Hit on some way of finding out about the flight documentation."

"I'd be happy to continue with that," she said. "I promise to be discreet."

"Go ahead," Wallander said. "But get a move on. Time's at a premium."

That same afternoon Wallander called a meeting of his investigative team, without Björk being there. They crammed into Wallander's office as the conference room was occupied by a meeting of police chiefs from all over the district, chaired by Björk. After they had heard what Höglund had to report about her meeting with the Bormans, Wallander informed them about his meeting with Harderberg at Farnholm Castle. Everybody listened intently, trying to find a lead, something he might himself have overlooked.

"My feeling that these murders and all the other incidents are linked to Harderberg is stronger now than it was before," Wallander said in conclusion. "If you agree with me, we'll go on following this line. But we can't rely on my feelings, we must acknowledge that we haven't solved anything yet. We could be wrong."

"What else do we have to go on?" Svedberg said.

"We can always go looking for a madman," Martinsson said. "A madman who doesn't exist."

"It's too cold-blooded for that," Höglund said. "It all seems to be so well planned. There's nothing to suggest a madman at work."

"We must continue to take every precaution," Wallander said. "Somebody is keeping an eye on us, whether it's Harderberg or somebody else."

"It's a pity we can't count on Kurt Ström," Svedberg said. "What we need is a contact inside the castle. Somebody who can move around among all those secretaries without drawing attention to himself."

"I agree," Wallander said. "It would be even better if we could find somebody who worked for Harderberg until recently. Especially somebody with a grudge."

"The fraud squad people maintain that there are only a handful of people who are close to Harderberg," Martinsson said. "And they've all been with him for many years. The secretaries are not very important. I don't think they know much about what goes on."

"Even so, we ought to have somebody there," Svedberg insisted. "Somebody who could tell us about daily routines."

The meeting was drifting towards stalemate.

"I have a proposal," Wallander said. "Let's shut ourselves away somewhere different tomorrow. We need peace and quiet to work our way through all the material. We have to define where we stand one more time. We need to use our time efficiently."

"At this time of year the Continental Hotel is practically empty," Martinsson said. "I'd have thought they'd have a conference room we could rent for next to nothing."

"I like it," Wallander said. "The symbolism is attractive. That's where Gustaf Torstensson met Harderberg for the first time."

They met on the first floor of the Continental Hotel. Discussions continued through lunch and every coffee break. Come evening, they agreed to go on the next day as well. Somebody phoned Björk, who gave his blessing. They shut out the outside world and worked their way through all the material yet again. They were well aware that time was running out. It was Friday, November 19.

It was late afternoon when they finally broke up. Wallander thought that Höglund had summed up the state of the investigation best.

"I get the feeling everything is here," she said, "but we can't see how it hangs together. If it is Harderberg pulling the strings, he's doing it very skilfully. Whichever way we turn he moves the goalposts and we have to start all over."

They were all exhausted when they left the hotel. But this was no vanquished army beating a retreat. Wallander knew something important had happened. Everybody had shared all they knew with everybody else. Nobody needed to be unsure about what ideas or doubts their colleagues had.

"Let's have a break this weekend," Wallander said. "We need some rest. We need to be fit and raring to go again by Monday."

Wallander spent Saturday with his father in Löderup. He managed to repair the roof, then sat for hours with his father in the kitchen, playing cards. Over dinner Wallander could see quite clearly that Gertrud was genuinely enjoying life with his father. Before he left, Wallander asked her if she was familiar with Farnholm Castle.

"They used to say it was haunted," she said. "But perhaps they say that about all castles?"

It was midnight when Wallander set off for home. The temperature was below freezing, and he was not looking forward to winter.

He slept in on Sunday morning. Then he went for a walk, and inspected the boats in the harbour. He spent the afternoon cleaning his flat. Yet another Sunday wasted on unproductive matters.

When Wallander woke up on the morning of Monday, November 22, he had a headache. He was surprised, as he hadn't had a drop to drink the previous night. Then he realised he hadn't slept well. He had had one horrific nightmare after the other. His father had died suddenly, but when he went to see him in his dream coffin, he hadn't dared to look as he knew it was really Linda lying there.

He got up reluctantly and dissolved two painkillers in half a glass of water. It was still below freezing. As he waited for the coffee water to boil, he thought that his nightmares were a prologue to the meeting he and Björk were due to have with Åkeson that morning. Wallander knew it was going to be tricky. Although he had no doubt Åkeson would give them the green light to continue concentrating on Harderberg, he knew that their results had been unsatisfactory so far. They had not been able to get their material to point in any one particular direction. The investigation was drifting. Åkeson would, with good reason, want to know how much longer the investigators could go on standing on one leg, as it were.

He scrutinised his wall calendar, coffee mug in hand. Just over a month to go before Christmas. He would say they needed as long as that. If they were no nearer to cracking the case by then, he would have to accept that they would need to start investigating other leads in the new year.

A month, he thought. Something needs to happen pretty fast.

He was interrupted by the phone ringing.

"I hope I didn't wake you up," Höglund said.

"I'm drinking coffee."

"Do you take *Ystad Allehanda*?" she said.

"Of course."

"Have you read it today?" she said.

"I haven't even collected it from the letter box."

"Do," she said. "Turn to the job adverts."

Wondering what was going on, he went out into the hall and fetched his paper. Telephone in hand, he started turning to the adverts.

"What am I supposed to be looking for?" he asked.

"You'll see," she said. "See you later."

She hung up. He saw it at once. An advertisement for a stablegirl at Farnholm Castle. To start immediately. That's why she had worded her call the way she did. She had not wanted to mention Farnholm Castle on the telephone.

This could be their chance. As soon as he had got through the meeting with Åkeson he would phone his friend Sten Widén.

As Wallander and Björk settled down in Åkeson's office, Åkeson told the switchboard they were not to be disturbed. He had a bad cold, and blew his nose frequently.

"I really ought to be at home in bed," he said, "but let's get through this meeting as arranged." He pointed to the heap of files before going on. "You won't be surprised to hear that with the best will in the world, I can't say the results you've achieved so far are satisfactory. A few extremely vague pointers in the direction of Alfred Harderberg is all we've got."

"We need more time," Wallander said. "This is a particularly complicated investigation. We knew it would be from the outset. This is the best lead we've got."

"If we can call it a lead," Åkeson interrupted. "You made a case for concentrating on Harderberg, but we haven't really got any further since then. Looking through the material, I'm forced to conclude that we're only

299

marking time. The fraud squad haven't come up with any financial irregularities either. Harderberg seems to be a remarkably honourable gentleman. We have nothing to link him or his businesses directly or indirectly with the murder of Gustaf Torstensson and his son."

"Time," Wallander said again. "That's what we need. We could also stand the whole thing on its head and say that the moment we can definitely exclude Harderberg from our deliberations, we'll be in a better position to approach the case from a different angle."

Björk said nothing. Åkeson looked hard at Wallander.

"I really ought to call a halt to it at this point," he said. "You know that. Convince me that we ought to carry on a little longer concentrating all our efforts on Harderberg."

"The justification is in the paperwork," Wallander said. "I'm still sure we're on the right track. The whole team agrees with me, come to that."

"I still think we ought to consider splitting the team and setting some of them to work from another angle," Åkeson said.

"We don't have another angle," Wallander said. "Who fakes an accident to cover up a murder, and why? Why is a solicitor shot in his office? Who plants a mine in an elderly lady's garden? Who blows my car up? Are we supposed to think it could be a madman who's decided for no reason at all that it would be fun to kill off everybody employed by a firm of solicitors in Ystad, and why not a police officer as well while we're at it?"

"You still haven't sifted through all the files of the solicitors' clients," Åkeson said. "There's a lot we don't know yet."

"I still think we need more time," Wallander said. "Not unlimited time. But more time."

"I'll give you two weeks," Åkeson said. "If you haven't come up with anything more convincing by then, we'll take a new approach."

"That's not enough," Wallander said.

"I could stretch it to three," Åkeson said with a sigh.

"Let's take Christmas as the landmark," Wallander said. "If anything crops up before then to suggest that we ought to change course, we can do that straight away. But let's keep going as we are until Christmas."

Åkeson turned to Björk. "What do you think?"

"I'm worried," Björk said. "I don't think we're getting anywhere either. It's no secret that I've never really believed that Dr Harderberg has anything to do with all this."

Wallander felt the urge to protest, but resisted the temptation. If needs be he would have to accept three weeks.

Åkeson turned to the pile of papers on his desk. "What's this about organ transports?" he said. "I read that you'd found a cool box for transporting human organs in Gustaf Torstensson's car. Is that true?"

Wallander told them what Nyberg had discovered, and what they had subsequently managed to find out.

"Avanca," Åkeson said. "Is that a company quoted on the Stock Exchange? I've never heard of it."

"It's a small company," Wallander said. "Owned by a family called Roman. They started in the 1930s, importing wheelchairs."

"In other words, it's not owned by Harderberg," Åkeson said.

"We don't know that yet."

Åkeson eyed Wallander up and down. "How can a company owned by a family called Roman also be owned by Harderberg? You'll have to explain that to me."

"I'll explain when I can," Wallander said. "But what I do know on the basis of what I've learned this last month is that the real owner of a company can be someone quite different from what it says on the company logo."

Åkeson shook his head. "You're a hard nut to crack," he said. He consulted his desk diary. "Let's say Monday, December 20. Unless we've made a breakthrough before then. But I'm not going to allow you a single day more if the investigation hasn't produced significant results by then."

"We'll make the most of the time," Wallander said. "I trust you realise that we're busting ourselves here."

"I know," Åkeson said. "But the bottom line is that I'm the prosecutor, and I have to do my duty."

The meeting was over. Björk and Wallander went back to their offices.

"It was good of him to give you as much time as that," Björk said as they parted in the corridor.

"Give *me* time?" Wallander said. "You mean *us*, don't you?"

"You know exactly what I mean," Björk said. "Let's not waste time discussing it."

"I entirely agree," Wallander said.

When he had got to his office and closed the door, he felt at a loose end. Somebody had put on his desk a photograph of Harderberg's jet parked at Sturup. Wallander glanced at it, then pushed it aside.

I've lost my touch, he thought. The whole investigation's gone to pot. I ought to pass it on to somebody else. I can't handle this.

He sat there in his chair, inert. His mind went back to Riga and Baiba. When he could no longer cope with doing nothing he penned her a letter, inviting her to Ystad for Christmas and New Year. To make sure that the letter would not just lie there or get torn to pieces, he put it in an envelope and without more ado handed it to Ebba in reception.

"Could you post that for me today?" he said. "It's really urgent."

"I'll take care of it myself," she said, with a smile. "Incidentally, you look shattered. Are you getting enough sleep?"

"Not as much as I need," Wallander said.

"Who's going to thank you if you work yourself to death?" she said. "Not me, for sure."

Wallander went back to his office.

A month, he thought. A month in which to wipe the smile off Harderberg's face. He doubted if it would be possible.

He forced himself to work, despite everything.

Then he phoned Widén.

He also made up his mind to buy some cassettes of opera recordings. He missed his music.

Chapter 13

At around noon on Monday, November 22, Kurt Wallander got into the police car that was still doing service as a temporary replacement for his own burned-out wreck and set off west from Ystad. He was heading for the stables next to the ruins of Stjärnsund Castle where Sten Widén ran his business. When he reached the top of the hill outside Ystad he turned off into the lay-by, cut the engine and stared out to sea. On the far horizon he could just dimly see the outline of a cargo vessel sailing out into the Baltic. All of a sudden he was overcome by a fit of dizziness. He was terrified that it was his heart, but then he realised it was something else, that he seemed to be about to faint. He closed his eyes, leaned his head back and tried not to think. After a minute or so he opened his eyes. The sea was still there and the cargo vessel was still sailing out to the east.

I'm tired, he thought. Despite having rested all weekend. The feeling of exhaustion goes deep, deep down, I'm only half aware of the causes, and there is probably nothing I can do about it. Not now that I've made up my mind to return to work. The beach on Jutland no longer exists as far as I'm concerned. I renounced it of my own free will.

He did not know how long he sat there, but when he began to feel cold he started the engine and drove on. He would have preferred to go home and disappear into the security of his flat, but he forced himself to continue. He turned off towards Stjärnsund. After about a kilometre the road deteriorated badly. As always when he visited Widén, he wondered how big horseboxes could negotiate such a wretchedly maintained track.

The path sloped steeply towards the extensive farm with row upon row of stable blocks. He drove down into the yard and switched off the engine. A flock of crows were screeching in a nearby tree.

He got out of the car and made for the red-brick building Widén used as a combined home and office. The door was ajar, and he could hear Widén talking on the phone. He knocked and went in. As usual it was untidy and smelled strongly of horses. Two cats were lying asleep on the unmade bed. Wallander wondered how his friend could put up with living like this year after year.

The man who nodded to him as he came in without interrupting his telephone call was thin, with tousled hair and an angry red patch of eczema on his chin. He looked just as he had twenty-five years back. In those days they had seen a lot of each other. Widén had dreamed then of becoming an opera singer. He had a fine tenor voice, and they had planned a future with Wallander acting as his impresario. But the dream had collapsed, or rather, faded away; Wallander had become a police officer and Widén had inherited his father's business, training racehorses. They had drifted apart, without either of them really knowing why, and it was not until the early 1990s, in connection with a lengthy and complicated murder case, that they had come into contact again.

There was a time when he was my best friend, Wallander thought. I haven't had another one since then. Perhaps he will always be the best friend I ever had.

Widén finished his call and slammed the receiver down.

"What a bastard!" he snarled.

"A horse owner?" Wallander said.

"A crook," Widén said. "I bought a horse from him a month ago. He has some stables over at Höör. I was going to collect it, but he's changed his mind. The bastard."

"If you've paid for the horse, there's not much he can do about it," Wallander said.

"Only a deposit," Widén said. "But I'm going to collect that horse no matter what he says."

Widén disappeared into the kitchen. When he came back Wallander could smell alcohol on his breath.

"You always come when I'm not expecting you," Widén said. "Would you like some coffee?"

Wallander accepted the offer and they went out to the kitchen. Widén shifted piles of old racing programmes to one side, exposing a small patch of plastic tablecloth.

"How about a drop of something stronger?" he asked, as he set about making the coffee.

"I'm driving," Wallander said. "How's it going with the horses?"

"It hasn't been a good year. And next year's not going to be any better. There isn't enough money in circulation. Fewer horses. I keep having to raise my training fees to make ends meet. What I'd really like to do is close down and sell up, but property prices are too low. In other words, I'm stuck fast in the Scanian mud."

He poured the coffee and sat down. Wallander noticed Widén's hand shaking as he reached for the cup. He's well on the way to drinking himself to death, he thought. I've never seen his hand shake like that in the middle of the day.

"What about you?" Widén asked. "What are you doing nowadays? Are you still off sick?"

"No, I'm back at work. A police officer again."

Widén looked bemused. "I didn't think so," he said.

"Didn't think what?"

"That you'd go back."

"What else could I do?"

"You were talking about getting a job with a security company. Or becoming head of security for some firm."

"I'll never be anything but a police officer."

"No," Widén agreed, "and I don't suppose I'll ever get away from these stables. That horse I've bought in Höör is a good 'un, by the way. Out of Queen Blue. Nothing wrong with its pedigree."

A girl rode past the window on horseback.

"How many staff have you got?"

"Three. But I can't afford more than two. I really need four."

"That's why I'm here, actually," Wallander said.

"Don't tell me you want a job as a stableboy," Widén said. "I don't think you've got the necessary qualifications."

"I'm sure I haven't," Wallander said. "Let me explain."

Wallander could see no reason why he shouldn't explain about Alfred Harderberg; he knew Widén would never breathe a word to anybody else.

"It's not my idea," Wallander said. "We've recently acquired a new woman police officer in Ystad. She's good. She was the one who saw the advert and told me about it."

"You mean I should second one of my girls to Farnholm Castle, is that it?" Widén said. "As a sort of spy? You must be out of your mind."

"Murder is murder," Wallander said. "The castle is impenetrable. This advert gives us an opportunity to get in. You say you have a girl too many."

"I said I had one too few."

"She can't be stupid," Wallander said. "She has to be wide awake and notice things."

"I have a girl who would fit the bill," Widén said. "She's sharp, and nothing scares her. But there is a problem."

"What's that?"

"She doesn't like the police."

"Why's that?"

"You know that I often employ girls who've gone off the rails a bit. Over the years I've found them pretty good. I cooperate with a youth employment agency in Malmö. I have a girl from there at the moment, 19 years old. Name's Sofia. She was the one riding past the window just now."

"We don't need to mention the police," Wallander said. "We can think up some reason why you need to keep an eye on what's cooking at the castle. Then you can pass on to me what she tells you."

"Only if I must," Widén said. "I'd rather not get involved. Alright, we don't need to tell her you're a police officer. You're just somebody who wants to know what's going on there. If I say you're OK, she'll take my word for it."

"We can try," Wallander said.

"She hasn't got the job yet," Widén said. "I expect there'll be lots of horsey girls interested in a job at the castle."

"Go and get her," Wallander said. "Don't tell her my name."

"What the hell shall I call you, then?"

Wallander thought for a moment. "Roger Lundin," he said.

"Who's he?"

"From now on it's me."

Widén shook his head. "I hope you're right about this," he said. "I'll go and fetch her."

Sofia proved to be thin and leggy with a mop of unkempt hair. She came into the kitchen, nodded casually in Wallander's direction, then sat down and drank what remained of the coffee in Widén's cup. Wallander wondered if she was one of the girls who shared his bed. He knew of old that Widén often had affairs with the girls who worked for him.

"You know I have to cut back here," Widén said. "But we've heard about a job that might suit you at a castle over at Österlen. If you take the job, or rather get it, things might pick up here later, and I promise to take you back if they do."

"What sort of horses are they?" she asked.

Widén looked at Wallander, who could only shrug his shoulders.

"I don't suppose they'll be Ardennes," Widén said. "What the hell does it matter? It's only going to be temporary. Besides, you'd be helping Roger here, who's a friend of mine. He'd like you to keep your eyes peeled and see what goes on there at the castle. Nothing special, just keeping your eyes open."

"What's the money like?" she asked.

"I've no idea," Wallander said.

"It's a castle, for God's sake," Widén said. "Stop being awkward."

He disappeared into the living room and came back with the paper. Wallander found the advert.

"Interview," he said. "Applicants should phone first."

"We can fix that," Widén said. "I'll drive you there tonight."

She suddenly looked up from the plastic tablecloth and stared Wallander in the eye.

"What sort of horses are they?" she asked.

"I really have no idea," Wallander said.

She cocked her head to one side. "I think you're police," she said.

"What on earth makes you think that?" Wallander said, astonished.

"I can feel it."

Widén interrupted her. "His name's Roger. That's all you need to know. Don't ask so many stupid bloody questions. Try to look comparatively respectable when we go there tonight. Wash your hair, for instance. And don't forget that Winter's Moon needs a bandage on her left hind leg."

She left the kitchen without another word.

"You can see for yourself," Widén said. "She's nobody's fool."

"Thanks for your help," Wallander said. "Let's hope she pulls it off."

"I'll drive her over. That's the best I can do."

"Phone me at home," Wallander said. "I need to know right away if she gets the job."

They went out to Wallander's car.

"I sometimes feel so desperately bloody tired of this whole business," Widén said.

"It would be nice if we could have our time over again," Wallander said.

"I sometimes say to myself, is that all it was? Life, that is. A few arias, loads of third-rate horses, constant money problems."

"Come on, it's not all that bad, is it?"

"Convince me."

"We have a reason to meet more often now. We can talk about it."

"She hasn't got the job yet."

"I know," Wallander said. "Phone me tonight."

He got into his car, nodded to Widén and drove off. It was still quite early in the day. He made up his mind to pay another visit.

Half an hour later he parked in a no-parking area in the narrow street behind the Continental Hotel and walked to Mrs Dunér's little pink house. He was surprised to see no sign of a police car in the vicinity. What had happened to the protection Mrs Dunér was supposed to be receiving? He grew annoyed and worried at the same time. He rang the doorbell. He would get on to Björk immediately.

The door opened a fraction, but when Mrs Dunér saw who it was, she seemed genuinely pleased.

"I apologise for not having phoned in advance," he said.

"It's always a pleasure to welcome Inspector Wallander," she said.

311

He accepted her offer of a cup of coffee, even though he knew he had drunk too much coffee already. While she was busy in the kitchen Wallander took another look at her back garden. The lawn had been repaired. He wondered if she was expecting the police to provide her with another phone directory.

In this investigation everything seems to have happened a long time ago, he thought, and yet it's only a few days since I threw the directory at the lawn and watched the garden explode.

She brought in the coffee, and he sat on the flower-patterned sofa.

"I didn't see a police car outside when I arrived," he said.

"Sometimes they're here, sometimes they're not," Mrs Dunér said.

"I'll look into it," Wallander promised.

"Is it really necessary?" she said. "Do you really think somebody is trying to harm me?"

"You know what happened to your employers. I don't believe anything else is going to happen, but we have to take all the precautions we can."

"I wish I could make sense of it all," she said.

"That's why I'm here," Wallander said. "You've had time to do some thinking. Often one needs to let a bit of time pass before things become clear, to let your memory warm up."

"I have tried. Day and night."

"Let's go back a few years," Wallander said. "To when Gustaf Torstensson was first offered the opportunity of working for Alfred Harderberg. Did you ever meet him?"

"No, never."

"You spoke to him on the phone?"

"Not even that. It was always one of the secretaries who called."

"It must have been a big deal for the firm to get a client like that."

"Oh yes, of course. We began to earn much more money than we'd ever done before. We were able to renovate the whole building."

"Even if you never met or spoke to Harderberg, you must have formed some idea of what he was like. I know you have a good memory."

She thought before answering. Wallander watched a magpie hopping about in the garden while he waited.

"Everything was always urgent," she said. "Whenever he called in Mr Torstensson, everything else had to be put to one side."

"Mr Torstensson must have discussed his client now and then," he said. "Told you about his visits to the castle."

"I think he was very impressed. And also fearful of making a mistake. That was very important. I remember him saying several times that mistakes were forbidden."

"What do you think he meant by that?"

"That if that happened Harderberg would go to another firm of solicitors."

"Weren't you curious about Harderberg, and about the castle?"

"I wondered what it was like, of course. But he never said much. He was impressed, but reticent. I remember he once said that Sweden should be grateful for all the things Dr Harderberg was doing."

"He never said anything negative about him?"

313

"Yes, he did, actually. I remember because it only happened once."

"What did he say?"

"I can tell you word for word. He said: 'Dr Harderberg has a macabre sense of humour.'"

"What do you suppose he meant by that?"

"I don't know. I didn't ask, and he didn't explain."

"When was this?"

"About a year ago."

"In what context did he say it?"

"He had just come back from Farnholm Castle. One of the regular meetings. I don't remember it having been anything out of the ordinary."

Wallander could see he wasn't going to get any further on that tack.

"Let's talk about something completely different," he said. "When a solicitor's at work, there's always a lot of paper around. But we hear from the representatives of the Bar Council that there's very little in the files concerning the work Mr Torstensson did for Harderberg."

"I was expecting that question," she said. "There were very special routines as far as work for Dr Harderberg was concerned. The only documents kept were the ones a solicitor regards as essential. We had strict instructions not to copy or save anything that wasn't absolutely necessary. Mr Torstensson took all the documents he worked on back to Farnholm Castle. That's why there's so little in the archives."

"That must have seemed very odd to you."

"The reason given was that Dr Harderberg's affairs were extremely sensitive. I had no reason not to accept that, so long as no rules were broken."

"I understand that Mr Torstensson gave financial advice," Wallander said. "Can you remember any details?"

"I'm afraid I can't," she said. "They were complicated agreements between banks and companies in all four corners of the world. It was generally one of Dr Harderberg's secretaries who typed the documents. I was only rarely asked to type anything Mr Torstensson was going to take to Dr Harderberg. He typed up quite a lot of things himself."

"But he didn't do that for other clients?"

"Never."

"How would you explain that?"

"I assumed they were so sensitive that not even I was allowed to see them," she said frankly.

Wallander declined the offer of a top-up for his coffee.

"Can you remember noticing any mention of a company called Avanca in any of the documents you saw?"

He could see she was trying hard to remember.

"No," she said. "It's possible I saw it, but I don't remember it."

"Just one more question," he said. "Did you know about the threatening letters the firm received?"

"Gustaf Torstensson showed them to me," she said. "But he said they were nothing to worry about. That's why they weren't put in the archives. I thought he had thrown them away."

"Did you know that the man who wrote them, Lars Borman, was a friend of Gustaf Torstensson?"

"No, and I am surprised to hear it."

"They met through an icons club or society."

"I knew about the club, but I did not know that the man who wrote those letters was a member."

Wallander put down his coffee cup. "I won't disturb you any longer," he said, rising to his feet.

She remained seated, staring at him. "Haven't you any news at all to tell me?" she said.

"We don't know yet who committed the murders," Wallander said. "Nor do we know why they did it. When we know that, we'll know why somebody planted a mine in your garden."

She stood up and took hold of his arm. "You *have* to catch them," she said.

"Yes," Wallander said. "But it could take time."

"I have to know what happened before I die."

"As soon as there is anything to tell you, I'll be in touch straight away," he said, knowing that this could not have sounded very satisfactory to her ears.

Wallander drove to the police station and was told that Björk was in Malmö. So he went to Svedberg and asked him to find out why there was no proper protection at Mrs Dunér's house.

"Do you really think she's at risk?" Svedberg said.

"I don't think anything," Wallander said. "But more than enough has happened already."

Svedberg handed him a note. "There was a call from somebody called Lisbeth Norin," he said. "You can get her on this number. She'll be there until 5.00."

It was a number in Malmö, not Gothenburg. Wallander went to his office and dialled the number. An old man's voice answered. After a pause Lisbeth Norin came to the phone, and Wallander introduced himself.

"I happen to be in Malmö for a few days," she said. "I'm visiting my father, he's broken his femur. I checked my answering machine and heard you'd been trying to reach me."

"Yes, I'd be grateful for a word with you," Wallander said. "Preferably not over the phone."

"What's it about?"

"I have some questions in connection with a case we're investigating at the moment," Wallander said. "I heard about you from a Dr Strömberg in Lund."

"I have some free time tomorrow," she said. "But it will have to be here in Malmö."

"I'll drive over," Wallander said. "Would 10 a.m. suit you?"

"That will do fine."

She gave him the address in central Malmö.

Wallander wondered how an old man with a broken femur could get to answer the phone. Then he realised he was extremely hungry. It was already late afternoon. He decided to work at home. He had a lot of material on Harderberg's business empire that he had not yet read. He found a plastic carrier bag in a drawer and filled it with files. He told Ebba that he would be working at home for the rest of the day.

He stopped at a grocer's and bought some food, and went into a tobacconist's to buy five lottery scratch cards. When he got home he cooked himself some blood pudding and had a beer with it. He looked in vain for the jar of lingonberry jam he thought he had. Then he washed up and checked his lottery cards. No luck. He decided he had had enough coffee for one day and lay on his unmade bed for a little rest before starting to go through the files.

He was woken up by the telephone ringing. He looked at the clock by his bed. It was 9.10 p.m.

He picked up the phone and recognised Widén's voice.

"I'm ringing from a phone box," he said. "I thought you'd like to know that Sofia got the job. She starts tomorrow."

Wallander was wide awake immediately.

"Good," he said. "Who gave her the job?"

"A woman called Karlén."

Wallander recalled his first visit to Farnholm Castle. "Anita Karlén," he said.

"A couple of cobs," Widén said. "Very valuable. That's what she'll be looking after. Nothing wrong with the wages either. The stables are small, but there's a one-room flat attached. I think Sofia has a much higher opinion of you now that she's had this opportunity."

"That's good," Wallander said.

"She's going to phone me in a few days' time. Just one problem: I can't remember your name."

Wallander also had to think hard before remembering. "Roger Lundin," he said.

"I'll write it down."

"I'd better do the same. Incidentally, better if she doesn't phone from the castle, tell her to use a call box the same as you're doing."

"There's a telephone in her flat. Why shouldn't she use that?"

"It could be bugged."

Wallander could hear Widén taking a deep breath at the other end of the line.

"I think you're out of your mind."

"I ought to be careful with my own phone, in fact," Wallander said. "But we keep a regular check on our police lines."

"Who is this Harderberg? A monster?"

"He's a friendly, suntanned man who's always smiling,"

Wallander said. "He's also elegantly dressed. There are lots of ways a monster can look."

Pips were sounding at the other end of the line. "I'll call you," Widén said, then he was cut off.

Wallander wondered if he ought to phone Höglund and tell her what had happened, but decided not to. It was getting late. He spent the rest of the evening poring over the contents of the plastic carrier bag. At midnight he took out his old school atlas and looked up some of the exotic places to which the tentacles of Harderberg's empire reached. It was clear that it was a huge operation. Wallander also had a nagging worry that he was pointing the investigation and his colleagues in the wrong direction. Perhaps there was another solution to the deaths of the two solicitors after all.

It was 1 a.m. by the time he went to bed. It struck him that it was a long time since Linda had been in touch. On the other hand, he should have phoned her ages ago.

Tuesday, November 23 was a fine, clear autumn day.

He had taken the liberty of lying in that morning. He had phoned the station a little before 8.00 and told them he was going to Malmö. He had made coffee and stayed in bed for another hour. Then he had had a quick shower and set off. The address Norin had given him was near the Triangle in the centre of the city. He left his car in the multi-storey car park behind the Sheraton Hotel, and rang the doorbell at dead on 10.00. A woman of about his own age answered. She was wearing a brightly coloured tracksuit, and he wondered if he had got the wrong address. She did not fit the image he had of her after hearing her voice on the telephone, nor did it correspond to the general and no doubt prejudiced idea he had of journalists.

"So you're the police officer," she said cheerfully. "I'd expected a man in uniform."

"Sorry to disappoint you," Wallander said.

She invited him in. It was an old flat with high ceilings. She introduced him to her father, who was sitting in a chair with his leg in plaster. Wallander noticed the cordless telephone on his knee.

"I recognise you," the man said. "There was quite a bit about you in the newspapers a year or so ago. Or am I mixing you up with somebody else?"

"No, that was probably me," Wallander said.

"And something to do with a car that burned out on Öland Bridge," the man said. "I remember it because I used to be a sailor before the bridge was built, getting in the way of the ships."

"Newspapers exaggerate things," Wallander said.

"I remember you were described as an exceptionally successful police officer."

"That's right," the daughter said. "Now you mention it, I recognise Inspector Wallander from the photos in the papers. Weren't you on some television discussion programme too?"

"You must be mixing me up with somebody else."

"Let's go and sit in the kitchen," she said.

The autumn sun was shining through the high window. A cat was curled up asleep among the plant pots. He accepted the offer of a cup of coffee, and sat down.

"My questions are not going to be very precise," Wallander said. "Your answers are likely to be far more interesting. Let me just say that the Ystad police are currently investigating a murder, possibly two murders, and there are certain indications to suggest that the transportation and illegal selling of body organs might be involved. I can't say for certain if that is the case, and I'm afraid I can't go into any more detail for technical reasons associated with the case."

Why can't I express myself more simply? he wondered, crossly. I speak like a parody of a police officer. I sound like a machine.

"I see why Lasse Strömberg gave you my name," she said, and Wallander could tell that her interest had been aroused.

"If I understand it rightly you're doing work on this horrific traffic," he said. "It would be a big help to me if you could give me an overview."

"It would take all day to do that," she said. "Possibly all night as well. Besides, you'd soon find there was an invisible question mark behind every word I said. It's a gruesome activity that practically nobody has dared look into, apart from a handful of American journalists. I'm probably the only journalist in Scandinavia who's started digging into it."

"I take it that's a pretty risky business."

"Maybe not here, and maybe not for me," she said. "But I know personally one of the American journalists involved, Gary Becker from Minneapolis. He went to Brazil to look into rumours about a gang said to be operating in São Paulo. He wasn't just threatened – one night as his taxi stopped outside his hotel someone fired a whole magazine at it. He booked the next flight and got the hell out of there."

"Have you come across any suggestion that Swedes could be involved in the trafficking?"

"No. Should I have done?"

"I was only asking," Wallander said.

She studied him without speaking, then leaned across the table towards him. "If you and I are going to have a conversation, you have to be honest with me," she said. "Don't forget that I'm a journalist. You don't have to pay for this visit because you're a police officer, but the least I can ask is that you tell me the truth."

"You're right," Wallander said. "There is a slight possibility that there might be a connection. That's the nearest I can go to telling you the truth."

"OK," she said. "Now we understand each other. But I want just one more thing from you. If in fact there does turn out to be a connection, I want to be the first journalist who knows about it."

"I can't promise you that," Wallander said. "It's against our regulations."

"No doubt it is. But killing people to take their body parts goes against something much more important than regulations."

Wallander considered what she had said. He was citing regulations that he had long since ceased to observe uncritically himself. In recent years his experiences as a police officer had taken place in a no man's land where any good he might have been able to do had always involved his having to decide which regulations to abide by, and which not. Why should he change now?

"You'll be the first to know," he said. "But you'd better not quote me. I'll have to remain anonymous."

"That's good," she said again. "Now we understand each other even better."

*

When Wallander looked back over all the hours he spent in that hushed kitchen, with the cat asleep among the pot plants and the rays of the sun moving slowly over the plastic tablecloth before disappearing altogether, he was surprised at how quickly the time had passed. They had started talking at 10 a.m. and it was evening by the time they finished. They had had a few breaks, she had prepared lunch for him, and her father had entertained Wallander with stories about his life as captain of various ships plying the Baltic coast, with occasional voyages to Poland and the Baltic States. Otherwise they had been alone in the kitchen, and she had talked about her research. Wallander envied her. They both worked on investigations, they both spent their time constantly up against crime and human suffering. The difference was that she was trying to expose crime to prevent it happening, while Wallander was always occupied in clearing up crimes that had already been committed.

What he remembered most from his time in that kitchen was a journey into an unimagined world where human beings and body parts had been reduced to market commodities, with no sign of any moral consideration. If she was correct in her assumptions, the trade in body parts was so vast that it was almost beyond comprehension. What shook him most, however, was her claim that she could understand the people who killed healthy human beings in order to sell parts of their bodies.

"It's a reflection of the world," she said. "This is how things are, whether we like it or not. When a person is sufficiently poor, he's ready to do anything at all to keep body and soul together, no matter how squalid his life might be. How can we presume to make moral judgments about what they do? When their circumstances are so far beyond our understanding? In the slums on the edge of cities like Rio or Lagos or Calcutta or Madras, you can hold up 30 dollars and announce that you want to meet somebody who's prepared to kill another human being. Within a minute you have a queue of willing assassins. And they don't ask who they're going to be required to kill, nor do they wonder why. And they're prepared to do it for 20 dollars. Maybe even ten. I'm aware of a sort of abyss in the middle of what I'm working on. I get shocked, I feel desperate, but as long as the world continues as it is, I recognise that everything I do could be regarded as meaningless."

Wallander had sat in silence for most of the time. From time to time he asked a question the better to understand what she was saying. But he could see that she really was trying to pass on everything she knew – or suspected, because there was so little anybody could be 100 per cent certain about.

And then, hours later, they had come to a stop.

"I don't know any more," she said. "But if what I've said is of help to you, I'm glad of it."

"I don't even know if I'm on the right track," Wallander said. "But if I am, I know we've identified a Swedish link to this abominable trade. And if we can put a stop to it, that surely has to be a good thing."

"Of course it does," she said. "One plundered corpse fewer in a South American ditch – that makes it all worthwhile."

It was almost 7 p.m. by the time Wallander left Malmö. He knew he ought to have phoned Ystad and told them what he was doing, but he had been too taken up by his conversation with Norin.

She had accompanied him to the car park where they had said their goodbyes.

"You've given me an awful lot to think about," Wallander said. "I can't thank you enough."

"Who knows," she said, "perhaps I'll get payment in kind one of these days."

"You'll be hearing from me."

"I'm counting on that. You'll normally find me in Gothenburg. Unless I'm on my travels."

Wallander stopped at a grill bar near Jägersro for something to eat. He was thinking all the time about what she had told him, and how he could fit Harderberg into that picture. But he couldn't.

He wondered if they would ever find an answer to the question of why the two solicitors had been killed. In all his years as a police officer, he had so far been spared the experience of being involved in an unsolved murder case. Was he standing now outside a door that would never open?

He drove home to Ystad that evening feeling the weariness seep through his body. The only thing he had to look forward to was phoning Linda when he got in.

But the moment Wallander stepped into his flat he knew that something was not as it had been when he left that morning. He paused in the hall, listening intently. Maybe it was his imagination. Yet the feeling would not go away. He switched on the light in the living room, sat down on a chair and looked around him. Nothing was missing, nothing seemed to have been moved. He went into the bedroom. The unmade bed was exactly as he had left it. The half-empty coffee cup was still on his bedside table next to the alarm clock. He went into the kitchen.

Only when he opened the refrigerator to get out the margarine and a piece of cheese was he sure that he was right. He looked hard at the opened packet of blood pudding. He had an almost photographic memory and he knew he had put it on the third of the four shelves. It was on the second shelf now.

The packet of blood pudding had been at the very edge and could easily have fallen out on to the floor – it had happened to him before. Then somebody had put it back on the wrong shelf.

He had no doubt at all that he remembered it rightly. Somebody had been in his flat during the day. And whoever had been there had opened his refrigerator, either to look for something or to hide something.

His first reaction was to laugh. Then he closed the fridge door and walked quickly out of the flat. He was scared. He had to force himself to think clearly. They're not far away, he thought. I'll let them think I'm still in the flat.

He went down the stairs to the basement. There was a door at the back leading to the rubbish room. He unlocked and opened it. He looked out at the parking places lined up along the back of the building. There was no-one about. He closed the door behind him and edged his way through the shadows along the wall. When he came to where it opened out into Mariagatan, he kneeled down and peered at waist height from behind the drainpipe.

The car was parked about ten metres behind his own. The engine was not running and the lights were off. He could make out a man behind the wheel, but could not be sure if there was anybody else in the car.

He pulled back his head and stood up. From somewhere he could hear the sound of a TV set. He wondered feverishly what to do next. Then he made up his mind.

He started running across the empty car park, turned left at the first corner and was gone.

Chapter 14

He was gasping for breath before he had got as far as Blekegatan. Once more Wallander thought he was about to die. He had taken Oskarsgatan from Mariagatan, it was not very far, and he had not been running flat out. Even so, the raw autumn air was tearing at his lungs and his pulse was racing. He forced himself to slow down, fearful that his heart would stop. The feeling of lacking the strength to do anything worried him more than the discovery that someone had been in his flat and was now sitting in a car in the street, keeping watch on him. He struggled to suppress the thought, but what was upsetting him was really his fear, the fear he recognised so clearly from the previous year, and he did not want it back. It had taken him almost twelve months to shake it off, and he thought he had succeeded in burying it once and for all on the beaches at Skagen – but here it was, back to haunt him.

He started running again. It wasn't far to the block of flats in Lilla Norregatan where Svedberg lived. He had the hospital on his right, then he turned downhill towards the town centre. A torn poster outside the kiosk in Stora Norregatan caught his eye, then he turned right and almost immediately left and could see that the lights were on in the top-floor flat where Svedberg lived.

Wallander knew the lights were often on all night. Svedberg was afraid of the dark; indeed, that might have been why he chose to become a police officer, to try to cure his fear. But he still left the lights on in his flat at night, so his career had not been any help.

Everyone is frightened of something, Wallander thought, police officers or not. He stumbled through the front door and ran up the stairs, then paused when he reached the top floor to get his breath back. He rang Svedberg's bell. The door was opened almost immediately. Svedberg had a pair of reading glasses pushed up on to his forehead, and was holding a newspaper. Wallander knew he would be surprised to see him. During all the years they had known each other, Wallander had only been in Svedberg's flat two or three times, and then only after making an arrangement to meet there.

"I need your help," Wallander said when the astonished Svedberg had let him in and closed the door.

"You look shattered," Svedberg said. "What's happened?"

"I've been running. I want you to come with me. It won't take long. Where's your car?"

"It's right outside the front door."

"Drive me back to my place in Mariagatan," Wallander said. "Let me get out shortly before we get there. You know the car I'm using at the moment, a police Volvo?"

"The dark blue one or the red one?"

"The dark blue one. Turn into Mariagatan. There's another car parked behind my Volvo, you can't miss it. I want you to drive past and see whether there's anybody in the car apart from the driver. Then come back to where you've dropped me off. That's all. Then you can go home to your paper."

"You don't want to arrest somebody?"

"That's exactly the last thing I want to do. I just want to know how many there are in the car."

Svedberg had taken off his glasses and put down the newspaper.

"What's going on?" he said.

"I think somebody's watching my flat," Wallander said. "I only want to know how many of them there are. That's all. But I want whoever it is in the car to think I'm still in my flat. I came out by the back door."

"I'm not sure I understand all this. Wouldn't it be best to make an arrest? We can ask for help."

"You know what we've decided," Wallander said. "If it's anything to do with Harderberg we should pretend we're not very wide awake."

Svedberg shook his head. "I don't like this," he said.

"All you need to do is to drive to Mariagatan and make an observation," Wallander said. "Then I'll go back to my flat. I'll phone you if I need help."

"I suppose you know best," Svedberg said, sitting on a stool in order to tie his shoelaces.

They went down to the street and got into Svedberg's Audi, then drove past Stortorget, down Hamngatan and left into Österleden. When they got to Borgmästaregatan they turned left again. Wallander asked Svedberg to stop when they came to Tobaksgatan.

"I'll wait here," he said. "The car's ten metres behind."

Minutes later Svedberg was back. Wallander got into the car again.

"There was only the driver."

"Thanks for your help. You can go home now. I'll walk from here."

Svedberg gave him a worried look. "Why is it so important to know how many there are in the car?" he asked.

Wallander had forgotten to prepare for that question. He was so focused on what he had decided to do that he had not taken Svedberg's natural curiosity into account.

"I've seen that car before," he lied. "There were two men in it then. If there's only the driver in it now, it could mean the other man isn't far away."

This explanation was pretty feeble, but Svedberg raised no objections.

"FHC 803," he said. "But I expect you've noted that down already."

"Yes," Wallander said. "I'll look it up in the register. You don't need to bother about that. Just go home now. I'll see you tomorrow. Thanks for your help."

He got out of the car and waited until Svedberg had disappeared down Österleden, then he started walking towards Mariagatan. Now that he was on his own again he could feel himself getting agitated, the nagging worry that his fear was making him weak.

He went in by the back door and left the stair lights off when he returned to his flat. If he stood on tiptoe on the toilet seat and looked through the little bathroom window, he could see the street below. The car was still there. Wallander went to the kitchen. If they had meant to blow me up, they'd have done that already, he thought. They must be waiting for me to go to bed, and for the lights to go out.

He waited until nearly midnight, then went back to the bathroom and checked to be sure the car was still there. Then he switched off the kitchen light and switched on in the bathroom. After ten minutes he switched off in the bathroom and switched on in the bedroom. He waited for ten more minutes, and switched off in there as well. Then he went rapidly down the stairs and left the building through the back door, crouched behind the drainpipe at the corner of the car park and waited. He wished he had put on a warmer jumper. A cold wind was getting up. He cautiously moved his feet about in an attempt to keep warm. By 1 a.m. the only incident of note was that Wallander needed to pee against the wall. Apart from the occasional car driving past, all was peaceful.

At about 1.40 he heard a noise from the street. He peered out from behind the drainpipe. The driver's door had opened, although the inside light had not come on. After a few seconds' pause the driver emerged and closed the door quietly behind him. He was staring up at Wallander's windows all the time. He was wearing dark clothes, and Wallander was too far away to make out his features. Even so, he was sure he had seen the man before. He tried to remember where. The man hurried across the street and vanished through the front entrance.

Then it came to Wallander where he had seen him. He was one of the men lurking in the shadows at the foot of the stairs at Farnholm Castle, on both occasions Wallander had been there. He was one of Harderberg's shadows. And now he was on his way up the stairs to Wallander's flat, perhaps with the objective of killing him. Wallander felt almost as if he were lying in bed, in spite of being where he was, outside in the street, in the cold.

I am witnessing my own death, he thought.

He pressed himself tightly against the drainpipe and waited. At 2.03 the door opened without a sound and the man emerged again into the street. He looked round, and Wallander drew back behind the corner. Then he heard the car take off in a racing start.

He's going to report to Harderberg, Wallander thought. But he's not going to tell him the truth because he would not be able to explain how I could be in the flat one minute, switch off the light and go to bed, and have disappeared the next.

Wallander could not exclude the possibility that the man had left some device in the flat, so he got into his car and drove to the police station. The officers on duty greeted him in surprise when he appeared in reception. He collected a mattress he knew was stored in the basement, then lay on the floor of his office. It was gone 3.00, and he was worn out. He had to get some sleep if he was going to be able to think clearly, but the man in the dark clothes followed him into his dreams.

Wallander woke up covered in sweat after a series of chaotic nightmares. It was shortly after 5 a.m. He spent a while thinking about what Norin had told him, then he got up and went to fetch some coffee. It tasted bitter after standing all night. He did not want to go back to his flat yet. He took a shower in the changing room downstairs. By 7.00 he was back at his desk. It was Wednesday, November 24.

He recalled what Höglund had said a few days earlier: "We seem to have all the data, but we can't see how it hangs together." That's what we must start doing now,

Wallander thought. Make everything fit together. He phoned Nyberg at home. "We have to meet," Wallander said.

"I tried to find you yesterday," Nyberg said. "Nobody knew where you were. We have some news."

"We? Who's we?"

"Ann-Britt Höglund and I."

"About Avanca?"

"I got her to help me. I'm a technician, not a detective."

"I'll see you in my office as soon as you can get here. I'll phone Höglund."

Half an hour later Nyberg and Höglund were sitting in Wallander's office. Svedberg put his head round the door. "Do you need me?" he said.

"FHC 803. I haven't got round to looking it up. Could you do that for me, please?"

Svedberg nodded and closed the door.

"Avanca," Wallander said.

"Don't expect too much," Höglund said. "We've only had a day in which to look into the company and who owns it, but we've already established that it's no longer a family business run by the Romans. The family let the company use their name – and their reputation – and they still have some shares, possibly quite big holdings. But for several years now Avanca has been part of a consortium comprising several different firms associated in some way or other with pharmaceuticals, health care and hospital equipment. It's incredibly complicated, and the firms all seem to be intertwined. The umbrella for the consortium is a holding company in Liechtenstein called Medicom. It is divided up in turn among several owning groups. They include a Brazilian company concerned mainly with producing and exporting coffee. But what's much more interesting is that Medicom has direct financial links with Bayerische Hypotheken-und-Wechsel-Bank."

"Why is that interesting?" Wallander said. He had already lost track of Avanca.

"Because Harderberg owns a plastics factory in Genoa," she said. "They make speedboats."

"I'm lost," Wallander said.

"Here comes the punchline," Höglund said. "The factory in Genoa is called CFP, whatever that stands for, and helps its customers to arrange funding by way of a sort of leasing contract."

"Avanca, please," Wallander said. "I couldn't care less about Italian plastic boats just now."

"Perhaps you should," Höglund said. "CFP's leasing contracts are drawn up in cooperation with Bayerische Hypotheken-und-Wechsel-Bank. In other words, there is a link with the Harderberg empire. The first one we've found since the investigation began."

"I can't make head nor tail of it," Wallander said.

"There could be even closer links," she said. "We'll have to ask the fraud squad to help us with this. I hardly know what I'm doing myself."

"This is impressive." Nyberg had not said a word until now. "Maybe we should find out if that plastics factory in Genoa makes other things besides speed-boats."

"Such as cool boxes for transplant organs?" Wallander said.

"For instance."

"If this turns out to be true," Wallander said, "it means that Harderberg is in some degree involved in the manufacturing and importing of these plastic containers.

He might even have control, even if at first glance it looks to be a maze of different but interconnected companies. Can it really be possible that a Brazilian coffee producer has links with a tiny firm in Södertälje?"

"That would be no more odd than the fact that American car manufacturers also make wheelchairs," Höglund said. "Cars cause car accidents, which in turn creates a demand for wheelchairs."

Wallander clapped his hands and stood up. "Right, let's turn up the pressure on this investigation," he said. "Ann-Britt, can you get the financial experts to draw up some kind of large-scale wall map showing what Harderberg's holdings really look like? I want everything on it – speedboats in Genoa, cobs at Farnholm Castle, everything we've found out so far. And Nyberg, can you devote yourself to this plastic container? Where it comes from, how it got into Gustaf Torstensson's car."

"That would mean that we blow the plan we've been working to so far," Höglund objected. "Harderberg's bound to find out that we're digging into his companies."

"Not at all," Wallander said. "It's all a matter of routine questions. Nothing dramatic. Besides, I'll talk to Björk and Åkeson and suggest it's high time we had a press conference. It will be the first time in my life I've ever taken *that* initiative, but I think it would be a good thing if we could give the autumn a helping hand to spread about a bit more mist and fog."

"I heard that Åkeson is still in bed with flu," Höglund said.

"I'll call him," Wallander said. "We're turning up the pressure, so he'll have to come whether he's got a cold or not. Tell Martinsson and Svedberg we're meeting at 2.00 today."

Wallander had decided to wait until everybody was there before he said anything about what had happened the previous night.

"Right, let's get going," he said.

Nyberg went out, but Wallander asked Höglund to stay behind. He told her that he and Widén had managed to place a stablegirl at Farnholm Castle.

"Your idea was an excellent one," he said. "We'll see if it produces the goods."

"Let's hope she comes to no harm."

"She'll just be looking after some horses," Wallander said. "And keeping her eyes open. Let's not get hysterical. Harderberg can't suspect everybody on his staff to be police officers in disguise."

"I hope you're right," she said.

"How's it going with the flight log?"

"I'm working at it," she said, "but Avanca took all my time yesterday."

"You've done well," Wallander said.

She was pleased to be told that, he noticed. We're far too reluctant to praise our colleagues, Wallander thought. Especially when there's no end to the amount of criticism and tittle-tattle we bandy about.

"That's all," he said.

She left, and Wallander went to stand at the window and ask himself what Rydberg would have done in this situation. But for once he felt that he had no time to wait for his old friend's answer. He just had to believe that the way he was running the investigation was right.

He used up a huge amount of energy over the rest of the morning. He convinced Björk of the importance of holding a press conference the next day, and he promised him that he would himself take care of the journalists once he had agreed with Åkeson what they were going to say.

"It's not like you to call in the mass media off your own bat," Björk said.

"Maybe I'm becoming a better person," Wallander said. "They say it's never too late."

After meeting with Björk he phoned Åkeson at home. It was his wife who answered, and she was reluctant to let Wallander talk to her husband, who was in bed.

"Has he got a temperature?" Wallander asked.

"When you're ill, you're ill. Full stop," Mrs Åkeson said.

"I'm sorry," Wallander insisted, "but I've got to speak to him."

After a considerable pause Åkeson came to the phone. He sounded worn out. "I'm ill," he said. "Influenza. I've been on the loo all night."

"I wouldn't disturb you if it weren't important," Wallander said. "I'm afraid I need you for a few minutes this afternoon. We can send a car to collect you."

"I'll be there," Åkeson said. "But I can take a taxi."

"Do you want me to explain why it's important?"

"Do you know who killed them?"

"No."

"Do you want me to approve a warrant for the arrest of Alfred Harderberg?"

"No."

"Then you can explain when I get in this afternoon."

Wallander next phoned Farnholm Castle. He did not recognise the voice of the woman who answered. Wallander introduced himself and asked if he could speak to Kurt Ström.

"He doesn't come on duty until this evening," the woman said. "No doubt you'll get him at home."

"I don't suppose you're prepared to give me his phone number," Wallander said.

"Why ever not?"

"I thought it might be against your rules, security and so on."

"No, not at all," she said, and gave him the number.

"Please pass on my greetings to Dr Harderberg, and thank him for his hospitality the other evening," Wallander said.

"He's in New York."

"Well, please tell him when he comes back. Will he be away for long?"

"We expect him back the day after tomorrow."

Something had changed. He wondered if Harderberg had issued instructions to respond positively to queries from the Ystad police.

Wallander dialled Ström's home number. He let it ring for some considerable time, but got no reply. He called reception and asked Ebba to find out where Ström lived. While he was waiting he went to fetch a cup of coffee. He remembered that he still had not been in touch with Linda, as he had promised himself he would be. But he decided to wait until evening.

Wallander left the station at around 9.30 and set off towards Österlen. Ström apparently lived in a little farmhouse not far from Glimmingehus. Ebba knew the area better than most, so she had drawn him a rough map. Ström had not answered the phone, but Wallander had a hunch he would find him there. As he drove through Sandskogen he tried to remember what Svedberg had told him about the circumstances in which Ström had been kicked out of the police force. He tried to anticipate what his reception would be. Wallander had occasionally come across police officers who had been involved in a crime, and he recalled such occasions with distaste. But he could not avoid the conversation in store for him.

He had no difficulty following Ebba's map, and he drove straight to a small white-painted house typical of the area, to the east of Glimmingehus. It was set in a garden that was no doubt very pretty in the spring and summer. When he got out of the car two Alsatians in a steel cage started barking. There was a car in the garage, and Wallander assumed he had guessed right: Ström was at home. He did not need to wait long. Ström appeared from behind the house, wearing overalls and with a trowel in his hand. He stopped dead on seeing who his visitor was.

"I hope I'm not disturbing you," Wallander said. "I did ring, but I got no answer."

"I'm busy filling in some cracks in the foundations," Ström said. "What do you want?"

Wallander could see Ström was on his guard.

"I've got something to ask you about," he said. "Maybe you can shut the dogs up."

Ström shouted at the dogs and at once they fell silent.

"Let's go inside," he said.

"No need," Wallander said. "We can stay here. It'll only take a minute." He looked around the little garden. "A nice place you've got here. A bit different from a flat in the middle of Malmö."

"It was OK there as well, but this is closer to work."

"It looks as though you live on your own here. I thought you were married?"

340

Ström glared at him with eyes of steel. "What's my private life got to do with you?"

Wallander opened wide his arms in apology. "Nothing," he said. "But you know how it is with former colleagues. You ask after the family."

"I'm not your colleague," Ström said.

"But you used to be, didn't you?"

Wallander had changed his tone. He was looking for a confrontation. He knew that toughness was the only thing Ström had any respect for.

"I don't suppose you've come here to discuss my family."

Wallander smiled at him. "Quite right," he said. "I haven't. I only reminded you that we used to be colleagues out of politeness."

Ström had turned ashen. For a brief moment Wallander thought he had gone too far, and that Ström would take a swing at him.

"Let's forget it," Wallander said. "Let's talk about something else. October 11. A Monday evening. Six weeks ago. You know the evening I mean?"

Ström nodded, but said nothing.

"I really only have one question," Wallander said. "But let's get an important thing out of the way first. I'm not going to let you get away with not answering on the grounds that you'd be breaking the security rules of Farnholm Castle. If you try that, I'll make life so hellish for you, you'll wonder what hit you."

"You can't do anything to me," Ström said.

"I wouldn't be so sure of that," Wallander said. "I could arrest you and take you to Ystad with me, or I could phone the castle ten times a day and ask to speak to Kurt Ström. They would soon get the feeling that the police were far too interested in their head of security. I wonder if they know about your past? That could be embarrassing for them. I doubt if Dr Harderberg would be pleased if the peace and quiet of Farnholm Castle were to be disturbed."

"Go to hell!" Ström said. "Get to the other side of that gate before I throw you out."

"I only want the answer to one question, about the night of October 11," Wallander said, unconcerned. "And I can assure you it won't go any further. Is it really worth risking the new life you lead? As I recall, when we met at the castle gates you said you were very happy with it."

Wallander could see that Ström was wavering. His eyes were still full of hatred, but Wallander knew he would get an answer.

"One question," he said. "One answer. But a truthful one. Then I'll be off. You can get on with your repairs and forget I was ever here. And you can carry on guarding the gates of Farnholm Castle till the day you die. Just one question and one answer."

An aeroplane flew past high above their heads. Wallander wondered if it was Alfred Harderberg's Gulfstream on its way back from New York already.

"What do you want to know?"

"That evening of October 11," Wallander said. "Gustaf Torstensson left the castle at 8.14 p.m. according to the printout of the gate checks I've seen. That could be forged, of course, but let's assume it's correct. We do know he did leave Farnholm Castle, after all. My question to you, Kurt Ström, is very simple. Did a car leave Farnholm Castle after Mr Torstensson arrived but before he left?"

Ström said nothing, but then he nodded slowly.

"That was the first part of the question," Wallander said. "Now comes the second part of the same question. Who was it who left the castle?"

"I don't know."

"But you saw a car?"

"I've already answered more than one question."

"Stop this shit, Ström. It's the same question. What make of car was it? And who was in it?"

"It was one of the cars that belong to the castle. A BMW."

"Who was in it?"

"I don't know."

"Your life will turn extremely unpleasant if you don't answer!"

Wallander discovered that he did not need to pretend to be furious. He was already furious.

"I honestly don't know who was in the car."

Wallander could see that Ström was telling the truth. He ought to have realised.

"Because the windows were fitted with dark glass," Wallander said. "So you can't see who's inside. Is that right?"

Ström nodded. "You've got your answer," he said. "Now get the hell out of here."

"Always a pleasure to bump into former colleagues," Wallander said. "And you're quite right, it is time I was off. Nice to talk to you."

The dogs started barking as soon as he turned his back. As he drove off Ström was still standing in the doorway, watching him go. Wallander could feel the sweat inside his shirt. He remembered that Ström could be violent.

343

But he had got a plausible answer to a question that had been troubling him. The starting point for what happened that October night when Gustaf Torstensson died, alone in his car. He had a good idea now how it had occurred. While Torstensson sat back in one of the sumptuous leather armchairs chatting to Harderberg and the Italian bankers, a car had left Farnholm Castle to lie in wait for the old man as he drove home. Somehow or other, by a display of force or cunning or convincing friendliness, they had got him to stop his car on that remote, carefully chosen stretch of road. Wallander had no idea if the decision to prevent Torstensson reaching home had been made that same night, or earlier; but at least he could now see the makings of an explanation.

He thought about the men lurking in the shadows in the entrance hall. Then he shuddered as he thought about what had happened the previous night.

Without realising it, he pressed harder on the accelerator. By the time he came to Sandskogen he was going so fast that if he had been stopped he would have had his licence suspended on the spot. He slowed down. When he reached Ystad he called at Fridolf's Café and had a cup of coffee. He knew what advice Rydberg would have given him.

Patience, he would have said. When stones start rolling down a slope, it's important not to start running after them right away. Stay where you are and watch them rolling, see where they come to a stop. That's what he would have said.

And he would have been right, Wallander thought. That's how we're going to proceed.

*

In the days to come Wallander had evidence once more of how he was surrounded by colleagues who did not stint on effort when it was really needed. They had already been working intensively, but nobody protested when Wallander announced that they were going to have to work even harder. It had started that Wednesday afternoon when Wallander called the team to the conference room, and Åkeson attended despite his diarrhoea and high temperature. They all agreed that Harderberg's business empire should be unravelled and mapped out with the greatest possible speed. While the meeting was in progress Åkeson phoned the fraud squads in Malmö and Stockholm. The others present listened in admiration as he described how the need for them to work harder and give the job the highest priority was more or less essential if the country were to survive. When he hung up, the meeting burst into spontaneous applause.

On Åkeson's advice they had decided that they themselves would continue to concentrate on Avanca without worrying about running into conflict with the work being carried out by the fraud squads. Wallander also established that Höglund was the best qualified officer for this task. Nobody objected, and from that moment on she was no longer a raw recruit but a fully fledged member of the investigative team. Svedberg took over some of the work she had been doing before, including the efforts to obtain the flight plans of Harderberg's aircraft. There was some discussion between Wallander and Åkeson as to whether this was a sufficiently valuable source of information to warrant the effort. Wallander argued that sooner or later they would have to establish Harderberg's movements, not least on the day Sten Torstensson died.

Åkeson maintained that if it really did now seem likely that Harderberg was behind what had happened, he would have access to state-of-the-art resources and could be in contact with Farnholm Castle even if he were crossing the Atlantic in his Gulfstream, or in the Australian outback, where the financial experts claimed he had substantial mining interests. Wallander could see Åkeson's point and was just about to cave in when Åkeson threw up his hands and said he had only been putting a personal point of view and did not want any obstacles in the way of work that was ongoing.

When it came to the recruitment of the stablegirl Sofia, Wallander made a presentation that Höglund went out of her way to congratulate him on in private afterwards. Wallander knew that not only might Björk and Åkeson protest, but that Martinsson and Svedberg might object to involving a complete outsider in the investigation. Without actually lying, although perhaps he was economical with the truth, Wallander explained that by chance they had acquired a source of information at Farnholm Castle, somebody Wallander happened to know, who was looking after the horses there. He provided this information more or less in passing, just as a tray of sandwiches had been delivered and nobody was listening with more than half an ear to what he was saying. He exchanged glances with Höglund, and could tell that she had seen through his tactic.

Afterwards, when they had finished the sandwiches and aired the room, Wallander described how his flat had been watched the previous night. He did not mention, however, that the man in the car had actually been inside his flat. He was afraid that information would lead Björk to apply the brakes and put restrictions on what they could or could not do for security reasons. Svedberg was able to supply the astonishing news that the car was registered to a person who lived in Östersund and was the manager of a holiday camp in the Jämtland mountains. Wallander insisted that the man be investigated, the holiday camp as well. If Harderberg had interests in Australian mines there was no reason why he should not also be involved in a winter sports establishment in the north of Sweden. The meeting ended with Wallander telling them about his meeting with Ström. On hearing his account the room fell silent.

"That was the detail we needed," Wallander said afterwards to Höglund. "Police officers are practical people. The little fact that a car left Farnholm Castle before old man Torstensson began his final journey means that all the vague and obscure aspects of the sequence of events now have a little detail to rest on at last. If that is what happened, and it could very well have been, we've also got confirmation of the fact that Torstensson was murdered in a cold-blooded and well-planned operation. That means we know we're looking for a solution to something where nothing is coincidental. We can forget accidents and dramatic passions. We know now where we don't need to look."

The meeting had ended in a mood Wallander interpreted as resolute determination. That was what he had been hoping for. Before Åkeson went home to bed he had joined in a discussion with Björk and Wallander. They talked about the press conference the following day. Wallander had urged that, without actually telling lies, they could maintain that they had a lead to follow, but that they could not yet give any details for reasons associated with the investigation.

"But," Åkeson wondered, "how are you going to describe the lead without Harderberg realising that it points to Farnholm Castle?"

"A tragedy arising from somebody's private life," Wallander said.

"That doesn't sound particularly credible," Åkeson objected. "It's also a suspiciously thin basis on which to call a press conference. Make sure you're fully prepared. You need to have detailed and definite answers to every likely question."

Wallander drove home after the meeting.

He examined his telephone to see if there was any sign of a bug. He found nothing, but nevertheless decided that from now on he would not discuss anything to do with Harderberg on the phone from home.

Then he had a shower and got changed.

He had supper at the pizzeria in Hamngatan. Then he spent the rest of the evening preparing for the press conference. Now and then he went to the kitchen window and looked down into the street, but there was only his own car parked outside.

The press conference went more smoothly than Wallander had expected. The murder of the two solicitors was apparently not considered by the media to be of great public interest, and so there were not many newspapers represented, no television, and the local radio station only ran a short item.

"That ought to keep Harderberg calm," Wallander said to Björk when the reporters had left the police station.

"Unless he can read our minds," Björk said.

"He can speculate, of course," Wallander said, "but he can't be completely sure."

When he got back to his office he found a message on his desk to phone Mr S. Widén. He dialled the number and after it had been ringing for a very long time, Widén answered.

"You rang," Wallander said.

"Hi there, Roger," Widén said. "Our friend called me a few minutes ago. She was in Simrishamn. She had something to say that I think might be of interest to you."

"What's that?"

"That her post is evidently going to be short-lived."

"What does she mean by that?"

"It looks as if her employer is preparing to leave his castle."

Wallander was struck dumb.

"Are you still there?" Widén said, eventually.

"Yes," Wallander said. "I'm still here."

"That was all," Widén said.

349

Chapter 15

By the time Ove Hanson returned to work in Ystad on the afternoon of November 25, he had been away for over a month. He had been in Halmstad attending a course on computerised crime-solving arranged by the National Police Board. After Sten Torstensson's murder he had contacted Björk and asked if he should abandon the course and return to duty in Ystad, but Björk had told him to stay on. That was when he first heard Wallander had come back to work. The same evening he had telephoned Martinsson from his hotel to check whether it could really be true. Martinsson had confirmed it, and added that personally he thought that Wallander seemed more energetic than ever.

Even so, Hanson had not been prepared for what was in store for him when he returned and paused outside the office he had been using while Wallander had been away. He tapped on the door and went straight in without waiting to be asked, but almost jumped out of his skin at what he saw, and made to leave again immediately. Wallander was standing in the middle of the room holding a chair over his head, and staring at Hanson with a look on his face that could only be described as lunatic. It all happened very quickly and

Wallander put the chair down, his expression returning to normal. But the image had burned itself into Hanson's memory. For a long time afterwards Hanson kept it to himself, and he wondered when Wallander would finally break down and go mad.

"I see I've come at a bad moment," Hanson said. "I was just going to say hello and tell you I'm back on duty."

"Did I scare you?" Wallander asked. "That wasn't the intention. I've just had a phone call that made me furious. It's a good job you came in when you did, or I'd have smashed the chair against the wall."

Then they sat down, Wallander behind his desk and Hanson on the chair he had inadvertently saved from destruction. Hanson was one of the detectives Wallander knew least well, although they'd been working together for many years. They were like chalk and cheese in character and approach, and often got into awkward discussions that turned into screaming arguments. Nevertheless, Wallander respected Hanson's ability. He could be abrupt and obstinate and difficult to work with, but he was thorough and persistent, and could occasionally surprise his colleagues with cleverly worked-out analyses that could make a breakthrough in a seemingly insoluble case. Wallander had at times missed Hanson over the past month. He had seriously considered asking Björk to call him back, but had never got round to doing anything about it.

He knew too that Hanson was probably the colleague who would have had fewest regrets if Wallander had never come back to work. Hanson was ambitious, which was not of itself a bad thing for a police officer, but he had never been able to accept that Wallander had taken over Rydberg's invisible mantle. Hanson thought he was the one who should have assumed it. But it was not to be, and as a result Hanson had never managed to overcome his antagonism.

From Wallander's side there were other factors, such as his irritation at Hanson spending so much of his time playing the horses. His desk was always piled high with racing cards and betting systems. Wallander was persuaded that Hanson sometimes spent half his working day trying to work out how hundreds of horses at courses up and down the country were going to perform at their next outings. And Wallander knew that Hanson couldn't bear opera.

But now they were facing each other across the desk, and Hanson was back on duty. He would strengthen the team, extend their scope. That was all that mattered.

"So you came back," Hanson said. "The last I heard you were about to resign."

"Sten's murder made me reconsider," Wallander said.

"And then you found out that his father had been murdered as well," Hanson said. "We had that down as an accident."

"It was cleverly disguised," Wallander said. "My finding that chair leg in the mud was pure luck."

"Chair leg?" Hanson sounded surprised.

"You'll have to set aside time to get up to speed on the detail of the case," Wallander said. "You're going to be crucial, make no mistake about it. Not least after that call I'd just received when you came in."

"What was it about?" Hanson said.

"It looks as if the man we're putting all our resources into pinning down intends to move out. That would cause us enormous problems."

"I'd better get reading."

"I'd have liked to give you a thorough rundown myself," Wallander said, "but I don't have the time. Talk to Ann-Britt. She's good at summarising what matters and leaving out what doesn't."

"Is she really?" Hanson asked.

Wallander stared at him. "Is she what?"

"Good. Is Höglund good?"

Wallander remembered something Martinsson had said when he had first come back to work, to the effect that Hanson thought his position was under threat thanks to Höglund's arrival on the scene.

"Yes," Wallander said. "She's a good police officer already, and she's going to get even better."

"I find that hard to believe," Hanson said, getting to his feet.

"You'll see," Wallander said. "Let me put it this way: Ann-Britt Höglund's here to stay."

"I think I'd prefer to talk to Martinsson," Hanson said.

"You do as you wish," Wallander said.

Hanson was already halfway out of the door when Wallander asked him another question.

"What did you do in Halmstad?"

"Thanks to the National Police Board, I had an opportunity to look into the future," Hanson said. "When police officers all over the world will be sitting at their computers, tracking down criminals. We'll be part of a communications network covering the whole world and all the information collected by forces in different countries will be available to everybody by means of cleverly constructed databases."

"Sounds frightening," Wallander said. "And boring."

"But probably also very efficient," Hanson said. "Mind you, I imagine we'll both be retired by then."

"Höglund will see it," Wallander said. "Is there a trotting course in Halmstad, by the way?"

"One night a week," Hanson said.

"How did you do?"

Hanson shrugged. "Swings and roundabouts," he said. "Usual thing. Some horses run as they should. Others don't."

Hanson left, closing the door behind him. Wallander thought of the fury that had welled up inside him when he heard that Harderberg was making preparations to move out. He rarely lost his temper completely, and he could not remember the last time he had so lost control that he had started throwing things around.

Now that he was alone again in his office, he tried to think calmly. The apparent fact that Harderberg intended leaving Farnholm Castle did not necessarily mean anything more than that he had decided to do what he had done many times before: move on to pastures new. There was no good reason to think that he was running away. What was there for him to run away from? And where would he run to? At worst it would make the investigation more complicated. Other police districts would have to be involved, depending on where he decided to settle.

It was a possibility that Wallander needed to look into without delay. He phoned Widén. One of the girls answered. She sounded very young.

"Sten's in the stables," she said. "The blacksmith's here."

"He has a telephone out there," Wallander said. "Put me through."

"The stables phone is out of order," the girl said.

"Then you'll have to go and fetch him. Tell him Roger Lundin wants to speak to him."

It was almost five minutes before he came to the phone.

"What is it now?" he asked. He was obviously annoyed at having been disturbed.

"Sofia didn't happen to say where Harderberg was going to move to, did she?"

"How the hell would she know?"

"I'm only asking. She didn't say anything about him intending to leave the country?"

"She only said what I told you. Nothing more."

"I have to see her. As soon as possible."

"Come off it, she has a job to do."

"You'll have to find some excuse. She used to work for you. You have some forms she needs to fill in. You must be able to fix that."

"I haven't time. The blacksmith's here. The vet's on his way. I have meetings arranged with several owners."

"This is important. Believe me."

"I'll do what I can. I'll call you back."

Wallander put down the receiver. It was 3.30 p.m. already. He waited. After a quarter of an hour he went to fetch a cup of coffee. Five minutes later Svedberg knocked on the door and came in.

"We can forget about the man in Östersund," he said. "His car with the registration number FHC 803 was stolen when he was in Stockholm a week ago. There are no grounds for not believing him. Besides, he's a local councillor."

"Why would a councillor be more trustworthy than anybody else?" Wallander objected. "Where was the car stolen? And when? Make sure we get a copy of his theft report."

"Is that really important?" Svedberg said.

"It might be," Wallander said. "And in any case, it

won't take long. Have you spoken to Hanson?"

"Only briefly," Svedberg said. "He's in with Martinsson at the moment, going through the investigation material."

"Give him the job, it's about right as something for him to start with."

Svedberg left. It was 4.00 and Widén still had not phoned. Wallander went to the cloakroom after asking reception to make a note of any incoming calls. He found an evening paper in the toilet and leafed through it, his mind elsewhere. He was back at his desk and had snapped twelve paper clips by the time Widén eventually called.

"I've invented a pack of lies," he said, "but you can meet her in Simrishamn an hour from now. I told her to take a taxi and that you'd pay. There's a café on the hill leading down to the harbour. Do you know the one I mean?"

Wallander did.

"She hasn't got much time," Widén said. "Take some forms with you so that she can pretend to fill them in."

"Do you think she's under suspicion?"

"How the devil should I know?"

"Thanks for your help anyway."

"You'll have to give her money for her taxi back to the castle as well."

"I'll leave right away," Wallander said.

"What's happened?" Widén said.

"I'll tell you when I know," Wallander said. "I'll phone."

Wallander left the police station at exactly 5 p.m. When he got to Simrishamn he parked by the harbour and walked up the hill to the café. As he had hoped, she was not yet there. He crossed the road and continued up the street. He stopped to look in a shop window while keeping an eye on the café. Not more than five minutes passed before he saw her coming up the street from the harbour, where she must have left the taxi. She went into the café. Wallander scrutinised the passers-by, and when he was as sure as he could be that she was not being followed, he went into the café. He should have taken somebody with him, to keep a lookout. She was sitting at a table in the corner. She watched him approach her table without greeting him.

"I'm sorry I'm late," he said.

"So am I," she said. "What do you want? I have to get back to the castle as quickly as possible. Aren't you going to pay for the taxi?"

Wallander took out his wallet and gave her a 500-kronor note. "Is that enough?" he asked.

She shook her head. "I need a thousand," she said.

"What? It costs a thousand kronor to get to Simrishamn and back?" He gave her another 500-kronor note, thinking that she was probably conning him. He was annoyed, but there was no time for that.

"What would you like?" he said. "Or have you already ordered?"

"I wouldn't mind a coffee," she said. "And a bun."

Wallander went to the counter and ordered. When he paid he asked for a receipt. He went back to the table with his tray.

Sofia was looking at him with an expression which Wallander recognised as being full of contempt.

"Roger Lundin," she said. "I don't know what your real name is, and I don't care either. But it's not Roger Lundin. And you're a policeman."

Wallander thought he may as well tell her the truth. "You're right, I'm not Roger Lundin. And I am a police officer. But you don't need to know my real name."

"Why not?"

"Because I say so," Wallander said, making it clear that he would brook no discussion. She noticed his attitude changed towards her, and she regarded him with something that might even be of interest.

"Listen carefully," Wallander said. "One day I'll explain to you why all this secrecy stuff is necessary. For now all I will say is that I'm a police officer investigating a bloody murder. Just so you realise this isn't a game. OK?"

"Perhaps," she said.

"Right now you're going to answer some questions," Wallander said. "And then you can go back to the castle."

He remembered the forms he had in his pocket. He put them on the table and passed her a pen.

"It could be that somebody's been following you," he said. "That's why you're now going to fill in these forms. Pretend this is what our meeting is about. Write your name at the top."

"Who's following me?" she said, looking round the café.

"Look at me," Wallander snapped. "Don't look anywhere else. If there is anybody following you we can be quite sure he can see you and that you won't see him."

"How do you know it's a man?"

"I don't."

"This is ridiculous."

"Drink your coffee, eat your bun, write in the form and look at me," Wallander said. "If you don't do as I say I'll make damn sure you never get back to Widén again."

She seemed to believe him. She did as she was told.

"Why do you think they're planning to move out of the castle?" he said.

"I was told I'd only be working there for a month, and that would be it. They'd be leaving the castle."

"Who told you that?"

"A man came to the stables."

"What did he look like?"

"He was sort of black."

"A black man?"

"No, but he was wearing dark clothes and had black hair."

"A foreigner?"

"He spoke Swedish."

"With a foreign accent?"

"Could be."

"Do you know his name?"

"No."

"Do you know what he does?"

"No."

"But he works at the castle?"

"I suppose he must do."

"What else did he say?"

"I didn't like him. In fact, he was horrible."

"In what way?"

"He wandered about the stables, watching me grooming one of the horses. He asked me where I was from."

"What did you say?"

"I said I'd applied for the job because I couldn't stay on with Sten."

"Did he ask anything else?"

"No."

"Why was he horrible?"

She thought before answering. "He asked questions in a way that made it seem he didn't want me to notice he was asking anything."

"Have you met anybody else?"

"Only the woman who took me on."

"Anita Karlén."

"I think that was her name, yes."

"Nobody else?"

"No."

"Is there nobody else looking after the horses?"

"No, only me. Two horses aren't much of a problem."

"Who looked after them before?"

"I don't know."

"Did they say why they suddenly needed a new stablegirl?"

"The Karlén woman said something about somebody being ill."

"But you didn't meet them?"

"No."

"What else have you seen?"

"What do you mean?"

"You must have seen other people. Cars coming or going."

"The stables are apart, out of the way. I can only see one of the gables. The paddock is further away in the other direction. And anyway, I'm not allowed to go to the castle itself."

"Who told you that?"

"Anita Karlén. I'd be sacked on the spot if I broke any rule. And I have to phone and get permission if I want to leave the castle."

"Where did the taxi pick you up?"

"At the gates."

"Is there anything else that you think might be of interest to me?"

"How do I know what you're interested in?"

He sensed that there *was* something else, but that she wasn't sure whether to mention it or not. He paused for a moment before going on, cautiously, as if he were feeling his way in the dark.

"Let's go back a bit," he said. "To that man who came to see you in the stables. Did he say anything else?"

"No."

"He didn't say anything about them leaving Farnholm Castle and moving abroad?"

"No."

That's true, Wallander thought. She's telling the truth. And I don't need to worry about her remembering wrongly, but there is something else.

"Tell me about the horses," he said.

"They are two really beautiful riding horses," she said. "One of them, Aphrodite, is nine years old. She's light brown. The other, Juno, is seven and black. It's ages since anybody has ridden them, that's for sure."

"How would you know that? I know very little about horses."

"I gathered."

Wallander smiled at her comment. But he didn't say anything, just waited for her to continue.

"They got really excited when I came with the saddles," she said. "You could see they were dying to have a gallop."

"And you gave them their heads?"

"Yes."

"You rode in the estate's grounds, I suppose?"

"I'd been told which paths I could go on."

A slight change of tone, barely perceptible, a hint of anxiety made Wallander prick up his ears. He was getting close to what she was wondering whether to mention or not.

"So you rode off."

"I started with Aphrodite," she said. "Meanwhile, Juno was careering round the paddock."

"How long were you out on Aphrodite?"

"Half an hour. The grounds are huge."

"Then you came back?"

"I let Aphrodite loose and saddled up Juno. Half an hour later I was back."

Wallander knew at once. It was while she was out with the second horse that something had happened. Her answer came much too quickly, as if she had been steeling herself to get past a frightening obstacle. The only thing to do, he decided, was to come straight to the point.

"I'm sure that everything you're telling me is true," he said, sounding as friendly as possible.

"I've nothing else to say. I have to be going now. If I'm late I'll get the sack."

"You can leave in a couple of minutes. Just a few more questions. Let's go back to the stables and that man who came to see you. I don't think you told me quite everything he said. Is that right? Didn't he also say that there were certain places you weren't to go anywhere near?"

"It was Miss Karlén who said that."

"Maybe she did too. But the man in the stables said

it in such a way that you were frightened? Am I right?"

She looked away and nodded slowly.

"But when you were out with Juno you took a wrong turning. Or maybe out of curiosity you took another path? It hasn't escaped my notice that you like to do whatever you want. Is that what happened?"

"I took a wrong turning." She was now speaking so softly that Wallander had to lean over the table to hear what she was saying.

"I believe you," he said. "Tell me what happened on that path."

"Juno suddenly reared up and threw me off. It was only when I was lying there that I saw what had scared him. It looked as if somebody had fallen on the path. I thought it was a dead body. But when I went to look I saw it was a human-sized doll."

Wallander could see she was still fearful. He recalled what Gustaf Torstensson had said to Mrs Dunér, about Harderberg having a macabre sense of humour.

"I'd have been frightened to death as well," he said. "But nothing's going to happen to you. Not if you keep in touch with me."

"I like the horses," Sofia said. "But not the rest of it."

"Stick to the horses," Wallander said. "And remember which paths you're not supposed to ride on."

He could see she felt relieved, now that she had told him what had happened.

"Go back now," he said, gathering up the papers on the table. "I'll stay here for a while. You're right, you mustn't be late."

She stood up and left. Half a minute later Wallander followed her into the street. He supposed she would have gone down to the harbour to get a taxi from there, but he was just in time to see her get into a taxi next to the newspaper stall. The car drove away, and he waited to make sure it was not followed. Then he went to his own car and drove back to Ystad, thinking about what she had said. He certainly could not, on her evidence, be sure about Harderberg's plans.

The pilots, he thought. And the flight plans. We have to be one step ahead of him if he really is going to move abroad.

It was time for another visit to Farnholm Castle. He wanted to talk to Harderberg himself again.

Wallander was at the police station by 7.45. He bumped into Höglund in the corridor. She nodded at him, curtly, and disappeared into her office. Wallander stopped in mid-stride, bewildered. Why had she been so abrupt? He turned back and knocked on her office door. When she responded he opened the door but did not go in.

"It's customary to say 'hello' in this police station," he said.

She went on poring over a file.

"What's the matter?"

She looked up at him. "I wouldn't have thought you needed to ask me that," she said.

Wallander stepped inside her office. "I don't understand," he said. "What have I done?"

"I thought you were different," she said, "but now I see that you're the same as all the rest of them."

"I still don't get it," Wallander said. "Would you mind explaining?"

"I've nothing else to say. I'd prefer you to leave."

"Not until I've had an explanation."

Wallander was not sure if she was about to throw a fit of rage, or burst into tears.

"I thought we were well on the way to becoming friends," he said, "not just colleagues."

"So did I," she said. "But no longer."

"Explain!"

"I'll be honest with you," she said, "even though that's the very opposite of what you've been with me. I thought you were someone I could trust, but you're not. It may take me some time to get used to that."

Wallander flung his arms out wide. "Do please explain."

"Hanson came back today," she said. "You must know that because he came to my office and told me about a conversation he had just had with you."

"What did he say?"

"That you were glad he was back."

"So I am. We need every officer we can get."

"The more so since you're disappointed in me."

Wallander stared at her in bewilderment. "He said that? That I was disappointed in you? He said I'd told him that?"

"I only wish you'd said it to me first."

"But it's not true. I said exactly the opposite. I told him you'd already proved yourself to be a good police officer."

"He sounded very convincing."

Wallander was furious. "That bloody Hanson!" he almost shouted. "If you like I'll phone him and tell him to get himself in here this minute. Surely you accept that not a word of what he said is true?"

"Why did he say it then?"

"Because he's nervous."

"Of me?"

"Why do you think he's away on courses all the time? Because he's afraid you'll overtake him. He hates to think that you are going to prove to be a better police officer than he is."

He could tell that she was beginning to believe him. "It's true," he said. "Tomorrow you and I are going to have a little talk with Mr Hanson. And it's not going to be a pleasant little talk as far as he's concerned, I can promise you that."

She looked up at him. "In that case, I apologise," she said.

"He's the one who needs to apologise," Wallander said. "Not you."

But the following day, Friday, November 26, the frost white on the trees outside the police station, Höglund asked Wallander not to say anything to Hanson. After sleeping on it, she had decided that she would prefer to speak to him herself, at some stage in the future, when she had had a chance to distance herself from it. Wallander was persuaded that she believed him now, so he raised no objection. Which did not mean that he would forget what Hanson had done. Later in the morning, with everybody seeming to be frozen stiff and out of sorts, apart from Åkeson who was fighting fit again, Wallander called a meeting. He told the team about his meeting with Sofia in Simrishamn, but it did not seem to improve the mood of his colleagues. On the other hand, Svedberg produced a map of the Farnholm Castle estate. It was very big. Svedberg told them that the extensive grounds had been acquired in the late nineteenth century when the castle belonged to a family with the strikingly unnoble name of Mårtensson. The head of the household had made a fortune building houses in Stockholm and then he had built what some would call a folly. Apparently, he was not only obsessed with grandeur, but may even have been close to actual lunacy. When Svedberg had exhausted all he had discovered about the castle, they continued to cross off their list aspects of the investigation that either had proved to be insignificant, or at the least could be put to one side for the present, being of little importance. Höglund had finally managed to have a detailed conversation with Kim Sung-Lee, the cleaner at the Torstensson offices. As anticipated, she had nothing of significance to say, and her papers had proved to be in order and her presence in Sweden totally legal. Höglund had also on her own initiative talked to the clerk, Sonia Lundin. Wallander could not help being pleased to note that Hanson was unable to conceal his disapproval of the way she had acted on her own initiative. Unfortunately, Sonia Lundin had nothing helpful to say either. One more possible lead could be crossed off. Eventually, when everybody appeared to be still more out of sorts and inert, and a grey fog seemed to have settled over the conference table, Wallander tried to bring them back to life by urging them to concentrate on the flight plans of Harderberg's Gulfstream. He also suggested that Hanson should make discreet enquiries about the two pilots. But he failed to blow away the fog, the inertia that had started to worry him, and it now seemed to him that their only hope was that the financial experts with all their computer expertise might be able to breathe new life into the investigation. They had undertaken a thorough investigation into the Harderberg empire, but they had been forced to ask for an extension of the deadline, and the meeting had been postponed until the following Monday, November 29.

Wallander had just decided to declare the meeting closed when Åkeson put his hand up. "We must talk about the state of play in the investigation," he said. "I've allowed you to concentrate on Alfred Harderberg for another month, but at the same time I can't ignore the fact that we have only extremely thin evidence to justify it. It's as if we're drifting further from something crucial with every day that passes. I think we'd all benefit from making one more clear and simple summary of where we've got to, based exclusively on the facts. Nothing else."

Everybody looked at Wallander. Åkeson's comments came as no surprise, even if Wallander would have rather not been confronted by them.

"You're right," he said. "We need to see where we are. Even without any results from the fraud squads' analyses."

"Unravelling a financial empire doesn't necessarily identify a murderer, let alone several," Åkeson said.

"I know that," Wallander said, "but nevertheless, the picture is not complete without their information."

"There is no complete picture," Martinsson said glumly. "There's no picture at all."

Wallander could see he would need to get a grip on the situation before it slid out of control. To give himself time to gather his thoughts he suggested they should have a short break and air the room. When they reassembled, he was firm and decisive.

"I can see a possible pattern," he began, "just as you all can. But let's approach it from a different angle and begin by taking a look at what this case *isn't*. There's nothing to convince us that we're dealing with a madman. It's true, of course, that a clever psychopath could have planned a murder disguised as a car accident, but there are no apparent motives, and what happened to Sten Torstensson doesn't seem to hang together with what happened to his father, from a psychopathic point of view. Nor do the attempts to blow up Mrs Dunér and me. I say me rather than Höglund because I think that's the way it was. Which brings me to the pattern that revolves around Farnholm Castle and Alfred Harderberg. Let's go back in time. Let's start with the day about five years ago when Gustaf Torstensson was first approached by Alfred Harderberg."

At that moment Björk came into the conference room and sat at the table. Wallander suspected that Åkeson had spoken to him during the short pause and asked him to be there for the rest of the meeting.

"Gustaf Torstensson starts working for Harderberg," Wallander began again. "It's an unusual arrangement – one wonders how on earth a provincial solicitor can be of use to an international industrial magnate. One might suspect that Harderberg intended to use Torstensson's shortcomings for his own advantage, expecting that he would be able to manipulate him if necessary. We don't know that, it's guesswork on my part. But somewhere along the line something unexpected happens. Torstensson starts to appear uneasy, or maybe I should say he appears to be depressed. His son notices, and so does his secretary. She even talks about him seeming to be afraid. Something else happens at about the same time. Torstensson and Lars Borman have got to know each other through a society devoted to the study of

369

icons. Their relationship suddenly becomes strained, and we may assume that this has a connection with Harderberg because he's somehow in the background of the fraud executed on the Malmöhus County Council. But the key question is: why did old man Torstensson start behaving in unexpected ways?

"I suspect that he discovered in the work he was doing for Harderberg something that upset him. Perhaps it was the same thing that upset Borman. We don't know what it was. Then Torstensson is killed in a stage-managed accident. Thanks to what Kurt Ström has told us, we can picture roughly what happened. Sten Torstensson comes to see me at Skagen. A few days later, he too is dead. He, no doubt, felt that he was in danger because he tries to set a false trail in Finland when in fact he's gone to Denmark. I'm convinced that somebody followed him to Denmark. Somebody watched our meeting on the beach. The people who killed Gustaf Torstensson were snapping at the heels of Sten Torstensson. They could not have known whether the father had discussed his discoveries with his son. Nor could they know what Sten said to me. Or what Mrs Dunér knew. That's why Sten dies, that's why they try to kill Mrs Dunér and why my car is torched. It's also the reason why I am being watched and not the rest of you. But everything leads us back to the question of what old man Torstensson had discovered. We are trying to establish whether it has anything to do with the plastic container we found on the back seat of his car. It could also be something else that the financial analysts will be able to tell us. Come what may, there is a pattern here that starts with the cold-blooded killing of Gustaf Torstensson. Sten Torstensson sealed his fate when he came to see me in Skagen. In the background of the pattern all we have is Alfred Harderberg and his empire. Nothing else – not that we can see, at least."

When Wallander had finished, no-one had a question.

"You paint a very plausible picture," Åkeson said when the silence began to feel oppressive. "You could conceivably be plum right. The only problem is that we don't have a shred of proof, no forensic evidence at all."

"That's why we must speed up the work that's being done on the plastic container," Wallander said. "We have to take the lid off Avanca and see what's underneath. There must be a thread we can start to pull somewhere inside there."

"I wonder if we ought to have a down-to-earth chat with Kurt Ström," Åkeson said. "Those men hanging around Harderberg all the time – who are they?"

"That thought had occurred to me too," Wallander said. "Ström might be able to throw a bit of light on matters. But the moment we contact Farnholm Castle and ask to speak to Ström, Harderberg will realise we suspect him of being directly involved. And once that happens, I doubt that we will ever solve these murders. With the resources he has at his disposal he can sweep the ground clean all around him. On the other hand, I think I'll pay him one more visit to lay our own false trail."

"You'll have to be very convincing," Åkeson said, "or he'll see through you immediately." He put his brief-case on the table and began packing away his files. "Kurt has described where we stand. It's plausible, but it's vague. However, let's see what the fraud squads have to say for themselves on Monday."

The meeting broke up. Wallander felt uneasy. His own words were resounding inside his head. Perhaps Åkeson was right. Wallander's summary had sounded plausible, but nevertheless would the course they were on end up by leaving them unable to prove anything?

Something's got to happen, he thought. Something's got to happen very soon.

When Wallander looked back on the weeks that followed, he would think of them as among the worst he had ever experienced in all his years as a police officer. Contrary to his expectations, nothing at all happened. The financial experts went through everything over and over again, but all they had to say was that they needed more time. Wallander managed to curb his impatience – or perhaps what really happened was that he managed to suppress his disappointment, because he could see that the fraud squads were working as hard as they could. When Wallander tried to contact Ström again, he found that he had left for Västerås to bury his mother. Rather than chase him up there, Wallander elected to wait. He never managed to make contact with the two Gulfstream pilots since they were always out and about with Harderberg. The only thing the team did achieve during this grim period was to get access to the flight plans of the private jet. Alfred Harderberg had an astonishing itinerary. Svedberg calculated that the fuel bill alone would come to many millions of kronor per year. The financial analysts copied the flight plans and tried to fit them in with Harderberg's hectic programme of business deals.

Wallander met Sofia twice, on both occasions at the café in Simrishamn; but she had nothing more to report.

It was December, and it seemed to Wallander that the investigation was close to collapse. Perhaps it had collapsed already.

Nothing of any use to them happened. Nothing at all.

On Saturday, December 4, Höglund invited him for dinner. Her husband was at home, a brief pause between his unending trips round the globe looking for faulty water pumps. Wallander had much too much to drink. The investigation was not mentioned once during the evening. It was very late by the time Wallander realised he should go home. He decided to walk. When he got to the post office in Kyrkogårdsgatan, he had to lean against a wall and throw up. When eventually he got home to Mariagatan, he sat with his hand on the telephone, meaning to call Baiba in Riga. But common sense prevailed and he called Linda in Stockholm instead. When she gathered who it was she was annoyed, and told him to ring back the next morning. It was only after the brisk exchange was over that Wallander realised that probably she was not alone. That thought worried him, and he felt guilty as a result, but when he telephoned her the next day he did not refer to the matter. She told him about her work as an apprentice at an upholstery factory, and he could hear that she was happy in what she was doing. But he was disappointed that she made no mention of coming to visit him in Skåne for Christmas. She and a few friends had rented a cottage in the Västerbotten mountains. Eventually she asked him what he was up to.

"I'm chasing a Silk Knight," he said.

"A Silk Knight?"

"One of these days I'll explain to you what a Silk Knight is."

"It sounds very attractive."

"But it isn't. I'm a police officer. We seldom chase anybody or anything attractive."

*

Still nothing happened. On Thursday, December 9, Wallander was well on the way to giving up. The next day he would suggest to Åkeson that they should start looking at some other leads.

But on Friday, December 10, something actually did happen. He did not know it at the time, but the wilderness days were over. When Wallander got to his office, there was a note on his desk asking him to phone Kurt Ström without delay. He hung up his jacket, sat at his desk and dialled the number. Ström answered immediately.

"I want to see you," he said.

"Here or at your home?" Wallander asked.

"Neither," Ström said. "I've got a cottage in Svartavägen in Sandskogen. Number 12. Can you be there in an hour?"

"I'll be there."

Wallander put down the receiver and looked out of the window. Then he stood up, put on his jacket and hurried out of the police station.

Chapter 16

Rain clouds scudded across the sky.

Wallander was nervous. Leaving the police station he had headed east, turned right down Jaktpaviljongsvägen and stopped when he came to the youth hostel. Despite the cold and the wind he walked down to the deserted beach. He felt as if he had been transported back a few months in time. The beach was Jutland and Skagen, and he was once more on patrol, pacing up and down his territory.

But that feeling passed just as quickly as it had come. He had no time for unnecessary daydreams. He tried to work out why Ström had made contact with him. His restlessness was due to the hope that Ström might be able to give him something that would lead to the breakthrough they so badly needed. But he knew that was wishful thinking. Ström not only hated him personally, he had no time at all for the force that had cast him out. They could not count on receiving help from Ström. Wallander had no idea what the man wanted.

It started raining. The raging wind sent him retreating to his car. He started the engine and turned up the heat. A woman walked past with her dog, heading for the beach. Wallander recalled the woman he kept seeing on the beach at Skagen. There was still almost half an hour to go before he was due to meet Ström in Svartavägen. He drove slowly back towards town and inspected the summer cottages at Sandskogen. He had no difficulty in identifying the red house Ström had described. He parked and walked into the little garden. The house looked like a magnified doll's house. It was in a poor state of repair. As there was no car outside, Wallander thought he must have got there first. But the front door opened and Ström was standing there.

"I didn't see a car," Wallander said. "I thought you hadn't come yet."

"But I had. You can forget about my car."

Wallander went in as bidden. He was met by a faint smell of apples. The curtains were drawn and the furniture was covered by white dust sheets.

"A nice house you have here," Wallander said.

"Who said it was mine?" Ström said, taking off two of the sheets.

"I have no coffee," he said. "You'll have to do without."

Wallander sat down in one of the chairs. The house felt raw and damp. Ström sat down opposite him. He was wearing a crumpled suit and a long, heavy overcoat.

"You wanted to see me," Wallander said. "Well, here I am."

"I thought we could strike a deal, you and me," Ström said. "Let's say that I have something you want."

"I don't do deals," Wallander said.

"You're too quick off the mark," Ström said. "If I were you I'd at least listen to what I have to say."

Wallander conceded the point. He should have waited before rejecting the offer. He gestured to Ström to continue.

"I've been off work for a couple of weeks, burying my mother," he said. "That gave me a lot of time to think. Not least about why the police were interested in Farnholm Castle. After you'd been to my place I could see of course that you suspected the murder of those two solicitors had something to do with the castle. The problem is simply that I can't understand why. I mean, the son had never been there. It was the old man who was dealing with Harderberg. The one we thought had died in a car accident."

He looked at Wallander, as if he were waiting for a reaction.

"Go on," Wallander said.

"When I came back and started work again, I suppose I'd forgotten all about your visit," he said. "But then something happened to put it in a new light."

Ström produced a packet of cigarettes and a lighter from an overcoat pocket. He offered the packet to Wallander, who shook his head.

"If there's one thing I've learned in this life," Ström said, "it's that you should keep your friends at arm's length. But you can let your enemies get as close to you as they can."

"I take it that's why I'm here," Wallander said.

"Could be," Ström said. "You should know that I don't like you, Wallander. As far as I'm concerned you represent the worst kind of upright bourgeois values the Swedish police force is stuffed so full of. But you can do deals with your enemies, or people you don't like. Pretty good deals, even."

Ström disappeared into the kitchen and came back with a saucer to use as an ashtray. Wallander waited.

"A new light," Ström said again. "I came back to find that I was being made redundant as from Christmas. I hadn't expected anything like that. But it was obvious that Harderberg had decided to leave Farnholm."

It used to be Dr Harderberg, Wallander noted. Now it's plain Harderberg, and he has trouble spitting even that out.

"Needless to say I was shattered," Ström said. "When I accepted the job of security chief, I was assured that it was permanent. Nobody mentioned the possibility of Harderberg leaving the place. The wages were good, and I'd bought a house. Now I was going to be out of work again. I didn't like it."

Wallander had been wrong. It was only possible that Ström had something important to tell him.

"Nobody likes being made redundant," Wallander said.

"What would you know about that?"

"Not as much as you do, obviously."

Ström stubbed out his cigarette. "Let's spell it out," he said. "You need inside information about the castle. Information you can't get without advertising the fact that you're interested. And you don't want to do that. If you did you'd have just driven up and demanded an interview with Harderberg. I don't care why you want information without anybody knowing about it. What is important, though, is that I'm the only one who can supply you with it. In exchange for something I want from you."

Wallander wondered if this was a trap. Was Harderberg pulling Ström's strings? He decided not. Too risky, too easy for Wallander to see through it.

"You're right," he said. "There are things I want to know, and without it being noticed. What do you want in return?"

"Very little," Ström said. "A piece of paper."

"A piece of paper?"

"I have to think about my future," Ström said. "If I have one, it's not going to be in the private sector security service. When I got the job at Farnholm Castle, I had the impression that it was an advantage to be on bad terms with the Swedish police force. But, unfortunately, that can be a disadvantage in other circumstances."

"What do you want on this piece of paper?"

"A positive reference," Ström said. "On police headed paper. Signed by Björk."

"That's not on," Wallander said. "It would obviously be a fake. You've never worked in Ystad. A check with National Headquarters and anyone could discover that you'd been kicked out of the force."

"You can perfectly well fix a reference, if you want to," Ström said. "I can deal with whatever they have in the National Police Archives myself, one way or another."

"How?"

"That's my problem. I don't want you to help in any way."

"How do you think I'm going to get Björk to sign a cooked-up reference?"

"That's your problem. It could never be traced to you anyway. The world is full of forged documents."

"In that case you can fix it with no input from me. Björk's signature could be forged."

"Of course it could," Ström said. "But the certificate would have to be a part of the system. In the computer database. That's where you come in."

Wallander knew Ström was right. He had once forged a passport himself. But still he found the idea objectionable.

"Let's say that I'll think about it," Wallander said. "Let me ask you a few more questions. We can regard your answers as sample goods. When I've heard what they are I can tell you whether I'll go along with you or not."

"I'm the one who'll decide whether enough questions have been asked," Ström said. "And we're going to sort this out here and now. Before you leave."

"I'll go along with that."

Ström lit another cigarette, then faced up to Wallander.

"Why is Harderberg doing a runner?"

"I don't know."

"Where's he going?"

"I don't know that either. Probably overseas."

"What makes you think that?"

"There've been quite a few visits recently from estate agents from abroad."

"What do you mean, foreign?"

"South America. Ukraine. Burma."

"Is the castle up for sale?"

"Harderberg generally hangs on to his properties. He won't be selling. Just because he's not living at Farnholm Castle doesn't mean that anybody else will be. He'll put it in mothballs."

"When's he going to move?"

"He could leave tomorrow. Nobody knows. But I reckon it will be pretty soon. Probably before Christmas."

Wallander had so many questions to ask, far too many. He couldn't make up his mind which ones were most important.

"The men in the shadows," he said eventually. "Who are they?"

Ström nodded in acknowledgment. "That's a pretty good way of describing them," he said.

"I saw two men in the entrance hall," Wallander said. "The night I visited Harderberg. But I also saw them the first time I went to the castle, and talked to Anita Karlén. Who are they?"

Ström contemplated the smoke rising from his cigarette. "I'll tell you," he said. "But it'll be the last sample you'll get."

"If your answer's right," Wallander said. "Who are they?"

"One of them is Richard Tolpin," Ström said. "He was born in South Africa. A soldier, mercenary. I don't think there's been a conflict or a war in Africa these last two decades where he hasn't been involved."

"On which side?"

"The side that paid better. But it looked like turning out badly at the start. When Angola kicked the Portuguese out in 1975 they captured about 20 mercenaries who were sent for trial. Fifteen of them were condemned to death. Including Tolpin. Fourteen of them were shot. I've no idea why they spared Tolpin. Presumably because he could be of use to the new regime."

"How old is he?"

"Young forties. Very fit. Karate expert. An excellent shot."

"And the other one?"

"From Belgium. Maurice Obadia. Also a soldier. Younger than Tolpin. Could be 34, maybe 35. That's all I know about him."

"What are they doing at Farnholm Castle?"

"They're called 'special advisers'. But they're just Harderberg's bodyguards. You couldn't find people who were more skilful, or more dangerous. Harderberg seems to enjoy their company."

"How do you know that?"

"Sometimes they have shooting practice in the grounds at night. Their targets are quite special."

"Tell me more."

"Dummies, big dolls, looking like people. They aim at their heads. And they usually score."

"Does Harderberg join in?"

"Yes. They sometimes keep going all night."

"Do you know whether either of them, Tolpin or Obadia, has a Bernadelli pistol?"

"I keep as far away from their guns as possible," Ström said. "There are some people you'd rather keep at arm's length."

"But they must have gun licences," Wallander said.

Ström smiled. "Only if they're resident in Sweden," he said.

"What does that mean? Farnholm Castle is in Sweden, surely?"

"There's something special about 'special advisers'," Ström said. "They've never set foot in Sweden. So you can't say that they are in this country."

Carefully he stubbed out his cigarette before he said: "There's a helicopter pad at the castle. It's always at night, the landing lights are switched on, a helicopter lands, sometimes two. They are off again before dawn. They fly low so they aren't tracked by radar. Whenever Harderberg is going to leave in his Gulfstream, Tolpin and Obadia disappear the night before by helicopter. Then they meet somewhere or other. Could be Berlin. That's where the helicopters are registered. When they come back, it's the same procedure. In other words, you could say they don't go through customs like ordinary folk."

Wallander nodded thoughtfully. "Just one more question," he said. "How do you know all this? You're confined to your bunker by the main gate. You can't possibly be allowed to roam about wherever you want."

"That's a question you'll never get the answer to," Ström said. "Let's just say it's a trade secret I don't want to pass on to anybody else."

"I'll fix that certificate for you," Wallander said.

"What do you know?" Ström said, with a smile. "I knew we'd strike a deal."

"You didn't know that at all," Wallander said. "When are you next on duty?"

"I work three nights in a row. I start tonight at 7.00."

"I'll be here at 3.00 this afternoon," Wallander said. "I'll have something to show you. Then I'll ask my question."

Ström stood up and checked through the curtains.

"Is there somebody following you?" Wallander asked.

"You can't be too careful," Ström said. "I thought you'd caught on to that."

Wallander went back to his car and drove to the police station. He paused in reception and asked Ebba immediately to summon a meeting of the investigation team.

"You look pretty stressed," Ebba said. "Has something happened?"

"Yes," Wallander said. "At long last something has happened. Don't forget Nyberg. I need him to be there."

Twenty minutes later they were ready to start, although Ebba hadn't been able to reach Hanson, who had left the building early that morning without saying where he was going. Åkeson and Björk came into the confer-ence room just as Wallander had decided he could not wait for them any longer. Without mentioning the fact that he had done a deal with Ström, he described their exchanges at the house in Svartavägen. The listlessness that had characterised recent sessions with the team was noticeably reduced, even though Wallander could read the doubt in his colleagues' faces. He felt a bit like a football manager trying to convince his players that they were about to enter a boom period even though they had lost every match for the last six months.

"I believe in this," he said in conclusion. "Ström can be very useful to us."

Åkeson shook his head. "I don't like it," he said. "The success of this investigation now seems to depend on a security guard who's been kicked out of the police force, but is nevertheless cast as our saviour."

"What choice do we have?" Wallander said. "Besides, I can't see that we're doing anything illegal. He was the one who came to us, not the other way round."

Björk was more scathing. "It's out of the question. We can't use a disgraced police officer for a grass. There would be a major scandal if this went wrong and the media got on to it. The National Police Commissioner would have my guts for garters if I gave you the go-ahead."

"Let him carve me up instead," Wallander said. "Ström is serious. He wants to help. As long as we do nothing illegal, we're hardly risking scandal."

"I can see the headlines," Björk said. "They're not nice."

"I see different headlines," Wallander said. "Something about two more murders the police haven't been able to solve."

Martinsson could see that the discussion was getting out of hand, and intervened. "It seems a bit odd that he didn't want anything in return for giving us a bit of help," he said. "Can we really believe that his being upset at having lost his job is sufficient reason for him to start helping the police whom he hates?"

"He hates the police, no doubt about that," Wallander said. "But I still think we can trust him."

You could have heard a pin drop. Åkeson poked at his upper lip, wondering what he ought to think. "Martinsson's question – you didn't answer it," he said.

"He didn't ask for anything in return," Wallander said, lying through his teeth.

"What exactly do you want us to do?"

Wallander nodded in the direction of Nyberg, who was sitting next to Höglund. "Sten Torstensson was killed by bullets that were probably from a Bernadelli pistol. Nyberg says that's a rare weapon. I want Ström to find out whether one of those bodyguards has a Bernadelli. Then we can go to the castle and make an arrest."

"We can do that anyway," Åkeson said. "People carrying guns, no matter what make they are, illegally resident in this country, that's good enough for me."

"But what then?" Wallander said. "We arrest them. We deport them. We've put all our eggs in one basket and then dropped it. Before we can point to those men as possible murderers we have to know whether either of them has a gun that could be the murder weapon."

"Fingerprints," Nyberg said. "That would be good. Then we can run a check with Interpol and Europol."

Wallander agreed. He had forgotten about fingerprints.

Åkeson was still poking at his upper lip. "Is there anything else you have in mind?" he asked.

"No," Wallander said. "Not at the moment."

He knew he was walking a tightrope and could fall at any moment. If he went too far, Åkeson would put a stop to any further contact with Ström, or at the very least hold things up. So Wallander did not mention everything he intended to do.

While Åkeson continued to think the matter over, Wallander looked across at Nyberg and Höglund. She smiled. Nyberg nodded almost imperceptibly. They've understood, Wallander thought. They know what I'm thinking. And they're with me.

At last Åkeson stopped arguing with himself. "Just this once," he said. "But this once only. No more contact with Kurt Ström in future without first informing me. I'll want to know what you intend asking him before I approve of any more contributions from that gentleman. You can also expect me to say no."

"Of course," Wallander said. "I'm not even sure there will be any more times."

When the meeting was over Wallander took Nyberg and Höglund into his office.

"I could tell that you had read my thoughts," he said when he had shut the door. "You didn't say anything, so I take it you agree with me that we should go a bit further than I led Åkeson to believe."

"The plastic container," Nyberg said. "If Ström could find a similar one at the castle, I'd be more than grateful."

"Exactly," Wallander said. "That plastic container is the most important thing we've got. Or the only thing, depending on how you look at it."

"But how is he going to be able to get away with it if he does find one?" Höglund said.

Wallander and Nyberg exchanged looks.

"If what we think is true, the container we found in Gustaf Torstensson's car was a substitute," Wallander said. "I thought we could give it back and replace it with the right one."

"I should have thought of that," she said. "Not thinking fast enough."

"I sometimes reckon it's Wallander who thinks too fast," Nyberg said quietly.

"I need it in a couple of hours," Wallander said. "I shall be seeing Ström again at 3.00."

Nyberg left, but Höglund stayed behind. "What did he want?" she asked.

"I'm not sure," Wallander said. "He said he wanted a certificate to say that he wasn't a bad police officer, but I think there's more to it than that."

"What?"

"I don't know yet, but I have my suspicions."

"And you don't want to say what your suspicions are?"

"I'd rather not just yet. Not until I know."

Nyberg came to Wallander's office with the plastic container just after 2.00. He had put it inside two black rubbish bags.

"Don't forget the fingerprints," Nyberg said. "Anything at all . . . glasses, cups, newspapers."

Half an hour later Wallander put the container on the back seat of his car and set off for Sandskogen. The rain was coming in off the sea in squalls. When he got out of his car Ström was in the doorway, already in uniform. Wallander carried the black rubbish bags into the red house.

"What uniform's that?" he said.

"Farnholm's own uniform. I've no idea who made it up."

Wallander took the container out of the plastic bags. "Have you seen this before?" he said.

Ström shook his head.

"There's an identical one somewhere at the castle," Wallander said. "There could be more than one. I want you to exchange this for one of them. Can you get into the main building itself?"

"I do my rounds every night."

"You're quite sure you've never seen this before?"

"Never. I wouldn't even know where to start looking."

Wallander thought for a moment. "Is there a cold-storage room anywhere?"

"In the cellar."

"Look there. And don't forget the Bernadelli."

"That'll be more difficult. They always have their weapons with them, probably they take them to bed too."

"We need Tolpin and Obadia's fingerprints. That's all. Then you can have your certificate. If that's what you really want."

"What else would I want?"

"I believe what you really want is to show that you're not as bad a police officer as a lot of people think."

"You're wrong," Ström said. "I have to think about my future."

"It was just a thought."

"Same time tomorrow," Ström said. "Here."

"One more thing," Wallander said. "If anything goes wrong I'll deny all knowledge of what you're doing."

"I know the rules," Ström said. "If that's all, you might as well push off."

Wallander ran through the rain to his car. He stopped at Fridolf's Café for a coffee and some sandwiches. It worried him that he had not told the whole truth at the morning meeting, but he knew he would be ready to concoct a certificate for Ström if that should prove to be necessary. His mind went back to Sten Torstensson, coming to ask for his help. He had turned him down. The least he could do now was to bring his murderers to light.

He sat in his car without starting the engine, watching the people hurrying through the rain. He thought of the occasion a few years back when he had driven home from Malmö while very drunk, and been stopped by some of his colleagues. They had protected him, and it had never been known about. That night he had not been an ordinary citizen: he had been a police officer, taken care of by the police force, instead of being punished, suspended or perhaps thrown out of the force. Peters and Norén, the officers who had seen him swerving all over the road and stopped him, had earned his loyalty. What if one day one of them tried to cash in on the favour they had done him?

In his heart of hearts Ström wanted to be back in the police force, Wallander was sure of it. The antagonism and hatred he displayed was only a superficial front. No doubt he dreamed of one day being a police officer again.

Wallander drove back to the station. He went to Martinsson's office, and found him on the phone. When he finished the call he asked Wallander how it had gone.

"Ström is going to look for an Italian pistol and he's going to collect some fingerprints," Wallander said.

"I find it hard to believe he's done that for nothing," Martinsson said.

"Me too," Wallander said. "But I suppose even somebody like Kurt Ström has a good side."

"He made the mistake of getting caught," Martinsson said. "And then he made another mistake by making everything seem so big and significant. Did you know he has a severely handicapped daughter, by the way?"

Wallander shook his head.

"His wife left him when the girl was very small. He looked after her for years. She has some form of muscle illness. But then it got so bad that she couldn't stay at home any longer, and she had to go into a special home. He still visits her whenever he can."

"How do you know all this?"

"I phoned Roslund in Malmö and asked him. I said I'd happened to bump into Ström. I don't think Roslund knew he works at Farnholm Castle, and I didn't mention it, of course."

Wallander stood staring out of the window.

"There's not much else we can do but wait," Martinsson said.

Wallander did not respond. It eventually dawned on him that Martinsson had said something. "I didn't hear what you said."

"All we can do is wait."

"Yes," Wallander said. "And right now there's nothing I find harder to do."

Wallander went back to his office, sat at his desk and contemplated the enlarged overview of Alfred Harderberg's worldwide empire they'd received from the fraud squad in Stockholm. He had pinned it to the wall.

What I'm looking at is really an atlas of the world, he thought. National boundaries have been replaced by ever-changing demarcation lines between different companies whose turnover and influence are greater than the budgets of many whole countries. He searched through the papers on his desk until he found the summary of the ten largest companies in the world that had been sent to him as an appendix by the fraud squad – they must have had a hyperactivity fit. Six of the biggest companies were Japanese and three American. The other was Royal Dutch/Shell, which was shared by Britain and Holland. Of those ten largest companies, four were banks, two telephone companies, one a car manufacturer and one an oil company. The other two were General Electric and Exxon. He tried to imagine the power wielded by these companies, but it was impossible for him to grasp what this concentration really meant. How could he when he did not feel he could get to grips with Harderberg's empire, even though that was like a mouse in the shadow of an elephant's foot compared with the Big Ten?

Once upon a time Alfred Harderberg had been Alfred Hansson. From insignificant beginnings in Vimmerby he had become one of the Silk Knights who ruled the world, always engaged in new crusades in the battle to outmanoeuvre or crush his competitors. On the surface he observed all the laws and regulations, he was a respected man who had been awarded honorary doctorates, he displayed great generosity and donations flowed from his apparently inexhaustible resources.

In describing him as an honourable man who was good for Sweden, Björk had given voice to the generally accepted view.

What I'm really saying is that there is a stain some-where, Wallander thought, and that smile has to be wiped from his face if we're going to nail a murderer. I'm trying to identify something which is basically unthinkable. Harderberg doesn't have a stain. His sun-tanned face and his smile are things we should, all of us Swedes, be proud of, and that's all there is to it.

Wallander left the police station at 6 p.m. It had stopped raining and the wind had died down. When he got home he found a letter among all the junk mail in the hall that was postmarked Riga. He put it on the kitchen table and looked hard at it, but did not open it until he had drunk a bottle of beer. He read the letter, and then, to be certain he had not misunderstood any-thing, read it through again. It was correct, she had given him an answer. He put the letter down on the table and pinched himself. He turned to the wall calendar and counted the days. He could not remember the last time he had been so excited. He had a bath, then went to the pizzeria in Hamngatan. He drank a bottle of wine with his meal, and it was only when he had become a bit tipsy that he realised he had not given a thought to Alfred Harderberg or Kurt Ström all evening. He was humming an improvised tune when he left the pizzeria, and then wandered about the streets until almost midnight. Then he went home and read the letter from Baiba one more time, just in case there was something in her English that he had misunderstood after all.

It was as he was about to fall asleep that he started thinking about Ström, and immediately he was wide awake again. Wait, Martinsson had said. That was the only thing they could do. He got out of bed and went to sit on the living-room sofa. What do we do if Ström doesn't find an Italian pistol? he thought. What happens to the investigation if the plastic container turns out to be a dead end? We might be able to deport a couple of foreign bodyguards who are in Sweden illegally, but that's about all. Harderberg, in his well-tailored suit, with that constant smile on his face, will depart from Farnholm Castle, and we'll be left with the wreckage of a failed murder investigation. We'll have to start all over again, and that will be very hard. We'll have to start examining every single thing that's happened as if we were seeing it for the first time.

He made up his mind to resign responsibility for the case if that did happen. Martinsson could take over. That was not only reasonable, it was also necessary. Wallander was the one who had pushed through the strategy of concentrating on Harderberg. He would sink to the bottom with the rest of the wreckage, and when he came up to the surface again it would be Martinsson who would be in charge.

When at last he went back to bed he slept badly. His dreams kept collapsing and blending into one another, and he could see the smiling face of Alfred Harderberg at the same time as Baiba's unfailingly serious expression.

He woke at 7 a.m. He made a pot of coffee and thought about the letter from Baiba, then sat down at the kitchen table and read the car adverts in the morning paper. He still had not heard anything from the insurance company, but Björk had assured him that he could use a police car for as long as he needed to. He left the flat just after 9.00. The temperature was above freezing and there was not a cloud in the sky. He spent a few hours driving from one car showroom to another, and spent a long time examining a Nissan he wished he could afford. On the way back he parked the car in Stortorget and walked to the music shop in Stora Östergatan. There was not much in the way of opera, and rather reluctantly he had to settle for a recording of selected arias. Then he bought some food and drove home. There were still several hours to go before he was due to meet Kurt Ström in Svartavägen.

It was 2.55 when Wallander parked outside the red doll's house in Sandskogen. When he knocked on the door there was no reply. He wandered around the garden, and after half an hour he started to get worried. Instinct told him something had happened. He waited until 4.15, then scribbled a note to Ström on the back of an envelope he had found in the car, giving him his phone numbers at home and at the station, and pushed it under the door. He drove back to town, wondering what he ought to do. Ström was acting on his own, and knew he had to take care of himself. He was perfectly capable of getting himself out of awkward situations, Wallander had no doubt, but even so, he felt increasingly worried. After establishing that nobody in the investigative team was still in the building, he went to his office and called Martinsson at home. His wife answered and told Wallander that Martinsson had taken his daughter to the swimming baths. He was about to phone Svedberg, but changed his mind and called Höglund instead. Her husband answered. When she came to the phone, Wallander told her that Ström had failed to turn up at their rendezvous.

"What does that mean?" she said.

"I don't know," Wallander said. "Probably nothing, but I'm worried."

"Where are you?"

"In my office."

"Do you want me to come in?"

"That's not necessary. I'll phone you back if anything happens."

He hung up and carried on waiting. At 5.30 p.m. he drove back to Svartavägen and shone his torch on the door. The corner of the envelope was still sticking out underneath, so Ström had not been home. Wallander had his mobile phone with him, and dialled Ström's number at Glimmingehus. He let it ring for about a minute, but there was no answer. He was now convinced that something had happened, and decided to go back to the station and get in touch with Åkeson.

He had just stopped at a red light on Österleden when his mobile phone rang.

"There's a Sten Widén trying to get in touch with you," said the operator at the police switchboard. "Have you got his number?"

"Yes, I have," Wallander said. "I'll phone him now."

The lights had changed and the driver of a car behind him sounded his horn impatiently. Wallander pulled in to the side of the road, then dialled Widén's number. One of the stablegirls answered.

"Is that Roger Lundin?" she asked.

"Yes," Wallander said, surprised. "That's me."

"I was to tell you that Sten is on his way to your flat in Ystad."

"When did he leave?"

"A quarter of an hour ago."

Wallander made a racing start to beat the amber light and drove back to town. Now he was certain something had happened. Ström had not returned home, and

Sofia must have contacted Widén and had something so important to tell him that Widén had felt it was necessary to drive to his flat. When he turned into Mariagatan there was no sign of Widén's old Volvo Duett. He waited in the street, wondering desperately what could have happened to Ström.

When Widén's Volvo appeared Wallander opened the door before Widén even had time to switch off the engine.

"What's happened?" he said, as Widén tried to extricate himself from the tattered safety belt.

"Sofia phoned," he said. "She sounded hysterical."

"What about?"

"Do we really have to be out here in the street?" Widén said.

"It's just that I'm worried," Wallander said.

"On Sofia's account?"

"No, Kurt Ström's."

"Who the hell is he?"

"We'd better go inside," Wallander said. "You're right, we can't stand out here in the cold."

As they went up the stairs Wallander noticed that Widén smelled of strong drink. He had better have a serious word with him on that score – one of these days when they had resolved who killed the two solicitors.

They sat at the kitchen table, with Baiba's letter still lying there between them.

"Who's this Ström?" Widén asked again.

"Later," Wallander said. "You first. Sofia?"

"She phoned about an hour ago," Widén said, pulling a face. "I couldn't understand what she was saying at first. She was off her rocker."

"Where was she calling from?"

"From her flat at the stables."

"Oh, shit!"

"I don't think she had much choice," Widén said, scratching his stubble. "If I understood her rightly, she had been out riding. Suddenly she comes across a dummy lying on the path ahead of her. Have you heard about the dummies? Life size?"

"She told me," Wallander said. "Go on."

"The horse stopped and refused to go past. Sofia dismounted to pull the dummy out of the way. Only it wasn't a dummy."

"Oh, hell!" said Wallander slowly.

"You sound as if you already know about it," Widén said.

"I'll explain later. Go on."

"It was a man lying there. Covered in blood."

"Was he dead?"

"It didn't occur to me to ask. I assumed so."

"What next?"

"She rode away and phoned me."

"What did you tell her to do?"

"I don't know if it was the best advice, but I told her to do nothing, to sit tight."

"Good," Wallander said. "You did exactly the right thing."

Widén excused himself and went to the bathroom. Wallander could hear the faint clinking of a bottle. When he came back Wallander told him about Ström.

"So you think he was the one there on the path?" Widén said.

"I'm afraid so."

Widén suddenly boiled over, and smashed his fist down on the table. Baiba Liepa's letter fluttered down to the floor.

"The police had bloody better get themselves out there right away! What the hell's going on at that castle? I'm not letting Sofia stay there a moment longer."

"That's exactly what we're going to do," Wallander said, getting to his feet.

"I'm going home," Widén said. "Call me as soon as you've got Sofia out of there."

"No," Wallander said. "You're staying here. You've been at the hard stuff. I'm not going to let you drive. You can sleep here."

Widén stared at Wallander as if he did not know what he was talking about. "Are you suggesting that I'm drunk?" he said.

"Not drunk, but you're over the limit. I don't want you getting into trouble."

Widén had left his car keys on the table. Wallander put them in his pocket. "Just to be on the safe side," he said. "I don't want you changing your mind while I'm gone."

"You must be out of your mind," Widén said. "I'm not drunk."

"We can argue about that when I get back," Wallander said. "I've got to go this very minute."

"I don't give a shit about your Kurt Ström," Widén said, "but I don't want anything to happen to her."

"I take it she's more than just a stablehand to you," Wallander said.

"Yes," Widén said. "But that's not why I don't want anything to happen."

"That's nothing to do with me," Wallander said.

"Too right. It isn't."

Wallander found a pair of unused trainers in his wardrobe. He had many times vowed to start jogging, but had never got round to it. He put on a thick sweater and a woollen cap, and was ready to leave.

"Make yourself at home," he said to Widén, who'd openly planted his whisky bottle on the kitchen table.

"You worry about Sofia, not about me," Widén said.

Wallander closed the door behind him, then paused on the dark staircase, wondering what to do. If Ström was dead, everything had failed. He felt as if he was back to where he had been the previous year, when death was waiting in the fog. The men at Farnholm Castle were dangerous, whether they smiled like Harderberg or skulked in the shadows like Tolpin and Obadia.

I've got to get Sofia out of there, he thought. I must phone Björk and organise an emergency call-out. We'll bring in every police district in Skåne if we have to.

He switched on the light and ran down the stairs. He rang Björk from his car, but as soon as Björk answered he switched off the phone.

I have to sort this out myself, he thought. I don't want any more dead bodies.

He drove to the police station and collected his handgun and a torch. He went to Svedberg's deserted office and switched on the light, then trawled through papers until he found the map of the Farnholm Castle grounds. He folded it and put it in his pocket. When he left the station it was 7.45. He drove to Malmövägen and stopped at Höglund's house. He rang the bell, and her husband opened the door. He declined the offer to go inside, saying that he only wanted to leave her a message. When she came to the door she was in a dressing gown.

"Listen carefully," he said. "I'm going to break into Farnholm Castle."

"Ström?" she said.

"I think he's dead."

She turned pale and Wallander wondered if she was going to faint.

"You can't go to the castle on your own," she said, when she had recovered her composure.

"I have to."

"Why do you have to?"

"I have to sort this out myself," he said, annoyed. "Please stop asking questions. Just listen."

"I'm going with you," she said. "You can't go there by yourself."

She had made up her mind. There was no point in arguing with her.

"Alright, you can come," he said, "but you'll wait outside. I can use somebody I can be in radio contact with."

She ran up the stairs. Her husband ushered Wallander in and closed the door.

"This is what she warned me would happen," he said with a smile. "When I get back home, she's the one who'll be going out on business."

"This probably won't take very long," Wallander said, though he could hear how lame it sounded.

A couple of minutes later she came back down wearing a tracksuit.

"Don't wait up for me," she said to her husband.

Nobody to wait up for me, Wallander thought. Nobody. Not even a dozy cat among the plant pots on a window ledge.

They drove to the police station and collected two radio telephones.

"Maybe I should get a gun," she said.

"No," Wallander said. "You'll wait outside the perimeter. And you're for the high jump if you don't do exactly as I say."

They left Ystad behind. It was a clear, cold night. Wallander was driving fast.

"What are you going to do?" she said.

"I'm going to find out what's happened."

She can see through me, he thought. She knows I haven't a clue what I'm going to do.

They continued in silence and reached the turn-off to Farnholm Castle at about 9.30. Wallander drove on to a parking place for tractors, switched off his engine and also the lights. They sat there in the dark.

"I'll be in touch every hour," Wallander said. "If you hear nothing for more than two hours, phone Björk and tell him to organise a full emergency call-out."

"You shouldn't be doing this, you know," she said.

"All my life I've been doing things I shouldn't be doing," Wallander said. "Why stop now?"

They tuned their radio telephones.

"Why did you become a police officer and not a vicar?" he said, looking into her eyes reflected in the dim light of the telephones.

"I was raped," she said. "That changed my whole life. All I wanted to do after that was to join the police force."

Wallander sat for a while in silence. Then he opened the door, got out and closed it quietly behind him. It was like entering another world. Höglund was nowhere to hand any longer.

The night was very calm. For some reason he was struck by the thought that in two days it would be Lucia, and all Sweden would be occupied with blonde girls wearing a crown of burning candles on their heads, singing "Santa Lucia" and celebrating what used to be thought of as the winter solstice. He positioned himself behind a tree trunk and unfolded his map. He shone his torch on it and tried to memorise the key elements. Then he switched off the torch, put the map into his pocket and ran down the road leading to the castle gates. It would be impossible to climb the double fence of barbed wire. There was only one way in, and that was through the gates.

After ten minutes he paused to get his breath back. Then he made his way cautiously along the road until he could see the bright lights at the gates, and the bunker that guarded them.

I must do what they least expect, he thought. The last thing they'll be waiting for is an armed man trying to get into the castle grounds on his own.

He closed his eyes and took a deep breath. He took his pistol out of his pocket. Behind the bunker was a narrow patch of shadow. He glanced at his watch: 9.57.

Then he made his move.

Chapter 17

The first call came after half an hour. She could hear his voice clearly, with no interference, as if he had not gone far from the car but was standing close by in the shadows.

"Where are you?" she said.

"I'm inside the grounds," he said. "Stand by for the next call in an hour from now."

"What's happening?"

But there was no answer. She thought there had been a temporary loss of contact and waited for him to call back, but then she realised that Wallander had switched off without replying to her question. There was no sound from the radio.

It seemed to Wallander that he was walking through the valley of the shadow of death. Nevertheless, getting in had been easier than he had ever dared to hope. He had sneaked swiftly to the narrow patch of shadow behind the bunker and been surprised to discover a small window. By standing on tiptoe he could see inside. There was only one person in the bunker, sitting in front of a bank of computer screens and telephones. Only one person, and a woman at that. She seemed to be knitting a child's jumper. Wallander could hardly believe his eyes.

The contrast with what was happening within the gates was too great, almost impossible to grasp. Obviously she could not possibly suspect that there would be an armed man just outside, so he walked calmly round the bunker and tapped on the door, trying to make it as *friendly* a knock as possible. Just as he had thought, she opened the door wide, not anticipating any threat. She had her knitting in her hand, and looked at Wallander in surprise. It had not occurred to him to draw his pistol. He explained who he was, Inspector Wallander from the Ystad police, and even apologised for disturbing her. He ushered her gently back inside the bunker and closed the door behind them. He looked to see whether there was a security camera inside the bunker as well, but there was no sign of one, and invited her to sit down. At that point it dawned on her what was happening, and she started screaming. Wallander drew his pistol. Holding the gun in his hand worried him so much that he felt sick. He avoided aiming at her, but ordered her to be quiet. She looked scared to death, and Wallander wished he had been able to calm her down, said she could carry on knitting the jumper which was no doubt for one of her grandchildren. But he thought about Ström and Sofia, he thought about Sten Torstensson and the mine in Mrs Dunér's garden. He asked if she had to keep reporting back to the castle, but she said she did not.

His next question was crucial. "Kurt Ström ought really to have been on duty tonight," he said.

"They phoned down from the castle and said I had to do his shift because he was ill."

"Who phoned?"

"One of the secretaries."

"Tell me exactly what she said, word for word."

"'Kurt Ström has been taken ill.' That's all."

As far as Wallander was concerned, he now had confirmation that everything had gone wrong. Ström had been unmasked, and Wallander had no illusions about the ability of the men around Harderberg to extract the truth from him.

He looked at the terrified woman. She was clinging to her knitting.

"There's a man just outside," he said, pointing to the window. "He's armed the same as me. If you sound the alarm after I've gone, you will not finish knitting that jumper."

He could see that she believed him.

"Whenever the gates open it's recorded up at the castle, is that right?" he said.

She nodded.

"What happens if there's a power cut?"

"A big generator cuts in automatically."

"Is it possible to open the gates by hand? Without it being registered by the computers?"

She nodded again.

"OK. Switch off the power supply to the gates," he said. "Open the gates for me, then close them behind me. Then switch the electricity back on."

He was sure she would do as he said. He opened the bunker door and shouted to the man who did not exist that he was coming out, that the gates were going to be opened and closed, and that everything was under control. She unlocked a box at the side of the gate to reveal a winch. When the gap was wide enough Wallander slipped through.

"Do exactly as I said. As long as you do, nothing will happen to you," he said.

Then he ran through the grounds towards the stables, picturing the route in his mind's eye from the map he had studied. All was very quiet, and when he was close enough to see the lights from the stables he paused and made the first call to Höglund. When she started asking questions he switched off. He went on walking cautiously towards the stables. The flat where Sofia lived was in an annexe built on to the main building. He stood for a considerable time in the shadow of a little coppice, observing the stables and the area round about. Occasionally he heard scrapes and thuds from the stalls. A light was on in the annexe. He made himself think completely calmly. The fact that Ström had been shot did not necessarily mean that they had realised there was a connection between him and the new stablegirl. Nor was it certain that the call she had made to Widén had been tapped. The uncertainty was the best Wallander could hope for. He wondered if they would have contingency plans to deal with a man having broken into the castle grounds.

He stayed in the shadows under the trees for several more minutes, then crouched and ran as fast as he could to the door of the annexe. He expected at any moment to be hit by a bullet. He knocked on the door, trying the handle at the same time. It was locked. Then he heard her voice, sounding very frightened, and he said who he was: Roger. Sten's friend Roger. He couldn't remember the surname he'd come up with. But she opened the door and he noted the expression of surprise mixed with relief on her face. The flat comprised a small kitchen and a living room with an alcove for a bedroom. He indicated with a finger to his lips that she should be quiet. They sat in the kitchen, facing each other across the table. He could hear the thuds from the stalls very clearly now.

Wallander said: "I don't have a lot of time and I can't explain why I'm here. So just answer my questions, please, nothing else."

He unfolded the map and laid it on the table.

"There was a man lying on a path," he said. "Can you point to where?"

She leaned across and drew a little circle with her index finger on a track marked to the south of the stables.

"About there," she said.

"I have to ask you if you had seen the man before."

"No."

"What was he wearing?"

"I don't remember."

"Was it a uniform?"

She shook her head. "I don't know. My mind's a blank."

There was no point in his pressing her further. Her terror had affected her memory.

"Has anything else happened today, anything out of the ordinary?"

"No."

"Nobody's been here to talk to you?"

"No."

Wallander tried to work out what that meant. But the image of Ström lying there in the darkness forced all other thoughts from his mind.

"I'm going now," he said. "If anybody comes, don't tell them I've been."

"Will you come back?" she said.

"I don't know. But you don't need to worry, nothing's going to happen."

He peered out through a crack in the curtains, hoping the assurance he had just given her really would turn out to be true. Then he opened the door quickly and ran to the back of the building. He did not stop until he was in the shadows again. A slight breeze had started blowing. Beyond the trees he could see the powerful beams lighting up the dark red façade of the castle. He could also see lights in several of the windows on all floors.

He was shivering.

After thinking hard once more about the map he had lodged in his memory, he set off again, torch in hand. He passed the site of an artificial lake that had been drained of water. Then he turned left and began looking for the path. He glanced at his watch and saw that he had 40 minutes before he was due to contact Höglund again.

Just as he was beginning to think he was lost, he found the path. It was about a metre wide, and he could see the tracks of horses' hooves. He stood still, listening. But it was silent everywhere, although the wind seemed to be getting stronger. He continued along the path, expecting to be grabbed at any moment.

After about five minutes he stopped. If she had indicated correctly on the map, he had walked too far. Was he on the wrong path? He went on, more slowly. After another hundred metres he was sure he must have passed the point she had marked by now.

He stood still, feeling uneasy.

There was no sign of Ström. The body must have been taken away. He turned and began to retrace his steps, wondering what to do next. He stopped again, this time because he needed a pee. He stepped into the bushes by the side of the path. When he had finished he took the map from his pocket and checked again, just to be certain that he had not mistaken the spot Sofia had circled, or taken the wrong path.

As he switched on the torch he caught sight of a naked foot. He gave a start and dropped the torch, which went out as it landed on the ground. He must have imagined it. He bent down to retrieve the torch. He switched it on again and found himself looking straight at Kurt Ström's dead face. It was ashen, the lips tightly clenched. Blood had drained away and coagulated on his cheeks. He had an entry wound in the middle of his forehead. Wallander thought about what had happened to Sten Torstensson. He stood up and hurried away. Leaned against a tree and threw up. Then he ran. He got as far as the empty lake and sank to his knees at its edge. Somewhere in the background a bird flew, clattering, from the top of a tree. He jumped down into the lake bed and crept to a corner. It was like being in a burial vault. He thought he could hear footsteps approaching and drew his pistol, but nobody appeared. He took a few deep breaths and forced himself to think. He was close to panic and felt that he would lose his self-control at any moment. Another 14 minutes and he was due to contact Höglund. But he did not have to wait, he could call her now and ask her to phone Björk. Ström was dead, shot through the head, and nothing was going to bring him back to life. They should call a full-scale emergency, Wallander would be waiting for them at the gates, and what would happen after that he had no idea.

But he did not make the call. He waited for 14 minutes and then reached for the radio telephone. She answered at once. "What's happening?" she said.

"Nothing yet," he said. "I'll call again in an hour."

"Have you found Ström?"

He switched off. Once again he was alone in the darkness. He had committed himself to do something, but did not know what. He had given himself an hour to fill without knowing how. Slowly he rose to his feet. He was freezing. He clambered up out of the lake bed and walked towards the light glimmering through the trees. He stopped where the trees came to an end and he found himself at the edge of the big lawn sloping up to the castle.

It was an impenetrable fortress, but somehow Wallander would have to force his way in. Ström was dead, but he could not be blamed for that. Nor could he be held responsible for the murder of Sten Torstensson. Wallander's guilt was different in kind, a feeling that he was going to let the side down once again, and when he could well be on the brink of solving the case.

There had to be a limit to what they were capable of doing, in spite of everything. They could not simply shoot him, an Ystad detective who was only doing his job. Then again, perhaps these people did not recognise any limits at all. He tried to unravel that conundrum, but he could not. Instead, he started making his way round to the back of the castle, a side of the building he had never seen. It took him all of ten minutes, despite walking briskly – not only because he was afraid, but also because he was so cold. He could not stop shivering. At the back of the castle was a half-moon-shaped terrace jutting out into the grounds. The left side of the terrace was in shadow: some of the hidden spotlights must have stopped working. There were stone steps from the terrace down on to the lawn. He ran as fast as he could until he was in the shadows again. He crept up the steps, his torch in one hand and his radio telephone in the other. The pistol was in his trouser pocket.

Suddenly he stopped dead and listened. What had he heard? It was one of his internal alarms going off. Something's wrong, he thought. But what? He pricked up his ears, but he could hear nothing apart from the wind coming and going. It's something to do with the light, he thought. I'm being drawn towards the shadows, and they are lying in wait for me.

When the penny dropped and he realised he had been tricked, it was too late. He turned to go back down the steps, but was blinded by a dazzling white light shining straight into his face. He had been lured into the shadowy trap, and now it had sprung. He held the hand holding the radio telephone over his eyes to keep out the light, but at the same time he felt himself being grabbed from behind. He tried to fight his way free, but it was too late. His head exploded and everything went black.

A part of his mind was conscious of what was happening all the time. Arms lifted him up and carried him, he could hear a voice speaking, somebody laughed. A door opened and the sound of footsteps on the stone terrace ceased. He was indoors, perhaps being carried up a staircase, and then he was set down on something soft. Whether it was the pain in the back of his head or the feeling of being in a room with the lights out, or at least dimmed, he did not know; but he came round, opened his eyes and found himself lying on a sofa in a very large room. The floor was tiled, possibly with marble. Several computers with flickering screens stood on an oblong table. He could hear the sound of air-conditioning fans and somewhere, out of his field of vision, a telex machine was clicking away. He tried not to move his head, the pain behind his right ear was too great. Then somebody started speaking to him, a voice he recognised, close by his side.

"A moment of madness," Harderberg said. "When a man does something that can only end with him being injured, or killed."

Wallander turned gingerly and looked at him. He was smiling. Further back, where the light barely penetrated, he could just make out the outlines of two men, motionless.

Harderberg walked round the sofa and handed him the radio telephone. His suit was immaculate, his shoes highly polished.

"It's three minutes past midnight," Harderberg said. "A few minutes ago somebody tried to contact you. I've no idea who it was, of course, and I don't care. But I assume somebody is waiting for you to get in touch. You'd better do that. I don't need to tell you, I am sure, that you shouldn't attempt to raise the alarm. We've had enough madness for one day."

Wallander called her up and she answered immediately.

"Everything's OK," he said. "I'll report again an hour from now."

"Have you found Ström?" she said.

He hesitated, unsure of what to say. Then he noticed that Harderberg was nodding at him encouragingly.

"Yes, I've found him," Wallander said. "I'll call again at 1.00."

Wallander put the radio on the sofa beside him.

"The woman police officer," Harderberg said. "I take it that she's in the vicinity. We could find her if we wanted to, of course. But we don't."

Wallander gritted his teeth and stood up.

"I have come in order to inform you," he said, "that you are suspected of being an accessory to a number of serious crimes."

Harderberg observed him thoughtfully. "I waive my right to have a solicitor present. Please go on, Inspector Wallander."

"You are suspected of being an accessory to the deaths of Gustaf Torstensson and his son Sten Torstensson. Furthermore, you are now also suspected of being implicated in the death of your own chief of security, Kurt Ström. In addition, there is the attempted murder of the solicitors' secretary, Mrs Dunér, and of myself and Police Officer Höglund. There are a number of other possible charges, including ones connected to the fate of the accountant Borman. The Public Prosecutor will have to sort out the details."

Harderberg sat down slowly in an armchair. "Are you saying that I am under arrest, Inspector Wallander?" he said.

Wallander felt on the point of fainting, and sat again on the sofa. "I don't have the necessary papers," he said. "But that doesn't affect the basic circumstances."

Harderberg leaned forward in his armchair, chin resting on one hand. Then he leaned back again and nodded. "I'll make things easy for you," he said. "I confess."

Wallander stared at him, unable to believe his ears.

"You're absolutely right," Harderberg said. "I admit to being guilty on all counts."

"Including Borman?"

"Including Borman, of course."

Wallander could feel his fear creeping up on him again, but this time colder, more threatening than before.

The whole situation was out of kilter. He was going to have to get out of the castle.

Harderberg watched him attentively, as if trying to read Wallander's thoughts. To give himself time to work out how he could get an SOS to Höglund without Harderberg realising, Wallander started asking questions, as if they'd been in an interrogation room. But still he could not tell what Harderberg was up to. Had he known Wallander was in the grounds from the moment he passed through the gate? What had Ström given away before he was killed?

"The truth," Harderberg said, interrupting Wallander's train of thought. "Does it exist for a Swedish police officer?"

"Establishing the line between a lie and a fact, the real truth, is the basis of all police work," Wallander said.

"A correct answer," Harderberg said approvingly. "But it's wrong all the same. Because there's no such thing as an absolute truth or an absolute lie. There are just agreements. Agreements that can be entered into, kept or broken."

"If somebody uses a gun to kill another human being, that can hardly be anything but a factual happening," Wallander said.

He could hear a faint note of irritation in Harderberg's voice when he answered. "We don't need to discuss what's self-evident," he said. "I'm looking for a truth that goes deeper than that."

"Death is deep enough for me," Wallander said. "Gustaf Torstensson was your solicitor. You had him killed. The attempt to disguise the murder as a car accident failed."

"I'd be interested to know how you reached that conclusion."

"A chair leg was left lying in the mud. The rest of the chair was in the car boot. The boot was locked."

"So simple! Pure carelessness."

Harderberg made no attempt to conceal the look he gave the two men skulking in the shadows.

"What happened?" Wallander said.

"Torstensson's loyalty began to waver. He saw things he shouldn't have seen. We were forced to ensure his loyalty, once and for all. Occasionally we amuse ourselves here at the castle with shooting practice. We use mannequins, tailors' dummies, as targets. We put a dummy in the road. He stopped. He died."

"And thus his loyalty was ensured."

Harderberg nodded, but seemed to be miles away. He jumped to his feet and stared at rows of figures that had appeared on one of the flickering computer screens. Wallander guessed they were share prices from some part of the world where it was already daytime. But then, did stock exchanges open on Sundays? Perhaps the figures he was checking were to do with quite different financial activities.

Harderberg returned to his armchair.

"We couldn't be sure how much his son knew," he said, as if he had never paused. "We kept him under observation. He went to visit you in Jutland. We couldn't be sure how much he had told you. Or Mrs Dunér, come to that. I think you have analysed the circumstances very skilfully, Inspector Wallander. But of course, we saw right away that you wanted us to think you had another lead you were following. I'm hurt to think that you underestimated us."

Wallander was beginning to feel sick. The cold-blooded indifference that oozed from the man in the armchair was something he had never encountered before. Nevertheless, his curiosity led him to ask more questions.

"We found a plastic container in the car," he said. "I suspect it was substituted for another one when you killed him."

"Why would we want to substitute it?"

"Our technicians could prove that it had never contained anything. We assumed that the container itself was of no significance: what was important was what it was meant to be used for."

"And what was that, pray?"

"Now you're asking the questions," Wallander said. "And I'm expected to answer them."

"It's getting late," Harderberg said. "Why can't we give this conversation a touch of playfulness? It's quite meaningless, after all."

"We're talking about murder," Wallander said. "I suspect that plastic container was used to preserve and carry transplant organs, cut out of murdered people."

Just for a moment Harderberg stiffened. It was gone in a flash, but Wallander noticed it even so. That clinched it. He was right.

"I look for business deals wherever I can find them," Harderberg said. "If there's a market for kidneys, I buy and sell kidneys, just to give one example."

"Where do they come from?"

"From deceased persons."

"People you've killed."

"All I have ever done is buy and sell," Harderberg said patiently. "What happens before the goods come into my hands is no concern of mine. I don't even know about it."

Wallander was appalled. "I didn't know people like you existed," he said in the end.

Harderberg leaned quickly forward in his armchair. "That was a lie," he said. "You know perfectly well such people exist. I'd go as far as to say that, deep down, you envy me."

"You're mad," Wallander said, making no attempt to conceal his disgust.

"Mad with happiness, mad with rage, yes, OK. But not plain mad, Inspector. You have to understand that I'm a passionate human being. I love doing business, conquering a rival competitor, increasing my fortune and never needing to deny myself anything. It's possible that I'm a restless Flying Dutchman, always seeking something new. But more than anything else I'm a heathen in the correct sense of the word. Perhaps Inspector Wallander is familiar with the works of Machiavelli?"

Wallander shook his head.

"Christians, according to this Italian thinker, say the highest level of happiness is to be attained through humility, self-denial and contempt for everything human. Heathens, on the other hand, see the highest level of goodness in mental greatness, bodily strength and all the qualities that make human beings frightening. Wise words that I always do my best to live up to."

Wallander said nothing. Harderberg looked at the two-way radio and then at his watch. It was 1 a.m. Wallander called Höglund, thinking that now he really had to work out how to convey to her his SOS. But yet again he told her that all was well, everything under control. She could expect him to be in touch again at 2 a.m.

Wallander made calls each hour through the night, but he could not get her to see that what he really wanted was for her to sound the alarm and send as many officers as possible to Farnholm. He had realised that they were alone in the castle, and that Harderberg was only waiting until dawn before leaving not just his castle but also his country, along with the still shadows in the background, the men who did his bidding and killed whoever he pointed a finger at. The only staff left were Sofia and the woman at the entrance gate. The secretaries had gone, all the ones Wallander had never seen. Perhaps they were already in another castle elsewhere, waiting for Harderberg?

The pain in Wallander's head had eased, but he was very tired. He had come so far and now he knew the truth, but he felt that that was not enough. They would leave him at the castle, possibly tied up, and when eventually he was discovered or managed to free himself, they would be up in the clouds and away. What had been said during the night would be denied by the lawyers Harderberg employed to defend him. The men who had actually pointed the guns, the ones who had never crossed Sweden's borders, would be no more than shadows against whom no prosecutor would be able to bring charges. They would never be able to prove anything, the investigation would crumble away through their fingers, and Harderberg would in the eyes of the world go on being a respectable citizen.

Wallander had the truth in his possession, he had even been told that Borman had been killed because he had discovered the link between Harderberg and the County Council fraud. And thereafter they had not dared to take the risk that Gustaf Torstensson would start seeing things he should not see. He had done, despite all their efforts to prevent it; but there again, it did not really matter. The truth would eventually consume itself, because the authorities would never be able to arrest anybody for this series of appalling crimes.

What Wallander would recall in the future, what would stay in his mind for a very long time to come as a horrifying reminder of what Harderberg was like, was something he said shortly before 5.00 that morning, when for some reason or other they had started talking about the plastic container again, and the people who were killed so that their body parts could be sold.

"You have to understand that it's but a tiny part of my activities. It's negligible, marginal. But it's what I do, Inspector Wallander. I buy and sell. I'm an actor on the stage governed by market forces. I never miss an opportunity, no matter how small and insignificant it is."

Human life is insignificant, then, Wallander had thought. That's the premise on which Harderberg's whole existence is based.

Then their discussions were over. Harderberg had switched off the computers, one after the other, and disposed of some documents in a shredder. Wallander had considered running away, but the motionless shadows in the background had never left. He had to admit defeat.

Harderberg stroked the tips of his fingers over his lips, as if to check that his smile was intact. Then he looked at Wallander one last time.

"We all have to die," he said, making it sound as if there were one exception: himself. "Even the span of a detective inspector has a limit. In this case, at my deciding." He checked his watch before continuing. "It will shortly be dawn, even though it is still dark. Then a helicopter will land. My two assistants will board it, and so will you. But you will only be in it for a short time. Then you will have an opportunity to see if you can fly without mechanical aids."

He never took his eyes off Wallander as he spoke. He wants me to beg for my life, Wallander thought. Well, he's going to be disappointed. Once fear reaches a certain point, it is transformed and becomes its opposite. That's one thing I've learned.

"Investigating the innate ability of human beings to fly was thoroughly researched during the unfortunate war in Vietnam," Harderberg said. "Prisoners were dropped, but at a great height, for a brief moment, they recovered their freedom to move, until they crashed into the ground and became a part of the greatest freedom of all." He stood up and buttoned his jacket. "My helicopter pilots are very skilful," he said. "I think they'll manage to drop you so that you land in Stortorget in Ystad. It will be an event that is recorded for ever in the annals of the town's history."

He's going clean off his rocker, Wallander thought.

"We must now go our different ways," Harderberg said. "We have met twice. I think I shall remember you. There were moments when you came close to displaying acumen. In other circumstances I might have been able to find a place for you."

"The postcard," Wallander said. "The postcard Sten Torstensson somehow sent from Finland when he was actually with me in Denmark."

"It amuses me to copy handwriting," Harderberg said. "It could be said that I'm rather good at it. I spent a few hours in Helsinki the day young Torstensson was with you in Jutland. I had a meeting – not a successful one, I'm afraid – with senior people at Nokia. It was like a game, like sticking a twig into an anthill. A game where the aim is to cause confusion. That's all."

Harderberg held out his hand to Wallander, who was so amazed that he shook it.

Then he turned on his heel and was gone.

Harderberg dominated the whole room whenever he was present. Now that the door had closed behind him there was nothing left. Wallander thought he left a sort of vacuum behind him.

Tolpin was leaning against a pillar, watching Wallander. Obadia was sitting, staring straight ahead.

Wallander refused to believe that Harderberg had given orders for him to be thrown out of a helicopter above the centre of Ystad. But he knew he would have to do something.

The minutes passed. Neither of the men moved.

So, he was to be thrown out, alive, to plummet on to the rooftops, or possibly on to the paving stones in Stortorget. Having to accept that led immediately to panic. It paralysed him, spreading through his body like poison. He could hardly breathe. He tried desperately to think.

Obadia slowly raised his head. Wallander could hear the faint noise of an engine rapidly coming closer. The helicopter was on its way. Tolpin gestured that it was time to go.

By the time they had emerged from the castle, there was still no hint of dawn light, but the helicopter was standing on the pad, its rotors unhurriedly spinning. The pilot was ready to take off the moment they climbed aboard. Wallander was still trying desperately to fashion a way of escaping. Tolpin was walking in front of him, Obadia a few paces behind with a pistol in his hand. They had almost reached the helicopter. Its rotor blades were still slicing the chilly night air. Wallander saw a pile of old broken-up concrete at one corner they were to pass to get to the pad: somebody had been repairing cracks but had not yet cleared away the debris. Wallander slowed down so that Obadia came momentarily between him and Tolpin. Wallander bent down and used his hands as shovels to scoop up as much of the concrete chunks as he could and hurled it up at the rotors. He heard loud, cracking bangs as fragments of concrete flew all around them. For just a moment Tolpin and Obadia thought that somebody was shooting at them and lost sight of what was happening behind them. Wallander flung himself with all his strength at Obadia and succeeded in wrestling his pistol from his grasp. He took a few steps backwards, stumbled and fell. Tolpin stared wide-eyed at what was going on without it properly sinking in, but now he reached into his jacket for his weapon. Wallander fired and hit him in the hip. Obadia hurled himself at Wallander, who fired again. He did not see where he had hit him, but Obadia fell, screaming with pain.

Wallander scrambled to his feet. The pilots might also be armed. But when he pointed the pistol at the open door of the helicopter, he could see only one young man there, and he had his hands above his head. Wallander examined the men he had shot. Both were alive but unlikely to go far. He pocketed Tolpin's pistol, then he walked up to the helicopter. The pilot still had his hands up. Wallander shouted that he should fly away. He took a few paces backwards and watched the helicopter take off then disappear over the roof of the castle, its searchlights probing the dark sky.

He seemed to be seeing everything through a fog. When he rubbed his cheek with his hand, it was covered in blood. A concrete chip had hit him in the face without his noticing it.

Then he ran towards the stables. Sofia screamed when she saw him. He tried to smile, but his face was stiff from his wound.

"Everything's alright," he said, trying to get his breath back. "But I've got to ask you to do something. Phone for an ambulance. There are two men with bullet wounds lying on the helipad. Once you've done that, I won't ask you to do anything more for me. You can go back to Sten and take him up on his promise. It's all over here now."

Then he remembered Harderberg. Time was very short.

As he ran from the stables he slipped in the mud churned up by the horses' hooves and fell. He struggled to his feet and ran towards the gates. He wondered if he would get there in time.

She had got out of the car to stretch her legs, and looked up to see him coming towards her. He saw the horrified expression on her face and realised how alarming he must look. He was covered in blood and mud, his clothes torn. But he had no time to explain. Only one thing mattered, and that was preventing Harderberg from leaving the airport. He shouted to her to get back into the car. Before she had closed her door he had reversed on to the road. He forced the car through the gears, slamming the accelerator hard down, and ignored the red light as he swung into the main road.

"What's the fastest way to Sturup?" he said.

She found a map in the glove pocket and told him the route. We won't make it, he thought. It's too far, we don't have enough time.

"Phone Björk," he said, pointing at the car phone.

"I don't know his home number," she said.

"Then ring the bloody police station and find out, for God's sake!" he yelled. "Use your head!"

She did as she was told. When the officer on duty wondered if it could not wait until Björk had come in for work, she too started shouting. The moment she had it, she dialled the number. "What shall I say?" she said.

"Tell him Harderberg's about to leave the country in his aircraft, and for good," Wallander said. "Björk has to arrange to have him stopped. He has half an hour maximum to do it in."

When Björk answered, Wallander listened as Höglund repeated word for word what he had said. She listened to the response in silence then handed the phone to Wallander.

"He wants to speak to you."

Wallander took the phone in his right hand and eased the pressure on the accelerator.

"What do you mean, I have to stop Harderberg's jet?" Björk's voice rasped over the phone.

"He arranged the murders of Gustaf and Sten Torstensson. Ström is dead too."

"Are you absolutely sure about what you're saying? Where are you right now? Why is the sound so bad?"

"I'm on my way from Farnholm Castle. I don't have time to explain. Harderberg is on his way to the airport now. He must be stopped immediately. If that plane takes off and he leaves Swedish air space, we've lost him."

"I have to say this all sounds very odd," Björk said. "What have you been doing at Farnholm Castle till this time in the morning?"

Wallander realised that Björk's questions were perfectly reasonable from his point of view. He wondered how he would have reacted if he had been in Björk's place.

"I know it sounds outlandish," he said, "but this time you *have to take the risk of believing me.*"

"I shall have to consult Åkeson," Björk said.

Wallander groaned. "There really is no time for that. You've heard what I said. There are police officers at Sturup. They have to be told to stop Harderberg."

"Ring me back in a quarter of an hour," Björk said. "I'll get in touch with Åkeson right away."

Wallander was so furious that he almost lost control of the car.

"Wind down that bloody window!" he said.

She did as he said. Wallander threw the telephone out.

"Now you can close it again. We'll have to sort this out by ourselves."

425

"Are you certain it's Harderberg?" she said. "What's happened? Are you wounded?"

Wallander ignored the last two questions.

"I'm certain," he said. "I also know we will never ever get him if he leaves the country."

"What are you going to do?"

He shook his head. "I don't know," he said. "In fact, I haven't the slightest bloody idea. I'll have to think of something."

But as they approached Sturup 40 minutes later, he still had no idea what he was going to do. With tyres screeching, he pulled up at the gates to the right of the airport building. The better to see, he clambered on to the roof of the car. All around passengers arriving for early flights paused to see what was going on. A catering truck inside the gates blocked his view. Wallander waved his arms and cursed in an attempt to attract the driver's attention and get him to move the truck. But the man behind the wheel had his head buried in a newspaper and was oblivious to the man on the roof of the car, ranting and raving. Then Wallander drew his pistol and shot straight up into the air. There was immediate panic among the watching crowd. People ran off in all directions, abandoning suitcases on the pavement. The driver of the truck had reacted to the shot and grasped that Wallander wanted him to move out of the way.

Harderberg's Grumman Gulfstream was still there. The pale yellow light from the spotlights was reflected by the body of the jet.

The two pilots, on their way to the aircraft, had heard the shot and stopped in their tracks. Wallander jumped off the car roof so that they would not be able to see him. He fell, hitting his left shoulder hard against the

426

road. The pain made him even more furious. He knew Harderberg was somewhere inside the yellow airport building and he had no intention of letting him get away. He raced towards the entrance doors, stumbling over suitcases and trolleys, Höglund a few paces behind him. He still had his pistol in his hand as he ran through the glass doors and headed for the airport police offices. As it was early on a Sunday morning there were not many people in the terminal. Only one queue had formed at a check-in desk, for a charter flight to Spain. As Wallander came charging up, covered in blood and mud, all hell broke loose. Höglund tried to reassure people, but her voice was drowned in the uproar. One of the police officers on duty had been out to buy a newspaper, and saw Wallander approaching. The pistol in his hand was the first thing he had seen. The officer dropped the paper and started feverishly keying in the door code, but Wallander grabbed him by the arm before he had finished.

"Inspector Wallander, Ystad police," he shouted. "There's a plane we have to stop. Dr Alfred Harderberg's Gulfstream. There's no bloody time to lose!"

"Don't shoot," gasped the terrified police officer.

"For heaven's sake, man!" Wallander said. "I'm a police officer myself. Didn't you hear what I said?"

"Don't shoot," the man said, again. Then he fainted.

Wallander stared in exasperation at the wretched man lying in front of him on the ground. Then he started belting on the door with his fists. Höglund had caught up.

"Let me try," she said.

Wallander looked round, as if expecting to see Harderberg at any moment. He ran over to the big windows overlooking the runways.

Harderberg was walking up the steps into the aeroplane. He ducked ever so slightly then disappeared inside. The door closed immediately.

"We're not going to make it!" Wallander yelled to Höglund.

He raced out of the terminal again. She was at his side all the way. He noticed that a car belonging to the airport was on its way in through the gates. He made one final effort and managed to squeeze through the gap before the gates closed. He banged on the boot and shouted for the car to stop, but the driver was obviously frightened out of his wits and accelerated away. Höglund was still outside the gates. She had not quite made it before they closed. Wallander flung out his arms in resignation. The Gulfstream was taxiing towards the runway. There were only 100 metres left before it would turn, accelerate and take off.

Right next to where Wallander was standing stood a tractor for towing baggage trailers. He had no choice. He climbed up, switched on the engine and steered towards the runway. He could see in his side mirror a long snake of trailers being towed along behind. He had not seen that they were connected to the tractor, but it was too late to stop now. The Gulfstream was just arriving at the runway and its engines were screaming. The baggage trailers had started tipping over as he cut across the grass between the apron and the runway.

Now he had reached the runway, where the black tyre marks made as the aircraft braked looked like wide cracks in the asphalt. He drove straight towards the Gulfstream, which was pointing its nose at him. When there were 200 metres still to go, he saw the plane begin to roll towards him. By then he knew he had managed it. Before the jet had got up enough speed to take off, the pilots would have to stop in order not to smash into the tractor.

Wallander applied the brakes, but something was wrong with the tractor. He pushed and pulled and slammed down his foot, but nothing happened. He was not moving fast, but the momentum was such that the nose wheel would be wrecked when the aircraft collided with the tractor. Wallander jumped off as the last trailers spilled loose, colliding with one another.

The pilots had switched off the engines to avoid an inferno. Wallander was struck on the head by one of the trailers, and rose unsteadily to his feet. He could scarcely see through the blood trickling into his eyes. Strangely, he was still holding the pistol in his hand.

As the door of the aeroplane opened and the steps were lowered, he could hear an armada of sirens approaching.

Wallander waited.

Then Harderberg emerged from the plane and walked down the steps on to the runway. It seemed to Wallander that he looked different. He saw what it was. The smile had disappeared.

Höglund jumped out of the first of the police cars to reach the aircraft steps. Wallander was busy wiping the blood out of his eyes with his torn shirt.

"Have you been hit?" she said.

Wallander shook his head. He had bitten his tongue, and found it hard to speak.

"You'd better phone Björk," she said.

Wallander stared at her. "No," he said. "You can do that. And deal with Dr Harderberg."

Then he started to walk away. She hurried to catch up.

"Where are you going?"

"I'm going home to bed," Wallander said. "I'm a bit on the tired side. And rather sad. Even if it turned out alright in the end."

Something in his voice discouraged her from saying more.

Wallander continued to walk away. For some reason, nobody tried to stop him.

Chapter 18

On the morning of Thursday, December 23, Wallander went rather reluctantly to Österportstorg in Ystad and bought a Christmas tree. It was distinctly misty – there was not going to be a white Christmas in Skåne in 1993. He spent a considerable time examining the trees, not at all sure what he really wanted, but in the end he picked one just about small enough to put on his table. He took it home and then spent ages searching in vain for a stand he distinctly remembered having: probably it disappeared when he and Mona had divided up their possessions after the divorce. He made a list of the things he needed to buy for Christmas. It was obvious that for the last few years he had been living in a state of increasing squalor. Every cupboard was bare. The list he made filled a whole page of A4. When he turned over to continue on the next page, he found there was something written there already. *Sten Torstensson.*

He recalled that this was the very first note he had made in the case, that morning at the beginning of November, almost two months ago, when he had decided to go back to work. He remembered sitting at this table and being intrigued by the death notices in *Ystad Allehanda*. Now, everything had changed.

That November morning seemed an age away.

Alfred Harderberg and his two shadows had been arrested. Once the Christmas holiday was over Wallander would get down to the investigation that seemed likely to keep on going for a very long time.

He wondered what would happen to Farnholm Castle.

He also thought he ought to phone Widén and find out how Sofia was faring, after all she had been through.

He stood up, went to the bathroom and examined himself in the mirror. His face looked thinner. But he had also aged. No-one could now avoid seeing that he was approaching 50. He opened his mouth wide and peered gloomily at his teeth. Despondent or annoyed, he couldn't make up his mind which, he decided he would have to make an appointment with the dentist in the new year. Then he returned to his list in the kitchen, crossed out the name Sten Torstensson, and noted that he would have to buy a new toothbrush.

It took him three hours, in the pouring rain, to buy all the things on his list. He had to resort to hole-in-the-wall machines twice to draw out more money, and he was outraged that everything was so expensive. He slunk home shortly before 1 p.m. with all his carrier bags, and sat down at the kitchen table to check his list. Needless to say, he had forgotten something: a stand for his Christmas tree.

The phone rang. He was supposed to be on holiday over Christmas, so he did not expect it to be from the police station. But when he picked up the receiver, it was Ann-Britt Höglund's voice he heard.

"I know you're on holiday," she said. "I wouldn't have phoned if it wasn't important."

"When I joined the force many years ago, one of the first things I learned was that a police officer is never on holiday," he said. "What do they have to say about that at Police Training College nowadays?"

"Professor Persson did talk about it once," she said. "But to tell you the truth, I haven't a clue what he said."

"What do you want?"

"I'm ringing from Svedberg's office. Mrs Dunér is in my room at the moment. She's very keen to talk to you."

"What about?"

"She won't say. She won't talk to anybody but you."

Wallander did not hesitate.

"Tell her I'll be there," he said. "She can wait in my office."

"Apart from that, there's nothing much happening here at the moment," Ann-Britt Höglund said. "There's only Martinsson and me here. The traffic boys are getting ready for Christmas. The population of Skåne is going to spend Christmas blowing into balloons."

"Good," he said. "There's too much of being drunk in charge. We have to stamp it out."

"You sometimes sound like Björk," she said, laughing.

"I hope not," he said, horrified.

"Can you tell me any kind of crime for which the figures are improving?" she said.

He thought for a moment. "The theft of black-and-white televisions," he said. "But that's about all."

He hung up, wondering what Mrs Dunér would have to say. He really could not imagine what it might be.

It was 1.15 when Wallander arrived at the police station. The Christmas tree was glittering away in reception, and

433

he remembered that he hadn't yet bought the usual bunch of flowers for Ebba. On his way to his office he called in at the canteen and wished everybody a merry Christmas. He knocked on Ann-Britt Höglund's door, but there was no reply.

Mrs Dunér was sitting on his visitor's chair, waiting for him. The left arm looked as if it would fall off the chair at any moment. She stood up when he came in, they shook hands and he hung up his jacket before sitting down. Wallander thought she looked tired.

"You wanted to speak to me," he said, trying to sound friendly.

"I'm sorry to disturb you," she said. "It's easy to forget that the police have so much to do."

"I have time for you," Wallander said. "What is it you want?"

She took a parcel out of the plastic carrier bag at the side of her chair, and handed it to him over his desk.

"It's a present," she said. "You can open it now, or wait until tomorrow."

"Why on earth would you want to give me a Christmas present?" Wallander asked in surprise.

"Because I now know what happened to my gentlemen," she said. "It's thanks to you that the perpetrators were caught."

Wallander shook his head and stretched out his arms in protest. "That's not true," he said. "It was teamwork, with lots of people involved. You shouldn't just thank me."

Her reply surprised him. "This is no time for false modesty," she said. "Everybody knows that you're the one we have to thank."

Wallander did not know what to say, and began to open the parcel. It contained one of the icons he had found in Gustaf Torstensson's basement.

"I can't possibly accept this," he said. "Unless I'm much mistaken, it's from Mr Torstensson's collection."

"Not any more it isn't," Mrs Dunér replied. "He left them all to me in his will. And I'm only too happy to pass one of them on to you."

"It must be very valuable," Wallander said. "I'm a police officer, and I can't accept such gifts. At the very least I'd have to talk to my boss first."

She surprised him yet again. "I've already done that. He said it was OK."

"You've spoken to Björk already?" Wallander said, astonished.

"I thought I'd better," she said.

Wallander looked at the icon. It reminded him of Riga, of Latvia. And most especially of Baiba Liepa.

"It's not as valuable as you might think," she said. "But it's beautiful."

"Yes. It's very beautiful. But I don't deserve it."

"That's not the only reason I'm here," Mrs Dunér said.

Wallander looked at her, waiting for what was coming next.

"I have a question for you," she said. "Is there no limit to human wickedness?"

"I'm hardly the right person to answer a question like that," Wallander said.

"But who can, if the police can't?"

Wallander carefully laid the icon on his desk.

"I take it you're wondering how anybody can kill another human being to get a body part to sell for profit," he said. "I don't know what to say. It's as incomprehensible to me as it is to you."

"What's the world coming to?" she said. "Alfred Harderberg was a man we could all look up to. How can anybody donate money to charity with one hand and kill people with the other?"

"We just have to fight it as best we can," Wallander said.

"How can we fight something we can't understand?"

"I really don't know," Wallander said. "But we have to do our best."

The brief conversation died out. Martinsson's cheerful laughter echoed down the corridor.

She rose to her feet. "I won't disturb you any longer," she said.

"I'm sorry I couldn't give you a better answer," he said, opening the door.

"At least you were honest," she said.

It occurred to Wallander that he had something to give her. He went to his desk and took the postcard with a picture of a Finnish landscape from one of the drawers.

"I promised to give you this back," he said. "We don't need it any longer."

"I'd forgotten all about it," she said, putting it into her handbag.

He escorted her out of the police station.

"May I wish you a merry Christmas," she said.

"Thank you," Wallander said. "And the same to you. I'll take good care of the icon."

He went back to his office. Her visit had made him uneasy. He had been reminded of the melancholy he had had to live with for so long. But he thrust it to one side, took his jacket and left the building. He was on holiday. Not just from his job, but from any thought that might depress him.

I may not deserve the icon, he thought, but I do deserve a few days off.

He drove home through the fog and parked.

Then he cleaned his flat. Before going to bed he improvised something to stand the Christmas tree in, and decorated it. He had hung the icon up in his bedroom. He studied it before putting the light out.

He wondered if it would be able to protect him.

The next day was Christmas Eve, the big day in Sweden. It was still foggy and grey outside. But Wallander felt that today he could rise above all the greyness.

He drove to Sturup airport at 2 p.m., despite the fact that the plane was not due until 3.30. He felt most uncomfortable as he parked his car and approached the yellow airport building. He had the feeling everybody was looking at him.

Nevertheless, he couldn't resist walking over to the gates to the right of the terminal.

The Gulfstream was no longer there. There was no sign of it.

It's all over, he thought. I'm putting a full stop behind it, here and now.

His relief was immediate.

The image of the smiling man faded away.

He went into the departure lounge, then out again, feeling more nervous than he could remember at any time since

437

he was a teenager. He counted the paving stones in the entrance, rehearsed his inadequate English, and tried in vain to think about anything but what was about to happen.

When the plane landed he was still standing outside the terminal. Then he hurried inside and positioned himself next to the newspaper stand, waiting.

She was one of the last to emerge.

But there she was. Baiba Liepa.

She was exactly as he remembered her.